Picture Perfect

Elara Westwood

Published by Elara Westwood, 2024.

This is a work of fiction. Similarities to real people, places, or events are entirely coincidental.

PICTURE PERFECT

First edition. October 2, 2024.

Copyright © 2024 Elara Westwood.

ISBN: 979-8227262240

Written by Elara Westwood.

Chapter 1: Shadows of the Past

I stand on the rooftop of my apartment, overlooking the vibrant skyline of Chicago, the sunset painting the sky in hues of orange and purple. The city hums beneath me, a living organism with its own heartbeat, throbbing with life, ambition, and the faintest undercurrent of nostalgia. The sun dips lower, casting long shadows over the buildings, each one a monument to dreams pursued and passions ignited. My name is Clara Lane, and I am a budding photographer, though the label feels precarious, as if it might slip away from me at any moment, like grains of sand between my fingers.

The wind tousles my hair, ruffling the edges of my oversized sweater, a familiar comfort in this bustling city that both inspires and intimidates me. I close my eyes, breathing in the mingled scents of roasting coffee beans from the café below and the faint hint of rain on the horizon. My camera hangs from my neck, a lifeline that allows me to capture snippets of beauty amidst the chaos. With each click, I strive to freeze moments that others might overlook, to encapsulate the emotion simmering just beneath the surface. But this evening, the sunset is not the only thing vying for my attention.

Just as the sky is splashed with vibrant colors, memories of my past flood my mind, haunting me like shadows in the twilight. I can almost hear the laughter we shared, a melody that feels bittersweet now. Ethan, my college sweetheart, who swept into my life with the kind of fervor that ignited every corner of my soul. We were young and naïve, wrapped in a cocoon of dreams and promises. But life, as it often does, unraveled those threads, leaving me tangled in a web of heartbreak. The memory of his touch lingers in the air around me, a ghost that refuses to fade.

Just when I think I've finally moved on, I catch sight of him, standing on the street below, his back turned to me. My breath catches in my throat, the familiar pang of recognition igniting the long-dormant feelings within me. Ethan has changed, yet somehow remained the same. His dark hair tousled by the wind, his tall frame silhouetted against the bustling street. I can't help but remember the way he would throw his head back and laugh, a sound that once wrapped around me like a warm blanket. The tension between us feels like a live wire, crackling with unspoken words, as if the very universe holds its breath in anticipation.

The reality of my own vulnerability crashes over me like a wave. I am no longer that girl who believed in happily-ever-afters. The scars of betrayal have etched themselves into my heart, each one a testament to the trust I once placed in him and the world around me. With trembling hands, I raise my camera, aiming it at him. A snapshot of the moment. A way to capture the tumult of emotions swirling within me. But just as I click the shutter, he turns, our eyes locking for the briefest instant. Time seems to freeze, and the cacophony of the city fades into a distant hum.

His gaze pierces through me, igniting memories both cherished and painful. I see the remnants of our shared history reflected in his eyes—the late-night talks, the dreams we sketched out beneath the stars, the warmth of his embrace that felt like home. But beneath that warmth lies a layer of hurt, a chasm that separates us now. My heart pounds like a drum, a cacophony of confusion and longing. He shifts slightly, as if sensing my presence, but I remain frozen in place, half hidden by the rooftop's edge, half wanting to leap into the fray of feelings swirling around us.

The city continues its relentless pace, oblivious to the emotional maelstrom brewing above. I lower my camera, knowing that this moment is too fraught to capture. The image I see is of a young woman standing on the precipice of her past, staring into the face of someone who once meant the world to her. I know that this encounter could unravel everything I have worked so hard to rebuild—the walls I have painstakingly erected to keep the pain at bay.

But then, something inside me stirs—a flicker of defiance against the fear that has held me captive for far too long. I step back from the edge, deciding to let the shadows of the past linger as they will. For now, I'll live in the present, capturing the vibrant world around me through my lens. I take a deep breath, feeling the crispness of the evening air fill my lungs, grounding me in the here and now. The city sparkles like a treasure trove, full of stories waiting to be told.

I turn my back on Ethan, but the decision feels less like an act of avoidance and more like a commitment to my own journey. I venture back inside, closing the door behind me, shutting out the bittersweet echoes of what once was. My heart still beats in time with the rhythm of the city, each pulse a reminder that I am alive, that I am still capable of creating beauty, even amidst the shadows. With renewed resolve, I pull out my camera, embracing the vibrant energy of Chicago, determined to transform my pain into art.

The soft chime of my phone pulls me back into the present, a gentle reminder that life outside the rooftop oasis is still pressing in. I glance at the screen, noticing a message from Jess, my best friend and most ardent supporter, accompanied by a picture of her latest culinary creation. Jess has an uncanny ability to turn even the simplest ingredients into works of art, her enthusiasm spilling over in both her cooking and her friendship. The text reads, Dinner tonight? Bring your camera. I made the most amazing truffle risotto!

The thought of truffle risotto piques my interest, a tantalizing invitation to indulge in comfort food while cloaking myself in the warmth of friendship. I shoot her a quick reply, a promise of my arrival, and reluctantly retreat from the rooftop. The echo of the city settles around me like a comforting embrace, the cacophony of voices and traffic swirling together into a familiar symphony. I weave through the maze of my apartment, gathering my things with an air of determination. I will not let the shadows of my past eclipse my present.

When I finally step out into the bustling streets of Chicago, the vibrant energy of the city invigorates me. The aroma of freshly baked bread wafts from a nearby bakery, mingling with the distant scent of roasted coffee, creating a heady mix that ignites my senses. I can feel the rhythm of the city thrumming beneath my feet, an unyielding reminder that life continues, with or without the ghosts that haunt me. Each step I take toward Jess's apartment feels like an act of rebellion against the fear that had threatened to envelop me earlier.

As I navigate through the throngs of people, I catch snippets of their conversations—laughter and debates, dreams and mundane grievances. In this melting pot of lives, I find solace. Chicago is a canvas, and its people are the brushstrokes that create its vibrant tapestry. I take a moment to pause, lifting my camera to capture a candid moment of a young couple, their faces lit with joy as they share a secret joke. The shutter clicks, freezing their laughter in time, a reminder that beauty often lies in the unexpected.

After a brisk walk filled with impulse shots and fleeting moments, I arrive at Jess's building. The brick facade, speckled with ivy, feels welcoming, as if it understands the burdens I carry. Jess's door swings open before I even knock, her face alight with excitement. She's wearing an apron that's splattered with vibrant colors, a testament to her culinary adventures, and her hair is pulled back in a messy bun that somehow enhances her charm.

"Clara! You made it!" she exclaims, pulling me into a hug that envelops me in warmth. The smell of something rich and savory wafts from the kitchen, and my stomach growls in anticipation.

"Can't resist truffle risotto, especially when you're the chef," I say, stepping into her inviting home. The cozy space is filled with eclectic decor, an array of mismatched furniture that somehow works harmoniously, reflecting her unique personality. Framed photographs of our adventures adorn the walls, each one a snapshot of joy and laughter, a stark contrast to the somber memories that linger in the corners of my mind.

As Jess busies herself in the kitchen, I take a moment to settle into her living room, filled with the gentle hum of a jazz playlist that floats through the air. The light from the window bathes the space in a golden glow, illuminating the small potted plants that line the sill. My fingers trace the edge of my camera, the familiar weight grounding me in the present. I can feel the tendrils of my earlier anxiety begin to dissipate, replaced by the reassuring cadence of Jess's chatter as she shares the day's mishaps in the kitchen.

"Did I tell you about the time I almost set my hair on fire while trying to flambé? It was a disaster!" she laughs, and I can't help but chuckle along with her. Her ability to find humor in her culinary catastrophes is one of the many reasons I cherish her friendship.

Dinner unfolds in a delightful flurry of flavors and stories. Jess serves the risotto with a flourish, each bite a creamy explosion of taste that dances on my tongue. We share our dreams and fears, the conversations weaving through topics as varied as our culinary preferences and the uncertainties of life. She notices my quieter moments, the shadows that flicker behind my smile, but she doesn't press, allowing me to share only what I'm ready to reveal.

As we finish dinner, I find myself drawn into a comforting rhythm of laughter and camaraderie, the worries of the day fading into the background. It feels good to be here, in this moment, surrounded by someone who sees me for all that I am, who embraces my flaws and celebrates my victories. Yet, even amidst the laughter, a shadow lingers at the edges of my consciousness—a reminder of Ethan and the past I'm trying to escape.

After dinner, we move to the living room, where Jess pours us both a glass of red wine. The rich liquid glimmers in the light, promising warmth and a touch of courage. We settle into her cozy couch, and Jess flips through her latest batch of photographs. "You've been shooting a lot lately, haven't you?" she asks, a hint of curiosity sparking in her eyes.

I nod, the memories of my recent outings flooding back. "Yeah, I've been trying to capture more of the city—its life, its stories," I reply, feeling a swell of pride. My camera has become a part of me, a tool that allows me to express emotions I often struggle to articulate.

She tilts her head, considering. "You know, Clara, your photographs have a way of telling stories. You capture moments that feel alive." Her praise washes over me like a warm wave, encouraging and uplifting.

"Thanks, Jess. That means a lot, especially now," I say, my voice softening. "I'm just trying to find my footing again."

As the evening stretches on, we continue to share stories, the laughter spilling over like the wine in our glasses. I can feel the healing power of friendship working its magic, gently stitching together the frayed edges of my heart. In this moment, I'm reminded that the shadows may linger, but they do not have to define me. I have the power to embrace the light and the connections that make life vibrant and full.

The evening deepens as Jess and I settle into a comfortable routine, the soft glow of the lamp casting a warm light over our impromptu photography critique session. She sips her wine, her eyes sparkling with enthusiasm as she flips through the images I've captured. Each photo sparks memories, the stories behind them weaving into our conversation like threads in a tapestry.

"Clara, this one is incredible!" she exclaims, pointing to a shot of the Chicago River at twilight, the water reflecting a kaleidoscope of city lights. "You've really captured the essence of the city. It feels alive." Her praise warms me, but beneath the surface, a nagging doubt lingers. Can I truly capture the essence of something so vast and complex, especially when my own feelings remain so tangled?

As Jess moves on to another image, I take a moment to glance around her cozy living room, each corner brimming with life. Shelves overflowing with books, plants thriving in every window, and a collection of quirky art pieces create an atmosphere that feels like a sanctuary. It's the kind of space that invites you to relax, to shed your burdens at the door and breathe a little easier. But even here, the shadows of my past cling to me, like stubborn cobwebs refusing to be swept away.

"Tell me about this one," Jess prompts, interrupting my reverie as she holds up a candid shot of a street musician lost in his craft, his weathered face lit by the soft glow of a nearby streetlamp. The image resonates with me, echoing the struggles and joys of those who dare to pursue their dreams in a city that sometimes feels indifferent.

"His name is Marco," I say, my voice tinged with nostalgia. "I met him on a particularly rough day when everything felt gray. He was playing the saxophone, pouring his soul into each note. I sat there, listening, and it was as if the music lifted the weight of the world from my shoulders." I pause, lost in the memory of the warmth of that day, the way Marco's music intertwined with my thoughts, making everything feel possible.

Jess watches me intently, her expression a mix of empathy and curiosity. "You have a gift for finding beauty in the ordinary," she replies, her voice gentle. "It's like you have this radar for moments that matter."

"I suppose I just want to see and share what's real," I admit, feeling vulnerable. "But sometimes, I worry that I'm not doing enough. That I'm just a spectator rather than a participant." The admission hangs between us, a delicate thread weaving through the evening's light-hearted banter.

"You're not just a spectator, Clara," Jess reassures me, her tone firm yet kind. "You're capturing the world as you see it, and that perspective is unique. Don't underestimate the power of your voice—your art." I feel a flicker of hope ignite within me, battling against the darkness that sometimes threatens to consume my thoughts.

As the night progresses, we share more stories, and laughter fills the room, brightening the shadows lurking in my mind. We lose track of time, our glasses refilled and the remnants of dinner pushed aside in favor of dessert—a slice of rich chocolate cake, courtesy of Jess's impeccable baking skills. I let the sweetness melt in my mouth, the taste a simple pleasure that grounds me in the moment.

It's during one of these tranquil pauses that my phone buzzes again, this time more insistent. I glance at the screen, my heart racing at the sight of Ethan's name lighting up my notifications. A brief moment of panic courses through me—should I answer? What could he possibly want after all this time? I swallow hard, forcing myself to breathe deeply as Jess raises an eyebrow, sensing my sudden shift in energy.

"Is everything okay?" she asks, her tone laced with concern.

I nod, but the truth is, I'm grappling with a whirlpool of emotions—anxious curiosity mixed with a long-buried longing that threatens to resurface. With a deep breath, I set my phone down, deciding not to let it steal my peace tonight. "I'm fine," I assure her, though the unease lingers just beneath the surface.

As the evening draws to a close, I help Jess clear the table, our playful banter making the task feel less like a chore and more like a ritual. She hums a tune, a catchy melody that carries me back to carefree moments in our friendship, the years spent laughing through life's ups and downs. It's a stark reminder that while shadows may linger, they do not define the light we create.

Finally, I gather my things, preparing to head back to my apartment. The night air greets me like an old friend, crisp and invigorating, wrapping around me as I step outside. The city feels alive beneath the stars, a tapestry of lights that twinkle like secrets waiting to be uncovered. I pause for a moment, taking in the view, and as I do, I catch sight of a familiar figure in the distance. It's Ethan again, standing on the corner across the street, his silhouette outlined by the glow of a streetlamp.

My heart races, the static electricity of our past surging to life once more. He seems to be deep in thought, the shadows playing tricks on his features, making him appear both vulnerable and untouchable. Memories crash over me like waves, each one pulling me deeper into the ocean of our shared history—the laughter, the arguments, the quiet moments that felt like eternity.

Before I can stop myself, I find my feet moving toward him, drawn by an invisible thread that binds us together despite the distance that time has woven. Each step feels heavy, yet somehow exhilarating, as if I am approaching a precipice from which I cannot turn back. The world around us fades, and all that matters is the electricity crackling in the air between us, the unspoken words lingering like a delicate dance on the edge of our hearts.

"Clara," he says, his voice a low murmur that stirs something deep within me. The tension between us flares, and in that moment, I can almost believe that the past can be rewritten. I have been building walls to protect myself from the pain, but standing here in the shadow of our shared memories, I feel the bricks beginning to crumble.

"What are you doing here?" I manage, my voice steady despite the whirlwind of emotions swirling within.

Ethan looks at me, and for a moment, I see the boy I once loved, the one who filled my days with laughter and my nights with dreams. The smile that breaks across his face is tentative yet genuine, and I realize that perhaps the shadows of the past don't have to dictate our future. Perhaps, just perhaps, there is still room for light amidst the darkness.

And as we stand on the edge of a new beginning, the city alive around us, I can feel hope flickering to life, a fragile flame that has the power to illuminate even the darkest corners of our hearts.

Chapter 2: Fractured Connections

The warm glow of morning light poured through the large windows of my photography studio, casting a golden hue over the scattered props and carefully arranged backdrops. I loved this place, my sanctuary nestled in the heart of downtown Charleston. The soft hum of the city outside blended with the gentle clinking of coffee cups, and the aroma of freshly brewed espresso enveloped me like a cozy blanket. My camera, an extension of myself, rested comfortably on the table, waiting for its next moment to capture.

As I adjusted the lens, I heard the door creak open, and my heart jolted. It was Ethan. The very name sent ripples of nostalgia through me, an electric current of emotions I thought I had neatly tucked away. He stepped in, a hesitant figure silhouetted against the brilliant sunlight, and for a moment, time stood still. His presence filled the room, overpowering the comforting smells and sounds, morphing my haven into a battlefield of buried feelings.

He looked different yet achingly familiar. The tousled dark hair that used to fall carelessly over his forehead was now cropped shorter, accentuating the sharp lines of his jaw. His deep-set eyes still held that captivating spark, but there was a flicker of uncertainty within them that tugged at my heart. A memory flooded my mind—a summer evening spent on the rooftop, sharing laughter and dreams beneath a blanket of stars. But now, the echoes of that night clashed with the weight of unspoken words hanging between us like a dense fog.

"Hey," he said, his voice soft and hesitant, as if testing the waters of a frozen lake. The casual tone was an illusion; the air crackled with tension as if the very universe was holding its breath.

"Hey," I replied, my heart racing at the simplicity of our exchange. I busied myself with rearranging the assortment of vintage cameras that lined the shelves, desperately searching for something—anything—to fill the silence. I caught a glimpse of myself in the reflection of a polished lens, hair slightly messy, cheeks flushed, and I mentally kicked myself. I couldn't afford to show any weakness.

"Do you have time to talk?" Ethan ventured, stepping further into the studio, the door swinging shut behind him with a soft thud. The finality of that sound sent a jolt through me.

"Is there something you need?" I asked, deliberately keeping my tone cool and professional, despite the way my stomach twisted. My voice betrayed me, quaking with the memories of the last time we'd been together. How had it come to this? The boy who once made my heart flutter with a single smile now stood before me as an uninvited reminder of everything I had lost.

Ethan shifted on his feet, his hands shoved deep into his pockets, as if to shield himself from the storm brewing between us. "I just... wanted to see how you've been. You know, since..."

"Since you left?" I interjected, the sharpness of my words surprising even me. The truth felt like shards of glass lodged in my throat. I tried to soften my expression, but the pain of his departure was still too fresh, like a wound that refused to heal.

A flicker of regret crossed his face, but he pressed on. "Yeah. I didn't mean to just disappear. I thought about you. A lot. I was—"

"Busy?" I supplied, crossing my arms defensively. The vulnerability of those summer nights, the whispered promises, now felt like a cruel joke. He had been the embodiment of my dreams, and yet he had vanished without a trace, leaving a gaping hole in their fabric.

"Things got complicated," he said, his voice dropping to a whisper. "I thought it would be easier to just... disappear for a while."

"Easier for who?" I shot back, frustration spilling over. "Because it wasn't easier for me."

He took a deep breath, the weight of my words hanging heavy in the air. I could see the internal battle raging within him, the desire to explain clashing with the realization that some wounds can't be dressed without reopening them. I felt my heart flutter and then falter at the thought of revisiting old wounds. "I've missed you," he finally said, his sincerity washing over me like a wave.

The truth of it struck me, a bittersweet chord resonating deep within. I missed him too, more than I cared to admit. But admitting it would mean facing the reality that he was standing here, now, in the very space where I had tried to rebuild myself after his abrupt exit. I couldn't afford to let him see how much I craved the comfort of his presence, how every ounce of my willpower struggled against the magnetic pull I felt toward him.

"I'm not sure what you expect me to say," I replied, keeping my voice steady. "I've had to piece my life back together, and you being here is... complicated."

"Complicated?" He echoed, his brow furrowing. "You mean painful, right? Because it hurts me too. Seeing you like this, knowing that I—"

"Ethan," I interrupted, my heart racing at the looming confrontation. "You don't get to walk back in here and pretend that everything is fine. It's not. You broke my trust when you left, and now you want to talk about feelings?"

The heat of our exchange filled the room, the air crackling with tension. His eyes softened, the storm of emotions swirling within them betraying the facade of confidence he tried to maintain. "I know I messed up. I know I hurt you, and I'm sorry. But I can't change what happened. All I can do is try to make things right now."

There was a sincerity in his voice that chipped away at the barriers I had so carefully erected. I longed to believe him, to melt into the warmth of our shared history. Yet the pain of his departure echoed in the corners of my mind, casting shadows over my heart.

I was terrified of what might happen if I allowed him back in, as if inviting the very storm that had once torn us apart.

I glanced around the studio, my gaze falling on the photographs hanging on the walls—frozen moments of laughter, joy, and love. They were remnants of the life I had built, but they also reminded me of the emptiness that followed Ethan's departure. I wanted to scream, to shake him and make him understand just how deeply his absence had cut. But instead, I stood there, torn between the desire to lash out and the longing to reach out.

"Why now, Ethan? After all this time?" My voice trembled, betraying my resolve.

He stepped closer, the distance between us closing in like the confines of my heart. "Because I can't go another day pretending that you don't matter to me. You've always mattered. I was a coward, and I hate myself for that. But I'm here now, and I want to make it right."

His words hung in the air, fragile yet potent, daring me to grasp them. As I stood there, the walls around my heart quaked under the weight of his sincerity. I felt the urge to throw caution to the wind and leap into the sea of emotions threatening to drown me. Yet, fear kept me anchored in place, leaving me teetering on the precipice of a choice I was not sure I was ready to make.

As Ethan stood just a breath away, the silence between us felt like a tightly stretched wire, ready to snap at the slightest touch. I could see the myriad of emotions flickering in his eyes—regret, hope, and that all-too-familiar spark of mischief that had once drawn me to him like a moth to a flame. I hated that I was still susceptible to it, the way his presence seemed to thaw the ice around my heart, even just a little.

"Can we just... start over?" he asked, his voice low and earnest, as if he were pleading for a chance he feared I might deny him. The vulnerability in his tone tugged at something deep within me. I wanted to say yes, to embrace the possibility of rekindling what we once shared. But my pride and the scars of the past kept me anchored in uncertainty.

I folded my arms tighter across my chest, a defensive barrier against the warmth of his gaze. "What's there to start over? You left without a word. You can't just waltz back in and expect everything to be fine." My words came out sharper than I intended, but I couldn't help myself. They were a shield, a way to push him away before I got too close and lost myself again.

Ethan's face fell, the light in his eyes dimming momentarily. "I know. I know I messed up," he said, his voice barely above a whisper. "But I had my reasons. It wasn't just about you. I thought I was protecting you, and maybe I was just being selfish."

His admission hung in the air, heavy and suffocating. I wanted to scream that I didn't want his protection; I wanted him. I wanted the carefree laughter we shared, the way he looked at me as if I were the only person in the room, the way we lost ourselves in our conversations until the sun dipped below the horizon. But all that seemed so far away, a distant memory blurred by the pain of his abrupt exit.

"I don't need your excuses, Ethan," I replied, my voice steadier than I felt. "What I need is for you to understand the damage you caused. I was left picking up the pieces of a life that you abandoned."

He took a step closer, and I felt the heat radiating from him, pulling me in against my better judgment. "You think I didn't feel it too? That I just walked away without a second thought? I think about it every day—what I lost when I lost you."

His words pierced through the barrier I had built, igniting a flicker of hope that danced dangerously close to my heart. But I squashed it down, determined not to fall into the trap of his charm again. "You have no idea what I've gone through, Ethan. You don't get to come back and act like you understand."

His brow furrowed, and for a moment, it felt as if we were both suspended in time, locked in this fragile dance of anger and longing. "I know it's not the same, but I'm trying to be here now. Isn't that something?"

My gaze flickered away from him, landing on the photographs lining the walls—moments frozen in time, each one a testament to the life I had built in the aftermath of his departure. I had poured my heart into my work, using the lens as a shield against the world. Each snapshot told a story, but none could capture the ache of losing the boy who had once been my everything.

"What do you want from me?" I asked, my voice tinged with frustration. "Do you want forgiveness? A chance to make things right? Because I don't know if I can give you that."

Ethan ran a hand through his hair, the familiar gesture bringing a wave of nostalgia. "I want to understand. I want to know how to fix this. I just want to be part of your life again."

His earnestness was disarming, and for the first time, I felt the foundations of my defenses tremble. It was the very thing I longed for but had spent so long convincing myself I didn't. Could I really let him back in? Was it worth the risk of getting hurt again?

The warmth in the studio seemed to amplify, wrapping around us like an embrace, but I resisted its pull. "It's not that simple, Ethan. Trust isn't something you can just rebuild overnight. You have to understand that."

"I do understand," he insisted, taking another step closer. The air crackled between us, charged with memories and unfulfilled desires. "And I'll do whatever it takes to earn your trust back. Just give me a chance."

There was sincerity in his voice that sent my heart racing, a familiar rhythm I had tried to silence for so long. "What does that look like? You want to take photos together? Laugh like nothing ever happened?" The bitterness in my words surprised even me, but I needed him to understand the depth of my hurt.

"No, it's more than that." Ethan's expression shifted, a blend of determination and vulnerability. "I want to show you that I'm different now. That I've grown. We both have. I just need you to meet me halfway."

His plea resonated deep within me, but I couldn't shake the fear that clung to my heart. The memories of the boy who had once made me feel invincible battled with the image of the man before me—someone who had walked away when I needed him most. "And what if it's just the same old story, Ethan? What if I open up and let you back in only for you to leave again?"

His gaze softened, and I caught a glimpse of the boy I once knew, buried beneath layers of time and regret. "I can't promise it won't be messy, but I can promise that I'll fight for you. I won't let you go again. You mean too much to me."

My heart thundered in my chest, the gravity of his words pulling me closer to a choice I had dreaded for so long. In that moment, I felt the walls I had painstakingly constructed begin to tremble. The urge to trust him again flickered within me, a small flame against the cold winds of doubt that howled in the corners of my mind.

"Okay," I finally said, my voice barely above a whisper. "But it's going to take time. I can't just forget how much you hurt me."

"I don't expect you to," he replied, relief washing over his features. "I just want the chance to prove that I can be someone you can count on. Someone who won't run away."

In that instant, a flicker of hope ignited within me. Maybe we could find our way back to each other. It wouldn't be easy, and I could feel the shadows of the past still lurking in the corners of my heart. But standing here, feeling the warmth of his presence and the sincerity in his eyes, I couldn't help but wonder if perhaps this time could be different.

I stepped back, creating a physical distance that mirrored my emotional one. "We'll see. I'm not ready to dive in headfirst just yet."

"Fair enough," he said, a hint of a smile breaking through the tension. "I'll take what I can get."

The air around us shifted, a fragile truce forged in the midst of chaos. My heart was still a battlefield, but for the first time in a long while, it felt like there was a possibility of healing. Maybe together, we could navigate this fractured connection and find our way back to a future we could both embrace.

The sunlight streaming through the windows painted the studio in hues of warmth, but the atmosphere felt frigid, a strange contradiction that mirrored the turmoil inside me. Ethan's presence—an uninvited specter—shifted the balance of my carefully crafted sanctuary. The sweet scent of coffee mingled with the lingering smell of varnish from a recent project, a comforting backdrop to a moment that felt anything but. I shifted my weight, hoping to ground myself, but my heart raced as if it were trying to escape the room.

"Okay," I finally conceded, my voice barely breaking the silence. "You want a chance to prove yourself? Then prove it. But understand that this is going to take more than just a few apologies."

Ethan nodded, an earnestness flooding his features that tugged at my heartstrings. "I'm willing to do whatever it takes. I just need to show you I'm not the same person who left."

With those words, a new kind of tension settled between us, laced with anticipation and fear. I felt as though we were two tightrope walkers, each trying to maintain our balance on a thin line stretched high above an uncertain chasm. The stakes were painfully high, and one misstep could send us both tumbling into an abyss of hurt we had once known too well.

"So, how do you propose we start?" I asked, my tone softer now but still laced with caution. "You can't just waltz back into my life like nothing happened."

"I get that," he replied, taking a deep breath, as if summoning the courage to forge ahead. "Let's start with something simple. Coffee? Just like old times?"

His suggestion hung in the air, a simple invitation that felt loaded with implications. The idea of slipping back into the familiar comfort of our shared moments sent a thrill through me. I envisioned us sitting in a quaint café, the soft hum of conversation surrounding us like a warm embrace. But just as quickly, doubt crept in, reminding me of the jagged edges that had resulted from his absence.

"Why don't we just stay here?" I suggested, gesturing to the coffee maker on the counter. "It's quiet, and we won't have to worry about anyone overhearing."

Ethan's expression brightened, and I felt a rush of satisfaction. He was willing to meet me halfway, to rebuild our connection in a space where I felt secure. "That works for me," he said, a grin breaking through his earlier tension.

As I busied myself preparing the coffee, the steam rising in soft curls, I could feel his gaze on me. It was a heady mix of warmth and nostalgia, drawing me back to lazy afternoons spent chatting over cups of coffee, where the world outside felt miles away. I could almost hear the soft laughter, the easy banter. But beneath that warmth lay the chill of past grievances, a reminder that our history was complex, threaded with pain and longing.

I handed him a steaming mug, our fingers brushing for just a moment, and I fought the rush of warmth that coursed through me. "So, what have you been up to?" I asked, trying to keep my voice casual, but I could feel the tension underlying my question.

"Honestly?" he said, leaning against the counter, his expression shifting from jovial to contemplative. "A lot of soul-searching. I spent some time in New York, trying to figure out what I wanted. I didn't know what I had until I lost it."

I couldn't help but scoff lightly. "You say that now, but what were you thinking back then?"

"I thought I was doing the right thing," he replied, the sincerity in his voice palpable. "But now I know I was just running away from my problems. From you."

I studied his face, searching for the flicker of truth in his eyes. "And you think just coming back is going to fix everything? You really believe we can just pick up where we left off?"

"No," he admitted, his voice steady. "But I hope we can build something new. I want to be a part of your life again, not just as the guy who hurt you but as someone who supports you."

His words struck a chord within me, resonating with a longing I had kept buried beneath layers of hurt. "And how do you plan to support me?" I challenged, my heart racing with a mixture of hope and skepticism.

"Let me help you with your photography. I know how much it means to you, and I'd love to learn more about it," he suggested, his enthusiasm palpable. "I can help set up shoots, brainstorm ideas, anything you need."

I arched an eyebrow, skepticism creeping in once more. "You want to be my assistant? You really think that's going to make everything okay?"

He chuckled, a sound that filled the room with warmth. "No, not an assistant. Think of it as a way for us to reconnect. A chance to create together. And who knows, maybe I'll even learn how to take a decent photo."

I couldn't help but smile at his genuine desire to be part of my world again. There was something oddly comforting about the idea of working together, of seeing him step outside of the shadows of our past and into the light of a shared passion. But my heart wavered, caught between the thrill of possibility and the fear of falling for the same illusion again.

"Alright," I relented, my tone softer now. "But don't think this is a free pass. You'll have to work for it. I'm not going to make it easy."

"Wouldn't dream of it," he replied, a spark of mischief lighting up his features. "I'm ready for the challenge."

As we sipped our coffee, the atmosphere shifted, no longer burdened by the weight of our past but filled with the faintest glimmer of hope. We exchanged stories, the easy banter returning like a familiar song, notes weaving through the air, mingling with laughter and the scent of fresh coffee. It felt good, but I remained cautious, determined not to lose myself in the moment.

"I'm serious about this," I said, the weight of my words pressing heavily upon us. "You can't just pop in and out of my life. I need consistency, Ethan. I can't go through this heartbreak again."

"I get it," he said, his gaze earnest. "And I'm willing to show you that I'm here to stay. Just give me time."

The honesty in his voice stirred something within me, a flicker of trust slowly igniting in the depths of my heart. "Time is all I can offer," I replied, my tone softening. "Let's see where this goes."

With each passing moment, it felt like we were carefully untangling the knots of our history, one thread at a time. Though I remained wary, I couldn't deny the magnetic pull between us, the familiar warmth that wrapped around me like a comforting blanket. As we navigated the contours of our new reality, I dared to dream of what might lie ahead, hoping that this time, we could create a future that was brighter than the past we had shared.

In that cozy studio filled with natural light and the scent of fresh coffee, a new chapter began to unfold, the possibilities shimmering before us like the sunlight streaming through the windows, illuminating the path ahead. As the city buzzed outside, a world of opportunity lay waiting, and I felt a fragile hope begin to bloom, tentatively but unmistakably, within my heart.

Chapter 3: Behind the Lens

The city was a living canvas, each street alive with the brushstrokes of a thousand artists, and as I wandered through the bustling neighborhoods of Chicago, I found myself entranced by the kaleidoscope of colors and cultures that surrounded me. The salty tang of the nearby Lake Michigan mixed with the scent of sizzling street food, wafting from the vibrant food trucks that lined the streets. The laughter of children echoed through the air, punctuated by the rhythmic beats of a nearby drummer, filling the atmosphere with a palpable energy that urged me to capture every fleeting moment. My camera dangled from my neck like a loyal companion, a steadfast ally in my quest to unveil the heart and soul of this magnificent city through the lens of my imagination.

    I stepped into Wicker Park, where every brick seemed to tell a story, every corner a new adventure waiting to unfold. I had come here with a mission: to photograph local artists whose creations breathed life into the urban landscape. My hands were clammy with anticipation, the coolness of the camera against my palm grounding me in the moment. It was more than just a project; it was my way of escaping the haunting echoes of my past, the remnants of insecurities that clung to me like the shadows of the alleys I traversed.

    As I strolled through the neighborhood, the murals on the walls sprang to life before my eyes, each one a vibrant testament to the creativity that flowed through this city like an unquenchable river. A bright phoenix adorned one wall, its feathers a riot of reds and oranges, symbolizing rebirth and resilience. I couldn't help but smile, the artist's spirit shining through the colors, igniting a flicker of courage within me. I raised my camera, framing the magnificent mural, clicking the shutter just as a burst of laughter echoed nearby.

    That's when I first spotted her—a whirlwind of energy and color. Mia stood before a blank wall, her overalls splattered with every hue imaginable. Her hair was a wild mane of curls, bouncing as she moved, a playful dance that mirrored her creative spirit. She was talking animatedly with a friend, her hands gesturing dramatically as she painted her dreams into reality. There was an unmistakable fire in her eyes, a passion that radiated from her like sunlight piercing through a storm cloud.

Compelled by an invisible thread, I approached, heart racing as if I were a moth drawn to her flame. "Hi!" I called out, hoping to break through the noise. She turned, her expression shifting from surprise to an infectious grin that lit up her face. "Hey there!" she replied, her voice a melodic lilt that instantly put me at ease.

"What are you working on?" I asked, gesturing to the expanse of untouched wall behind her, the air charged with potential.

"I'm about to bring this wall to life," Mia exclaimed, her excitement palpable. "It's going to be a tribute to the local community—a vibrant representation of all the people who make this place what it is. Want to help?" Her enthusiasm was so genuine, so inviting, I felt a flutter of possibility in my chest.

I hesitated, unsure of how to respond. "I'm not really an artist," I confessed, my self-doubt creeping in like an unwelcome fog. "I just take pictures."

"Exactly! You see the world differently. You can help me capture the essence of this project." Her eyes sparkled, and I felt a warmth spreading through me that I hadn't experienced in ages. "Come on! Grab your camera and let's get started!"

Before I knew it, I found myself beside her, my camera suddenly feeling like more than just a tool—it became a bridge connecting me to this vibrant world, a means to express the emotions I often kept buried. We worked side by side, my heart racing as I clicked the shutter, capturing Mia's every brushstroke. She poured herself into her art, each stroke of her brush echoing her laughter, her fervor infecting me with newfound courage.

As the mural began to take shape—a fusion of colors and figures that danced together—I learned more about Mia. She spoke of her dreams and aspirations, her voice an exhilarating melody that carried me along with it. She was an artist not just in the way she painted but in the way she approached life, with reckless abandon and fearless joy. Her fire ignited something dormant inside me, coaxing me out from behind my self-imposed barricades.

"Why do you hide?" she asked one afternoon as we took a break, the sun dipping low in the sky and casting a warm glow over the city. We sat on the curb, the cool concrete beneath us, the day winding down around us like a whispered secret. "Your photos have so much life in them. You need to let that shine through."

I looked away, the weight of her question settling heavily in the air between us. "It's complicated," I finally said, my voice barely above a whisper. "I've always felt like I'm not good enough. Like there's something... wrong with me."

Mia's expression softened, her fiery demeanor giving way to a genuine empathy. "There's nothing wrong with you. Everyone has their struggles. But you can't let your past dictate your future. Your art is beautiful, just like you."

Her words hung in the air, a gentle challenge, nudging me toward the precipice of my own potential. I took a deep breath, feeling the warmth of her encouragement wrap around me like a cozy blanket. Maybe it was time to let go of the weight that had anchored me to the ground for too long. The shadows of self-doubt started to dissipate, replaced by the vibrant hues of possibility that Mia effortlessly embodied.

I returned to my photography with renewed vigor, capturing not just the subjects but the emotions and stories woven into each frame. Each click of the shutter became an act of defiance against the doubts that had once consumed me. I was no longer just a spectator;

I was a participant in the colorful tapestry of life, every image I took a step closer to embracing who I truly was.

As the mural took its final form, bursting with life and stories waiting to be told, I realized that in capturing Mia's world, I was also beginning to reclaim my own. The city thrummed around us, alive with the promise of tomorrow, and for the first time in a long while, I felt a flicker of hope lighting my path.

The city pulsed with life, a heartbeat that quickened with each passing day. The sun rose over Chicago, casting a golden hue across the skyline, illuminating the towering buildings that stood like sentinels of ambition. It was in this lively landscape that I found my sanctuary, a realm where each shutter click unraveled layers of vibrant stories waiting to be told. My camera, a compact companion, became an extension of my soul, a vessel through which I sought connection and expression, while simultaneously cloaking the turmoil within.

Each day, I explored new neighborhoods, uncovering artistic enclaves nestled within the urban sprawl. On a crisp autumn morning, I found myself in Pilsen, where the streets were alive with the scent of freshly baked conchas wafting from local bakeries, mingling with the spicy aroma of tacos from food carts. The walls burst with murals—each a tapestry of color and emotion—depicting stories of resilience, love, and cultural heritage. My lens drank in the beauty around me, eager to capture not just the images but the very essence of the lives lived here.

I wandered into a cozy coffee shop, its warm ambiance inviting me to stay a while. The air was thick with the comforting aroma of espresso and cinnamon, and I settled into a corner booth, my camera resting on the table like a loyal friend. As I sipped my drink, I noticed a small group of artists gathered in the corner, their animated discussions punctuated by laughter. They spoke of upcoming projects, ideas swirling around like the steam from their mugs, each artist bringing their unique flair to the conversation.

It was then that I saw her again—Mia. She was perched on a barstool, her eyes sparkling with mischief as she animatedly gestured with a paintbrush in hand, splattered with colors that seemed to reflect her vibrant personality. It was impossible not to be drawn to her; there was a magnetic quality to her presence that felt electric, igniting a warmth in the pit of my stomach. I hadn't anticipated how much her energy would awaken something within me, a reminder that life, much like art, was meant to be lived boldly.

After gathering my courage, I approached the table, my heart fluttering with the thrill of new connections. "Hey, Mia," I called out, trying to sound nonchalant as I joined them. She turned, a grin blooming on her face that felt like sunlight breaking through clouds.

"Glad to see you! You're just in time to hear about my latest masterpiece," she exclaimed, her enthusiasm contagious. The other artists welcomed me with open arms, and I found myself swept into their world, where creativity flowed as freely as the coffee.

As they discussed their works in progress, I listened intently, soaking in their passion like a sponge. Mia spoke about her mural project, the symbolism woven into every color and shape. "Art should challenge, inspire, and evoke emotions," she declared, her voice ringing with conviction. "I want people to stop and feel something, anything, when they see my work." Each word dripped with her fiery spirit, and I felt an urge to capture that very essence in my photographs.

"Would you let me take some portraits of you while you work?" I asked, my voice steady despite the fluttering in my chest. "I'd love to capture the passion that drives you."

Mia's eyes lit up, and she nodded enthusiastically. "Absolutely! But only if you promise to join me in the paint! It's a collaboration, after all." Her laughter was infectious, a melodic sound that wrapped around me like a warm embrace.

What was I getting myself into? The thought sent a wave of apprehension coursing through me, yet I felt an undeniable thrill at the idea of stepping outside my comfort zone. "Alright, you've got a deal," I replied, a smile creeping onto my face.

That afternoon, we ventured to her favorite mural spot—an expansive wall on a quiet street, adorned with the remnants of forgotten art. The space was draped in an aura of history, and I could feel the anticipation crackling in the air as we prepared to breathe new life into it. As I set up my camera, Mia began to sketch out her vision, her hands moving with a confidence I envied.

With each brushstroke she laid down, I captured her in action, the vibrant colors reflecting off her face, illuminating her features with an ethereal glow. She was a force of nature, and I felt honored to witness her transformation of a blank canvas into a world bursting with life and meaning. The brush danced across the wall, and with it, my inhibitions began to peel away like old paint.

As I clicked the shutter, I felt an exhilaration that I hadn't experienced in ages, a rush of creativity that surged through me like an electric current. I was no longer just an observer; I was part of something greater—a partnership born from our shared love for art. Mia's laughter rang out like music, lifting my spirits, and as the mural evolved, I felt a sense of camaraderie blossom between us.

"Your turn!" Mia announced, stepping back to admire her work. She handed me a paintbrush, its bristles still glistening with fresh paint. "Now it's your turn to add your mark."

I hesitated, fear bubbling up inside me like a shaken soda can. "But I don't know how to paint," I stammered, my insecurities clawing at my confidence.

"Neither do I when I started!" she laughed, her voice light. "It's all about experimentation and finding your voice. Just go for it! Trust yourself."

With a deep breath, I dipped the brush into a swirl of bright yellow paint, hesitantly applying it to the wall. It felt foreign and exhilarating, a rush of adrenaline coursing through my veins as the colors began to blend together. Mia encouraged me, her presence a guiding light that helped dispel my fears. Each stroke became a revelation, a burst of color that freed me from the shackles of self-doubt.

The mural became a visual representation of our collaboration—two distinct voices merging to create something entirely new. The sun dipped lower in the sky, casting long shadows that danced across our work, and I felt as if the city itself was applauding our efforts, the vibrant heartbeat of Chicago echoing our shared triumph.

As we stood back to admire our creation, I felt a warmth radiating from within, a glow that had nothing to do with the setting sun. In that moment, I understood that embracing the unfamiliar didn't just enhance my art; it was a pathway to self-discovery. I had stepped beyond the confines of my own fears, and in the process, I began to see the world through a lens colored with hope and possibility.

As the mural emerged, a vivid tapestry of our combined imaginations, I felt the boundaries of my own self-doubt begin to dissolve. The colors, bold and unapologetic, spoke of stories long buried, of resilience and hope that thrived against the urban landscape. Each brushstroke we applied seemed to echo the laughter and chatter of the neighborhood, the backdrop alive with the sound of children playing and the distant thrum of music seeping from nearby cafes. Chicago was not merely a city; it was a vibrant tapestry woven from countless threads of creativity, culture, and life, and I was beginning to understand my place within it.

Mia and I worked late into the evening, the setting sun casting a warm glow that bathed our mural in a golden hue. The air was crisp, tinged with the scent of autumn leaves and the faintest hint of woodsmoke. Mia's laughter danced in the air as she showed me her favorite painting techniques, explaining how colors could evoke emotion, how shadows could tell stories. "Art is like a conversation," she said, her voice a melody of passion. "You have to listen to it as much as you speak."

With each word, I felt more of my own voice begin to emerge, no longer trapped within the confines of my past. I embraced the vibrant energy surrounding us, letting it seep into my bones and fill the gaps that had long felt hollow. My camera, now resting against my chest, felt like an extension of my heart, pulsing with life and possibility.

By the time we stepped back to admire our work, the mural was a riot of color and form—dynamic shapes that twisted and turned, punctuated by symbols that reflected the community's spirit. We had woven together elements that spoke of unity, diversity, and the raw beauty of artistic expression. As I looked at our creation, I realized I had captured not just a moment, but a heartbeat—an imprint of who we were in that instant.

Mia wiped her hands on her overalls, a satisfied grin plastered on her face. "We did this," she said, glancing back at the mural, her eyes alight with triumph. "And it's only the beginning."

Her words hung in the air, resonating deep within me. What did the beginning mean? It felt like an invitation to something greater, a beckoning towards a future I had never dared to imagine. My mind spun with possibilities, a world unfolding before me that was rich with potential, waiting for me to step into it.

The following days were a whirlwind of creativity and collaboration. We began to organize a community event—a mural unveiling that would celebrate not only our work but the artists and residents of Pilsen. Flyers scattered across coffee shops and art studios, inviting everyone to join the festivities. As the date approached, the energy in the neighborhood grew palpable, charged with anticipation.

Mia and I spent our mornings finishing the mural, while the afternoons were filled with preparation—decorating the area, gathering supplies, and enlisting the help of local musicians and food vendors. Each interaction reinforced the bonds we were forming within the community, and I could feel my own fears being replaced by a sense of belonging. I was no longer just an outsider with a camera; I was becoming part of a tapestry woven from the threads of connection, creativity, and resilience.

On the day of the unveiling, the sun shone brightly, casting a radiant glow over the street. The smell of freshly made tacos mingled with the sweet scent of pastries, creating an aroma that felt like a celebration itself. The street was lined with tables adorned with colorful tablecloths, showcasing local art and handmade crafts. Children giggled and chased each other, their laughter mingling with the vibrant sounds of live music that echoed through the air.

As the moment of the unveiling approached, I stood beside Mia, both of us bubbling with excitement and nerves. "Are you ready?" she asked, her voice barely containing the thrill that coursed through her.

"Ready as I'll ever be," I replied, my heart racing in time with the pulsating beat of the drums from a nearby band. The crowd had gathered, their faces lit with curiosity, and I felt a surge of pride swell within me. This was our moment, our creation—a reflection of the love and effort we had poured into every inch of that wall.

When the time came to unveil the mural, Mia's hand clasped mine tightly, an anchor amidst the whirlwind of emotions. Together, we pulled back the fabric that concealed our work, revealing the explosion of colors and forms that danced upon the wall. Gasps of awe rippled through the crowd, followed by applause that washed over us like a warm wave.

I could see the faces of the community, their eyes wide with admiration and recognition. They saw themselves in the art—a tapestry of their lives, woven into a narrative that transcended individual stories. Mia and I exchanged glances, and in that moment, I realized how much I had changed. This mural was no longer just a project; it was a celebration of every struggle, every victory, and every shared experience that had shaped us.

As the day unfolded, laughter and music filled the air, each moment a vibrant stroke on the canvas of life. Conversations sparked between strangers, connections blossomed as people mingled, and the energy was intoxicating. I drifted through the crowd, capturing the joy and camaraderie that swirled around us. My camera clicked away, each shot a testament to the resilience and beauty of community, to the magic of art that had the power to bring people together.

Later, as the sun began to set, painting the sky in hues of orange and pink, I found Mia sitting on the curb, a contented smile gracing her face. I joined her, the moment heavy with unspoken gratitude and shared triumph. "You know, I never thought I'd feel this way again," I confessed, my voice quiet against the backdrop of laughter and music.

"Feel what?" she asked, her gaze steady, inviting me to share more.

"Alive," I replied, the truth echoing in the space between us. "I had almost forgotten what it felt like to be part of something bigger, to embrace the moment without fear."

Mia looked at me, her expression softening. "That's what art does, isn't it? It reminds us of our humanity. It brings us together, even when we're alone."

In that moment, surrounded by the vibrant tapestry of life, I knew I had discovered a piece of myself. The world stretched before me like a blank canvas, and for the first time, I felt ready to pick up the brush and paint my own story—a story defined not by the shadows of my past but by the radiant colors of hope and connection that lay ahead.

Chapter 4: Unexpected Encounters

The hum of laughter and soft clinks of glasses mingled in the air as we stepped into the gallery, the walls adorned with vibrant splashes of color that danced before my eyes. The arts district, a colorful tapestry of creativity, sprawled out around me like an invitation to lose myself. Every corner of the street pulsed with life—street musicians serenaded passersby, while food trucks wafted savory scents of gourmet tacos and spicy barbecue. I inhaled deeply, allowing the scents to weave through me, filling the void left by the anticipation of the evening.

Mia tugged me forward, her enthusiasm a force of nature that propelled us toward the entrance of the gallery. "You're going to love this exhibit," she exclaimed, her eyes sparkling with a childlike excitement that reminded me why I adored her so much. With her wild curls bouncing around her shoulders and her eclectic mix of patterns and colors, she embodied the very essence of artistic freedom, a stark contrast to the careful way I always seemed to present myself.

We stepped inside, the atmosphere instantly wrapping us in an intimate embrace. Dim lights hung above, spotlighting the artwork as if to say, "Look here! Marvel at my beauty!" I found myself captivated by a piece—a swirling depiction of a tumultuous ocean, vibrant blues and greens colliding with stark whites, echoing the very chaos I felt within. I reached out, fingers grazing the cool surface of the frame, lost in thought, when suddenly, my world tilted.

The sharp collision of bodies jolted me back to reality. I stumbled, catching a glimpse of a familiar figure—a face that sent my heart into a chaotic dance of emotions. Ethan stood before me, his dark hair slightly tousled, framing a face that still looked as if it belonged in a classic movie poster. My heart raced as I registered the surprise in his deep-set eyes, which sparkled with recognition and something else—was it warmth? I took a step back, attempting to regain my composure, but it felt futile against the tide of memories flooding my mind.

"Hey! Long time no see!" he said, his voice a mix of smooth confidence and genuine surprise. It wrapped around me like a soft blanket, both comforting and overwhelming. I could feel Mia beside me, the excitement in her eyes almost palpable as she beamed at us.

"Ethan! Wow, this is... unexpected." I struggled to keep my voice steady, as if the very act of talking might shatter the delicate moment we were suspended in. I could feel the weight of our shared history—the late-night study sessions, the inside jokes, and the bittersweet memories of unfinished conversations.

"I know, right?" He rubbed the back of his neck, a gesture that was achingly familiar, making me acutely aware of the space between us, a chasm I'd tried to ignore since graduation. "I just got back from a trip abroad. I'm still trying to shake off the jet lag, but seeing you here definitely helps."

His smile was both apologetic and hopeful, igniting something within me. I had spent so long burying the remnants of our past, the laughter we once shared now mingling with uncertainty. The gallery buzzed around us, but in that moment, time stood still.

"Are you still doing the design work?" he asked, tilting his head slightly, as if trying to read the layers of my emotions.

"Yeah, I've been freelancing for a couple of local companies. It's a bit of a rollercoaster," I replied, my voice more animated than I intended. "But I love the freedom it gives me. How about you? I saw some of your photos online—absolutely stunning!"

He flushed slightly, the pink coloring his cheeks making him look boyish and approachable. "Thanks! It's been a dream, really. Traveling has opened my eyes to so many stories. I've just returned from a project in Greece, capturing the landscapes and the people. It was surreal."

The knot in my stomach tightened at the mention of his travels. I forced a smile, pushing down the whirlwind of insecurities that threatened to unravel me. "Greece sounds incredible. I'd love to hear more about it." The words felt forced, each syllable coated in an anxiety I was desperately trying to conceal.

Ethan's expression shifted to one of genuine eagerness. "Why don't we grab a coffee? It's been ages since we've caught up, and I'd love to share more."

My heart raced at the thought, a mixture of excitement and dread battling within me. I glanced at Mia, who was practically vibrating with enthusiasm, silently urging me to accept. "Sure," I finally said, trying to sound casual. "Let's do it."

We wandered out of the gallery, the cool evening air enveloping us as we strolled down the sidewalk lined with art installations and murals, each piece telling its own story. The cafe he led me to had a bohemian vibe, with mismatched furniture and colorful light fixtures that seemed to float like stars in a darkened sky. As we settled into a cozy nook, the ambiance transformed into something more personal, the buzz of the crowd fading into the background.

"I missed this," Ethan said, his voice warm as he stirred his coffee. "I missed us."

The simple words hung in the air, heavy with unspoken histories. I met his gaze, feeling the vulnerability and truth behind them. Memories flooded back—our laughter echoing in the empty hallways of college, the late-night conversations where we dreamed about the future, the moments that left me breathless and longing for more.

As we reminisced, my laughter broke free, filling the space between us. Each shared story, each wave of nostalgia brought me closer to the person I had once been—the girl unafraid to love fiercely and dream boldly. Yet, just as I began to feel the warmth of familiarity, he casually mentioned the places he had traveled to, and the knot tightened painfully in my stomach.

"While I was in Santorini, I met this incredible girl. We really hit it off. It's wild how quickly you can form connections when you're out there, living in the moment," he said, his tone light, but I could hear the gravity behind it.

The laughter caught in my throat, the warmth from earlier evaporating into an icy chill. I fumbled with my coffee cup, the porcelain feeling foreign in my grip. Suddenly, the stories we shared felt less like a reunion and more like a reminder of the distance that had grown between us. I tried to mask the hurt that flickered across my face, but it felt impossible as the echoes of my own insecurities began to drown out the joy of our conversation.

And so, we sat together, the familiar warmth of our connection juxtaposed against the cold reality of my uncertainty.

The coffee shop hummed with the soft sounds of conversation and the rich aroma of freshly brewed espresso. I took a moment to inhale deeply, trying to capture the comforting blend of coffee and baked goods that filled the air. The space was warm and inviting, with worn wooden tables and mismatched chairs that added a touch of character. I could hear the gentle clink of ceramic cups as patrons engaged in soft conversations, their voices merging into a symphony of casual intimacy. The atmosphere felt alive, yet it contrasted sharply with the rising tension knotting my stomach.

Ethan leaned back in his chair, the light from the vintage-style lamp casting a soft glow on his face. There was something disarming about him—an easy charm wrapped in layers of nostalgia and a hint of mischief. I watched as he took a sip of his coffee, his eyes momentarily closed in bliss, and I felt a strange longing to reach out and touch that moment, to hold onto it like it was a fragile piece of art. The laughter we had shared moments earlier still echoed in my ears, but as he spoke of his recent adventures, I felt that echo fading, replaced by uncertainty.

"Greece was surreal," he continued, a faraway look in his eyes. "The sunsets were incredible—like the sky was on fire. I even took a ferry to a few of the islands. You know me and my obsession with sunsets." He laughed softly, a sound that once filled my heart with warmth but now made it clench in confusion.

I nodded, forcing a smile while internally battling the uncomfortable twist in my gut. "That sounds amazing. You always had a knack for finding the most picturesque places." The compliment slipped out before I could stop it, and I felt an uncomfortable flush creep up my neck. What was I doing? Was I really sitting here, complimenting him on his adventures while battling my own insecurities?

The conversation meandered through the familiar landscapes of our shared history, weaving in and out like a well-loved tapestry. We spoke of professors who had shaped our minds and late-night study sessions fueled by caffeine and half-hearted attempts at preparing for exams. Each story felt like a step backward into the safety of our past, where everything had been uncomplicated and filled with promise.

Then Ethan mentioned the girl from Greece—an offhand comment that caught me off guard. "Her name was Mira," he said, a slight smile playing on his lips. "She had this infectious laugh, and we shared a couple of nights just wandering the markets. It was refreshing, you know?"

The words pierced through the warmth of our reunion, sending a chill down my spine. My heart sank as I felt the weight of those words. I glanced down at my coffee, swirling the dark liquid as if I could erase the implications swirling in my mind. How was it possible that a moment of reconnecting could morph into a moment of sheer vulnerability? My laughter felt hollow now, echoing like a distant memory as I navigated the treacherous waters of jealousy and insecurity.

"Sounds like quite the adventure," I replied, forcing a smile that felt more like a mask. The coffee shop's chatter faded into the background, replaced by the rushing sound of my heartbeat. "I'm glad you're experiencing all of that. It seems... liberating."

Ethan's eyes softened, and I couldn't tell if he noticed the shift in my demeanor. "It was. But you know, sometimes I miss the simpler things. The late-night talks, the ridiculous debates about which pizza joint was better." He leaned forward, his gaze intense. "I didn't realize how much I'd missed you until I got back."

The confession hung between us, heavy with significance. I felt my pulse quicken, the flutter of hope battling against the iron grip of doubt that had settled within me. "I've missed you too," I admitted, the truth escaping my lips before I could think to restrain it. "But life got in the way, didn't it?"

The corner of his mouth quirked upward, and for a fleeting moment, the shadows of our shared past brightened the space between us. "Yeah, life has a way of complicating things. But it's nice to think that some things haven't changed."

The warmth of his words wrapped around me like a comforting blanket, igniting a spark of hope that flickered within me. I could still feel the remnants of the laughter we had shared, the joy that had been so easily revived between us. Perhaps there was a chance—however slim—that the connection we once had could be rekindled.

But just as quickly as that thought ignited, the fire of hope dimmed, a stark reminder that we were no longer the carefree college kids, with the world at our fingertips and dreams waiting to be chased. I fiddled with the paper napkin on the table, my mind racing as I tried to balance the possibilities against the reality of his newfound adventures.

"Where do you see yourself going next?" I asked, attempting to steer the conversation away from the intimacy we had slipped into. "Any more travel plans?"

He took a moment, his expression thoughtful. "I've been considering going to Japan. The culture, the food—it all seems fascinating. Plus, I've heard the cherry blossoms in spring are breathtaking."

"Sounds incredible," I replied, a bittersweet smile spreading across my face. I pictured him wandering through vibrant streets, surrounded by new experiences and faces I could never know. It stung more than I wanted to admit, the image of him finding joy and adventure without me.

His gaze flickered back to me, concern shadowing his features. "What about you? Any plans to travel? I remember you talking about wanting to explore the West Coast."

I hesitated, the weight of my dreams pressing down on me like a lead anchor. "I've thought about it," I admitted, trying to muster some excitement that I didn't quite feel. "But for now, I'm just focused on my work. Building something for myself."

"Building something?" he asked, his brow raised in genuine interest. "What does that look like for you?"

I paused, searching for the right words, feeling a surge of vulnerability rise within me. "I guess I'm just trying to carve out my own space in this city. I've always wanted to create something meaningful, maybe even something that connects people."

"Like art?" he mused, leaning back in his chair, his expression shifting to one of admiration. "You've always had an artist's heart."

His words sparked something inside me, a flicker of the passion I had buried beneath layers of doubt. "Yeah, art has always been a part of me. I just want to find a way to make it a bigger part of my life."

"I believe you will," Ethan replied, his voice steady, cutting through the haze of my insecurities. "You always had that fire in you."

For a moment, the weight of uncertainty lifted, replaced by a shared understanding that sparked between us. I smiled genuinely this time, feeling lighter than I had in ages, as if our conversation had reignited a dormant part of my spirit. But as the minutes passed and the world continued its relentless march forward, I couldn't shake the sensation that our brief reconnection was destined to become another cherished memory, leaving me to wonder if the path we had once walked together could ever be crossed again.

As we continued to sip our coffee, the comforting warmth of the mugs in our hands momentarily distracted me from the underlying tension I felt. I watched Ethan, noting how he appeared to be the same yet so different—an evolution marked by his experiences and travels. His laughter resonated in my ears, a melody I had once taken for granted, now tinged with an unfamiliarity that felt both refreshing and alarming.

He shared more about his time in Greece, the sun-drenched landscapes, and the intricate labyrinth of ancient ruins that had captured his imagination. "You should see the way the light hits the Parthenon at sunset," he said, his eyes sparkling with enthusiasm. "It's like the whole structure comes alive. It made me think about how history feels so present there—like you could reach out and touch it."

A part of me was captivated, drawn into the narrative he spun with such ease. I could almost picture the scene—the golden hues of the sun setting over the ancient stone, the laughter of locals echoing through the streets, and the bustling marketplaces filled with life. My heart ached at the thought of him in those moments, weaving stories with strangers who would fade into the background of his life, while I remained a ghost of his past.

"You've always had a knack for storytelling," I replied, trying to keep my voice steady. "I remember those late-night tales you'd spin about your dreams of traveling the world."

His smile turned soft, nostalgia swimming in his gaze. "Yeah, I guess some dreams don't fade. But honestly, they're even better when you live them. I didn't realize how much I needed to break out of my comfort zone."

Comfort zone. The phrase echoed in my mind, wrapping around me like a weighted blanket. I had been so focused on building a life in the same city, the same familiar routines, that I hadn't truly considered what it might mean to step outside my own boundaries. Perhaps my art had become my way of experiencing the world—a canvas for the dreams I hadn't dared to chase.

"What about you? Have you found your own adventures?" Ethan asked, his tone shifting, genuine curiosity illuminating his features.

I hesitated, my mind racing through memories of failed attempts and stifled dreams. "I've been working a lot, really. Trying to establish my career as a designer." The words felt like a disclaimer, an explanation for why I hadn't traveled, why I hadn't experienced the world in the same way he had.

"Isn't that an adventure in its own right?" he countered, leaning closer. "Creating something new? Isn't that what art is all about?"

A flicker of warmth ignited within me at his encouragement. "I suppose it is. Sometimes I get caught up in the daily grind and forget how transformative the creative process can be." I sighed, the tension in my shoulders easing slightly. "But I do long for something more, something that feels as vibrant as the colors on a canvas."

The words hung in the air, charged with a truth I rarely allowed myself to explore. As if sensing the shift, Ethan's expression turned contemplative. "You should let yourself experience it. Take that leap, whatever it looks like. Sometimes the best art comes from chaos, from stepping into the unknown."

His words were a soothing balm against my uncertainties, but as soon as they resonated, a wave of doubt crashed over me. "But what if it's not enough? What if I fail?"

Ethan shook his head, his dark hair catching the light. "Failure is just part of the journey. Every artist I've met has a story of setbacks and missed opportunities. It's what makes the success worth it. Besides, you won't know until you try."

I felt my resolve wavering, pulled between the comfort of the known and the excitement of the unfamiliar. The conversation turned lighter again, as we exchanged stories of friends and mutual acquaintances from college, each name evoking laughter and nostalgia. It was a beautiful distraction, a reminder of a time when possibilities felt endless.

"Do you remember that art showcase we put together?" he asked, a grin spreading across his face. "The one where you created that giant mural of the skyline? I still think it was the highlight of the event."

A laugh escaped me, bubbling up like champagne. "I do! I spent three sleepless nights working on it, but seeing everyone's reactions made it worth it. I never thought I could create something that would resonate with so many people."

"Exactly," he replied, his voice earnest. "You've always had that gift. Maybe it's time to rediscover it."

Before I could respond, a flash of movement at the entrance of the café caught my eye. A couple entered, their laughter ringing out like a bell, drawing the attention of everyone in the room. They looked utterly captivating, a whirlwind of style and charisma that felt like a stark contrast to our more subdued presence.

Ethan turned his head, glancing at the couple as they exchanged flirty banter. "Some people just have that energy, don't they?" he mused, a hint of envy lacing his tone.

"Yeah, it's almost contagious," I replied, watching as they seamlessly navigated their surroundings, completely at ease. A pang of longing shot through me—how easy it looked, how effortless their connection seemed.

"Do you ever feel like you're missing out?" Ethan asked suddenly, his eyes focused on me. "Like there's a whole world out there that's passing you by?"

I contemplated his words, feeling the weight of his gaze as he searched for an answer. "Sometimes. It's hard not to when you see people living so boldly, so fearlessly."

"What holds you back?" he pressed, his tone soft but insistent.

The question cut through my thoughts, exposing the fragile layers of my insecurities. "I don't know. Fear of failure, maybe? Fear of change?"

He nodded, understanding evident in his eyes. "Change can be terrifying, but it can also be the catalyst for something extraordinary."

As our eyes locked, a sense of clarity washed over me. This conversation, this moment, felt like a turning point, the beginning of something new. I was sitting across from the boy who had once known me so well, and here we were, confronting the ghosts of our past while contemplating the paths ahead.

"Maybe it's time to step outside that comfort zone," I murmured, almost to myself.

Ethan's smile widened, and for the first time, I could see the flicker of possibility mirrored in his eyes. "Let's make a pact," he said, leaning forward with a playful intensity. "We'll take a leap together. You help me with a photography project I've been wanting to explore, and I'll help you plan your next adventure—no matter where it leads."

A smile broke free on my face, hope bubbling within me like champagne once more. "Deal."

The rest of the world faded away, leaving just the two of us in our little café oasis, wrapped in laughter and dreams. Whatever came next felt less daunting, as if we were both standing at the edge of a vast horizon, ready to leap into the unknown together. And in that moment, the knots in my stomach began to unravel, replaced by a growing sense of excitement for the adventure that awaited us, hand in hand.

Chapter 5: The Art of Healing

The vibrant pulse of the city reverberated around me as I prepared for the photoshoot, the sun casting golden rays that danced over the graffiti-covered walls of downtown Atlanta. Each stroke of paint told a story, and as I stood before Mia's latest mural, a stunning tapestry of color and emotion, I felt an exhilarating mix of excitement and trepidation. The air was rich with the scent of wet paint and the faint aroma of street food wafting from a nearby vendor, each whiff anchoring me in the moment. This wasn't just another project; it was a revival of sorts, not just for the city but for me as well.

Ethan arrived with that effortless charm that always managed to render me speechless. His tousled hair caught the sun just right, creating a halo effect that made my heart flutter. With a camera slung casually around his neck, he approached with a confidence that both intrigued and unnerved me. As he stood beside me, we exchanged smiles that felt like electric currents, sparking an undeniable chemistry that made the walls I had so carefully constructed begin to waver.

"Ready to capture some magic?" he asked, his voice smooth and inviting, as if we were the only two people in the world at that moment. I nodded, a playful smile creeping onto my face, trying to mask the fluttering in my stomach. We began to set up, Ethan taking the lead with an enthusiasm that made my heart swell. He adjusted the camera, his fingers brushing the lens with a delicacy that seemed to carry unspoken promises. The way he focused on the details—the vibrant hues of the mural, the interplay of light and shadow—reminded me that beneath his playful demeanor was a profound sensitivity, an understanding of the beauty in imperfection.

As the first click of the camera echoed in the air, the world around us faded away. I stepped back to observe, marveling at the artistry that Mia had poured into her work. It was a kaleidoscope of dreams, aspirations, and raw emotion, each stroke reflecting the heartbeats of those who passed by, each color a voice yearning to be heard. I could feel my heart align with the rhythm of the mural, a symphony of hope that echoed in my soul.

"Let's try a few with you in the frame," Ethan suggested, a glint of mischief in his eyes. My heart raced at the idea. The thought of being part of the mural felt both exhilarating and terrifying. Yet, his gaze, warm and inviting, coaxed me into the moment. I positioned myself against the mural, letting the colors envelop me, feeling the weight of their stories pressing against my skin. Ethan clicked the shutter, each snap capturing a piece of my vulnerability, a moment of trust I wasn't entirely sure I was ready to give.

The afternoon melted into a dance of light and laughter as we moved through different angles, trying to capture the essence of Mia's work. With every shared glance, my walls began to feel less formidable, less like an impenetrable fortress and more like a delicate veil that might soon be lifted. We joked and teased, our laughter echoing in the alleyway, mixing with the distant sounds of the bustling city. I could see in Ethan's eyes that he felt it too—the magic that seemed to weave around us, a tapestry of connection that both thrilled and terrified me.

But beneath the surface, the anxiety stirred. I grappled with the fear that had rooted itself in my heart, a persistent whisper that warned me of the fragility of our situation. Could I trust him again? Could I trust myself to open up? As we reviewed the photos on the camera, I saw glimpses of our shared energy, the warmth radiating between us, igniting hope that maybe our connection wasn't as broken as I had thought.

In one of the photos, I caught a fleeting moment of laughter—my eyes crinkled in delight, Ethan's expression one of pure joy. I felt a flutter in my chest as I studied the image. It was beautiful, but it also felt like a dare, challenging me to confront my fears head-on. As the sunlight began to dip below the horizon, painting the sky in hues of pink and orange, I realized that the moment was fleeting, and I didn't want to let it go without a fight.

"Let's try something different," I said, my voice steadying as a new idea sparked within me. "Let's take a few shots with you in front of the mural, too. I want to capture your perspective."

Ethan looked surprised, a smile creeping onto his lips. "You want to include me in the art?"

"Why not? You're a part of it now," I replied, a sudden surge of confidence empowering my words. I gestured for him to step forward, and as he positioned himself, I felt a rush of excitement. It was a simple gesture, yet it felt monumental—a step toward bridging the gap between us.

The camera clicked, and I focused on his expression, the way he lit up under the backdrop of vibrant colors. The intimacy of the moment forced me to confront the reality that perhaps, just perhaps, we could rebuild the trust that had been so easily shattered.

Each shot became a testament to our unfolding story—a narrative filled with laughter, vulnerability, and unspoken promises. I knew I had a long way to go, that healing was not a straight path but rather a winding road filled with bumps and detours. Yet as I stood there, capturing the essence of our shared experience, I felt the weight of my fears begin to lighten, replaced by a fragile but undeniable sense of hope.

As the sun sank lower, casting long shadows over the alley, I realized that this moment was just the beginning, an awakening of sorts. With Ethan by my side, I felt ready to embrace the uncertainties ahead, to dance with my fears rather than let them dictate my journey. It was an exhilarating thought, one that ignited a fire within me, pushing me to step further into the light.

With the sunset bleeding into the evening sky, we decided to take a break from shooting and wandered down a nearby street alive with the sounds of laughter and clinking glasses. The air was fragrant with the smoky aroma of grilled meats and sweet spices from food trucks that had lined the sidewalks, each offering a mouthwatering array of delights. As we ambled, Ethan and I exchanged playful banter, the rhythm of our conversation as effortless as the gentle breeze that rustled the leaves above us.

"Okay, I have to ask," Ethan began, a teasing glint in his eye, "what's your go-to order at a food truck? Are you a taco person, or are you secretly judging the world from a safe distance with a salad?"

I laughed, swatting at his arm playfully. "Salad? Please! Tacos all the way. You can't judge a good taco without getting a little messy, and I am all about the mess."

His eyes sparkled with mischief. "Then let's find you the messiest taco in Atlanta."

As we wove through the crowd, the sound of sizzling meats and vibrant conversations enveloped us, creating a warm cocoon of community. I couldn't help but feel that this moment was a reprieve from everything that weighed me down—the worries, the fears, and the lingering doubts about my past. With Ethan beside me, laughter came easily, and the world felt expansive, filled with possibilities.

We stopped at a truck decorated with colorful murals, the vibrant colors reflecting the artistic spirit of the city. I ordered a taco loaded with barbacoa, guacamole, and a heaping pile of fresh salsa, while Ethan opted for a simple chicken taco with just a hint of lime. As we waited for our food, I watched the busy cook flip tortillas, the flames licking at the edges, the sizzling sound a delightful prelude to the feast ahead.

When our tacos finally arrived, we stepped to the side, finding a small patch of curb to sit on. I took a hearty bite, the flavors exploding in my mouth, and I couldn't help but moan in delight. "This is heaven," I declared, eyes wide as I savored every bite.

Ethan grinned, a playful smirk dancing across his lips. "Told you! You're going to have to share your secret taco source with me later."

Between bites, we shared stories about our favorite local spots, trading recommendations like precious currency. I told him about a hidden bookstore down the street, filled with worn leather chairs and dusty shelves that seemed to whisper secrets. He spoke of his favorite coffee shop, where the barista knew how to make a perfect espresso that could coax a smile out of even the most miserable of mornings.

As the sun dipped below the horizon, painting the sky in deep purples and oranges, our conversation shifted, turning more serious, the laughter subsiding into thoughtful contemplation. "So, what about you?" Ethan asked, his tone gentle but probing. "What do you want out of all this? The mural, the project... and me?"

I paused, my taco halfway to my mouth. It was a loaded question, one I hadn't truly examined. The truth was, I had avoided thinking about what I really wanted, the fear of disappointment looming larger than my hopes. "I guess I just want to feel... alive," I finally admitted, the words tumbling out before I could second-guess them. "After everything, I want to create something that matters. I want people to feel something when they see the mural—joy, inspiration, hope."

Ethan nodded, his gaze steady and earnest, the kind of look that made me feel seen. "You're already doing that," he said softly. "Mia's mural is a reflection of your heart. Your energy fuels it."

The weight of his words sank deep, igniting a flicker of warmth within me. I wanted to believe him. I wanted to embrace the notion that perhaps I was more than just the shadows of my past, more than the girl who had stumbled through the darkness for so long. "What about you?" I asked, shifting the focus back to him. "What do you want?"

His smile faded slightly, and I could see the flicker of uncertainty in his eyes. "Honestly? I want to create something that lasts, too. I want to tell stories that matter, whether through photos or film. There's so much beauty in the world, and I want to capture it all."

In that moment, under the canopy of a starlit sky, something shifted between us. Our shared vulnerability created a bridge, one I hadn't realized we were building. Each layer of laughter, every candid glance, now seemed to draw us closer, dissolving the remnants of my reservations like sugar in the rain.

As we finished our tacos, the laughter returned, bubbling up like effervescent soda, sparkling with a newfound intimacy. I was acutely aware of the way his shoulder brushed against mine, the electric warmth radiating between us, like a shared secret that pulsed beneath the surface.

Later, we wandered back toward the mural site, the streets now aglow with the soft light of street lamps. I could feel the energy of the city wrapping around us, welcoming and warm. When we arrived, the mural stood tall and majestic, as if it had absorbed all our laughter and fears and transformed them into something vibrant and real.

"Want to take one more set of photos?" I asked, my heart racing at the thought of capturing this moment. The idea of preserving the night, of solidifying our connection in a tangible way, felt exhilarating.

Ethan's grin was infectious as he nodded. "Absolutely. Let's make it unforgettable."

As I positioned myself again in front of the mural, the glow of the lights illuminating the colors around me, I could feel my confidence surge. This was more than just a photoshoot; it was a testament to our shared journey, a record of two souls learning to trust again. I struck poses, playful and bold, and with each click of the camera, I felt a piece of my heart unfurl, a tentative yet hopeful embrace of the future.

Ethan captured me, not just as I was but as I aspired to be—bold, vibrant, alive. The laughter bubbled between us, mingling with the night air, and I realized that perhaps the art of healing wasn't a solitary journey after all. It was woven into the threads of connection, a tapestry of moments shared and memories created, each one painting a more vivid picture of who I could become.

The evening sun surrendered to the horizon, casting a soft, velvety glow across the vibrant mural. Each stroke of color seemed to pulse with life, mirroring the thrill and apprehension that coursed through me. I felt a rush of gratitude for this space, this moment, where the past began to feel like a distant whisper instead of a haunting echo. With Ethan beside me, the air thickened with possibilities, and for the first time in a long while, I felt the flutter of excitement nudging away my doubts.

"Let's experiment a little," I suggested, my voice light but my heart pounding. "Why don't we try some candid shots? Just us, being... us." I bit my lip, wondering if I had just opened a floodgate of vulnerability.

Ethan's eyes sparkled at the idea, a mischievous grin breaking across his face. "Candid? So you mean I can catch you in a moment of pure taco-induced joy?"

"Precisely!" I replied, laughter spilling from my lips, a sound that felt liberating. "But only if you promise to look equally ridiculous. Deal?"

"Deal," he affirmed, the playful challenge igniting a spark between us.

I positioned myself at the edge of the mural, playfully leaning against it, my heart racing as he lifted the camera. With each click, the shutter captured snippets of our spontaneity—the way my hair caught the light, the sparkle in Ethan's eyes, the genuine joy of being free in that moment. We danced around each other, pretending to pose while laughing at our antics, letting our inhibitions dissolve in the warmth of shared silliness.

But as we played, the atmosphere shifted. The sun dipped lower, and a chilly breeze swept through the alley, sending a shiver down my spine. I shuddered, realizing how quickly the warmth of the day had faded, but Ethan stepped closer, his body brushing against mine, a comforting warmth that ignited a fire beneath my skin. "You okay?" he asked, concern threading through his voice.

"Yeah, just a bit cold," I replied, offering a reassuring smile. But inside, I was battling a tempest of emotions, an urgency growing in my chest—a longing to connect, to break free from the chains of my past and fully embrace this moment.

"Let's head to that coffee shop," Ethan suggested, nodding toward the inviting glow of a nearby café. "They have the best hot chocolate. You'll warm up in no time."

The thought of sharing a cozy drink with him filled me with anticipation. "That sounds perfect," I agreed, and as we made our way down the street, the city buzzed with life around us, the streets adorned with the twinkling lights of nearby shops and the laughter of people milling about.

Once inside the café, the rich scent of roasted coffee and sweet pastries enveloped us like a warm blanket. We found a small table by the window, the glass reflecting our animated conversation. The barista, a cheerful woman with bright pink hair, greeted us with a wide smile, and I couldn't help but feel that this was one of those rare moments that made life feel beautifully serendipitous.

As we sipped our drinks—Ethan indulging in a spiced latte while I savored the decadent hot chocolate—our conversation deepened, weaving through stories of our pasts, our dreams, and our artistic aspirations. I discovered that Ethan had a knack for photography that went beyond the lens; he saw stories in every captured moment, threads of connection in the mundane.

"What do you think it is that draws us to art?" I asked, curiosity lacing my tone. "Why do we feel so compelled to create?"

He paused, a thoughtful expression crossing his face. "I think it's our way of processing the world. Art allows us to express what we can't put into words, to transform pain into beauty. Sometimes, it's the only way to find clarity."

His words resonated deeply within me, striking a chord that reverberated in the quiet corners of my heart. In that moment, I felt a shift—a realization that we were not just creating art for others, but for ourselves, a way to mend the pieces of our fractured souls.

The conversation flowed effortlessly, yet a small part of me still wrestled with the remnants of my fears. I wanted to tell him everything—the doubts, the shadows that haunted me—but the words clung to the back of my throat, unwilling to escape.

"Can I ask you something?" Ethan's voice broke through my reverie, his gaze steady and sincere.

"Of course," I replied, my pulse quickening at the intensity of his expression.

"Why are you so hesitant to let people in? I mean, you're an incredible artist, and yet I feel like there's so much you hold back."

His question hung in the air like a delicate crystal chandelier, shimmering with vulnerability. My heart raced, and I felt the walls I had built around my past begin to tremble. This was my chance to be real, to strip away the layers I had so carefully constructed.

"I guess... I'm scared," I confessed, my voice barely above a whisper. "Scared of opening up, scared of getting hurt again. I've been in places where trust felt like a luxury I couldn't afford."

Ethan leaned closer, his expression softening with understanding. "You're not alone in that. I've been there too. But sometimes, the greatest risks lead to the most beautiful rewards."

His words struck a deep chord, igniting something within me that I had buried for too long. As we continued to talk, the barriers I had erected slowly began to dissolve, revealing the vibrant essence of who I truly was beneath the weight of fear and self-doubt.

The night wore on, and as the café began to empty, we lingered over our drinks, the laughter between us weaving a tapestry of connection that felt unbreakable. I reveled in the moments—his laughter echoing against the backdrop of our shared stories, the warmth radiating between us, the way he listened with rapt attention, making me feel like the only person in the room.

When we finally stepped outside, the cool night air greeted us like an old friend. The streets sparkled under the soft glow of streetlights, and I felt alive—truly alive—for the first time in ages. We strolled together, the conversation flowing like the river nearby, deep and unending.

As we approached the mural once more, Ethan reached for my hand, his touch igniting a warmth that spread through me like wildfire. "Let's make a promise," he said, his voice low and earnest. "Let's keep exploring this—whatever this is—together. No more holding back."

My heart soared at his words, a sweet blend of hope and excitement enveloping me. "I promise," I replied, my voice steady. In that moment, I knew I was ready to embrace this journey of healing, to allow the light of connection to seep through the cracks of my past.

Together, we stood before the mural, its vibrant colors reflecting our newfound bond. The beauty of art lay not just in its creation but in the way it breathed life into our stories, weaving a narrative of hope, healing, and trust that would guide us forward. As we looked into each other's eyes, the world faded away, leaving just the two of us—two artists ready to paint our futures anew.

Chapter 6: The Truth Unveiled

The gallery buzzes with life, a symphony of voices blending with the soft clinking of wine glasses and the rustle of crisp gallery brochures. The walls are adorned with Ethan's photographs, each frame a portal to a different world, a frozen moment in time that whispers stories of adventure, loneliness, and uncharted emotions. I weave through the crowd, drawn deeper into the labyrinth of images that reflect his journey—snapshots of sun-drenched beaches, bustling city streets alive with color, and quiet moments under starry skies that seem to beckon the heart. Each photograph feels like a thread, weaving a tapestry of his experiences, pulling me closer to him in ways I never thought possible.

The scent of fresh paint lingers in the air, mingling with the faint aroma of sandalwood from the candles flickering on tables scattered throughout the gallery. I pause before a photograph of a deserted pier, the sky painted in hues of pink and orange as the sun dips beneath the horizon, and my chest tightens. It echoes my own feelings of isolation and longing, capturing the bittersweet beauty of solitude. Just as I'm lost in thought, a voice breaks through the cacophony—a low murmur filled with warmth.

"Do you see it?" Ethan's voice wraps around me like a familiar embrace. I turn, and the moment I meet his gaze, the world around us fades into a blur. His eyes, a deep shade of blue reminiscent of the ocean depths, hold a sincerity that roots me to the spot. "It's called 'The Edge of Reflection.' I took it on a trip to the coast last summer." He steps closer, and the warmth radiating from him mingles with the evening air, creating an electric tension that makes my pulse quicken.

"It's beautiful," I breathe, my voice barely above a whisper. "It feels so… lonely, yet there's hope in it." I can't help but feel vulnerable, exposed under the weight of his scrutiny. The gallery is alive, but in this moment, it's just the two of us—two souls navigating the delicate dance of connection.

Ethan's expression softens, and he gestures toward another photograph. "Every place has a story. I want people to feel something when they look at my work." His passion is palpable, a fire flickering just beneath the surface of his calm demeanor. "But it's not just the places—it's the emotions that come with them. The fear of being alone, the joy of discovery... they're all intertwined."

Before I can respond, he takes my hand gently, leading me away from the thrumming heart of the gallery to a quieter corner, where the noise becomes a distant hum. The moment feels intimate, charged with unspoken words. I can feel my heart racing, a drumbeat echoing the urgency of the moment. He turns to me, his eyes searching mine as if looking for something he's afraid to name.

"Lily," he starts, his voice low and earnest. "There's something I need to tell you." The gravity in his tone draws me closer, as if the air itself thickens around us, filled with anticipation. "When I left the mansion... it wasn't just about the curse. It was about me. I was scared." The vulnerability in his admission cuts through the air like a blade, and I can almost feel the weight of his confession settle between us.

"Scared?" The word escapes my lips, laced with disbelief. How could someone as vibrant and talented as Ethan ever feel fear? "You? But you're so..." I falter, searching for the right words. "You're amazing, Ethan. Your art speaks to people. It's filled with life."

His gaze drops for a moment, as if the compliment carries an unseen burden. "Thank you, but it's not about that. Art can be a mask, you know? It can hide the truth, but it can't change it." He takes a deep breath, and I watch as the vulnerability washes over him, a tide pulling back to reveal the rocky shore beneath. "I've always struggled with feelings of inadequacy. I thought leaving would make things easier for everyone, but I was wrong. I didn't want to drag you or my family down with my fears."

The revelation strikes me like a bolt of lightning. I had always seen him as the strong one, the anchor in the storm of my life. But now, standing here, I recognize the fractures in his facade. My heart aches for him, resonating with the truth of our shared struggles. "You're not alone, Ethan. You never have to be alone. We can face this together." The words spill out before I can think them through, raw and honest, a lifeline thrown into the turbulent sea between us.

His eyes meet mine again, and there's a flicker of something—hope, maybe. "I want that," he admits, the tension easing slightly. "But I also don't want to pull you into my darkness." His voice wavers, and I can see the internal battle waging within him.

"You're not pulling me into anything." I squeeze his hand, grounding us both in the moment. "We've both faced our shadows, and if we're going to walk this path together, we need to share those burdens. I want to understand you, Ethan. All of you."

The honesty of my words hangs between us like a fragile thread, and I feel the air shift. He exhales slowly, as if the weight of his fears is finally lifting. "Then let's be honest with each other, starting now." His voice is firm, the resolve in his eyes igniting a flame within me.

Around us, the gallery hums with laughter and conversations, but in this sacred space, time feels suspended. We stand on the precipice of something beautiful, a bond forged through the honesty of our fears and the courage to confront them together. And in that moment, as I gaze into Ethan's eyes, I realize that we are both still navigating our own stormy seas. Yet, together, we could find our way back to the shore.

Ethan's words linger in the air between us, a fragile promise that hangs like the last note of a symphony. The gallery's bustle becomes a distant murmur, fading into the background as I allow myself to fully absorb his confession. His vulnerability shines a light on the shadows I've carried, illuminating the unspoken fears that have woven themselves into the fabric of my being. I can see the weight of his struggles mirrored in my own—an invisible thread connecting our hearts, drawing us closer with each heartbeat.

As we stand there, the world around us begins to swirl back into focus. A couple nearby laughs too loudly, a wine glass clinks against a ceramic plate, and an artist passionately discusses their own work. Yet none of it distracts from the intensity of this moment. I take a deep breath, summoning courage as I ask, "What are you afraid of, Ethan? What haunts you?" The question hangs between us like a challenge, daring him to delve deeper into the recesses of his soul.

He hesitates, his gaze drifting to the ground as he weighs his thoughts, a battle of emotions playing out on his face. Finally, he meets my eyes again, and in that moment, I see the flicker of an unguarded truth. "I'm afraid of being a disappointment. I've always felt like I'm not living up to expectations—mine, my family's, or even those of the people who look at my work. Every time someone praises my photos, I wonder if they see the real me or just the images I create." His voice quivers with sincerity, and I can sense the heavy burden of self-doubt he's carried for so long.

"Ethan, your art is an extension of who you are. It speaks volumes, even if you don't see it." I gently squeeze his hand, wanting to impart the strength I feel surging through me. "But the truth is, no one expects you to be perfect. We're all just trying to navigate this chaotic world, aren't we?"

He nods slowly, and a flicker of relief dances across his features. "Maybe you're right. But it's hard to shake off the fear that if they knew the whole truth about me, they wouldn't look at me the same way anymore." His admission cuts deeper than I anticipated, resonating with my own insecurities and reminding me that vulnerability can be both a blessing and a curse.

"Then let's rewrite that narrative together," I suggest, a sudden surge of determination swelling in my chest. "Let's show them who we really are—flaws, fears, and all." The conviction in my voice surprises me, igniting a spark of hope in Ethan's eyes.

Before he can respond, an exuberant art critic approaches, his enthusiasm cutting through our intimate exchange like a knife. "Ethan! Your work is simply breathtaking!" The critic gestures animatedly, pulling Ethan into a conversation that leaves me hovering on the outskirts, a bittersweet smile plastered on my face. It's fascinating to watch Ethan interact with someone who sees him as an artist, a source of inspiration. Yet, I can't help but feel a twinge of longing for our earlier moment of connection.

While they discuss the intricacies of photography, I allow myself to wander back to the photographs lining the walls, each one pulling me into its narrative. A haunting black-and-white image of a crumbling building brings back memories of my own childhood, filled with echoes of laughter and the slow decay of dreams I thought I'd left behind. I could almost hear the whispers of the past seeping from the walls, a reminder of how fragile our lives truly are.

Ethan's laughter breaks through my reverie, warm and infectious, reminding me of the lightness I've missed in my life. When the critic finally drifts away, I find myself drawn to him once more, eager to reclaim the conversation that has been suspended in the air.

"I could hear you smiling from across the room," I tease, a playful grin on my face as I step back into his orbit. "You know, I almost forgot that the world has a pulse of its own outside of us."

He chuckles softly, the sound a melodic balm to the tension that had been lingering. "It's a strange feeling, being celebrated for something so personal. Sometimes, I forget how much I need that connection." He pauses, then adds, "But I also need the quiet moments—the ones that feel like home."

"Like this?" I gesture around us, the gallery brimming with life, yet still feeling somehow secluded. "Is this where you find home?"

"It is now," he admits, his gaze locking onto mine with an intensity that sends a shiver down my spine. "But home isn't just a place; it's a feeling. It's being seen for who you are, not just for what you create."

Those words resonate deeply within me, the echoes of my own journey wrapping around my heart. I want to be seen. I want to peel back the layers of my own fears and insecurities, revealing the truth of who I am. With Ethan standing before me, I feel a flicker of courage igniting in my chest, urging me to share my own stories.

"I've struggled with feeling invisible," I confess, my voice barely above a whisper. "Like I'm floating through life, just out of reach of the connections I crave. It's terrifying to think that I might never truly belong anywhere."

Ethan's expression shifts, a soft understanding replacing the earlier spark of warmth. "I get it. We're all just trying to find our place, aren't we? But I want you to know that you belong here—with me." The sincerity in his voice wraps around me like a warm blanket, easing the tension that has coiled tightly in my chest.

In that moment, I realize that vulnerability isn't just about exposing our fears; it's about building bridges through shared experiences. We're not alone in our struggles, and the connections we forge can illuminate the darkest corners of our lives.

As we stand together, surrounded by the vibrant energy of the gallery, I can feel the tides of change beginning to shift. Our pasts, though marked by pain, now seem like stepping stones leading us toward something more—something beautiful, raw, and real. The gallery may echo with the laughter of strangers, but here, in this quiet corner of understanding, I feel at home. With Ethan beside me, ready to unveil our truths, I take a breath and step boldly into the future, knowing that together, we can face whatever shadows lie ahead.

The energy of the gallery swirls around us, a mixture of laughter, soft conversations, and the clinking of glasses that somehow feels like background music to the unfolding drama of our lives. Ethan's revelation hangs heavy in the air, creating a sacred space that sets us apart from the vibrant chaos around us. I can't help but be drawn into the depth of his sincerity, and I can feel my heart thundering, echoing the rhythm of my thoughts.

The gallery's walls, adorned with his photographs, become an extension of our conversation. Each image seems to pulse with the raw emotions he has poured into them, a visceral representation of his internal battles. I step closer to a striking photograph of a crowded market in a distant city, the colors exploding in a frenzy of life. "I feel like this captures a part of you," I say, my finger tracing the outline of the bustling scene. "It's chaotic yet beautiful, just like everything you've shared with me tonight."

Ethan tilts his head, considering my words. "That's the thing about chaos," he replies, his voice barely rising above the din of the gallery. "It can feel overwhelming, but within it, there are moments of clarity. That's what I try to capture—the small pieces of beauty hidden in the noise."

I nod, feeling the weight of his wisdom settle in my chest. The parallels between his art and my life are startling, and I find myself longing to share my own journey with him. "I think we both understand that feeling. There's so much beauty in the struggle, isn't there?" I take a step back, locking eyes with him, the space between us electric with possibility.

"Exactly," he says, the spark in his eyes reigniting. "It's about finding the light in the darkness. That's why I left—because I needed to confront my fears. But I've realized that running only makes them grow stronger."

The vulnerability in his admission pulls at my heartstrings, a gentle tug that feels like the beginning of something profound. "You're brave for facing those fears, Ethan. Most people would rather hide behind their insecurities than confront them." My voice softens, wanting to reassure him. "But you don't have to face them alone anymore."

A smile flickers across his lips, a hesitant yet hopeful expression. "Maybe that's the key, then. Maybe the real strength lies in sharing that burden." His hand brushes against mine, a soft contact that sends a wave of warmth cascading through me. The gallery, with all its vibrancy, suddenly feels like a cocoon, shielding us from the outside world.

As we stand there, I notice the way the light dances across his face, casting shadows that flicker like the insecurities we've both wrestled with. I want to reach out, to pull him closer into my world, to show him that he isn't alone in his journey. "Ethan," I begin, my voice steady despite the uncertainty churning within me, "I've been navigating my own struggles too. There's so much I haven't shared."

He looks at me, his expression a mix of curiosity and empathy. "I'm here, Lily. You can tell me anything."

And just like that, the dam holding back my emotions begins to crack. I take a deep breath, feeling the weight of my past pressing against my chest. "After my mother died, I felt lost. I didn't know how to process that grief, so I buried it deep inside. I think I've spent most of my life trying to pretend everything is fine, all while feeling like a ghost."

Ethan's eyes widen, and I can see the gears turning in his mind as he processes my words. "You've been carrying that alone?" His voice is laced with concern, and I can sense the empathy radiating from him.

"It's easier to hide," I admit, a bitter taste lingering on my tongue. "But hiding doesn't make the pain go away. It just festers." The truth spills from my lips, a cathartic release that leaves me feeling both vulnerable and liberated. "I've always felt like I'm standing on the edge of a cliff, afraid to leap into the unknown."

He nods, the understanding in his gaze deepening. "It's terrifying, isn't it? But maybe that leap is what we need—both of us." His voice softens, and I can feel the weight of his words wrapping around us like a gentle embrace.

In that moment, the gallery seems to fade into the background once more, leaving just the two of us standing at the precipice of something monumental. "We can help each other find that leap," I say, my heart racing at the thought of taking that step together. "We can learn to embrace our fears, not let them dictate our lives."

A glimmer of hope sparkles in Ethan's eyes, igniting a fire within me. "Let's do it, then. Let's face our fears, one photograph and one story at a time."

The resolve in his voice sends shivers down my spine. We stand there, two souls intertwined in a moment of clarity, ready to embark on a journey that promises to be both exhilarating and terrifying.

As the crowd continues to swirl around us, I realize that this is the beginning of something beautiful—a partnership rooted in vulnerability, understanding, and the promise of growth. We may not have all the answers, but we are ready to navigate the chaos together, illuminating the shadows that have long haunted us.

With a newfound sense of purpose, I pull Ethan closer, our shared warmth enveloping us in the midst of the bustling gallery. Together, we take a step into the unknown, ready to embrace the beauty that lies within the chaos, forging a path toward healing and connection. And as I look into his eyes, I know that whatever challenges lie ahead, we will face them side by side, our hearts open to the possibility of love, trust, and the power of shared stories.

Chapter 7: Crossing Boundaries

The moment we stepped out of Ethan's old Jeep, the tranquility of the woods enveloped us like a thick, warm blanket. Towering pines, their needles shimmering with morning dew, framed the secluded cabin like nature's embrace. I inhaled deeply, filling my lungs with the crisp, pine-scented air, and for the first time in a long while, I felt the weight of the world lift, if only slightly. The chaos of our lives seemed to dissolve into the soft rustle of leaves and the distant call of a woodpecker, transforming the atmosphere into a gentle cocoon where the outside noise faded away.

Ethan turned to me, his hazel eyes sparkling with an infectious enthusiasm. "Ready to make some memories?" he asked, a playful smile tugging at the corners of his lips. I nodded, unable to suppress a smile of my own. It was easy to forget everything else here, amidst the towering trees and the soft sounds of nature. I felt a flutter of excitement as he led the way to the cabin, the crunch of gravel under our feet punctuating the serene stillness that surrounded us.

The cabin itself was a rustic charm, built from weathered logs and adorned with touches of modern comfort. Inside, the living room welcomed us with its cozy fireplace, a sturdy oak table, and mismatched chairs that spoke of countless gatherings and shared laughter. I marveled at the simple beauty of it all, the space rich with the aroma of cedar and the faint trace of wood smoke. As I moved around, I felt like a guest in a warm embrace, the surroundings wrapping around me, filling me with a sense of belonging.

We wasted no time. Ethan and I dropped our bags by the door and headed outside to explore the trails that snaked through the woods. The ground was soft beneath our feet, a carpet of leaves and moss that muffled our footsteps as we ventured deeper into the embrace of the forest. Sunlight filtered through the branches above, casting dappled shadows that danced across our skin. The world felt alive, vibrant with color and sound, and with each step, I felt more at home.

As we walked, we talked—endless conversations that flowed effortlessly. Ethan's laughter echoed like music in the stillness, and I found myself laughing right alongside him, losing myself in the warmth of his presence. We shared stories, peeling back the layers of our lives, revealing secrets and dreams in a way that felt raw and authentic. I told him about the time I climbed a tree in my grandmother's backyard, convinced that if I reached the top, I could see the whole world. He shared his own childhood escapades—hilarious mishaps involving his younger brother, a garden hose, and a particularly aggressive family of squirrels.

As the sun dipped lower in the sky, we found a perfect clearing by a babbling brook, its crystal-clear water glimmering in the fading light. The sound of the water, a gentle murmur, added a soothing backdrop to our conversation. Ethan plopped down on a rock, motioning for me to join him. I perched beside him, the cool stone grounding me as I gazed out at the cascading water.

"Isn't it amazing?" he mused, his voice barely above a whisper. "How something so simple can be so beautiful?" I nodded, completely entranced by the scene before us. The sun's golden rays danced on the surface of the brook, and for a fleeting moment, I forgot about everything—the pressures, the expectations, and the uncertainty that loomed over us like dark clouds. It was just us, the forest, and the gentle song of nature.

As night fell, we returned to the cabin, where the chill of the evening air hinted at the approaching autumn. Ethan built a fire in the hearth, its flames crackling and popping, casting flickering shadows that danced across the wooden walls. We settled on the floor, wrapped in a blanket, the warmth radiating from the fire mixing with the warmth of his body beside me. I could feel the tension that had accompanied us dissipate, replaced by a growing intimacy that felt both exhilarating and terrifying.

"Do you ever wonder what it would be like if we could just stay here forever?" Ethan asked, his gaze locked onto mine, the firelight reflecting in his eyes. I could see the vulnerability in his expression, a fleeting glimpse of the boy behind the confident facade. My heart raced at the thought. The world outside felt like a distant memory, a chaotic blur that I longed to escape.

"Every day," I admitted, my voice barely above a whisper. "It's hard to remember what it felt like to just breathe without the weight of everything else." He nodded, understanding threading through his gaze as we sat in companionable silence, the warmth of the fire casting a golden glow around us. The intimate atmosphere was electric, and I felt an undeniable pull toward him, a desire to close the distance and let the boundaries between us blur even further.

Our conversation flowed naturally, exploring the depths of our fears and aspirations, weaving our lives together in a tapestry of shared vulnerability. The stars above peeked through the cabin windows, their light twinkling like diamonds against the velvet night sky. It was in this cocoon of warmth and light that I began to question everything I had thought I knew about love and trust. What if, amidst the chaos, I had found something truly profound with Ethan? What if we could forge a connection that transcended the challenges awaiting us beyond these woods?

As the fire crackled softly, I felt a shift within me, a burgeoning hope that perhaps we could redefine our boundaries—not just as friends, but as something deeper. Each laugh, each shared glance, felt like a step toward something more, something that could change the course of our lives. And in this secluded cabin, surrounded by the whispered secrets of the woods, I dared to dream of what that might look like.

The following day dawned with a light mist hanging in the air, the sun's rays piercing through the trees like golden arrows. Ethan and I emerged from the cabin, each carrying a sense of anticipation as we prepared to embark on our first real adventure of the trip. He suggested we hike to a nearby overlook that promised a breathtaking view of the valley below. The prospect excited me; it felt like a metaphor for our relationship, climbing toward something beautiful and new.

As we walked along the trail, the earth felt alive beneath our feet. Each step kicked up a delicate perfume of pine and damp soil, mingling with the sweetness of wildflowers that dotted the path. Ethan, with his easy gait and infectious enthusiasm, took the lead, occasionally glancing back to share a grin that made my heart flutter. He pointed out various plants and wildlife, weaving in snippets of knowledge that revealed a side of him I hadn't seen before—a softer, more thoughtful essence that contrasted with his usual bravado.

"I can't believe you've never been here before," he exclaimed as we rounded a bend. "This place is magical. Just wait until you see the view!" His excitement was palpable, igniting a spark within me. I had always been a creature of comfort, content to dwell in the known, but with Ethan, I felt emboldened to step beyond the boundaries I had set for myself. The thrill of discovery was intoxicating, filling me with a sense of possibility that I never wanted to end.

After what felt like an eternity of climbing, we finally reached the overlook, and I gasped at the sight that greeted us. The valley stretched out like a patchwork quilt, vibrant greens interspersed with splashes of color from blooming flowers. A river meandered through the landscape, catching the sunlight and shimmering like a silver ribbon. Ethan stood beside me, his presence warm and reassuring, as we both took in the view in silence, letting the beauty wash over us.

"Isn't it incredible?" he said, his voice barely above a whisper, as if he were afraid to break the spell. I nodded, my heart swelling with gratitude for this moment, for this experience shared with him. It was as if the world had fallen away, leaving just the two of us and the breathtaking expanse before us.

We settled down on the edge of a rocky outcrop, the ground cool beneath us. I leaned back against a boulder, feeling the warmth of the sun on my face, while Ethan pulled out a small picnic basket he had packed. The simple act of sharing lunch felt like a sacred ritual, a bridge between our lives and the quiet world we had temporarily claimed as our own.

"Turkey and avocado sandwiches," he announced with a flourish, pulling out the neatly wrapped sandwiches. "And for dessert, chocolate chip cookies—homemade, of course." He grinned, clearly pleased with himself. I laughed, charmed by his enthusiasm for something as simple as a meal.

As we munched on our sandwiches, the conversation flowed easily. We traded stories about our families, our childhoods, and the silly things that made us who we were. I learned about Ethan's obsession with baseball as a kid, how he'd spent hours perfecting his pitching arm in his backyard, dreaming of one day playing for the major leagues. In turn, I shared my own childhood antics, the times I'd gotten in trouble for climbing trees or pretending to be a superhero.

"Did you ever want to be anything other than a superhero?" he teased, a playful smirk tugging at his lips. I shot him a mock glare, knowing full well how ridiculous my dreams had been. "Okay, fine. Maybe I also wanted to be an astronaut. Or a marine biologist. Anything that involved adventure."

His eyes sparkled with mischief as he leaned closer. "So, you're saying that being stuck in a classroom all day just doesn't cut it for you?"

"Exactly! There's a whole world out there, waiting for us to explore," I replied, my voice thick with conviction. His laughter was infectious, and in that moment, the boundaries that had once defined us began to dissolve even further.

After finishing our lunch, we lay back on the grass, watching the clouds drift lazily across the sky. I turned my head to catch a glimpse of Ethan, his face softened in the gentle light, the corners of his mouth turned up in a contented smile. I felt a warmth spreading through me, a connection that ran deeper than friendship. It was an exhilarating feeling, like standing on the edge of a cliff and daring to jump, trusting that the air would catch me.

The afternoon unfolded slowly, a beautiful dance of laughter and shared secrets, until the shadows grew long, signaling that our day was coming to an end. As we hiked back to the cabin, I found my heart racing with the realization that our connection had shifted—deepened—into something more profound. The air felt charged, heavy with unspoken words and glances that lingered just a moment longer than necessary.

When we reached the cabin, I helped Ethan gather wood for a fire. As the sun dipped below the horizon, the sky transformed into a canvas of oranges, purples, and deep blues, the vibrant colors reflecting the shift in our relationship. We arranged the logs and lit the fire, the flames crackling to life, illuminating our faces and casting dancing shadows around us.

We settled beside the fire, the warmth enveloping us in a comforting embrace. Ethan pulled a guitar from the corner of the cabin, a slightly worn instrument that hinted at countless evenings spent playing music. He strummed a few chords, the melody floating into the night air like a gentle caress. I closed my eyes, letting the sound wash over me, creating a perfect backdrop for our burgeoning intimacy.

"Do you know any songs?" he asked, glancing at me with a playful challenge in his eyes. I shook my head, feeling a little self-conscious, but the encouragement in his gaze sparked something inside me.

"Okay, maybe just a few," I admitted, surprised at my own willingness to share. As I began to sing softly, the words felt like a bridge between us, a way to express everything I had been feeling but hadn't yet said. With every note, I could see Ethan listening intently, his focus solely on me, and in that moment, I felt utterly seen.

As the fire crackled and the stars began to twinkle overhead, I realized that this weekend getaway had morphed into something far more significant than I could have imagined. It wasn't just an escape from the chaos of our lives; it was a transformative experience, a chance to redefine who we were and what we could be together. In the safety of the cabin, surrounded by the whispers of the forest, I began to understand that love, in all its complexity, might be waiting for me just beyond the shadows.

The crackling fire flickered in front of us, casting an inviting glow that danced against the walls of the cabin, enhancing the rustic charm of our surroundings. Ethan's soft strumming filled the air, weaving a musical tapestry that seemed to harmonize perfectly with the sounds of the night. I could hear the distant hoot of an owl, its call echoing through the trees, punctuating our laughter and shared stories. This place was a world away from our daily lives, an enchanting sanctuary where time felt suspended, allowing us to explore not only the landscape around us but the uncharted territory of our hearts.

As the firelight flickered, I leaned closer to Ethan, drawn in by the warmth of the flames and his presence. Each shared glance felt charged, electric, as if we were both acutely aware of the unspoken words lingering between us. With every chord he played, the music seemed to dissolve the last remnants of any hesitation I had felt. I couldn't help but admire how effortlessly he created beauty, the gentle strumming wrapping around us like a comforting embrace.

"Do you ever think about what's out there?" he asked, breaking the comfortable silence that had settled like a warm blanket around us. I turned my gaze to the sky, where countless stars twinkled in defiance of the darkness. The universe felt infinite, each star a whisper of possibility.

"All the time," I admitted, my voice soft and contemplative. "I wonder if there's more to life than just what we see every day."

Ethan's eyes sparkled with curiosity, and I could tell he understood. "Like adventures waiting for us beyond the trees?"

"Exactly," I replied, emboldened by his enthusiasm. "Somewhere out there, beyond this place, there are stories yet to be lived."

With that, a sense of daring washed over me. I reached out, brushing my fingers against the back of his hand, the warmth radiating from his skin igniting a spark within me. It was a simple gesture, but it spoke volumes, an invitation that lingered in the air between us. He turned his hand over, our palms touching, and the warmth of our connection felt electric.

As the night deepened, the conversations flowed freely, revealing layers of our dreams, fears, and hopes. I discovered that Ethan had aspirations of becoming a wildlife photographer, driven by a desire to capture the beauty of nature and share it with the world. He spoke passionately about the animals he had encountered and the fleeting moments that could be frozen in time through his lens.

"What about you?" he asked, curiosity piquing in his voice. "What do you want to do with your life?"

I hesitated, caught off guard by the question. My dreams had always seemed distant and nebulous, but sitting there with him, surrounded by the serenity of the woods, I felt a newfound courage. "I've always wanted to write," I confessed. "To create worlds with words, to transport people into stories they can lose themselves in."

Ethan's expression shifted, a look of genuine admiration in his eyes. "You should do it. You have a gift for storytelling. I'd read everything you write."

His encouragement ignited something within me—a flicker of determination. Maybe this weekend was more than just a break from reality; it was a catalyst for change, a chance to embrace who I truly was, both for myself and for him.

As the fire began to wane, I could feel the chill of the night creeping in, wrapping around us like a shroud. Ethan shifted closer, our shoulders brushing, the warmth of his body a comforting presence against the growing cold. It was an unspoken invitation, a silent acknowledgment of the shift in our relationship. The boundaries that had once defined us began to melt away, replaced by something far more profound and complex.

Suddenly, the tranquility was interrupted by the sound of rustling in the underbrush. My heart raced as I instinctively pressed closer to Ethan, seeking his reassurance. "What was that?" I whispered, a mix of excitement and fear swirling in my chest.

"Probably just a raccoon," he replied with a grin, attempting to ease my anxiety. "But let's go check it out."

With an adventurous gleam in his eye, he stood, extending his hand toward me. I took it, feeling the rush of adrenaline as we moved toward the edge of the clearing. The moonlight bathed the landscape in silvery hues, casting eerie shadows that danced between the trees.

As we ventured into the dark, the forest came alive with sounds—the rustle of leaves, the distant croak of frogs, and the soft whisper of the wind. My heart pounded in my chest, a thrilling reminder that we were at the mercy of nature, unbound by the confines of our everyday lives.

The rustling grew louder as we approached, and I couldn't help but feel a thrill of excitement. We rounded a thick trunk, and suddenly, there it was—a pair of curious eyes reflecting the moonlight, a deer standing gracefully in the clearing. It watched us with a mixture of wariness and curiosity, its delicate frame silhouetted against the trees.

Ethan and I stood in awe, breathless at the sight. Time seemed to suspend as we took in the beauty of this moment, united in our shared wonder. The deer, sensing no immediate threat, took a tentative step closer, and in that instant, I felt an overwhelming connection to the wild, to the world around us, and to Ethan beside me.

"Isn't it incredible?" he murmured, his voice barely above a whisper, as if speaking too loudly might scare it away. I nodded, entranced by the gracefulness of the creature. In that shared moment, I realized how much I had yearned for connection—not just with Ethan, but with the world itself.

As the deer darted away into the underbrush, the spell was broken, but the magic lingered in the air. We returned to the cabin, the fire now reduced to glowing embers, leaving us in a cozy twilight glow. I turned to Ethan, his face illuminated by the flickering light, and felt a surge of emotions I could no longer ignore.

"Ethan," I began, my voice trembling slightly, "I don't want this weekend to end. I want to explore everything with you, not just the woods but whatever comes next."

He looked at me, surprise flickering in his eyes before a slow smile broke across his face. "Neither do I," he admitted, his voice steady and sincere. "This feels right."

In that moment, the boundaries that had once defined our relationship shattered, replaced by the potential for something deeper, something beautiful. And as the fire's glow faded, I knew that whatever awaited us beyond the trees, we would face it together. In the quiet of the woods, surrounded by the whispers of nature, I discovered that love had a way of crossing boundaries, forging connections that could illuminate even the darkest nights.

Chapter 8: Embracing Vulnerability

The air was thick with the sweet scent of blooming magnolias as we wandered through the shadowy expanse of the park, the moonlight casting silver pools on the grass. Each step felt deliberate, as if the universe was pausing to listen to our unspoken thoughts. The world was muffled, the distant sounds of the city—a siren wailing, laughter bubbling from a nearby bar—felt like whispers in a dream, and it was just us in our little cocoon of twilight.

Ethan walked beside me, a presence that felt as grounding as the earth beneath our feet. The faint rustle of leaves danced around us, mingling with the sound of our footsteps, forming a melody that played softly in the background. I could feel the warmth radiating from his body, a quiet assurance that drew me in like gravity, making the weight of my own insecurities feel lighter.

"What are you thinking about?" he asked, his voice low and sincere, a soft caress against the evening hush. I glanced up, catching a glimpse of his profile, the way the moonlight accentuated the sharp lines of his jaw and the faint stubble that framed his lips. I had never noticed how much vulnerability could glow in someone's eyes until I saw it reflected back at me from his.

"I'm just..." My words trailed off, a hesitant flutter in my throat. How could I articulate the swirl of feelings that tugged at my heart like the tides? "I'm just afraid of how easy it is to let someone in," I finally confessed. The admission hung in the air between us, fragile and exposed, like a threadbare secret that had found its way to the surface.

Ethan stopped, turning to face me fully, and the intensity of his gaze sent a tremor through me. "What if you let me in anyway?" he asked, his voice steady and warm, wrapping around my uncertainty like a comforting blanket. "What's the worst that could happen?"

The question hung heavy, demanding a response I wasn't ready to give. My heart raced, pounding against my ribcage as if it wanted to escape, to leap into the unknown. I thought of past wounds, the scars that marred my spirit like ghostly reminders of love lost and trust broken. "I've just been hurt before," I admitted, my voice barely a whisper.

"Me too," he replied, a flicker of understanding passing through his eyes. "But maybe that's why we can trust each other. We know what it feels like to be vulnerable." There was a strength in his words, a shared experience that bridged the gap between us, making the darkness around us seem less intimidating.

With that, we resumed our walk, the silence pregnant with possibilities. The stars above shimmered, like distant memories whispering promises of hope. I found myself stealing glances at him, noticing how he ran a hand through his tousled hair, the light catching the soft curls as they fell over his forehead. There was something so undeniably captivating about him, something that made my heart ache with an inexplicable yearning.

We eventually reached a clearing, where an old wooden bench sat, weathered yet sturdy. As we sank onto the bench, the coolness of the wood pressed against my skin, grounding me as the weight of my thoughts swirled. I looked up at the night sky, its vastness echoing the turmoil within me, and I let out a shaky breath.

"What are you afraid of?" he asked, his voice a gentle probe, coaxing me to peel back the layers of my heart. I wanted to scream, to unleash the turmoil of insecurities and fears that clawed at my mind, but the words felt trapped in my throat.

"What if I let you in, and it all falls apart?" I confessed, the words escaping in a rush, raw and untamed. "What if I'm not enough, or worse, what if I'm too much?" The vulnerability poured from me like a torrential rain, each word freeing a piece of my guarded heart.

Ethan's gaze softened, and he leaned closer, the warmth of his presence igniting a fire deep within me. "You are enough, and you're never too much for me. I want to know you, all of you—the messy, the beautiful, the broken pieces. You don't have to pretend with me." His words wrapped around me like a cocoon, enveloping me in the safety I had craved for so long.

In that moment, I felt a shift—a softening of the walls I had meticulously built around my heart. I leaned into him, letting the warmth of his body seep into my own, our breaths mingling in the quiet space between us. It was terrifying yet exhilarating, a dance on the precipice of something monumental. The fear that had clung to me like a shadow began to fade, replaced by an electrifying hope that danced just beyond my grasp.

Then, in a heartbeat, it happened. Ethan leaned in, his intentions clear as the space between us dwindled to nothing. The world around us faded, and it was just him, just me, suspended in time. Our lips met, tentative at first, like a gentle exploration of uncharted territory. The kiss was soft, an invitation, and as it deepened, a fire ignited within me—a flame I thought had long been extinguished by doubt and heartache.

Every worry, every fear, shattered like glass under the intensity of our connection. I felt alive, vibrant, as if the kiss breathed new life into the dormant parts of my heart. But just as quickly, doubt crept back in, icy fingers wrapping around my chest. What if this was just a fleeting moment, a spark that would extinguish as quickly as it ignited?

I pulled away, breathless, my heart racing with conflicting emotions. The realization of what had just happened rushed over me like a cold wave, overwhelming and dizzying. There was a moment of silence, the air charged with unsaid words and unresolved tension. Ethan searched my face, his expression a mixture of concern and hope, and I knew that I had to make sense of this whirlwind of feelings before I could let myself fall completely.

The silence that followed our kiss lingered in the air, heavy with unspoken emotions and a vulnerability that felt both exhilarating and terrifying. I could hear the gentle rustling of leaves overhead, the night creatures stirring in the shadows, but all I could focus on was the warmth radiating from Ethan's body next to mine, an anchor in the tumultuous sea of my thoughts. The intensity of his gaze pierced through the haze of doubt that threatened to consume me, and I could sense the weight of expectation hanging between us.

"What was that?" I finally managed to whisper, my voice barely more than a breath. The question felt ridiculous as soon as it left my lips, but it encapsulated the whirlwind of feelings swirling inside me—an intoxicating blend of desire and fear, excitement and uncertainty.

Ethan's smile was a soft curve, illuminating his features in the moonlight. "It was a kiss," he replied, his tone teasing yet sincere, and I felt my cheeks flush under his gaze. "But it meant more than that, didn't it?" He leaned closer, the space between us charged with an electric current, pulling me in like a moth to a flame.

I looked down, suddenly shy under his unwavering attention. My heart raced as I replayed the moment in my mind, the soft brush of his lips against mine, the way it had felt like coming home. Yet I couldn't shake the nagging voice in my head that whispered warnings of past heartaches, reminding me of every time I had allowed myself to trust and been met with disappointment.

"It did," I admitted reluctantly, my voice trembling slightly. "But what if it's just a moment? What if I'm just imagining things?" The vulnerability in my words hung in the air like a fragile promise, and I hoped he could see through my doubts to the truth buried beneath.

He reached for my hand, his touch sending shivers racing up my arm. "Moments can lead to something more if we let them," he said, his thumb brushing over my knuckles in soothing circles. "But we have to be willing to take that leap. I'm not going to pretend that it's all easy, but I think we owe it to ourselves to find out what this is."

The sincerity in his voice wrapped around me, weaving a sense of comfort through my anxieties. I looked up, meeting his gaze, and in that moment, I saw a reflection of my own fear mirrored back at me, but there was something else too—an undeniable spark of hope, the promise of a connection that felt too precious to dismiss.

We remained there, locked in each other's eyes, the world around us fading into a distant hum. I felt like we were the only two people on Earth, suspended in a moment that could either shatter into a million pieces or bloom into something beautiful. I took a deep breath, tasting the crisp night air tinged with the fragrance of jasmine and honeysuckle, and allowed myself to relax into his presence.

"What do you want?" I asked, my voice steadying as I ventured into uncertain territory. "What do you want from us?"

Ethan's expression shifted, the lightheartedness fading into something deeper, more contemplative. "Honestly?" he began, searching for the right words. "I want to understand you. I want to know what makes you laugh, what makes you cry, and what keeps you up at night. I want to share those things with you, to build something real together."

His honesty struck me like a bolt of lightning, illuminating the shadows of my doubt. I had spent so long protecting my heart, constructing barriers against the possibility of pain that I had nearly forgotten what it felt like to truly connect with someone. The prospect of allowing myself to be vulnerable, of opening up to Ethan completely, both thrilled and terrified me.

"I don't want to rush into anything," I said softly, my heart racing with both excitement and apprehension. "But I also don't want to miss this chance. It's just... everything feels so intense, and I'm not sure I'm ready for it."

Ethan nodded, his expression softening. "I get that. We can take it slow. Let's just see where this goes. No pressure, no expectations—just you and me figuring it out as we go."

The relief that washed over me was palpable. I felt a weight lift, and the corners of my lips turned up into a tentative smile. "Okay," I whispered, the word feeling like a promise rather than just an agreement.

We sat together in the warm embrace of the night, the stars above twinkling like distant dreams waiting to be realized. I felt a surge of courage bubbling within me, igniting a flicker of hope that perhaps this was the beginning of something beautiful, something that could rise from the ashes of my past.

With our fingers intertwined, Ethan and I continued to share fragments of our lives—the silly quirks that made us laugh, the moments that had shaped us into who we were today. I opened up about the time I accidentally dyed my hair neon pink for a school project, and he roared with laughter, his joy infectious, and I found myself grinning in return.

As the night deepened, we spoke of dreams, hopes, and the fear of failing. Ethan revealed his aspirations of traveling the world, capturing its beauty through his photography. I found myself leaning closer, captivated by his passion, my earlier reservations fading into the background. His voice painted vivid pictures in my mind, the sights and sounds of faraway places becoming tangible as he spoke.

"Maybe we can explore those places together someday," I said, my voice barely above a whisper, but the suggestion hung in the air between us, tantalizing and full of promise.

"Maybe," he replied, a soft smile playing on his lips, but I could see the spark in his eyes, the same spark that ignited my own. It was a small step, but it felt monumental, as if we were laying the foundation for something that could grow beyond our wildest imaginations.

As the night began to wane, a sense of peace settled over me, wrapping around my heart like a cozy blanket. I realized that this moment was more than just a fleeting encounter; it was the opening of a door I had kept shut for far too long. I felt a warmth blossom inside me, urging me to embrace the uncertainty that lay ahead, to step into the light of vulnerability with Ethan by my side.

It was a thrilling prospect, one that whispered promises of adventure, laughter, and perhaps even love. And for the first time in a long time, I felt a flutter of excitement dance through my chest, the thrill of possibility unfurling like a flower in bloom. As the first hints of dawn began to lighten the sky, I knew that whatever came next, I was ready to face it—together.

The remnants of that kiss lingered in the air like the last notes of a haunting melody, a reminder of what had just transpired. I shifted on the bench, the wood cool beneath me, grounding me as I grappled with the tumultuous whirlpool of emotions roiling inside. Ethan's hand was still in mine, a solid reminder that this moment was real, yet a flutter of uncertainty swept through me like a gentle breeze rustling the leaves overhead.

"What's wrong?" he asked, his brow furrowing slightly as he studied my face, which I was certain betrayed my inner turmoil. His concern was palpable, a silent plea for me to share the storm brewing within. I took a deep breath, willing myself to speak through the heaviness pressing against my chest.

"I guess I'm just scared," I admitted, my voice trembling slightly. "Scared that we're rushing into something without really knowing each other." The honesty spilled from me, a cathartic release that felt both terrifying and liberating. "What if this connection isn't as real as it feels right now?"

Ethan squeezed my hand gently, his grip reassuring. "Every connection starts somewhere. We'll figure it out together, won't we?" His smile was genuine, filled with warmth and encouragement, and it sparked a flicker of hope within me. "Life is about taking chances. If we don't take that first step, how will we ever know?"

His words resonated deeply, echoing my own thoughts and fears. I had spent so much time building walls, fortifying myself against pain and disappointment. Yet here he was, offering me a glimpse of a different path, one paved with possibility and trust. I could feel my heart, usually so guarded, edging closer to a leap of faith.

As the night deepened, the stars twinkled above us like a cosmic audience, watching over our tentative exploration. I leaned against the bench, allowing the weight of my thoughts to settle for the moment. With Ethan by my side, I felt a flicker of courage beginning to kindle in my chest.

"What do you want?" I asked, a question that had been simmering just below the surface. It felt critical to understand his intentions, to navigate this delicate dance together. "I mean, what do you really want from all this?"

Ethan hesitated, the easygoing charm flickering momentarily as he considered his answer. "I want to know you, the real you," he replied earnestly. "I want to share experiences, laugh together, and even face challenges together. It's about building something authentic, not just a fleeting moment."

There was something in his voice that made my heart ache with recognition. I could feel the sincerity radiating from him, cutting through the barriers I had erected. I took a deep breath, searching for the words that would articulate my own desires.

"What if we just… take our time?" I suggested tentatively, the words tumbling out in a rush. "No pressure to define what this is right now. Just enjoy the moments, see where they lead us."

A smile broke across his face, illuminating the darkness like a beacon. "That sounds perfect," he said, relief washing over his features. "Moments are what we make of them, anyway. So let's make them count."

As we sat there, the night wrapping around us like a comforting embrace, I realized how much I craved this—this connection, this openness. I felt my worries ebbing away, replaced by the warm glow of possibility.

In that instant, the park transformed around us, each tree and shadow blending into a backdrop for our newfound understanding. I could almost see the memories we would create, etched against the starry canvas.

As dawn approached, the first hints of light began to filter through the trees, casting a soft glow on the world around us. I felt a surge of gratitude wash over me—a profound appreciation for this moment, this choice to embrace vulnerability. I turned to Ethan, and in that quiet space, I realized that this was only the beginning of a journey neither of us could fully comprehend yet, but one that promised to be richly woven with laughter, tears, and everything in between.

"I've never met anyone like you," I said, my voice soft and sincere. "You make it easier to be honest about how I feel."

His smile widened, a sparkle in his eye that made my heart flutter. "You're pretty amazing yourself. I'm just glad you're willing to share this part of yourself with me."

The sun began to rise, painting the horizon in shades of pink and gold, and I felt the warmth on my skin, a tangible reminder of the hope that lay ahead.

As we left the park, hand in hand, the city stirred to life around us. The aroma of freshly brewed coffee wafted through the air, mingling with the distant sounds of laughter and chatter. I glanced at Ethan, his face glowing with anticipation for the day ahead. The vibrant tapestry of life unfolded before us, an invitation to embrace whatever came next.

We ventured toward a quaint café that had quickly become a favorite haunt of mine, nestled between two bustling storefronts. The bell jingled as we entered, and the familiar scent of pastries and brewed coffee enveloped me like a warm hug. I spotted a corner table bathed in sunlight and led Ethan toward it, feeling a flutter of excitement at the prospect of sharing a meal together.

As we settled in, I glanced around, taking in the eclectic decor—vintage posters of classic films adorned the walls, and mismatched furniture gave the place a cozy, inviting charm. The barista, a cheerful woman with vibrant pink hair, greeted us with a smile.

"What can I get you two lovebirds today?" she asked, her tone teasing but warm.

Ethan chuckled, shooting me a playful glance. "What do you recommend?"

"Everything!" she exclaimed with enthusiasm. "But if you want something special, the cinnamon rolls are legendary."

I nodded enthusiastically, and soon we placed our order—two steaming cups of coffee and a cinnamon roll to share. As we waited, I felt a sense of comfort settle over me, the ambience buzzing with life and conversation, a backdrop to the blossoming connection between us.

Once our order arrived, the warm, gooey roll sat between us, a decadent centerpiece. We laughed and shared bites, each morsel punctuated by playful banter and teasing glances.

"This is amazing," I said, savoring the sweetness that danced on my palate. "I think I might come here every day if I could."

"Only if I get to join you," he replied, his eyes sparkling with mischief.

I felt my cheeks heat, and in that moment, I realized just how much I had missed this—this lightheartedness, this sense of belonging. I could see the future unfurling before us, a tapestry of shared moments and laughter.

As we finished our breakfast, Ethan leaned back in his chair, a thoughtful expression crossing his face. "You know, I used to think vulnerability was a weakness," he said, his tone serious. "But now, I see it as strength. It takes courage to let someone in."

His words resonated deeply, wrapping around my heart like a gentle embrace. "It really does," I agreed, feeling a swell of admiration for him. "And I'm glad we're choosing to be brave together."

We left the café, stepping into the world that now felt ripe with possibilities. The sun shone brightly overhead, illuminating our path as we strolled through the lively streets, side by side. Each step felt like a small victory, a testament to our decision to embrace vulnerability and take a chance on each other.

As the day unfolded, I felt an overwhelming sense of hope blooming within me, each moment bursting with potential. I knew that this journey would have its challenges, but I also understood that with Ethan beside me, I could face whatever came our way. Together, we would explore the intricacies of connection, weaving our stories into a shared narrative filled with laughter, adventure, and love.

Chapter 9: Shadows Return

The city of Chicago enveloped me like a thick fog as I stepped off the train, the familiar skyline piercing the gray horizon, each building a monument to the life I had left behind. The air was heavy with the scent of roasted coffee mingling with the faint, bitter tang of the lake, a reminder of home and all its complexities. In my mind, I replayed the moments we had shared—the laughter echoing against the walls of the cafe, the soft glances exchanged beneath the flickering lights of the art gallery, and the warmth of his hand intertwined with mine. Yet, as the train doors slid shut behind me, sealing my past in its metallic womb, the thrill of those memories felt increasingly distant, overshadowed by a creeping sense of dread.

I walked through the bustling streets, the sound of city life swelling around me like a tidal wave—horns blaring, people shouting, and the soft murmur of conversations that felt as foreign as they were familiar. The heart of Chicago pulsed with a frenetic energy that should have excited me, but instead, it settled in my chest like a stone. Ethan's presence, which had once ignited my spirit, felt more like a flickering candlelight now, barely holding its ground against the wind of my insecurities. We had built something beautiful in the summer haze, but the looming specter of reality now threatened to extinguish it.

The sky darkened as I made my way toward our favorite park, a green oasis tucked between the concrete giants. I could almost hear the whispers of the willow trees beckoning me closer, their leaves dancing in the cool breeze like gentle spirits. It was there that we had shared countless secrets, where the world melted away, and it had been just us—two souls finding solace in one another. But as I approached, the laughter and chatter of children playing on the swings sounded like a cruel reminder of the happiness that felt just out of reach.

When I spotted Ethan seated on a bench, his expression was solemn, his brow furrowed in deep thought. A chill slithered down my spine. I could sense the tension radiating off him, thick and oppressive, as if he were struggling with invisible chains. His usual spark was dimmed, leaving only a flicker that worried me more than I cared to admit. What had changed between us? Had the summer warmth begun to fade before autumn even arrived?

"Hey," I said softly, approaching him, trying to mask the tremor in my voice. He turned to me, and for a fleeting moment, our eyes locked—his gaze searching, as if he were trying to decipher a riddle that had no answer. A slight smile graced his lips, but it didn't reach his eyes. That hollow depth was new, an unwelcomed visitor I wished to banish.

"Hey," he replied, his voice low, almost lost amidst the sounds of the park. The warmth I had longed for felt like a distant memory. The distance between us was palpable, stretching like a chasm filled with unspoken words and unresolved fears. I took a seat beside him, the bench creaking under our combined weight, a metaphor for the delicate balance we were trying to maintain.

As we sat in silence, the laughter of children drifted closer, their innocence a stark contrast to the turmoil brewing within us. I wished I could grasp that lightheartedness, wrap it around me like a comforting blanket, but the shadows of my thoughts began to take shape, and I couldn't help but wonder about the conversation I had overheard just days before, a phantom that haunted me.

It was a chance encounter, overheard in a crowded café, the murmur of voices blending into a chaotic symphony. Ethan's tone was sharp, his words laced with frustration as he spoke to Jake, a mutual friend who had seen us through the highs and lows of our relationship. "I don't want to drag her into my past," he had said, his voice heavy with the weight of regret. "I can't let her see that part of me again. It would ruin everything."

My heart twisted painfully at the realization that the shadows we had fought to escape were still lurking, threatening to devour us whole. Had I been so blinded by the warmth of our connection that I had ignored the darkness clinging to Ethan? The thought settled in my stomach like a stone, heavy and unyielding. Would he always be running from the demons of his past, unable to step fully into our future together?

"I heard some of your conversation with Jake," I finally admitted, the words spilling out before I could stop them. Ethan stiffened, a frown creasing his brow. "I'm sorry," I added quickly, my voice trembling. "I didn't mean to eavesdrop, but I... I can't help but feel like there's something you're not telling me."

Ethan's shoulders sagged, and he let out a heavy sigh, the weight of his unspoken thoughts evident in the way he clenched his fists. "It's complicated," he murmured, his eyes drifting toward the ground, as if searching for the right words buried beneath the earth.

"Everything we've built together is complicated, but that doesn't mean we have to face it alone," I urged, desperation creeping into my tone. I reached out, placing my hand gently on his knee, willing him to feel the connection we shared. "I want to help you carry that burden, but you have to let me in. You can't keep pushing me away."

His gaze lifted to meet mine, and I saw a flicker of something—fear, perhaps, or vulnerability—but it was gone as quickly as it came. "I'm scared, okay?" he admitted, his voice breaking slightly. "I'm scared that if I open up to you about my past, I'll ruin everything. I can't go back to that place, not when we're finally finding something real."

The confession hung in the air, heavy and laden with the truth of our circumstances. My heart ached for him, for the struggles that had shaped him into the man I had fallen for. "We're not going to ruin anything," I promised, my voice steady despite the turmoil within. "We're stronger together, even in our brokenness."

As I spoke, I could feel the distance between us beginning to shrink, the invisible barriers eroding under the weight of our honesty. Yet, doubt loomed like a shadow, whispering insidious thoughts that threatened to unravel the fragile thread of hope we had woven. Would our bond withstand the test of reality? Or would the shadows of our pasts drag us back into the darkness we had fought so hard to escape?

The park was alive with the symphony of late summer, the rustling leaves performing a gentle dance in the breeze while the warm sun cast a golden glow over everything. Yet here I sat, a silent observer to a conversation filled with unspoken fears, as if the very essence of joy was slipping through our fingers like sand. Ethan's brow furrowed deeper, and his eyes drifted toward the ground, avoiding my gaze as though I were a mirror reflecting truths he was not ready to confront.

"I just don't want to hurt you," he finally said, the admission slipping from his lips like a reluctant confession. The weight of his words hung heavily between us, intertwining with the tendrils of unease that had begun to strangle our budding relationship. I could feel the tension building, a slow crescendo that echoed the heartbeat of the city around us.

"Hurt me?" I echoed, a touch incredulous. "Ethan, we're in this together. We can't move forward if you're always looking back." My own words rang hollow, a faint echo of the certainty I wished I felt. It was easy to preach resilience when I was the one feeling strong, but what about when his ghosts began to seep into our reality?

He turned toward me, his expression a mix of longing and trepidation. "What if my past becomes our present? I can't let that happen. You deserve better than the remnants of my mistakes."

I reached for him, grasping his hand, feeling the warmth of his skin beneath my fingers, a reminder of all the moments we had shared. "You're not those mistakes, Ethan. You're so much more than that. You've fought to change, to be better. Just let me in. I promise I'll be here, through the chaos and the quiet."

But as I spoke, a flicker of doubt crept into my heart. Hadn't I spent years running from my own shadows? I had built walls to shield myself, not realizing that they also confined my heart. What if the very act of inviting him into my world invited chaos I wasn't prepared to handle?

A dog barked in the distance, drawing Ethan's attention momentarily, and in that brief interlude, I could see the memories wrestling within him, battling for dominance. He was a fortress, and I was the hopeful invader, desperately wishing to breach the walls but knowing that I risked triggering a disaster.

"Can you promise me something?" he asked, his voice barely above a whisper, a thread of vulnerability weaving through his tone.

"Anything."

"Promise me you won't give up on me, no matter how hard it gets." His gaze was fierce, demanding, as if he were asking me to sign a contract with my heart.

"I can promise you that," I replied, squeezing his hand, feeling the tension ease just slightly. "But you have to meet me halfway. I can't be the only one fighting for us."

For a moment, it felt like we were standing on the edge of a precipice, the vast unknown stretching out before us. Then, the sun broke through the clouds, casting a warm halo around us. It felt like a sign, an affirmation that perhaps we could navigate the complexities of our intertwined lives together.

With a deep breath, Ethan nodded, his resolve appearing to solidify. "Okay, then. Let's try." The words hung in the air like a promise—a fragile but steadfast commitment to face the uncertainties together. I couldn't help but smile, a mix of relief and exhilaration flooding through me.

The chatter of nearby picnickers pulled us from our intimate bubble, reminding me that life continued around us, vibrant and chaotic. Children ran past, their laughter a joyful melody that tugged at something deep within my heart. It made me long for the carefree days of summer, when every moment felt infinite and filled with possibility.

"Let's get out of here," I suggested, the impulse for adventure bubbling to the surface. "We could head to the Art Institute. I want you to see this exhibit I've been raving about."

Ethan hesitated, his expression flickering with uncertainty. "I don't know, maybe we should just—"

"Come on! A little culture never hurt anyone. Besides, it's one of our favorite spots. Let's remind ourselves of the good things."

He chuckled, the sound a mixture of amusement and reluctant acceptance. "Alright, but if we get lost in the art, I'm blaming you."

The journey to the institute was filled with an ease that felt foreign yet comforting, like slipping into a favorite sweater. We walked shoulder to shoulder, our fingers intertwined, a silent acknowledgment of the journey we were embarking on. The streets buzzed with life—tourists snapping pictures, street musicians pouring their souls into their performances, and the aroma of deep-dish pizza wafting through the air, tempting our senses.

As we reached the entrance of the Art Institute, the majestic building loomed above us, a bastion of creativity amidst the urban sprawl. I led Ethan through the grand atrium, where the light filtered through the towering glass ceiling, illuminating the marble floors like a stage set for our own unfolding drama.

We navigated through the galleries, each piece of art igniting conversation and laughter. I watched Ethan's face as he engaged with the works, his passion shining through the shadows that had clung to him. It was in those moments that I saw the man I had fallen in love with, a vibrant soul eager to share his thoughts and insights.

As we paused before a breathtaking Monet, the colors swirling like a vivid dream, I couldn't help but lean into him, savoring the warmth radiating from his body. "Isn't it beautiful?" I mused, my voice barely above a whisper, as if speaking too loudly might shatter the moment.

"It's incredible," Ethan replied, his eyes dancing over the canvas. "It makes me feel... alive."

I turned to face him, the weight of his past slipping from my shoulders as I absorbed the sincerity in his gaze. "Then let's hold onto this feeling. We're not just surviving; we're living. You and I, together."

His smile brightened the room, the shadows retreating like specters in the light. We were carving out a space for ourselves, one filled with art, laughter, and unyielding hope. As we continued to explore, I felt the threads of our connection tighten, each shared glance and touch weaving a tapestry of resilience against the storm of uncertainty that threatened to engulf us.

But deep down, I knew that the journey ahead would be far from easy. We were only beginning to scratch the surface of our intertwined struggles, and the shadows would always linger, waiting for a moment of vulnerability to creep back into our lives. Yet, as I stood there beside him, surrounded by beauty and possibility, I clung to the belief that love—our love—could be the light that pierced through the darkness.

Amid the hum of the Art Institute, the air thick with the smell of varnish and polished wood, I felt a strange combination of exhilaration and trepidation. The artwork around us captured the spectrum of human emotion, each brushstroke a story begging to be told, and yet, despite the vibrancy of our surroundings, the gravity of our earlier conversation clung to me like a stubborn stain. Ethan had started to emerge from the depths of his past, but I wondered if I was simply a momentary reprieve from the battles he had yet to fight.

We wandered through the gallery, our fingers still intertwined, but there was an invisible thread of tension woven between us, fraying at the edges. It was when we reached a modern installation, a sprawling web of colored yarn draped against stark white walls, that the conversation shifted once more. The artist had captured chaos and order in a single frame, a stark contrast that felt almost personal.

"Look at that," I said, gesturing toward the piece, my voice infused with false enthusiasm. "It's like life—beautifully chaotic, yet somehow still makes sense."

Ethan's gaze drifted to the installation, but I could see that his mind was miles away. "Yeah," he replied, his voice distant, devoid of the spark I craved. "I guess that's one way to put it."

The knot in my stomach tightened. "What's going on in that head of yours?" I pressed, refusing to let the moment slip into silence. "You're miles away, and it's making me worry."

He hesitated, the uncharacteristic reluctance weighing down the air between us. "I just... I don't want to drag you into my mess," he confessed, finally meeting my eyes. "This art, it makes me think about all the tangled threads in my life—how easy it is for them to get knotted up, and I don't want to pull you into that chaos."

I could see the shadows flickering behind his gaze, ghosts of past mistakes and fears that had yet to be exorcised. "But we're already tangled together, aren't we?" I challenged gently, taking a step closer. "You can't just unravel what we've built because you're scared of where it leads. Life is messy, Ethan. Let's embrace the chaos together."

His silence was a weight pressing down on my chest, and I could feel my resolve wavering. I wanted to pull him close, to reassure him that he wasn't alone, but I also feared that my touch might only deepen his reluctance. It felt as if we were two artists, standing before a blank canvas, each too afraid to make the first stroke, terrified of what might come from it.

"Maybe we need a change of scenery," he finally suggested, his voice stronger, a flicker of determination breaking through the clouds. "I know a place. It's not too far from here. We could go—just the two of us."

The shift in his tone was enough to coax a smile from my lips, igniting the hope I had nearly surrendered. "Lead the way," I replied, squeezing his hand tighter, feeling the warmth of his skin beneath mine as we stepped into the thrumming life of the city outside.

We wandered down the streets of Chicago, the city alive with the pulse of summer. Street performers filled the sidewalks with music, the notes weaving through the air like colorful ribbons, while the scent of roasted nuts and cinnamon danced in our noses, drawing us closer to a nearby vendor. I watched Ethan's expression shift from concern to a reluctant smile as we shared a bag of warm pretzels, the dough soft and chewy, slathered in coarse salt that made our lips glisten.

"See? This isn't so bad," I teased, nudging him playfully. "A little street food and art therapy. Who needs therapy when you have this?"

He chuckled, the sound breaking through the tension that had enveloped us. "You may be onto something," he replied, a glint of mischief lighting up his eyes. "Next time, we'll add hot dogs and a baseball game. Nothing screams Chicago more than that."

With each shared laugh and bite of pretzel, I felt the weight of our earlier conversation begin to lift, but I knew we were only skimming the surface. It was when we arrived at the hidden gem Ethan had promised—a quaint rooftop garden tucked above a small bookstore—that the true magic began to unfold.

The view was breathtaking, an unexpected sanctuary nestled amidst the concrete giants. The skyline stretched out before us, the buildings reaching for the sky like fingers grasping for dreams. As we settled onto the soft grass, surrounded by vibrant flowers, I could feel the tension finally release its grip on my heart.

"This place is amazing," I breathed, taking in the riot of colors and the gentle hum of life around us. "How did you find it?"

"It's a bit of a secret," he replied, leaning back on his elbows, the sunlight bathing him in a golden glow. "I used to come here when I needed to escape. It feels like a different world up here, doesn't it?"

"It really does," I agreed, lying back beside him, the grass cool beneath my skin. I let my eyes wander over the clouds, imagining them as fluffy ships sailing across an endless sea of blue. "It's perfect."

We fell into a comfortable silence, the sounds of the city below fading into a distant murmur. I could sense Ethan's presence beside me, the warmth radiating from him grounding me as I let myself be enveloped in the beauty of the moment. Yet, despite the serenity, I felt a lingering uncertainty, a flicker of doubt that dared to creep back into my mind.

"Ethan," I said softly, my voice breaking the stillness like a pebble thrown into a pond. "I know you're scared. I see it in the way you hesitate, in the shadows that pass over your face. But I'm here, and I'm not going anywhere."

He turned his head, his gaze searching mine. "I want to believe that," he admitted, vulnerability lacing his words. "But what if I drag you down with me? What if my past comes back to haunt us?"

"Then we face it together," I replied firmly, my heart racing at the weight of my own promise. "You're not just a collection of your mistakes, Ethan. You're more than that. You're the man who makes me laugh, who sees the world in colors I never knew existed. I refuse to let fear dictate our story."

His expression softened, a flicker of hope igniting in his eyes. "You make it sound so easy," he murmured, a hint of a smile breaking through the facade.

"It's not easy, but it's worth it," I replied, the determination solidifying within me. "Every day will be a choice, but I'd rather choose to fight than to give up. Love isn't just a feeling; it's an action."

As the sun began to dip below the horizon, painting the sky in hues of orange and pink, I felt the moment shift, as if the universe were aligning for us. We leaned in, and in that breathless second, our lips met—a tentative brush that ignited a spark between us. It was a promise sealed in warmth, an acknowledgment of our pasts and the willingness to embrace the unknown.

As we pulled back, breathless and wide-eyed, the worries that had once held us captive felt lighter, as if the shadows were retreating in the face of our connection. We were two flawed souls finding refuge in one another, ready to navigate the winding roads ahead. The chaotic tapestry of our lives might remain tangled, but we had made a choice—a choice to weave our stories together, one colorful thread at a time.

And as night fell over the city, the stars began to emerge, twinkling above us like whispers of hope. In that moment, enveloped in the magic of our newfound commitment, I felt a sense of peace wash over me. The shadows would always linger, but they would never overshadow the love we were learning to cultivate. Together, we could face whatever storms might come. Together, we were finally learning to live.

Chapter 10: The Art of Letting Go

The morning sun poured into my studio, drenching everything in a warm golden glow that danced across the floor like laughter spilling out of a bottle. Dust motes twirled lazily in the air, caught in the beams of light streaming through the large bay window. I stood there, half-awake and barely focused, surrounded by the chaos of my creative sanctuary—a maze of half-finished canvases stacked precariously against one another, splashes of paint dotting the wooden floor like a child's reckless joy. The scent of turpentine hung in the air, mingling with the faint sweetness of my coffee, which had long gone cold.

Ethan's laughter echoed in my mind, a haunting melody that lured me deeper into reverie. I felt a pang of regret, an ache in my chest that was as familiar as the gentle creaking of the old house settling around me. I reached for my camera, fingers trembling slightly, half-excited and half-nervous as I fumbled with the settings. It was time to document the essence of healing, to transform my swirling emotions into something tangible.

The dancer arrived just as I was beginning to lose hope. Her name was Mia, a wild spirit wrapped in layers of vibrant fabric that swirled around her like living flames. Her dark hair bounced in soft waves, glistening under the studio lights, and her energy filled the room, an electric charge that made my heart race. We exchanged pleasantries, and I could sense the strength hidden behind her gentle smile. There was a comfort in her presence, an unspoken understanding that connected us.

As she began to move, I felt my breath catch. Mia's body flowed like water, each motion a whisper of resilience. The way she arched her back and lifted her arms toward the sky spoke of struggles overcome, of battles fought and won. I lifted my camera, the shutter clicking rhythmically as if it were keeping time with the very heartbeat of the moment. With each photograph, I was capturing not just an image but a story—her story, woven into the fabric of her movements.

I became lost in her dance, the world around us fading into a soft blur. Colors blended together, and sounds transformed into a symphony of grace and strength. My mind began to wander, drawing parallels between Mia's journey and my own. I had been clinging to the past, to the fragments of what Ethan and I had shared. But as I watched her spin and leap, I understood that to truly embrace life, I needed to let go. Let go of the shadows that loomed over me, the fears that had held me captive for far too long.

The studio transformed into a sanctuary, each click of the camera a release, a step toward liberation. I captured her delicate balance, the way she hovered on the precipice between flight and fall, a metaphor for my own hesitation. What if I chose to take that leap? What if I embraced the uncertainty that awaited me beyond the walls of my safe haven? With every shutter click, I was sending pieces of my heart into the universe, hoping they would find their way back to me—transformed, renewed.

After an hour, Mia paused, breathless and radiant. She approached me, eyes sparkling with a fierce joy. "You have an incredible eye," she said, her voice a melodic echo of gratitude. "I felt every click of your camera. It was like you were dancing with me."

Her compliment wrapped around me like a warm embrace, and I couldn't help but smile. "It was all you," I replied, feeling a rush of warmth bloom in my chest. "Your spirit is so alive."

As we continued to talk, I found myself opening up in a way I hadn't expected. "I've been struggling," I admitted, the words spilling out like paint from an overturned tube. "With letting go of the past, especially with someone I thought I could trust." My voice trembled slightly, revealing the vulnerability I often tried to mask.

Mia nodded, her expression shifting to one of understanding. "Letting go isn't easy. It's like shedding skin; it can feel painful but is necessary for growth." She glanced around the studio, her gaze landing on a canvas I had left half-finished, splashes of vibrant colors swirling together in a chaotic dance. "Maybe your art can help you find that release."

The thought struck a chord within me. I had always turned to my art as a refuge, a place where I could explore the depths of my emotions without fear of judgment. Maybe Mia was right; perhaps it was time to take that leap, to pour my feelings onto the canvas and create something beautiful from the pain.

I set to work, the brush gliding across the surface like a dancer's foot caressing the stage. With each stroke, I felt the weight of my heart lift, the colors spilling out my emotions, my fears, and my hopes. I painted the essence of healing—the tumultuous storm of grief swirling into a gentle sea of tranquility, the bright bursts of color symbolizing joy breaking through the darkness. It felt liberating, cathartic, as if I was allowing myself to breathe again.

As the day faded into evening, I stepped back to admire my creation. The canvas glowed with the promise of healing, a testament to the journey I had embarked on. I turned to Mia, who watched me with a knowing smile. "You've done it," she said, her voice filled with warmth. "You've captured the essence of letting go."

In that moment, I realized that letting go was not a singular act; it was a journey, one that required time and patience. Just as Mia had transformed her pain into art, I could transform mine into a tapestry of hope and resilience. As the shadows lengthened in the studio, I felt a flicker of light within me, a reminder that while the past may linger, the future was mine to shape. And in that uncertainty, there was beauty.

With the final stroke of the brush, I felt the rush of accomplishment settle over me like a warm blanket on a chilly evening. The canvas before me, vibrant and full of life, shimmered with every hue I had poured into it, each color telling a story of its own. It was a wild fusion of emotions—anguish swirling into euphoria, like a turbulent sea suddenly calmed by a gentle breeze.

Mia, now resting on the studio floor, stretched her limbs like a contented cat. I offered her a grin, a mixture of pride and disbelief. "I didn't realize how cathartic that would be," I confessed, wiping my hands on a paint-splattered rag. "It's like I've shed a layer of skin, a burden I didn't know I was carrying."

She beamed back at me, her eyes sparkling with shared joy. "That's the magic of art. It's not just a reflection; it's a process of transformation."

As we both gazed at the canvas, a sense of peace washed over me, yet the lingering shadow of Ethan loomed just beyond the edges of my newfound clarity. My heart tugged with a bittersweet nostalgia, the weight of what had been and what could have been draped over me like a heavy cloak. I could almost hear his voice, soft and reassuring, as if he were standing right beside me.

But I quickly shook the thought away. This was my moment, one that I had created for myself, a stepping stone toward reclaiming my life. I had come to the studio to heal, not to dwell.

The evening light shifted, bathing the studio in a dusky hue. As the sun dipped behind the horizon, I felt a wave of weariness wash over me. Mia gathered her things, thanking me profusely for the experience. Her gratitude echoed in the small space, wrapping around me like a comforting embrace.

As she stepped out, I realized how empty the studio felt without her vivacious energy filling the air. I let out a soft sigh, taking a moment to relish the quietude, the silence punctuated only by the soft creaking of the old wooden floor. Alone with my thoughts, I picked up my camera again, drawn to the pile of photographs lying scattered across the table.

Each image was a snapshot of a moment, a fragment of my past that now seemed both precious and heavy. I flicked through them, capturing the stories behind each shot. There was Ethan, his smile a beacon of warmth, and another where we stood by the river, the sun kissing our skin as we shared laughter that felt like a gentle promise. Those memories felt like ghosts now—haunting yet beautifully tragic.

The clock on the wall ticked rhythmically, the sound grounding me. I found solace in the act of creation, diving back into my project. I knew I needed to explore the relationship between healing and memory, how we hold onto moments that shape us but can also weigh us down.

With my camera in hand, I ventured outside, stepping into the crisp evening air. The world outside the studio felt alive, a pulsating entity filled with potential. As I walked through the neighborhood, the scent of fallen leaves and distant woodsmoke lingered in the air, a reminder of the autumn that had quietly settled around us.

I wandered aimlessly at first, allowing the scenery to seep into my senses. A small park caught my eye, bathed in the soft glow of lamplight. It was quiet, save for the rustling of leaves and the distant laughter of children playing, oblivious to the bittersweet melodies of heartbreak.

Finding a bench, I sat and watched as shadows danced under the streetlamps, flickering like memories caught between light and darkness. I raised my camera, snapping candid shots of the evening's essence. Each click was another breath, another moment released into the universe. The trees stood tall, their branches a tapestry of gold and crimson, whispering stories of change and resilience.

Suddenly, a figure caught my eye—a young couple walking hand in hand, their laughter infectious and bright. For a moment, I felt a pang of longing. I wanted to capture the beauty of their connection, the effortless way they leaned into one another, lost in a world of their own. It reminded me of Ethan, of the ease we had once shared, the joy that flowed between us like an unbreakable thread.

I trained my lens on them, heart fluttering as I focused on the little details—the way her hair caught the wind, or how he brushed his thumb across her knuckles. With every shot, I felt a gentle nudge, a reminder that love, in all its forms, was still out there, waiting to be discovered.

After they passed, I let out a breath I didn't realize I'd been holding. I leaned back against the bench, feeling the weight of my heart shift slightly, as if a lock had been turned, allowing light to seep in. I needed to embrace the possibility of new connections, new moments, even if the specter of the past still lingered.

As the night deepened, the air grew cooler, and I decided to head back to the studio. With each step, I found myself humming a soft tune, a melody born of hope and resilience. Inside, I returned to my canvas, drawn back to the colors that spoke of my journey. I mixed paints, creating new shades to reflect the changes brewing within me, letting the brush glide over the surface as I added layers of depth and emotion.

I painted late into the night, the world outside fading into a distant murmur. Each stroke felt like a release, an act of defiance against the shadows that sought to confine me. I wasn't merely letting go; I was actively choosing to embrace the uncertainty that lay ahead.

As the clock ticked on, I felt a sense of belonging settle around me, an affirmation that this space, this art, was mine. And while Ethan's memory still lingered, I understood that I had the power to create a new narrative, one filled with light, love, and endless possibilities.

The next morning dawned crisp and clear, a bright blue canvas painted with streaks of gold and orange that beckoned me to step outside. I could feel the city coming alive as I prepared for the day, the sound of distant traffic mixing with the soft rustle of leaves outside my window. There was something invigorating about the early hours, a chance to breathe in fresh possibilities. I donned my favorite oversized sweater, the one that enveloped me in warmth, and slipped on my well-worn boots, the soles scuffed from countless walks through the ever-changing streets of Philadelphia.

The scent of fresh coffee wafted through the air as I strolled down the sidewalk, the world pulsating around me. I passed by quaint cafés, their windows fogged with warmth, and bakeries bursting with the sweet aroma of pastries freshly pulled from the oven. The brick buildings, adorned with ivy that clung like a lover, whispered stories of the past while the laughter of friends gathered at sidewalk tables painted a picture of community that felt almost tangible.

As I made my way toward the art supply store, the chatter of the city enveloped me in its vibrant embrace. I couldn't shake the feeling that every moment was a brushstroke on the canvas of my life, every interaction a color added to my palette. I spotted a street musician playing a soulful tune, the notes rising and falling like the tide. I paused for a moment, captivated by the rhythm of his guitar and the deep, resonant voice that echoed against the walls. The music wrapped around me, filling the space left by Ethan's absence, igniting a flicker of hope that danced just beyond my reach.

After purchasing fresh supplies, I returned to my studio, my mind buzzing with new ideas. I had decided to focus on a series of portraits that captured the essence of healing and resilience, not only through the lens of the dancer but through the myriad experiences that had shaped me. Each portrait would tell a story, a visual narrative of the journey through pain to strength, interwoven with the threads of my own life.

I set to work immediately, arranging my materials and creating a makeshift backdrop that mirrored the autumnal colors of the outside world. The warm hues filled my space, casting a glow that made the room feel alive. I could almost hear the whispers of encouragement as I began to transform the blank canvas into a world bursting with emotion.

Each stroke of my brush became a dialogue, an exploration of the nuances of healing. I painted with abandon, layering colors in a frenzied dance, letting the brush guide me as I lost myself in the process. I recalled the dancer's grace, the way her movements conveyed her struggles, and I infused that energy into my work. I wanted to capture the vulnerability, the strength that arose from confronting fears head-on.

Hours melted away as I painted, the light shifting in the studio like the seasons changing. It was only when I paused to catch my breath that I noticed the shadows creeping in. A gentle tapping at my window caught my attention. I turned to see Mia standing outside, her face aglow with the excitement of being part of this unfolding story.

"Mind if I join you?" she asked, her voice bright and welcoming as she entered, shedding the chill of the outside world like a snake shedding its skin.

"Of course! I'd love the company," I replied, gesturing to the assortment of canvases.

Mia immediately fell into a rhythm beside me, sharing her insights as I painted. She had a natural talent for observation, and her perspective added richness to the experience. "You know, it's like you're unearthing something beautiful that was buried beneath the surface," she mused, leaning over to inspect a particularly vibrant piece that represented resilience.

"Exactly! It's about peeling back the layers and showing what lies beneath," I said, my excitement building as I shared my vision.

With Mia by my side, our conversation flowed effortlessly, weaving between the personal and the profound. I felt a sense of camaraderie that soothed the remnants of my lingering doubts. With every stroke of the brush, I began to imagine the exhibit showcasing our art, stories of healing threaded together like a tapestry.

As the afternoon sun waned, casting long shadows across the floor, a sudden thought struck me. "What if we created an installation that intertwines our work?" I suggested, my voice bubbling with enthusiasm. "An immersive experience that draws people in and encourages them to confront their own journeys?"

Mia's eyes widened with excitement. "Yes! We could incorporate movement, sound, and even written reflections from visitors. It would be a space for everyone to share their healing stories."

The idea ignited a spark between us, the room buzzing with possibilities as we brainstormed ways to blend our talents. I envisioned a space where colors danced on walls, stories floated through the air, and people connected through their shared vulnerabilities. The prospect of this project became a lifeline, pulling me away from the confines of my self-doubt and back into the embrace of creativity.

As the evening approached, I set aside my brush and grabbed my camera, feeling a renewed sense of purpose. I wanted to capture the essence of this collaboration, the joy radiating from Mia as she moved gracefully across the studio, embodying the spirit of resilience.

Each click of the shutter was a moment preserved, a fragment of our journey encapsulated in time. I captured her laughter, the way her hair danced around her face, and the determination that shone in her eyes. These images would be part of the exhibit, a visual narrative intertwined with our art, a testament to the power of connection and healing.

With the studio bathed in the soft glow of evening light, I realized that I was no longer bound by the shadows of my past. The weight of my memories had transformed into fuel for creativity, igniting a fire within me that had long been dormant. Mia and I worked late into the night, our laughter echoing through the studio, mingling with the sound of our brushes gliding across canvas.

In that shared space, I felt my heart begin to unfurl, opening up to the possibility of what lay ahead. Letting go of Ethan didn't mean erasing our moments together; instead, it meant honoring them and allowing them to coexist with the new experiences waiting just beyond the horizon.

As I looked around at the studio, now filled with color and light, I knew that I was on the brink of something beautiful. This was just the beginning of my journey—a canvas still stretching, waiting to be filled with laughter, love, and the vibrant hues of healing. The world outside continued to pulse with life, and I was finally ready to step into it, brush in hand, heart wide open.

Chapter 11: A Broken Reflection

The gallery hums with a life of its own, a vibrant organism pulsating beneath the muted glow of pendant lights. The walls, draped in soft white fabric, serve as a canvas for my photographs—snapshots of moments that reflect the kaleidoscope of my soul. Each image tells a story: the tender laughter of a child chasing fireflies in a sun-drenched field, the wistful gaze of an elderly couple sharing secrets over steaming cups of coffee at a quaint café, and the wild beauty of the ocean crashing against rugged cliffs under a lavender sky. As I survey my work, a symphony of nerves and anticipation courses through me, making my fingers tremble slightly around the delicate stem of the wine glass I clutch.

Friends and family mill about, their laughter a harmonious backdrop to my racing thoughts. I catch snippets of their conversations, punctuated by the occasional burst of applause or a delighted gasp at a particularly evocative photograph. My heart swells with gratitude for their support, but anxiety coils tighter around my chest. What if they don't see the beauty I've tried to capture? What if my art fails to resonate, like echoes in an empty chamber? Just then, the door swings open, and the cool evening air rushes in, carrying with it a flurry of laughter and the unmistakable silhouette of Ethan.

His presence transforms the atmosphere; the room brightens as if a switch has been flipped. Dressed in a crisp white shirt that emphasizes the strong lines of his frame, he strides in with an ease that seems to command attention. The moment our eyes meet, a spark ignites between us, electric and warm. My stomach flutters, and my breath catches as I watch him approach, weaving through the crowd with a grace that belies his size.

"Wow," he breathes, pausing in front of the photograph that I've titled "Endless Summer." It features a young girl with sun-kissed hair, twirling in a field of wildflowers, her laughter seemingly captured in the very fabric of the image. "This is stunning, Lily."

I can feel the heat rising to my cheeks at his praise, and I muster a smile that feels both genuine and slightly shaky. "Thank you. It's one of my favorites." My voice trembles slightly as I speak, the weight of my insecurities pushing against the back of my throat. I want to convey confidence, to show him that I believe in my work, but I feel like an imposter in this beautiful space, surrounded by whispers of admiration that seem to cling to the walls like ivy.

He shifts his gaze to me, and I catch a glimpse of admiration in his eyes that warms me from the inside out. "You have an incredible talent, you know that?" His words wrap around me like a blanket, and I allow myself to bask in his sincerity for just a moment. "Each photograph feels like a piece of your heart."

His compliment settles around me, yet the shadows of doubt linger just beyond the periphery. I glance at a nearby mirror, my reflection flickering back at me—a girl with bright, expressive eyes framed by waves of chestnut hair that spill over my shoulders. But what I see beneath the surface is a jigsaw of broken pieces, scars of past heartaches and dreams that once felt too distant to grasp. Each fragment tells a story, a history that weighs heavily on my soul. It's a reminder of who I was before, and even as I've started to piece myself back together, the remnants of that girl remain, fragile and uncertain.

Ethan leans closer, his voice a conspiratorial whisper. "You know, I was worried I'd be the only one here who thought you were a genius." There's a playful spark in his tone that makes me laugh, a genuine sound that chases away the edges of my anxiety, if only momentarily.

I can't help but smile at his teasing. "You're definitely not alone in that. I think half the crowd is in love with your compliments." I gesture towards a group of friends animatedly discussing one of my pieces, their enthusiasm infectious.

Ethan chuckles, a deep sound that rumbles through the air like a gentle wave. "Well, they have great taste, obviously." He pauses, his expression turning earnest. "But seriously, your work deserves to be seen. You're capturing moments that most people would overlook."

A warmth spreads through me, and I'm suddenly aware of the space between us, a magnetic pull that seems to deepen with every shared glance. As we continue to discuss my work, the noise of the gallery fades into a distant hum. It feels as if we are suspended in time, two souls intertwining in a world created from snapshots and memories. The intimacy of the moment unravels the anxiety that had gripped me earlier, replacing it with a sense of belonging that envelops my heart.

But the ghost of my insecurities lingers, casting shadows on this beautiful evening. I can't shake the feeling that I'm teetering on the edge of something monumental, something that could either elevate me or shatter the delicate peace I've fought so hard to build. The reflection in the mirror becomes a haunting reminder—a woman piecing together her life while standing on the precipice of vulnerability.

As the evening unfolds, the laughter and clinking of glasses blend into a melody, a chorus that sings of support and friendship. I watch as my friends admire my photographs, their joy a balm to my wounded spirit. But amid the applause and cheers, Ethan's unwavering gaze anchors me, a lighthouse guiding me through the storm of self-doubt.

"Can I show you something?" he asks suddenly, pulling me from my reverie. Before I can respond, he takes my hand, leading me through the gallery. I can feel the warmth of his touch seep into my skin, a pulse of comfort that calms the storm inside me. He stops in front of a piece titled "Reflections," a close-up of a girl staring into a pond, her expression a mix of wonder and contemplation.

"This one speaks volumes," he says softly, his eyes scanning the photograph. "It's like she's searching for something deeper within herself."

I nod, suddenly aware of how closely his words mirror my own internal battle. "That's exactly it. I wanted to capture that moment of introspection—the way we all sometimes feel lost, like we're searching for a part of ourselves."

He turns to me, his expression earnest. "You've done that beautifully, Lily. It's as if you've poured your soul into every piece."

His words wash over me, and for a fleeting moment, the fractured pieces of my heart seem to align, forming a mosaic of hope. In this sanctuary of art, surrounded by the people I love and the man who sees me, I begin to believe that perhaps, just perhaps, I am worthy of the beauty I've created.

As the night unfolds, I become increasingly aware of the subtle choreography of emotions around me. The gallery is a living, breathing entity, each person contributing to the vibrant tapestry of the evening. Laughter bubbles like champagne, filling the air with a lightness that contrasts with the weight of my own insecurities. I steal glances at Ethan, who seems to radiate warmth, engaging effortlessly with my friends as they bask in the glow of my photographs.

The gentle hum of conversation ebbs and flows like the tide, and I find myself momentarily lost in the way the light dances off the surfaces of the framed images. Each reflection captures a moment suspended in time, and yet I feel like a ghost haunting my own exhibition, a spectator in a world I created. A wave of uncertainty crashes over me, and I clutch my wine glass a little tighter, feeling the cool stem against my palm, grounding me amidst the whirlwind of emotions.

Suddenly, a wave of laughter breaks my reverie. I turn to see Sarah, my childhood friend, gesturing animatedly, her expressive face alive with excitement. "Lily, you have to see this one!" she calls out, her voice bright and inviting. She pulls me toward a photograph of a golden autumn landscape, where sunlight filters through the trees, creating a tapestry of reds and oranges. "It feels like you're inviting us into that moment. I swear I can hear the leaves crunching underfoot."

A warm smile spreads across my face at her enthusiasm. "That was my favorite spot last fall. I spent hours just soaking it in." I lean closer, appreciating the way she sees my work. Her joy feels infectious, and I can't help but feel a surge of pride at her words.

"Look at how it draws you in! It's like you can almost step through the frame." She takes a step back, tilting her head as if she's seeing the photograph for the first time. "You're capturing emotions, not just moments, and that's what makes it art."

Her words resonate deep within me, reigniting that flicker of confidence I had momentarily lost. I watch as she drifts away, leaving me standing in front of my work, the buzz of the gallery enveloping me like a cozy blanket. Yet, even as the admiration from my friends fills the room, there's an undercurrent of doubt that threatens to tug me back into shadow.

I glance at Ethan, who is now deep in conversation with Lucas, animatedly discussing one of my black-and-white portraits. The lines of his face are sharp, and the way he gestures as he speaks makes me appreciate the strength of his character even more. But what catches my breath is the way he looks at me when he thinks I'm not paying attention. There's something tender in his gaze, a warmth that sparks a longing within me, and for a moment, the world outside the gallery dims, leaving only him in sharp focus.

A soft melody begins to play in the background, the soothing strains of a piano filling the air. It becomes a backdrop to the murmurs and laughter, a gentle reminder that this evening is not just about art but about connection, celebration, and perhaps a hint of something more. I take a breath, allowing the music to wrap around me, and let my insecurities drift further away.

A group of friends approaches, their faces alight with enthusiasm, and I feel a familiar flutter in my stomach as they surround me. "You did it, Lily! This is incredible!" One of them, Mia, beams at me, her eyes sparkling like the stars outside. "I can't believe how talented you are."

"Seriously, this should be in a gallery in New York or something!" another chimes in, and the compliment washes over me, mixing with the earlier words of Sarah, creating a buoyant feeling that lifts my spirits.

I laugh, the sound bubbling up, genuine and unrestrained. "You're all too kind. But really, I just wanted to share what I love with all of you." My voice catches slightly as I look around, seeing the faces of my friends, the familiar comfort of their presence warming me like a sunbeam.

As the night progresses, I find myself moving from group to group, sharing stories behind my photographs, the moments that inspired each shot, and the challenges I faced in capturing them. The more I talk, the more I realize how much I cherish this connection with my art and those who appreciate it. I can feel my heart begin to swell, infusing the night with newfound confidence.

But amidst this newfound joy, a fleeting glance toward Ethan stirs something within me. He's engaged in a conversation, but every now and then, his eyes drift toward me. It's a subtle connection, a thread woven between us, fragile yet strong. I want to reach out, to bridge that gap, but an invisible barrier holds me back—fear that he'll see through my carefully crafted facade, that he'll catch a glimpse of the broken pieces I still struggle to reconcile.

In a moment of impulsiveness, I excuse myself from the lively conversation, seeking a moment of solitude. I step outside onto the gallery's terrace, where the crisp night air greets me like an old friend. The stars glitter overhead, each one a beacon of possibility, and I lean against the cool railing, allowing the quiet to wash over me.

As I breathe in deeply, the scent of night-blooming jasmine mingles with the sharpness of the autumn air, grounding me in this beautiful moment. I close my eyes, surrendering to the peaceful sounds of the night—a soft rustle of leaves, the distant hum of traffic, the faint laughter spilling from the gallery. In this cocoon of tranquility, I let my thoughts drift.

The sound of footsteps pulls me from my reverie, and I open my eyes to find Ethan standing a few paces away, his expression a blend of concern and curiosity. "Hey," he says softly, his voice wrapping around me like a warm blanket. "You okay out here?"

I nod, forcing a smile that doesn't quite reach my eyes. "Just needed a breather. It's a little overwhelming in there."

He steps closer, the space between us shrinking, and for a moment, I feel as if the world outside fades into oblivion. "You know, you really are amazing. Watching you tonight, I realized how much heart you put into your work."

I feel a warmth creep up my neck, and my heart races in response to his sincerity. "Thanks, Ethan. It means a lot, especially coming from you."

His eyes hold mine, and in that moment, everything else falls away—the gallery, the laughter, the weight of expectations. It's just us, suspended in time, with an unspoken understanding that seems to bind us.

The night air carries a gentle breeze that rustles through the leaves, and I can't help but feel that this moment, however fleeting, holds something significant—a shift, perhaps, in the fragile dynamics of our friendship. Just then, I find myself wishing that this connection would deepen, that the walls I've built around my heart might begin to crumble, allowing the light of possibility to seep in.

The warmth of Ethan's presence lingers in the air like an embrace, and I can hardly bear the weight of the moment. His gaze holds mine, intense and searching, as if he's trying to read the unspoken words trapped within my heart. The world around us fades, and the symphony of laughter and chatter feels distant, a mere echo of the joy that surrounds us. There's a pull between us, magnetic and exhilarating, igniting a flicker of hope that maybe, just maybe, I'm not as alone as I sometimes feel.

"Can I ask you something?" he says, breaking the silence, his voice a low, soothing balm that calms the storm of my insecurities. I nod, willing him to continue, though my heart races with anticipation.

"What inspired you to choose photography? It seems so... personal." The question hangs in the air, heavy with possibility. His genuine curiosity prompts a rush of emotions within me, a swirl of memories and experiences that have led me to this moment.

I take a deep breath, feeling the cool night air infuse me with a sense of clarity. "It's like capturing a heartbeat, you know? Each photograph is a pause in time, a chance to see beauty in the mundane." I gesture toward a piece featuring a worn wooden bench beneath an ancient oak tree, sunlight filtering through the leaves, creating a dappled effect on the ground. "That bench holds stories, laughter, secrets. It's a reminder that even the simplest things can hold extraordinary significance."

Ethan nods, his eyes glinting with understanding. "You have a way of seeing the world that most people overlook." He pauses, as if weighing his next words. "It's rare to find someone who captures the heart of life so beautifully."

My breath catches at his words, a delicate butterfly alighting on my heart, filling the void left by my fears. It's not just his admiration that touches me; it's the way he sees me. I'm no longer just the girl with a camera; I am an artist, a storyteller, and perhaps even a dreamer.

As we continue to talk, I become acutely aware of the magic brewing around us. The gallery feels alive, the vibrant energy a palpable force that pulses with every word we exchange. I share anecdotes of late-night editing sessions, the thrill of capturing a fleeting moment, and the countless hours spent wandering city streets, seeking inspiration in unexpected places. Each tale seems to draw Ethan closer, the distance between us shrinking until it feels almost insignificant.

But just as I begin to lose myself in this bubble of connection, a shadow flits across my mind, the familiar specter of self-doubt creeping back in. I wonder if he truly understands the weight of the darkness I carry. Beneath the surface of my laughter and passion lies a fragility I've worked so hard to conceal—a collection of heartaches and disappointments that have shaped me into the woman I am today.

In that moment of vulnerability, I find the courage to voice my fears. "Sometimes, I worry that I'm just pretending to be someone I'm not. Like I'm still that girl who doesn't quite fit in, always on the outside looking in." The admission feels raw, almost painful, and I brace myself for his response, anxiety fluttering like a caged bird in my chest.

Ethan's expression softens, his eyes searching mine. "You're not pretending. You're evolving. We all have our struggles. What matters is how we rise from them." His voice, steady and reassuring, resonates deep within me. "The real magic happens when we embrace our scars. They're what make us unique."

A wave of gratitude washes over me as his words sink in. I realize that he isn't just seeing my art; he's seeing me. With a newfound clarity, I step closer to him, feeling the warmth radiating from his body as the night air cools around us. I want to reach out, to bridge the gap between us that has persisted for far too long.

"Thank you, Ethan. For believing in me," I whisper, my voice barely more than a breath, laden with meaning.

He leans in slightly, the distance between us now negligible. "You're worth believing in, Lily." The sincerity in his eyes sparks something deep within me, a flame flickering to life in the hollow spaces of my heart.

Just then, the gallery door swings open, and a rush of laughter spills onto the terrace. My friends have come looking for me, their voices a cacophony of joy and curiosity. The spell we shared shatters for a moment, reality crashing back in as they pull me into their circle, eager to share their thoughts on the exhibition.

But as I listen to their chatter, my gaze finds Ethan again. He stands at the periphery, watching me with a smile that seems to hold secrets of its own. There's an unspoken promise lingering in the air, a connection that feels more profound than mere friendship. My heart flutters at the thought, a heady mix of hope and fear swirling within me.

The night progresses with a mix of art and laughter, each photograph eliciting admiration from my friends as they recount their favorite pieces. They gather around a photo I call "Two Hearts," capturing the candid joy of a couple dancing in the rain, their expressions a blend of bliss and abandon. "This is everything," Mia declares, her eyes sparkling. "It makes me believe in love all over again."

Their enthusiasm warms me, but a part of me can't shake the sensation that tonight is merely a prologue to something larger, something that whispers promises of change.

As the evening winds down, I step outside again, drawn by the pull of the night sky. The stars twinkle above like diamonds scattered across velvet, and I take a moment to breathe, inhaling the crisp air that dances with the scent of jasmine.

Suddenly, Ethan appears beside me, leaning against the railing with an ease that draws me closer. "Can I tell you a secret?" he asks, his tone playful yet earnest. I nod, eager to hear what he has to say, intrigued by the glint in his eyes.

"I think tonight was just the beginning for you, Lily. Your work deserves to be seen by so many more people." His voice carries a weight of conviction, and I can't help but feel a flicker of possibility ignite within me.

I turn to him, the warmth of his presence a soothing balm. "What if they don't love it?" I challenge softly, the old insecurities bubbling back to the surface.

"Then they're missing out," he replies without hesitation. "But I know they will love it. You have a gift."

His unwavering belief acts as a tether, grounding me amidst my swirling thoughts. There's a determination in his gaze that stirs something deep within, urging me to take a leap of faith. "Maybe I should try for a bigger exhibition," I muse, testing the waters, my heart racing at the thought.

"Absolutely. I'll help you however I can," he says, his enthusiasm infectious. "Let's make it happen."

As I look into his eyes, I realize that this moment is more than just about art. It's about stepping into the light, embracing the shadows, and finding strength in vulnerability. In Ethan's unwavering support, I see the possibility of a future that extends beyond the confines of my fears—a future filled with new beginnings, uncharted territories, and a love that dares to blossom amidst the chaos.

With the night wrapping around us like a protective cloak, I reach out and take his hand, feeling the warmth of his palm against mine. It's a simple gesture, yet it feels monumental—a promise of what lies ahead, a bond that has been forged in honesty and understanding. As the stars twinkle above us, I realize that this night is a turning point, a moment where everything shifts, and the path before me is suddenly filled with light.

Chapter 12: Flickering Flames

The air was thick with the scent of pine and the warm, comforting aroma of cinnamon as the late afternoon sun filtered through the tall trees lining the edge of the sprawling park. Golden rays danced upon the surface of the nearby lake, creating a mesmerizing shimmer that beckoned me closer. I often found solace in this place, a serene refuge from the cacophony of the world beyond. It was where I felt the pulse of life thrumming around me, the sound of leaves rustling, birds chirping, and the gentle lapping of water against the shore providing a backdrop for my thoughts. Today, though, my mind was anything but calm.

Ethan had pulled away, like the tide receding from the beach, leaving me stranded on the shore, grasping at grains of sand that slipped through my fingers. I replayed our last conversation in my mind, searching for clues that might explain his sudden withdrawal. We had been lying on my porch, the stars above us twinkling like distant diamonds, discussing everything and nothing. It was blissful, filled with laughter and quiet moments that made my heart swell. But now, those memories felt tainted, overshadowed by the uncertainty that loomed between us like an ominous storm cloud.

I had seen the flicker in his eyes—the way they would shine when he spoke of his dreams, the passion that ignited when he talked about his art. But that spark had dimmed, and I couldn't shake the feeling that I had somehow extinguished it. My heart ached as I remembered the warmth of his laughter, the way it wrapped around me like a cozy blanket. I longed to feel that warmth again, to bask in the light of his presence. But every time I reached out, he seemed to slip further away.

As I strolled along the winding path that hugged the lake's edge, I recalled the day I had first met Ethan. It was a typical summer afternoon, one of those sticky days where the air felt thick enough to chew. I had been wandering through the local art fair, a riot of colors and sounds, when I stumbled upon his booth. His paintings, vibrant and pulsating with life, drew me in like moths to a flame. I could feel the raw emotion radiating from each stroke, each splatter of paint speaking to something deep within me. And then there he was, standing behind the easel, his presence as captivating as his work.

His dark hair fell in soft waves across his forehead, and those deep-set eyes, pools of intensity, seemed to capture the very essence of the world around him. We struck up a conversation, a natural ebb and flow that felt as though we had known each other for years. Every word he spoke painted a vivid picture in my mind, every laugh resonating like music in my ears. I remember thinking how easy it was to connect with him, how effortlessly our souls intertwined, as if we were two pieces of a puzzle that had finally found their place.

But now, that connection felt fragile, like a delicate glass ornament on the verge of shattering. I couldn't help but wonder if I had said something wrong, if my past had reared its ugly head again, casting a shadow over something so beautiful. My insecurities began to spiral, taunting me with whispers of inadequacy. Perhaps he had realized that I was just a girl from a small town, with dreams that often felt too big for me to grasp. I had fought to cultivate a sense of worth within myself, but with every moment that passed, I felt it slipping away like sand through my fingers.

As I meandered past a group of children laughing and splashing in the water, I was reminded of simpler times. I used to be that carefree girl, chasing after fireflies and catching the scent of summer on my skin. But adulthood had a way of weighing heavy on the heart, tethering dreams to the ground while simultaneously stirring a longing for flight. I had fought hard to find my footing, to believe that I deserved love and happiness, yet here I was, standing at the edge of despair, fearful that I might lose the very thing I had fought so hard to find.

Taking a deep breath, I inhaled the fresh, invigorating scent of the surrounding trees, allowing it to wash over me like a balm. I needed to confront Ethan, to uncover the reasons behind his retreat and bridge the distance that had formed between us. I turned my gaze toward the horizon, where the sun began its descent, casting a golden glow over the lake. It was beautiful, breathtaking even, yet it served as a stark reminder that light could fade into darkness in an instant.

Determined, I headed back home, a flurry of emotions swirling within me. I could hear my heart pounding in my ears, each beat urging me forward. Ethan had become my anchor, the one person who understood the depths of my soul, and I refused to let fear dictate my actions any longer. If I wanted to salvage what we had, I had to confront the uncertainty head-on.

The warmth of the evening enveloped me as I made my way toward my porch, a familiar comfort waiting at the end of the journey. I spotted him sitting there, silhouetted against the setting sun. His gaze was lost in thought, a portrait of quiet contemplation. As I stepped closer, the world around us faded away, leaving only the soft rustle of leaves and the distant sound of laughter echoing from the park.

"Ethan?" I ventured softly, my voice barely above a whisper.

He turned, his expression momentarily surprised, before a veil of sadness washed over his features. My heart twisted painfully in my chest at the sight. It felt like he was a canvas slowly losing its vibrancy, and I yearned to bring back the colors that had once danced in his eyes.

"I need to talk to you," I said, my voice steadier than I felt.

He nodded, and I took a seat beside him, the warmth of his presence a balm to my frayed nerves. The flickering flame of hope ignited within me, urging me to fight for what we had, to bridge the gap that had formed in the shadow of our uncertainty.

The silence between us hummed like the distant chirping of crickets, the soft rustle of leaves weaving an intricate tapestry of sound that enveloped the night. The evening stretched out before us, a blanket of stars overhead, their light shimmering in the depths of Ethan's dark eyes. He seemed lost in a world of his own, an artist captivated by a vision only he could see. I could feel the weight of unspoken words pressing down on us, creating a palpable tension that danced between hope and despair.

"Ethan," I began, my voice trembling slightly. "What's going on? You've been... distant." The words tumbled from my lips, an admission of my own vulnerability. I studied him closely, searching for any flicker of the warmth that had initially ignited our connection. There was a flicker, yes, but it seemed shrouded in shadows.

He ran a hand through his hair, a gesture I had come to recognize as a sign of his inner turmoil. "It's just... a lot to take in," he said slowly, his voice almost a whisper. "You know how it is when something feels too good to be true." His gaze drifted toward the lake, reflecting the myriad stars above like scattered diamonds on a dark velvet cloth.

I could sense the truth behind his words, the fear lurking beneath the surface, gnawing at his resolve. I shifted closer, the wooden porch creaking beneath us as if echoing my anxious heart. "You don't have to carry it alone," I urged gently. "I'm here, Ethan. I want to share this with you. Whatever it is."

He turned to me then, those deep-set eyes piercing through my defenses, searching for the truth of my intentions. "What if I mess it all up? What if I ruin what we have?" The vulnerability in his voice cut through the air, and I could see the weight of his fears etched into the lines of his face.

I felt a rush of empathy wash over me, understanding all too well the crippling anxiety of wanting something desperately while fearing its inevitable loss. "We'll figure it out together," I promised, my heart pounding with the earnestness of my words. "I'm not going anywhere. You're worth the risk, Ethan."

For a moment, silence enveloped us, a thick blanket of tension that crackled with unspoken possibilities. Then, he reached for my hand, his fingers brushing against mine, sending a jolt of warmth racing through my body. The world around us faded into a soft blur, the noise of the night dimming in the face of our connection. In that instant, everything felt right.

But just as quickly as the warmth ignited, a shadow crossed his features. "What if I'm not enough?" he murmured, pulling his hand away as if it were scalding hot. The flicker in his eyes dulled, replaced by a distant melancholy that mirrored the darkness of the lake behind him.

"Ethan," I said, my voice steadying as I tried to bridge the chasm that had opened between us. "You're more than enough. You're talented, kind, and you see the world in ways that others can't. You bring light to those around you." I paused, searching for the right words, the ones that would reach him. "I'm not here because of your art. I'm here because of you. I care about you."

His eyes softened for a moment, but the shadow of doubt still loomed large. "It's just hard to believe," he admitted, his voice barely a whisper. "I've spent so long feeling like I have to prove myself to everyone. It's like I'm stuck in this endless cycle of self-doubt."

I took a deep breath, feeling the weight of my own insecurities rise to the surface. "I get it. I've been there too. But you don't have to prove anything to me. I'm not looking for perfection. I'm looking for you—the real you." I held his gaze, willing him to see the truth in my words.

For a heartbeat, the distance between us felt like it was narrowing. I could see the gears turning in his mind, the flicker of hope battling against the shadows of his past. But just as quickly, the shadows surged back, stronger than before.

"I need time," he said finally, his voice heavy with resignation. "I want to be what you deserve, but I don't know if I can be that person right now."

The words hit me like a cold wave crashing against the shore, and my heart sank. The fear of losing him gripped me tightly, and I struggled to hold onto the fragments of our connection. "Time," I echoed softly, letting the word hang in the air. "I understand. But don't shut me out, Ethan. Please. I don't want to lose what we have."

He looked away, the internal battle playing out behind his eyes. I could see the struggle etched across his face, a mixture of longing and fear. I wanted to reach out, to pull him closer, but I felt the invisible barrier between us solidifying, a wall constructed of his doubts.

"I'll try," he finally said, the words heavy with unspoken limitations. "But I can't make any promises."

I nodded, a bittersweet acceptance coursing through me. "That's all I can ask for," I replied, forcing a smile, though it felt shaky and fragile. I wanted to believe that we could weather this storm together, but doubt lingered in the back of my mind, whispering fears of what could happen if he remained adrift.

The night stretched on, filled with the soft symphony of nature—the crooning of frogs, the gentle rustle of leaves in the breeze. Each sound felt magnified in the stillness, echoing the turmoil within me. I couldn't help but wonder if we had reached a turning point, a precipice from which we could either soar or fall.

As the stars twinkled above, I made a silent vow to myself. I wouldn't let this connection slip away without a fight. I would push through the uncertainty, shattering the walls he had built around himself, even if it meant wading through his fears. I had once believed in the magic of flickering flames; now, I would nurture it, keeping it alive against the odds, hoping that in the end, it would illuminate our path forward.

But for now, we sat in silence, each lost in our thoughts, the tension between us an unspoken promise of what might still be. The flicker of hope remained, fragile yet resilient, waiting for the right moment to reignite into something beautiful and lasting.

The weeks rolled on, each day stretching into the next, and the tension between Ethan and me wove itself into the very fabric of my existence. The park became our sanctuary, the place where I would seek him out, a moth drawn to the flame that flickered hesitantly between us. I would often find him sitting on that weathered bench, sketchbook in hand, the pages filled with swirling lines and bold strokes that captured the very essence of his soul. I wanted so desperately to be a part of that world he painted, to weave myself into the narratives that spilled forth from his imagination. Yet, there were days when he seemed unreachable, lost in thought, as if the shadows from his past had seeped into the present, casting a veil over his heart.

One crisp autumn afternoon, as the leaves turned to hues of amber and crimson, I approached him with a determination that thrummed in my veins. The sun dipped low on the horizon, casting a warm glow across the landscape, the golden light enveloping us in a gentle embrace. I settled onto the bench beside him, the comforting scent of earth and leaves mingling in the air.

"Can we talk?" I asked, my voice steady despite the fluttering in my chest.

He looked up, surprise flashing in his eyes before he nodded, a hint of apprehension lurking just beneath the surface. "Yeah, of course."

I took a deep breath, summoning the courage to push past the uncertainty. "I miss you," I confessed, the words spilling from my lips like water from a broken dam. "I miss the way we used to talk, the way everything felt so easy. I don't want to lose that."

Ethan's gaze dropped to his sketchbook, the pencil in his hand trembling slightly. "It's not that I don't want to be here," he murmured, his voice barely above a whisper. "I just... I don't know how to be the person you need me to be."

The vulnerability in his admission cracked open my heart, revealing the raw emotions I had buried beneath layers of doubt. "I don't need you to be perfect," I said, urgency lacing my words. "I just need you to be you. That's all I've ever wanted."

He met my eyes then, a flicker of uncertainty dancing within the depths of his own. "But what if who I am isn't enough?" The question hung heavy in the air, filled with an intensity that made my heart ache for him.

I leaned closer, resting my hand over his, feeling the warmth radiate from his skin. "You are enough, Ethan. You're an incredible artist, and more importantly, you're a good person. You've already brought so much light into my life." I paused, watching the conflict play out on his face. "Just let me in. Let's face this together."

He hesitated, the internal struggle clear as day in the furrow of his brow. Then, slowly, he nodded. "I'll try," he said, the words a fragile promise that felt both like a lifeline and a weight.

Our conversation unfurled like the autumn leaves around us, each word a step forward, each confession a brushstroke against the canvas of our relationship. The warmth of connection began to seep back in, dispelling the chill of doubt that had hung over us for too long. I could sense the flickering flame reigniting, its glow warming my heart.

As we talked, the world melted away, leaving just the two of us amidst the trees swaying gently in the breeze. We shared stories of our pasts—his haunted by whispers of insecurity, mine laced with shadows of regret. There was something liberating about unveiling our truths, laying bare our vulnerabilities like the changing leaves that surrendered to the earth. In that moment, we became intertwined, not just as individuals but as a tapestry of shared experiences, hopes, and fears.

But the specter of his hesitation still lingered, an unwelcome guest that threatened to pull him back into the depths of his doubts. I could see the flicker dim once more as the conversation waned, and I knew I had to keep fanning the flames. "What about your art?" I prompted, hoping to draw him back to the passion that had ignited our initial connection. "What's inspiring you right now?"

His eyes brightened slightly, the spark of creativity lighting up his features. "I've been working on a new piece," he admitted, his voice gaining strength as he spoke. "It's about the idea of finding solace in chaos. It's this big canvas, full of swirling colors, representing how beauty can emerge from disorder."

"Can I see it?" I asked, eager to glimpse the world through his eyes, to witness the transformation of his emotions into art.

"Yeah," he replied, a tentative smile breaking through the tension. "It's not finished yet, but I think you'll like it."

We stood together, hand in hand, and as we made our way to his studio, I felt a sense of hope swell within me. The flickering flame between us began to burn brighter, casting away the darkness that had threatened to suffocate our connection.

Ethan's studio was a whirlwind of colors, canvases leaning against the walls like soldiers standing guard over their territory. The air was heavy with the smell of paint and turpentine, a heady mix that stirred something creative within me. I glanced around, my heart racing as I took in the beauty surrounding us.

And then I saw it—a massive canvas, almost consuming an entire wall, splashed with vibrant hues that seemed to pulse with life. It was a cacophony of color, an explosion of emotions that captivated me instantly. "It's beautiful," I breathed, stepping closer to examine the details.

The colors swirled together in a chaotic dance, yet somehow they harmonized, creating a stunning visual representation of his inner turmoil and hopes. "I'm trying to capture how it feels to be caught in the storm, yet still find moments of beauty amidst the chaos," he explained, his voice filled with passion. "It's how I feel most days—torn between my fears and the desire to embrace life fully."

I turned to him, my heart swelling with admiration. "You've done it. You've captured the essence of it all." I gestured to the canvas, my eyes shining with emotion. "It's raw, it's real, and it resonates with everything we've talked about. It's a testament to your journey."

Ethan smiled, a flicker of pride illuminating his features. In that moment, I saw a glimpse of the boy I had first met—the one unafraid to dream and unashamed to express himself through his art. The flame between us flickered again, brighter this time, fueled by the vulnerability we had shared.

As we stood there, surrounded by creativity and possibility, I knew that the journey ahead wouldn't be without challenges. There would be moments of doubt and hesitation, but together, we could navigate the darkness and embrace the light. With each brushstroke, with each conversation, we were building something beautiful—something worth fighting for.

In the heart of that studio, amidst the chaos of colors and dreams, I felt a new beginning unfurling before us, a tapestry woven from our hopes, fears, and the flickering flame of our connection, ready to illuminate the path we would walk together.

Chapter 13: The Chase

The rain tapped insistently against the window, a rhythmic serenade that accompanied my thoughts like a haunting melody. I nestled deeper into the plush corner of the coffee shop, my favorite refuge tucked away in the heart of New Orleans, where the scent of freshly brewed coffee danced with the sweet notes of beignets dusted in powdered sugar. The wooden beams of the ceiling loomed above, adorned with delicate fairy lights that twinkled like stars, casting a warm glow that enveloped us in a cocoon of intimacy.

Ethan sat across from me, his dark hair slightly damp from the drizzle outside, and his intense gaze seemed to pierce through the flickering candlelight, making my heart race in a way that felt both exhilarating and terrifying. I had always admired the way he wore his emotions on his sleeve, though today, his expression was a complicated blend of thoughtfulness and hesitation. I could sense the weight of the unspoken words hanging between us, thick enough to cut through the air.

"Why do you keep pulling away?" I asked, my voice barely above a whisper, yet it felt as if I had shouted the words into the stillness that surrounded us. The clinking of cups and the murmured conversations of other patrons faded into the background as I laid my emotions bare before him, hoping he could somehow grasp the tumult within me. "I need to know what's going on in your head."

He hesitated, fingers nervously tracing the rim of his cup as if contemplating the storm raging within his own heart. "It's complicated," he finally admitted, his voice low and earnest. "I'm trying to make sense of everything. My art, my life… and you."

My breath caught in my throat, the intensity of his gaze igniting a fierce determination within me. "What do you mean? Is it me? Do I make things complicated?" The vulnerability in his eyes mirrored the chaos swirling within my chest, a poignant reminder of the emotional tightrope we had been walking.

"No," he said quickly, almost too quickly, his eyes softening as they locked onto mine. "It's just that..." He sighed, running a hand through his hair, and I could see the frustration etched on his face. "I want to pursue my art career with everything I have, but every time I start to take a step forward, I find myself thinking about you, and it distracts me."

A flicker of hope danced in my chest. I had expected the familiar refrain of self-doubt or fear of commitment, but instead, he was admitting that his feelings for me were intertwined with his passion. "Then don't let it distract you," I urged, leaning forward, my palms pressed against the warm wood of the table. "Use it. Chase your dreams with the same fervor you chase my heart."

Ethan's brow furrowed in contemplation, and I could see the gears in his mind turning. The vulnerability that had once held him captive now seemed to shift into something more potent—a spark of realization. "You really believe that?" he asked, a hint of disbelief lacing his tone.

"Absolutely," I replied, a smile breaking through the tension that had gripped us both. "Art is an expression of who you are, and if I'm part of that, then embrace it. Let your feelings fuel your creativity instead of stifling it." My heart raced as I spoke, a fervor igniting within me that propelled my words like an unstoppable force.

He remained silent for a moment, his eyes searching mine as if he were peeling back layers I hadn't even realized existed. "You make it sound so easy," he said finally, a hint of skepticism in his voice.

"Maybe it is, and maybe it isn't," I countered, my voice steady and firm. "But what I do know is that if you don't chase your dreams, you'll always wonder what could have been. And I can't stand the thought of you regretting something you didn't try." My heart swelled with a mixture of affection and determination, a bond that transcended our fears.

Ethan's shoulders relaxed, and a hint of a smile crept onto his lips. "You always know how to get under my skin, don't you?" he said, a teasing lilt returning to his voice, lightening the weight of the conversation.

"Only because I know how amazing you are when you let yourself be," I shot back, reveling in the playful banter that had always characterized our relationship. It was as if the rain outside had washed away some of the heaviness that had lingered, leaving room for something more hopeful to blossom.

He leaned back in his chair, contemplation etched across his features as he took a sip of his coffee. "You know, I've been so focused on trying to succeed that I've forgotten what it feels like to just create without that pressure," he admitted, his voice thoughtful. "Maybe it's time I reminded myself why I fell in love with art in the first place."

The realization hung in the air between us, electric and charged, and I couldn't help but feel that something had shifted. The distance that had felt insurmountable only moments ago was beginning to bridge, leaving behind a fragile but undeniable connection.

"I want to be there for you, Ethan," I said softly, a sincerity that seemed to resonate with the very essence of my being. "I don't want you to feel like you have to choose between your dreams and me. They can coexist; they should coexist."

Ethan met my gaze, his eyes shimmering with something akin to gratitude and warmth. "You have no idea how much that means to me," he said, his voice laced with sincerity. "I've spent so long pushing people away, and here you are, pulling me back to what matters most."

The moment lingered, sweet and poignant, as we sat there surrounded by the aroma of coffee and the melody of the rain outside. In that dimly lit café, it felt like we had carved out a piece of the universe for ourselves—a sanctuary where dreams and love intertwined, igniting a spark of hope that shimmered brighter than any candle flickering on our table.

As we settled into a newfound rhythm, the coffee shop transformed into a sanctuary of sorts—a haven where time seemed to pause, allowing the world outside to blur into an indistinct backdrop. The rain continued its gentle patter against the windows, and the murmur of conversation enveloped us like a warm embrace. I couldn't shake the feeling that we were cocooned in our little bubble, a safe space where vulnerability became a strength instead of a burden.

Ethan leaned forward, his elbows resting on the table, and for a fleeting moment, I caught a glimpse of the artist within him—the spark of inspiration igniting beneath the surface. "You make me want to create again," he said, the corners of his mouth twitching into a smile that lit up his entire face. "It's been a while since I felt that way. Life has a funny way of making you forget what truly matters."

"Life is just an elaborate distraction sometimes," I mused, my fingers curling around the warmth of my cup, drawing comfort from the rich brew. "But the key is to find those moments that remind you why you started. Why you fell in love with the process in the first place."

His gaze held mine, a mixture of admiration and disbelief. "You really have a way with words. I wish I could paint them as beautifully as you say them." He paused, and for a heartbeat, I wondered if he was seeing me—or perhaps seeing himself reflected in my eyes. "It's just… I don't want to chase my dreams just for the sake of it. I want to pour my heart into something that matters, something that resonates with people."

"Then do just that," I encouraged, leaning in closer, as if sharing a secret that only we were meant to know. "Pour your heart into your art, and let it speak for itself. You have a voice, Ethan, and it deserves to be heard." The words rolled off my tongue, infused with an honesty that felt both liberating and empowering.

"Sometimes I feel like I'm too scared to put myself out there," he admitted, vulnerability creeping back into his tone, darkening the vibrant energy that had filled the air moments before. "What if people don't understand me? What if they judge me for what I create?"

"Then you'll learn from it," I replied, my heart aching at the thought of him being held back by the chains of self-doubt. "Not everyone will love what you do, and that's okay. What matters is that you're expressing yourself. The right audience will find you, but only if you let your art breathe."

He nodded slowly, absorbing my words, and the light in his eyes flickered like the candle flame dancing on our table. "You always know what to say to shake me awake," he murmured, a hint of gratitude lacing his voice. "It's like you can see the best parts of me even when I can't."

"Maybe that's because I see how much potential you have," I said softly. "You're not just an artist; you're a storyteller. Each piece you create tells a story that only you can share. Don't let fear dim your light."

With every word that escaped my lips, I felt a connection strengthening between us—a bond woven through our shared dreams and fears. Ethan reached across the table, his fingers brushing against mine in a fleeting touch that sent a spark of electricity racing up my arm. "You make me want to fight for my dreams, you know that?" he said, his voice low and earnest. "I can't let you down."

"You'll never let me down," I assured him, squeezing his hand gently. "You're stronger than you realize. Just remember, I'm here to support you, not to hold you back. We're in this together."

The warmth of our fingers interlaced seemed to create a bubble around us, isolating us from the world outside, where the rain fell relentlessly, washing away the grime of the day. The soft chatter of patrons blended into a harmonious background hum, but for us, the coffee shop had become a realm unto itself—a space where dreams were born and nurtured.

As the minutes slipped by, the atmosphere transformed. The weight of uncertainty began to lift, replaced by a lightness that danced through the air like the fragrant steam rising from our cups. I could see the wheels turning in Ethan's mind, the way his expression shifted from doubt to possibility. "Maybe I should start small," he mused, his brow furrowing in contemplation. "What if I set a goal to create one piece every week? Just for myself?"

"That sounds perfect," I encouraged, my heart swelling with pride at his determination. "Let the process be your guide. Who knows what might blossom from it?"

Ethan's eyes sparkled with newfound enthusiasm, and I felt a warmth spread through me, igniting the space between us. "And what about you?" he asked, his voice teasing but genuinely curious. "What dreams do you want to chase?"

I hesitated, suddenly feeling exposed under the weight of his gaze. My dreams had always been wrapped in layers of doubt and insecurity, buried beneath the expectations that loomed like heavy clouds. "I've always wanted to write," I confessed, my voice barely above a whisper. "But it's one of those things I keep pushing aside, thinking there will be a better time."

"Then what's stopping you?" he countered, his expression unwavering. "If you have a story to tell, you need to start telling it. Don't let fear hold you back."

The intensity of his gaze made my pulse quicken, and I felt a mixture of fear and exhilaration wash over me. "You really believe I can?" I asked, my voice trembling slightly.

"Absolutely," he said, the conviction in his tone unwavering. "You have so much to say, and the world deserves to hear it."

With each encouraging word, a fire ignited within me, slowly pushing away the shadows that had clouded my aspirations. It was in that moment, surrounded by the comforting chaos of the coffee shop, that I realized how intertwined our dreams had become. Ethan was not just my muse; he was a mirror reflecting the depths of my own unfulfilled desires. Together, we were embarking on a journey—one that promised to be both thrilling and terrifying.

As the candle flickered, casting playful shadows across our table, I felt a deep-seated connection between us solidify into something more than mere friendship. It was a bond forged in shared vulnerability, a pact to chase our dreams hand in hand, ready to face whatever challenges lay ahead. The rain continued to dance outside, but inside, our hearts pulsed with the promise of possibility, echoing the rhythm of our newfound resolve.

As our conversation deepened, the coffee shop became more than just a cozy retreat from the downpour outside; it morphed into a sanctuary of our aspirations and fears. The walls, lined with eclectic art from local artists, seemed to nod in approval as we unveiled pieces of ourselves, shedding the layers of hesitation that had clung to us like a second skin. The world outside, with its relentless drizzle, faded away, allowing us to carve out our own reality—a realm where dreams felt tangible, just waiting for us to reach out and grab them.

Ethan's eyes sparkled with determination, a shift that didn't go unnoticed. "You know," he began, his voice brimming with newfound energy, "I've always thought of art as a solitary pursuit. I'd convince myself that my creations were meant for my eyes alone. But now, sitting here with you, I realize I don't have to do this alone."

The corners of my mouth curled into a smile. "Exactly. You have a community of people who want to see you succeed, starting with me. Let's lift each other up. You inspire me, and I want to be your biggest supporter." The warmth of my words wrapped around us like a blanket, soothing any lingering doubts that had threatened to cloud our progress.

"Alright, let's do this," Ethan said, his voice steady, almost resolute. "I'll commit to creating something new every week. And you—" He leaned in closer, his eyes narrowing playfully. "You need to write. No excuses."

My heart raced at the thought. "Deal," I replied, feeling the weight of the challenge settle comfortably on my shoulders. The thrill of accountability electrified the air between us, turning the moment into a pact that felt as significant as it was simple.

In that moment of mutual resolve, the candlelight flickered more brightly, as if the universe itself had recognized our intentions. As I glanced around the shop, I could see other patrons caught up in their own worlds, each immersed in conversations and daydreams, but none as vibrant as ours. I envisioned the stories yet to be written, the canvases yet to be painted, and the lives yet to be lived—all waiting in the wings, ready to be summoned forth by our hands.

As the minutes melted into one another, Ethan shifted the conversation to the artistic community in New Orleans. "There are so many galleries and events that celebrate local talent," he said, excitement tinging his voice. "We could check out an art walk this weekend. It might give me some ideas, and I'd love to share that experience with you."

I nodded enthusiastically, feeling a thrill of anticipation bubble within me. "That sounds amazing! I've always wanted to see the art scene here from that perspective. Plus, it'll give you a chance to meet other artists—maybe even find inspiration in their work."

"I've got to start somewhere," he said, a self-deprecating smile crossing his lips. "Who knows? Maybe I'll find a gallery that will take me seriously."

"And if they don't, who cares?" I teased, leaning forward, my voice low and conspiratorial. "Just consider it a stepping stone. The right place will come along when the time is right."

With our spirits lifted, we spent the rest of the afternoon entwined in conversation, sharing dreams and laughter that chased away the clouds of doubt. I marveled at how quickly the tension that had once shrouded our relationship melted away, replaced by a vibrant energy that felt almost tangible.

The rain began to lighten, the rhythmic sound transforming into a gentle patter, creating a soothing backdrop to our discussions. As we both sipped our drinks—Ethan opting for a rich mocha and me indulging in a chai latte—the fragrant steam rising from our cups swirled around us like a welcoming mist, encouraging our thoughts to flow freely.

"What if I showcased a piece at the art walk?" Ethan mused, his brow furrowing as he contemplated the possibilities. "Just a small display, something that captures where I am right now."

"Absolutely! Why not? Show them what you've got!" I responded, the excitement palpable in my voice. "You can create something that embodies your journey—your struggles, your triumphs, and everything in between."

The idea seemed to take root in his mind, blossoming as he spoke. "Maybe I'll paint our coffee shop," he suggested, a hint of mischief dancing in his eyes. "The flickering candlelight, the rain outside, us... It could be a portrait of this very moment."

"Now that would be something special," I said, the warmth spreading through me. "A snapshot of us, here, right now—vulnerable yet hopeful."

As Ethan shared his vision, his enthusiasm infectious, I found myself swept up in the moment, a wave of creativity crashing over me. "What if I write a short story to accompany your painting?" I suggested, my mind racing with ideas. "We could display them side by side—your art and my words, telling a single story. It would be like a mini-exhibit."

Ethan's eyes widened, a spark igniting within him. "That's brilliant! A narrative that intertwines our journeys, showcasing not just the art, but the bond behind it."

With each idea exchanged, the world around us faded further into the background, leaving only the echo of our dreams hanging in the air. The outside world continued its march—cars splashed through puddles, pedestrians hurried along the sidewalks, and the scent of rain mingled with the rich aroma of coffee—but inside our little bubble, nothing else mattered.

As we prepared to leave, the storm had passed, leaving a fresh, invigorating scent wafting through the air. The sun had broken through the clouds, casting a golden hue over the streets, painting the world anew.

"Let's get to work," Ethan said, his eyes gleaming with determination as we stepped outside. The sun warmed our faces, and I couldn't help but feel that this was just the beginning of something beautiful—something that might change everything.

Side by side, we walked along the cobblestone streets, the vibrant life of New Orleans unfolding around us like a canvas waiting to be painted. Musicians played lively tunes nearby, filling the air with a rhythm that mirrored the excitement thrumming in my veins.

The possibilities stretched out before us like an open road, brimming with potential. It wasn't just about the art or the words we would create; it was about embracing the journey together. In that moment, I realized that love could be a muse, a catalyst for dreams yet to be realized.

With Ethan by my side, I felt a profound sense of hope—a belief that we could conquer our fears, chase our aspirations, and create something magical. Hand in hand, we stepped into the vibrant tapestry of life, ready to weave our stories together, one brushstroke and one word at a time. The future beckoned, and we were ready to embrace it with open arms.

Chapter 14: Dancing in the Rain

The storm had rolled in without warning, dark clouds swirling like a tempestuous dance partner as they cloaked the sun. The air was thick with the scent of rain-soaked asphalt, a smell that both grounded me and sent my heart racing. I stood beneath the awning of a small café on the corner of Clark Street, watching as the world transformed into a vibrant watercolor painting. Raindrops fell in torrents, each droplet racing to join its brethren in forming shimmering puddles that reflected the chaotic beauty of the city above.

Ethan appeared like a hero emerging from the shadows, a playful grin stretching across his face as he stepped out into the rain. His dark hair, slicked back by the downpour, framed his face perfectly, accentuating the mischievous spark in his eyes. I couldn't help but smile back at him, feeling an inexplicable pull toward the spontaneity he embodied. With an audacious flourish, he extended his hand toward me, a silent invitation that ignited a thrill deep within my chest.

"Come on! You can't let a little rain stop you from having fun," he urged, his voice a mix of challenge and promise. The world around us faded, the storm cocooning us in a lively bubble filled with laughter and the steady drum of rain on rooftops.

With my heart pounding like a drum in my ears, I slipped my hand into his, and together we stepped into the rain. The cool water splashed against my skin, soaking through my clothes in an instant, the fabric clinging to my body. The sensation was exhilarating, a jolt of electricity that danced along my spine, washing away the burdens I had carried for far too long. Ethan twirled me around, our laughter mingling with the sound of rain, each movement a vibrant note in this impromptu symphony.

We spun and twirled, arms flailing as we danced in the middle of the street, the glistening pavement beneath our feet glimmering like shards of broken glass under the streetlights. The city became a blur, the usual hustle and bustle replaced by the serene rhythm of the rain. I felt weightless, free from the clutches of reality, as if the storm had washed away not just the water but also my worries, fears, and the shadows of my past.

Ethan's grip on my hand was firm yet tender, his laughter a melodic echo that seemed to bounce off the buildings surrounding us. "You know, they say that dancing in the rain washes away your troubles," he shouted above the cacophony of droplets crashing around us, his voice filled with a joyful exuberance that made my heart swell.

"Is that so?" I replied, my voice barely a whisper amidst the roaring storm.

"Absolutely!" He pulled me closer, our bodies moving in sync, my heart racing not just from the thrill of dancing but from the magnetic connection that was undeniable. "It's like a reset button for your soul."

We moved as if the rain were our choreographer, guiding our steps in a waltz only we could hear. In that moment, it felt as though the universe conspired to bring us together, two souls adrift in a world that often felt indifferent. I couldn't remember the last time I had allowed myself to be so carefree, to truly feel alive. This was a moment suspended in time, a sweet interlude in the chaos of life.

As we danced, I caught glimpses of our reflections in the puddles, two radiant figures splashing joyfully through the chaos. I could see the freedom in my own eyes, the weight of my past giving way to something new and thrilling. I wanted to capture this feeling forever—the intoxicating mix of laughter, connection, and the intoxicating scent of rain-soaked earth.

But even amidst the joy, a flicker of doubt wormed its way into my mind, lingering at the edges of my happiness. What if this moment was fleeting? What if the storm passed, leaving us soaked but alone? The thought was like a dark cloud creeping back in, threatening to overshadow our laughter. But I refused to let it dampen my spirit.

"Let's keep dancing!" I shouted, determined to chase away the shadows of uncertainty. Ethan's eyes sparkled with delight as he nodded, his laughter echoing through the storm as we continued our whirlwind of movement, each step taken was a testament to our defiance against whatever lay ahead.

For a brief eternity, the rain became our sanctuary, and I felt the connection between us deepening. Each drop seemed to weave an invisible thread that bound us together, reminding me that I was not just a girl lost in a storm; I was someone deserving of joy, of love, and of moments like these.

We danced until our legs grew weary, until our laughter faded into the soft patter of the rain, the world around us becoming a distant memory. As the storm began to relent, the raindrops softened, transforming from a downpour to a gentle drizzle, a soothing caress against our flushed cheeks. I looked up, my gaze lost in the clouds parting to reveal the first hints of a starry sky, a sight that felt like a promise of brighter days ahead.

Ethan's hand remained firmly clasped in mine, a grounding presence amidst the lingering uncertainty. I could see the warmth in his smile, the way his eyes sparkled even in the dim light, a beacon guiding me toward hope.

"I think we just made a memory worth keeping," he said softly, his breath warm against my ear, igniting a flutter deep within me.

"Yes," I replied, my voice filled with conviction, "and it's just the beginning."

In that moment, as the last of the storm faded away, I realized that no matter what awaited us in the future, I was ready to face it—especially if it meant dancing in the rain again with Ethan by my side.

With the rain gradually tapering off, the world around us shimmered in a kaleidoscope of colors, as if the city had been dipped in a vibrant paint palette. Puddles reflected the neon lights from nearby shops, creating little pools of electric blue and bright pink that danced beneath our feet. The air was crisp and fresh, infused with the scent of damp earth and a hint of distant cinnamon from a bakery nearby, enticing and warm.

As the last remnants of the storm faded into a gentle drizzle, Ethan and I finally slowed our frenzied dance, breathless and exhilarated. The energy that had sparked between us in the downpour still crackled in the air, charging the atmosphere with unspoken words. He brushed a damp strand of hair away from my forehead, his fingers lingering a moment too long, sending an unexpected thrill coursing through me.

"Do you think we'll get arrested for dancing in the street?" he teased, his voice playful, the hint of a challenge in his eyes.

"Maybe," I replied with a mock-seriousness that made him chuckle. "But it's a small price to pay for such an epic moment." I nudged him gently with my shoulder, feeling the warmth of his laughter wrap around me like a cozy blanket.

As the last echoes of raindrops faded, we stood in the aftermath of our impromptu celebration, our laughter blending into the soft sounds of the city awakening once more. I could see people peeking out of their homes, curious gazes darting our way, but in that moment, we were oblivious to the world outside our little bubble of joy. All I could focus on was the way Ethan looked at me, as if he could see into the depths of my soul and was willing to dive in.

"Let's find somewhere to dry off," he suggested, nodding toward the café from which I had just emerged. "They have the best hot chocolate in the city."

"Hot chocolate sounds perfect," I agreed, my heart fluttering at the thought of continuing this enchanting evening. We walked side by side, the intimacy of our shared experience still lingering in the air. The streets, glistening like diamonds, shimmered under the glow of streetlights as we made our way through the heart of Chicago.

The café was small and cozy, a hidden gem tucked away between larger buildings. Inside, the warm glow of yellow lights illuminated the rustic wooden tables, each adorned with potted plants that added a splash of life to the space. The barista, a cheerful woman with a warm smile, greeted us as we entered, her laughter ringing like chimes in the air.

"Two hot chocolates?" she asked, her eyes twinkling as she recognized the playful energy between us.

"Yes, please!" Ethan replied, his tone bright. I couldn't help but notice the way he spoke with such ease, making every interaction feel personal and genuine.

We found a small table by the window, the raindrops on the glass providing a gentle soundtrack to our conversation. As we waited for our drinks, I felt a comfortable silence envelop us, an unspoken connection that was both exciting and terrifying.

"So, what's the wildest thing you've ever done?" Ethan asked, leaning forward, his elbows resting on the table. His gaze was intense, drawing me in, and I felt a sudden urge to share my truth, to peel back the layers I had carefully built around myself.

I hesitated for a moment, considering the question. "I once decided to sneak into an amusement park after hours with a couple of friends," I said, a grin creeping onto my face as I recalled the thrill of that night. "We climbed over the fence, and for about an hour, we had the entire place to ourselves—riding the Ferris wheel, running through the arcade, the works. It felt so rebellious and exhilarating."

Ethan chuckled, his eyes sparkling with mischief. "That's amazing! I wish I had been there. I'm sure you were the mastermind behind it all."

"Oh, you have no idea," I laughed, feeling the heat rise to my cheeks. "But I'd say I've mellowed out since then. Nowadays, I settle for dancing in the rain."

He looked at me, his expression shifting to something more serious, almost contemplative. "You know, it takes courage to let loose like that. Most people are too afraid to step outside their comfort zones."

I shrugged, the weight of his words settling over me. "Maybe I'm just tired of living in fear of what could happen. Sometimes you have to take a leap of faith, even if it means getting wet."

He nodded thoughtfully, as if my words resonated with him. "I get that. Life can be a lot sometimes. It's easy to get caught up in what you think you're supposed to be."

Our drinks arrived, steaming mugs filled to the brim with rich hot chocolate topped with fluffy whipped cream. I took a sip, the warm liquid spreading through me like a comforting embrace, melting away the chill from the rain.

"Delicious," I murmured, relishing the sweet taste.

Ethan grinned, clearly pleased with my reaction. "I knew you'd love it. It's one of my favorite spots to unwind."

We continued to share stories, weaving our lives together with laughter and sincerity. Ethan talked about his love for photography, how he found beauty in the mundane, capturing moments that others overlooked. I shared my dreams of becoming a writer, of wanting to weave my thoughts into stories that made people feel.

In the midst of our conversations, I felt a sense of ease I hadn't experienced in years. There was something undeniably magnetic about Ethan, something that made me want to peel back my layers and let him see the real me. I found myself wanting to show him every piece of my world, to let him in on my fears and my hopes.

As the evening wore on and the café began to fill with more patrons, the outside world slowly faded into the background. It was just Ethan and me, two kindred spirits discovering each other under the twinkling lights of the café. The air was thick with potential, a promise of what could be. I glanced at him, captivated by the way he spoke with his hands, the passion in his voice illuminating every word.

"I'm glad we ran into each other tonight," he said, his tone shifting slightly, the weight of his words sinking in.

"Me too," I replied, my heart swelling with a mixture of gratitude and longing.

The night was young, and as we sat there, enveloped in warmth and laughter, I couldn't help but feel that perhaps, just perhaps, this was the start of something extraordinary.

With our mugs of hot chocolate cradled between our hands, the warmth radiating through the ceramic felt like a reassuring hug against the cool air of the café. The atmosphere was alive with the mingling scents of roasted coffee beans and freshly baked pastries, creating a sanctuary amidst the bustling streets of Chicago. The soft chatter and the clinking of cups formed a comforting backdrop as Ethan and I shared stories, our words flowing as effortlessly as the rain that had just enveloped us.

"Do you have a favorite spot in the city?" I asked, genuinely curious. I had spent my life searching for the hidden gems that lay tucked away in the bustling metropolis, the places that felt like a refuge from the chaos.

Ethan leaned back, his gaze drifting toward the window where the last remnants of the storm faded into a soft mist. "I love the Art Institute. There's something magical about walking through the galleries, losing myself in the paintings. It's like stepping into another world."

His passion was infectious, and I could picture him wandering through the sprawling halls, each artwork resonating with him on a level I could only imagine. "I've always wanted to explore more art,"

I admitted, a spark of inspiration igniting within me. "There's a story behind every piece, and I can't help but wonder what the artist was feeling when they created it."

"Exactly! Art is like a conversation across time," he replied, his enthusiasm lighting up his face. "It captures emotions we sometimes can't put into words."

As we chatted, the world outside continued to transform under the glow of streetlights, the rain having washed the city's usual grime away, leaving behind a cleaner, fresher essence. It was as if the storm had cleansed not just the streets but our spirits as well.

"What about you?" he asked, bringing me back to the moment. "Where do you feel most at home?"

I took a moment, reflecting on the places that had shaped my life. "There's a little park near my apartment," I started, my thoughts drifting to the green space lined with cherry blossom trees. "In the spring, it's like stepping into a dream. The petals fall like confetti, and everything feels alive. It reminds me that beauty exists even in the smallest moments."

Ethan nodded, captivated. "I'd love to see that."

The conversation flowed seamlessly, weaving between our dreams and desires, our hopes and fears. I found myself sharing more than I intended, recounting tales of my childhood, the struggles that had shaped me, and the aspirations I held close to my heart. Each word felt like an unburdening, a revelation of my true self that had long been hidden beneath layers of uncertainty.

Just as I began to delve into the darker chapters of my past, the atmosphere shifted, like a cloud momentarily obscuring the sun. Ethan leaned forward, his expression earnest. "You don't have to share anything you're not comfortable with," he said, his voice a soothing balm. "I'm here to listen, not to judge."

His kindness enveloped me, easing the hesitation that clung to my thoughts. "It's just... sometimes it's hard to trust. I've always felt like I was carrying a weight, a fear of being vulnerable," I confessed, my voice barely above a whisper. "But with you, it feels different."

He smiled softly, the sincerity in his gaze encouraging me to continue. "I understand that feeling. I've been there too," he replied, his words resonating with my own experiences. "But vulnerability can be a strength. It's what connects us."

In that moment, I felt a flicker of hope igniting within me, a belief that perhaps I could let go of the chains that had bound me for so long. The comfort of his presence made the weight of my past feel lighter, almost bearable.

Our drinks grew colder as we lost track of time, each moment threading us closer together, creating a tapestry of connection that felt both fragile and enduring. Outside, the rain transformed into a gentle drizzle, the city alive with the soft hum of life continuing, despite the earlier storm.

When the café's bell chimed to signal the arrival of a new customer, it pulled me from my reverie. I glanced around, taking in the surroundings. It was a simple place, filled with wooden tables, mismatched chairs, and quirky decorations that gave it an inviting charm. I wondered how many stories had unfolded within these walls, how many connections had been made over steaming cups of coffee.

"Want to go for a walk?" Ethan suggested, his eyes twinkling with the thrill of adventure. "I think the rain has finally let up."

"Absolutely," I replied, excitement bubbling within me.

We stepped outside, the cool air invigorating as it wrapped around us like a refreshing blanket. The streets glistened, the pavement reflecting the vibrant colors of neon signs, giving the city an otherworldly glow. Hand in hand, we wandered through the streets, the rhythm of our footsteps syncing with the heartbeat of the city.

As we walked, I felt a sense of freedom, a thrilling sensation of possibility. We strolled past a small park where children chased after the remnants of summer, their laughter blending with the soft whispers of the evening breeze. It reminded me of my own childhood, a simpler time when worries felt distant and joy was an everyday occurrence.

"Do you miss it?" Ethan asked, noticing my gaze lingering on the children playing.

"Sometimes," I admitted, my voice soft. "But I think it's also important to cherish the memories and move forward."

He squeezed my hand gently, a gesture of understanding that warmed my heart. "You're right. It's all part of our journey."

We continued to explore, crossing streets and winding through alleyways adorned with vibrant murals, each telling a story of its own. The city felt alive, pulsing with energy as if it were sharing its secrets with us. The night unfolded like a storybook, and I was lost in the narrative we were weaving together.

As we reached the waterfront, the calmness of Lake Michigan spread before us, its waters reflecting the stars that had begun to twinkle in the night sky. Ethan and I paused, taking in the breathtaking view. The moonlight shimmered on the water, creating a magical aura that seemed to envelop us in its embrace.

"This is beautiful," I murmured, feeling a sense of peace wash over me.

"It is," he replied, his gaze fixed on the horizon. "But not as beautiful as the moments we create together."

His words lingered in the air, and I felt my heart flutter with hope. In that instant, surrounded by the beauty of the city and the warmth of our connection, I realized that maybe, just maybe, I had found a place where I truly belonged.

As the night deepened, we sat on a bench overlooking the lake, our shoulders touching, the silence wrapped around us like a soft embrace. I could hear the gentle lapping of the waves, a soothing melody that accompanied our shared breaths. It felt like a moment suspended in time, a serene oasis amidst the chaos of life.

With Ethan beside me, I felt lighter, freer. The world was vast and unpredictable, but here, under the starlit sky, it seemed perfectly crafted, as if destiny had conspired to bring us together on this very night. In that moment, I dared to dream of what could be, to imagine a future filled with possibilities, laughter, and love.

Chapter 15: When Walls Come Crumbling Down

The scent of pine and fresh water washed over me as I stepped out of the car, the crisp autumn air invigorating my senses. The sprawling lake house stood majestically at the edge of Lake Windham, its wooden beams glowing in the golden light of the setting sun. I could hardly contain my excitement. This was more than just a getaway; it felt like a promise of something deeper between Ethan and me. I glanced at him, his eyes sparkling with anticipation, and I felt the butterflies flutter in my stomach as I took in the way his smile lit up his entire face. He stepped closer, his fingers brushing against mine as he led me toward the door, the warmth of his touch igniting a spark of hope.

Inside, the house was a blend of rustic charm and modern comfort. The living room boasted a massive stone fireplace, its mantle adorned with a collection of seashells, a remnant of summers spent at the beach. The rich scent of cedar lingered in the air, weaving through the cozy space like a familiar tune. I could almost hear the crackling of the fire as I imagined us curled up together, sharing stories and laughter. Ethan set about making dinner, the sound of pots clanging and water boiling filling the room, creating a symphony of domestic bliss.

As I gazed out the large windows overlooking the lake, I lost myself in the beauty of the scene. The water mirrored the vibrant colors of the sky, rippling gently as a soft breeze danced across the surface. Shades of orange, red, and purple melded together like a painter's palette, each stroke more breathtaking than the last. My heart swelled with contentment. This was exactly the escape I had needed.

But the tranquility shattered like glass when I heard the crunch of tires on gravel. A car pulled into the driveway, and I felt a sudden pang of unease ripple through me. Ethan, oblivious to my growing anxiety, continued to hum softly as he stirred the pasta. I forced myself to breathe deeply, brushing off the sensation as merely the remnants of city stress clinging to my nerves.

When the door swung open, revealing a girl with sun-kissed hair and an effortless smile, I felt as if the ground had been pulled from beneath my feet. Claire. She stepped into the house like she owned the place, her laughter ringing through the air like chimes in the wind. Ethan's face lit up at the sight of her, and I felt the world tilt on its axis. My heart sank, each beat drumming a melody of jealousy and insecurity in my chest.

"Ethan!" she exclaimed, her voice warm and inviting. She crossed the room, throwing her arms around him, and my breath hitched in my throat. The familiarity between them was palpable, a connection I wasn't a part of. It felt as though I had stumbled into a scene from a movie, one where I was merely a spectator to their history. I stood frozen, the walls I had carefully constructed around my heart beginning to crack under the weight of uncertainty.

As they pulled apart, Ethan's eyes sparkled with something I couldn't quite place—nostalgia, perhaps? Claire turned to me, her gaze assessing as she took in the space between us. "And you must be Lily! Ethan's told me so much about you."

The warmth of her greeting felt as hollow as the laughter that echoed in my mind. I managed a smile, but it felt brittle, as if it might shatter at any moment. "Nice to meet you," I said, my voice barely above a whisper.

The three of us settled into the living room, the atmosphere thick with unspoken tension. I watched as Ethan and Claire reminisced, their shared stories weaving a tapestry of friendship that I desperately wanted to be a part of, yet felt utterly excluded from. I tried to engage, to inject humor into the conversation, but my attempts felt feeble and awkward. Each laugh they shared struck like a gong, reverberating through my core, and I felt myself withdrawing into a shell of self-doubt.

After dinner, we headed outside, the cool evening air wrapping around us like a soft blanket. The moon hung low in the sky, casting silver beams across the lake, transforming it into a shimmering canvas of dreams. But as Ethan and Claire shared stories under the stars, I felt like an outsider in a world that was meant to be ours. The fire crackled softly, but my heart felt heavy, burdened by unvoiced fears.

"I've missed this place," Claire said, her voice laced with nostalgia. "Remember those summer nights we spent out here? Just us and the stars?"

Ethan chuckled, and I could see the memories playing behind his eyes, each one a thread woven into the fabric of their friendship. "Yeah, we'd stay up until dawn, talking about everything and nothing."

I forced a smile, but the knot in my stomach tightened. I wanted to be the one sharing those memories, to laugh about the past in a way that felt effortless and free. Instead, I was stuck in a limbo of jealousy, my heart fluttering like a trapped bird seeking escape.

The conversation shifted, and they began to plan a boat trip for the next day. "Lily, you're coming with us, right?" Ethan asked, looking at me with those earnest eyes that always made my heart race.

I hesitated, a part of me wanting to retreat, to hide from the shadows of my insecurities. "Sure, sounds fun," I replied, the words tasting bitter on my tongue. I knew I should be excited, but the prospect of spending a day with Claire looming over me felt like a challenge I wasn't sure I could face.

As the night wore on, I felt the cracks in my emotional fortress deepen. I wrapped my arms around myself, the chill of the night seeping into my bones as I wrestled with the feeling that I was losing Ethan, even if he didn't realize it.

The morning sun filtered through the curtains, casting playful shadows across the wooden floorboards of the lake house. I lay in bed, cocooned in a blanket that smelled faintly of cedar and the remnants of last night's fire. The faint sounds of laughter drifted in from the kitchen, where I could imagine Ethan and Claire preparing breakfast, the scent of coffee wafting through the air, tempting me to join them. I forced myself to sit up, a battle raging within me between the desire to sink back into the warmth of my dreams and the pull of reality waiting just beyond the door.

After a few moments of deliberation, I pushed the blanket aside, steeling myself for the day ahead. My heart pounded as I crossed the room, each step echoing with uncertainty. I peeked into the kitchen, my breath catching at the sight of Ethan, his back turned to me as he flipped pancakes on the stove. Claire stood at the counter, her hair pulled back in a carefree ponytail, humming softly as she chopped fresh strawberries. Their easy camaraderie struck a nerve deep inside me, a reminder of how easily he fit into her world—one I had only just entered.

"Morning, sleepyhead!" Ethan called over his shoulder, his voice bright and inviting. He turned around, and his smile felt like a warm embrace. I couldn't help but smile back, though it felt slightly strained. "I hope you're hungry. Claire made her famous strawberry pancakes."

I stepped into the kitchen, the rich aroma of coffee and sweet batter enveloping me. "I can't resist a good pancake," I said, my tone attempting to convey enthusiasm, though I felt more like a reluctant participant in their morning ritual.

As I sat at the table, Ethan's warmth radiated around me, yet I couldn't shake the cold presence of Claire. She plopped a generous stack of pancakes in front of me, the strawberries glistening like rubies, and I couldn't help but feel the need to compete with the sparkle in her eyes. "I hope you like them," she said, her voice sweet, almost too sweet. "I made sure to make extra."

"Wow, thanks!" I replied, forcing a smile while attempting to drown out the unease bubbling beneath the surface. I picked up my fork, determined to savor the moment, but the first bite felt heavy in my mouth, the flavor overshadowed by the tension lingering in the air.

As we ate, the conversation flowed easily between Ethan and Claire, their shared stories a reminder of the bond I was only beginning to understand. I watched them exchange glances, laughter spilling over like syrup on pancakes, and I felt my own laughter fade into the background. Ethan spoke animatedly about his childhood memories at the lake house, and Claire chimed in with her own snippets, weaving a tapestry of nostalgia that left me feeling like an interloper.

Once breakfast was finished, Ethan suggested we take the boat out on the lake. "It'll be great! Just the three of us, soaking up the sun," he said, his enthusiasm infectious. I nodded, trying to match his excitement, but deep down, I hesitated. The thought of spending the day alone with Claire felt like a perilous endeavor.

With the sun shining brightly, we made our way down to the dock, the boards creaking beneath our feet. Ethan expertly maneuvered the boat into the water, and soon we were gliding across the shimmering surface, the gentle ripples creating a rhythmic lullaby. I leaned back against the seat, the wind whipping through my hair, trying to drown out the inner turmoil brewing inside me.

Claire leaned forward, her voice raised above the sound of the engine. "Remember that summer we tried to wakeboard? You fell so many times, Ethan! I thought you'd never get the hang of it!"

Ethan laughed, the sound rich and full, and for a moment, I felt a flicker of joy for him. "I was determined! I must have swallowed half the lake trying to impress you," he replied, shaking his head in disbelief at the memory.

As I sat there, a mix of emotions swirled within me—admiration for Ethan's playful spirit, yet an acute awareness of the shadows Claire cast over our time together. I forced myself to join in the banter, but it felt hollow, like I was a third wheel clumsily trying to ride the coattails of their shared history. Each laugh felt like an admission of my own inadequacies, each memory recounted another nail in the coffin of my confidence.

"Hey, Lily, want to give it a try?" Ethan asked, breaking through my thoughts. He motioned toward the wakeboard, a glint of mischief dancing in his eyes.

"Me? Wakeboarding?" I stammered, my heart racing at the prospect. I had never done it before, and the idea of falling flat on my face—literally—terrified me. Yet, there was something about the challenge that ignited a spark of determination within. "Sure, why not?"

Ethan grinned and handed me the wakeboard, a hint of pride flickering in his expression. "Just hold on tight and let the boat do the work. I promise it'll be fun!"

With Claire watching, I felt an unspoken pressure to succeed, to prove that I could belong in their world. I strapped on the board, the plastic cold against my skin as I waded into the water. The moment I felt the cool lake embrace me, I took a deep breath, steeling myself for the adventure.

As I climbed onto the board, I could hear Claire's voice calling out tips and encouragement. "Just keep your knees bent and lean back!" she shouted, her enthusiasm unwavering. But beneath her words was an undertone of competition, a silent battle for Ethan's attention that fueled my nerves.

Ethan revved the engine, and as the boat surged forward, I felt the rush of adrenaline surge through my veins. I gripped the handle, my heart pounding in sync with the thrum of the boat's motor. The water splashed against my legs, and for a fleeting moment, I was free—unburdened by doubt, surrounded by the beauty of the lake and the warmth of the sun.

And then I was up—briefly. The thrill of standing on the wakeboard sent exhilaration coursing through me, but it was short-lived. The board slipped from beneath me, and suddenly I was plunged into the cold depths of the lake. The water enveloped me, silencing the world above, and as I surfaced, I couldn't tell if I was laughing or crying. I glanced back at the boat, Ethan's face beaming with delight, and Claire's expression caught somewhere between admiration and amusement.

I couldn't help but smile, even through the frustration of my fall. It was a reminder that I was here, amidst the laughter and camaraderie, and even though the walls of my insecurities threatened to close in, I was determined to break through them.

The boat cut through the water, its engine thrumming beneath me like the heartbeat of some colossal creature. I took a deep breath, relishing the crisp autumn air as I bobbed in the water, strands of hair plastered to my forehead. Ethan's laughter floated toward me, bright and buoyant, and I felt a flicker of resolve spark within. With a deep inhale, I clutched the wakeboard tightly, ready to give it another go. This time, I wouldn't let my insecurities pull me under.

As I clambered back onto the board, the chill of the lake nipped at my skin, a reminder of the world I had temporarily left behind. I felt my heart rate steadying, each thump resonating with the determination swirling in my chest. Ethan's voice carried over the roar of the engine, filled with encouragement. "You got this, Lily! Just focus!"

With a confident shout of "Hit it!" Ethan gunned the throttle, and I was off again, adrenaline flooding my veins. I leaned back, knees bent, my body swaying in rhythm with the boat. This time, I felt the water beneath me—its ripples and waves were allies rather than adversaries. As I skimmed the surface, I caught sight of Claire, her smile bright as the sun, and for a moment, I dared to hope that I could prove myself, not just to her, but to Ethan, too.

The thrill of the ride coursed through me, an intoxicating mix of fear and freedom. I was gliding, and the world blurred into a kaleidoscope of colors—blue sky, shimmering water, and the golden hues of autumn trees lining the shore. My laughter mixed with the wind, a sound untainted by the doubts that had swirled around me since Claire's arrival.

But in an instant, the wave beneath me shifted, and I felt the board slip again. This time, I barely had time to brace myself before I was tumbling back into the cold embrace of the lake. Submerged in the depths, I couldn't help but laugh again, the bubbles of air escaping my lips like giggles. As I resurfaced, sputtering, I spotted Ethan grinning from ear to ear, Claire shaking her head in playful disbelief.

"Okay, maybe wakeboarding isn't my thing!" I shouted, splashing water in their direction as I climbed back onto the boat. But the truth was, each fall made me feel a little lighter, chipping away at the weight of my insecurities. For the first time that weekend, I felt a sense of belonging—however fragile it might be.

As the afternoon wore on, we switched gears and decided to take a break from wakeboarding, opting instead for a peaceful paddle around the lake. I nestled between Ethan and Claire in the small kayak, the vessel rocking gently as we glided across the still waters. The sun hung low in the sky, painting everything in golden light, and I couldn't help but feel that the beauty around us was at odds with the turmoil brewing inside me.

"What's your favorite lake memory, Ethan?" Claire asked, her voice carrying a hint of nostalgia that made my stomach twist. The question felt like a trap, a pitfall hidden in the shimmer of the lake, and I braced myself for whatever answer would come.

Ethan's face lit up, and I knew instantly that this was his moment. "There was this one summer, right after Claire and I graduated high school. We stayed out all night fishing and ended up getting lost on the way back to the house. We were convinced we'd never find our way home, but we ended up seeing the most incredible meteor shower." His eyes sparkled with the memory, and I couldn't help but notice how effortlessly he slipped back into a time when Claire was his constant companion.

I forced a smile, aware of the tightness in my chest. "That sounds amazing," I said, trying to inject enthusiasm into my voice, but it felt strained. I could practically feel the familiar walls creeping back up, the layers of jealousy and self-doubt threatening to suffocate me.

Claire laughed, her voice warm and inviting, drawing Ethan's gaze like a moth to a flame. "We were so scared we wouldn't make it back," she continued. "But it turned into one of the best nights of our lives." Her eyes sparkled with a kind of mischief that only made my heart race faster.

With every word they exchanged, I felt as if I were being pushed further from their shared history, stuck in a moment that belonged to a version of Ethan I barely knew. The easy banter, the laughter—it was a rhythm I struggled to join, and I silently chastised myself for feeling this way. Why couldn't I just let go?

Suddenly, Ethan turned to me, his expression shifting as he sensed the change in the atmosphere. "What about you, Lily? What's your favorite memory?"

Caught off guard, I blinked, the pressure of their expectations suddenly heavy. I thought for a moment, searching for something worthy of the moment—a story that would capture their attention, something that would bridge the gap between my world and theirs. "Um, well, I used to go camping with my family every summer," I started, my voice steadier than I expected. "We'd find some remote spot in the mountains, and my dad would teach us how to fish and build a fire. One year, we got caught in a storm, and we all huddled under this massive tree, waiting for it to pass. It was terrifying, but also… magical in a way. We sang songs and told stories, and it felt like we were the only people in the world."

As I spoke, I saw Ethan's eyes soften, and Claire's smile turned genuine. For a moment, I felt a connection, a thread linking our stories together. It wasn't about who had the best memories; it was about sharing the pieces of ourselves that made us who we were.

The sun dipped lower in the sky, painting everything in hues of pink and orange, and the world began to slow. We paddled in comfortable silence for a while, the sounds of the water lapping against the kayak soothing my frayed nerves. The tension that had defined my thoughts began to dissipate, replaced by the tranquil beauty of our surroundings.

As evening descended, we headed back to the dock, the sun a fiery orb on the horizon. Ethan pulled the kayak onto the shore while Claire gathered the supplies. I stood back, taking a moment to breathe in the atmosphere, the scent of damp earth and fallen leaves mingling with the crispness of the approaching night.

Once the boat was secured, we gathered around the fire pit, the warmth from the flames crackling in the evening air. Claire expertly arranged the wood, and soon we were enveloped in the comforting glow of the fire. I could feel my heart settling as we roasted marshmallows, the gooey sweetness melting in my mouth, laughter flowing freely.

As we shared stories beneath the blanket of stars, I found myself drifting closer to Ethan, the barrier that had felt so insurmountable earlier in the day beginning to erode. He turned to me, his expression earnest. "I'm really glad you're here, Lily," he said softly, his gaze unwavering.

I felt my heart swell with gratitude, a surge of warmth wrapping around me like the flames before us. "I'm glad to be here too," I replied, my voice barely above a whisper.

With the fire crackling, I realized that the walls I had built around my heart were not impenetrable after all. Perhaps it was okay to let a little light in, to allow myself to be vulnerable in the presence of people who truly cared. As we sat together, the night stretching out before us, I couldn't help but feel that the weekend was not just an escape, but a chance to redefine what it meant to belong—to embrace the uncertainties and find comfort in the connections we forged, even in the most unexpected of circumstances.

Chapter 16: Heartbeats and Confessions

The fireplace crackled softly, its flames dancing in a warm ballet of orange and gold, casting flickering shadows across the expansive living room of the Rowen mansion. I sat on the plush, oversized rug that felt like a warm embrace beneath me, while Ethan lounged on the leather couch, his expression a mixture of concern and contemplation. The faint scent of cedarwood from the logs mingled with the rich aroma of hot cocoa we had prepared together, a comforting blend that wrapped around us like a familiar blanket on this chilly Vermont night.

Outside, the first snowflakes of winter drifted down in a delicate choreography, dotting the windows with whimsical patterns. The world beyond felt ethereal, shrouded in white, but inside, the air buzzed with an unspoken tension that hung between us like an intricate spider web—fragile yet unyielding. I had spent too many nights with these fears coiling around me, suffocating my thoughts, and tonight, they seemed to spill from my lips as if released by some unseen force.

"Ethan," I began, hesitating as I searched for the right words. "What's going on with you and Claire?" My voice was steadier than I felt, but the moment the question left my mouth, I wished I could reel it back.

He straightened slightly, his brow furrowing as if my words had struck a nerve. "Claire was part of my past. She's not a threat to us," he replied, his tone measured, yet there was a flicker of something—maybe annoyance or disappointment—behind his eyes.

A part of me wanted to believe him, to cling to the reassurance that our relationship was solid and unshakeable, but the remnants of insecurities clawed at my heart. The past has a way of lurking in the shadows, waiting for the moment when your guard is down, ready to pounce with all the ferocity of a panther.

I looked down at the soft fibers of the rug, tracing patterns with my finger, suddenly finding the intricate weaving far more interesting than the man sitting across from me. "I just... I can't help but worry," I admitted, my voice barely above a whisper. "What if she tries to come back? What if I'm not enough?"

The silence that followed felt heavy, as though the air itself had thickened with the weight of my confession. Ethan shifted, and I could see the turmoil swirling behind his calm facade. "You are more than enough, Lily. I wouldn't be here if I didn't feel that way." His voice was low, earnest. "You have no idea how much I care about you. It terrifies me."

My heart skipped at his admission. The vulnerability in his gaze sent warmth flooding through my veins, erasing the chill of doubt. There was something liberating about speaking our fears aloud, laying them bare before each other like fragile glass ornaments, so easily shattered yet so beautifully crafted.

I leaned closer, the space between us shrinking as the heat of the fire enveloped us. "Then tell me," I urged gently, my breath mingling with the sweet scent of cocoa, "what are you afraid of?"

His fingers raked through his tousled hair, a gesture that I had come to associate with his own brand of anxiety. "I'm afraid of failing you, of not living up to the expectations I put on myself." The confession hung in the air, raw and powerful. "Sometimes, I feel like I'm just a boy trying to be a man, and it's all too much."

A warmth spread through my chest, and I couldn't help but smile at the man before me—the complicated, layered soul who wore his heart on his sleeve, even when it was vulnerable to the elements. "Ethan, it's okay to feel scared. We're both just figuring this out," I said softly, leaning even closer, encouraged by the honesty that was creating an invisible thread connecting us. "I'm scared, too. Scared of losing you, scared of the future. But I want to face it with you."

His gaze flickered to mine, and in that moment, it felt as though we were suspended in time, the chaos of the outside world fading away. "You really want to face it together?" he asked, a hint of disbelief lacing his tone, as if he were afraid the answer might be too good to be true.

"Absolutely," I replied, my voice unwavering. "We're stronger together. I want you to know that you're not alone in this. I'll fight for us."

Ethan smiled, a genuine expression that illuminated his features, softening the harsh lines of worry that had etched themselves into his brow. The warmth radiating from him was more potent than the flames licking the logs, and I felt a surge of affection that nearly took my breath away.

"Then let's promise to keep talking. No more secrets," he said, and I nodded, feeling the weight of unspoken promises hanging in the air.

As we sat there, hearts racing and souls laid bare, the room felt smaller yet more intimate. I was hyperaware of the heat radiating from the fire and the rhythmic beating of our hearts echoing in sync. The space between us had transformed from an abyss of doubt into a bridge of shared vulnerabilities, and for the first time in what felt like forever, I felt anchored—not just to him, but to the possibility of us.

Time slipped away as we delved deeper into each other's worlds, sharing stories that had shaped us, dreams that beckoned just beyond the horizon. Each word was a thread, weaving a tapestry of trust that enveloped us, shielding us from the cold outside.

In that cozy, flickering sanctuary, I couldn't help but marvel at how beautifully flawed we were, two souls navigating the tangled web of emotions. With every shared fear and heartfelt confession, I felt the distance between us shrink, until it seemed we were no longer just two individuals, but one entity—a singular force against the uncertainties that loomed outside the mansion's walls.

The air around us was electric, a charged current that crackled with the revelations we had just shared. I could feel the vulnerability lingering like the sweet aftertaste of dark chocolate, rich and bittersweet. Ethan leaned back slightly, his arms outstretched along the back of the couch, a casual pose that belied the intensity swirling between us. It was as if the entire universe had converged into this moment, the flickering light of the fire illuminating not just our faces but the intricate pathways of our emotions.

We sat in comfortable silence for a heartbeat longer before the stillness was broken by the soft patter of snow against the window, each flake a delicate messenger from the world outside. I turned my gaze to the swirling white, watching how it transformed the familiar landscape into a winter wonderland, an enchanted realm that felt miles away from the emotional chaos we had just unraveled. I had always found comfort in the changing seasons, but this particular night felt different—imbued with a sense of possibility and warmth that I had long craved.

"Do you ever think about what's next for us?" I asked, my voice barely a whisper against the rhythmic crackling of the fire. The question hung in the air, a fragile thread connecting our hopes and fears, woven through the intimate tapestry of our shared truths.

Ethan hesitated, a fleeting look of uncertainty crossing his features before he nodded slowly. "I do," he replied, his voice steady. "But sometimes it feels overwhelming. I want to be everything you need, but I also don't want to promise more than I can give."

His admission struck a chord deep within me, resonating with my own fears of inadequacy. The vulnerability we had embraced moments ago now morphed into an uncharted territory filled with questions and potential pitfalls. "What if we just take it one day at a time?" I suggested, my heart racing with the thrill of possibility. "We don't have to have all the answers right now."

The corners of his mouth turned upward in a wry smile, the tension in his shoulders easing slightly. "One day at a time sounds manageable. But I can't promise I won't overthink everything," he chuckled softly, and I couldn't help but laugh with him, the sound a balm to the rawness that had lingered between us.

The laughter faded, leaving behind an intimate quiet that wrapped around us like a shawl. I reveled in the feeling of being so close to him, the warmth radiating from his body a comforting contrast to the coldness that nipped at the edges of the room. My heart beat steadily, a metronome keeping time with the unspoken promises woven into the fabric of our conversation.

"I wish I could just lock you away in a safe little bubble," he said suddenly, a playful glint in his eyes. "You know, keep you away from all the craziness in the world."

"Ah, yes, the infamous safe bubble," I teased, leaning back against the couch. "But then I'd miss out on all the fun."

"Fun?" he repeated, raising an eyebrow. "You call hiding out in the woods with a bunch of shape-shifters fun?"

"Okay, fair point," I admitted, a laugh escaping me. "But it's also... exciting. There's never a dull moment."

Ethan leaned closer, lowering his voice as if sharing a secret. "You're not afraid of the dark, are you?"

"Only when there are monsters lurking in the shadows," I replied, a playful smile gracing my lips. "But thankfully, I have a knight in shining armor to protect me."

He chuckled, shaking his head, and the warmth in his gaze made my heart flutter. "More like a guy who's still figuring out how to wield his sword," he said, feigning modesty.

"Every knight has to start somewhere," I countered, feeling the weight of my earlier fears begin to lift. "And the fact that you're trying means more than anything."

The moment hung, thick with unspoken understanding, as we drifted into a comfortable silence. Outside, the snow continued to fall, blanketing the world in quiet. The glow of the fire flickered, creating a soft dance of light that flickered over the contours of Ethan's face, illuminating the sincerity in his eyes.

I shifted slightly, wanting to savor this moment, this unique connection that felt fragile yet powerful. "What if we made some plans?" I suggested, emboldened by our earlier conversation. "Like a winter adventure. Just you and me."

His brow furrowed in thought, and I could see the wheels turning in his mind. "What did you have in mind?" he asked, intrigued.

"We could go sledding, build a snowman, or have a snowball fight. And then, maybe we can find a cozy café and warm up with some hot drinks afterward," I proposed, my voice bubbling with enthusiasm as I envisioned the possibilities.

Ethan grinned, his earlier worries momentarily forgotten. "A snowball fight, huh? I'm not sure you're ready for my expert snowball-throwing skills."

"Oh please," I scoffed, waving my hand dismissively. "I've faced worse foes. You should see me in action."

"Is that a challenge?" he asked, a playful glint in his eye that ignited my competitive spirit.

"Absolutely," I replied, my heart racing at the thought of not just the snow but the thrill of being out there with him, where laughter and joy overshadowed our fears. "May the best snow warrior win."

We shared a smile, a spark of excitement igniting between us, and I could feel the invisible thread of connection tightening, wrapping us in warmth and comfort. I took a deep breath, letting the magic of the moment wash over me, and in that space, I realized that even amidst the uncertainties, there was a newfound courage in vulnerability.

"Let's do it," Ethan said suddenly, his voice infused with determination. "Let's make our own adventures."

"Together?" I asked, my heart swelling with hope and anticipation.

"Always," he replied, and the sincerity in his voice melted away the last vestiges of doubt that clung to me.

In that simple word, a world of possibilities unfurled before us—an open road leading us toward a future where we could weave our stories together, shaping our own narrative amidst the chaos of our lives.

The fire crackled again, sending sparks soaring into the air, a perfect reflection of the feelings blossoming within me. I could envision us, side by side, building our own unique story, full of laughter, warmth, and the occasional snowball. And as the snow continued to fall outside, I couldn't help but think that, just maybe, this was the beginning of something extraordinary.

The warmth of the fire painted a soft glow across the room, its light flickering like our shared thoughts, illuminating the cracks in our hearts that had previously been hidden in the shadows. Outside, the snow continued to fall in lazy, swirling patterns, creating a serene backdrop that contrasted with the storm of emotions brewing within us. As the night deepened, the atmosphere felt charged, imbued with an unspoken promise that hung in the air like the sweet aroma of hot cocoa.

Ethan leaned closer, resting his elbows on his knees, his expression a blend of contemplation and affection. "You know," he began, his voice dropping to a more intimate register, "I never thought I'd find myself here, in this moment with you. It feels... right."

The sincerity in his tone sent warmth blooming in my chest, and I felt as if I were suspended between the warmth of the fire and the coolness of the window, a beautiful intersection of safety and risk. "It feels right to me, too," I replied, finding my voice steady, even as my heart raced at the weight of his words.

"What are we doing?" he asked, his brow furrowing slightly, as though he were trying to decipher a riddle. "I mean, really. With all the craziness surrounding us, with the Rowens and the curse—" he hesitated, clearly grappling with the enormity of our reality.

I considered his question, the weight of it pressing against my chest. The Rowens were a world apart, filled with secrets and burdens, their lives intricately tied to a legacy that felt heavy enough to crush a soul. Yet here we were, navigating our own labyrinth of emotions, each turn leading us deeper into uncharted territory. "I think we're creating something of our own," I said softly, willing him to understand that our connection, no matter how fragile, was worth fighting for. "Something real."

He smiled, but it was tinged with uncertainty. "Real is a big word, Lily. With my family's history, with Claire..." His voice trailed off, the mention of her name throwing a shadow over our warmth.

"Then let's redefine it together," I urged, reaching out to rest my hand on his. "Let's take every bit of this chaos and make it ours. We have the power to shape our story, even with all the darkness around us."

The fire crackled, and for a heartbeat, I swore I could see the flames nodding in agreement, as if the universe conspired to encourage our audacity. Ethan's gaze locked onto mine, and I saw a flicker of resolve flare in his eyes. "You're right. We can't let the past dictate our future. But it's going to take work, right?"

"Work is what makes it worthwhile," I replied, my spirit buoyed by the thought of us facing whatever came next side by side. "And

I'm willing to put in the effort. We'll build our own rules, our own adventures."

Ethan squeezed my hand, and in that small gesture, a spark ignited between us—an affirmation that we were ready to embrace the unpredictable, to dance in the rain of uncertainty that life poured upon us. "Okay," he said, a new determination coloring his voice. "Let's do it. Let's write our own story."

With the unspoken agreement, we settled into a comfortable rhythm, our conversation flowing freely, punctuated by laughter and shared memories that intertwined like threads in a tapestry. We talked about our dreams, the way the world felt like a vast expanse of possibility before us, and how our individual paths had led us to this very moment. Each word woven into the fabric of our connection, bringing us closer together as the night wore on.

As the flames flickered low, I noticed the shadows stretching across the walls, the flickering light creating an enchanting display that danced around us. The outside world seemed to fade away, leaving only the cozy sanctuary of the Rowen mansion. I marveled at the history of this place—the whispers of generations echoing in the ornate woodwork, the secrets hidden within its walls, and how, despite everything, it had become a backdrop for our burgeoning relationship.

But the weight of the Rowen curse lingered just beneath the surface, a reminder that our world was anything but ordinary. "Have you ever thought about how we might help the Rowens?" I asked, my tone shifting as the warmth of our earlier conversation faded into the shadows of concern.

Ethan's expression shifted, and I could see the tension return to his shoulders. "I've thought about it a lot. They're a family bound by a curse that seems impossible to break. I want to help, but it's like trying to fight an unseen enemy," he said, his voice heavy with frustration.

"What if we dug deeper? What if we uncovered more about the curse?" I suggested, emboldened by the resolve that had settled between us. "There has to be something we can do—some way to help them reclaim their lives."

A flicker of hope ignited in Ethan's eyes. "You really think we could make a difference?"

"I believe we can," I replied, feeling the weight of determination swell within me. "We've faced down chaos together already. Why not tackle this next challenge? After all, if we're committed to each other, why not extend that to the people we care about?"

Ethan leaned back, his expression thoughtful as he considered my words. "It would be risky," he warned. "The Rowens have lived under this shadow for so long. They might not even want our help."

"Maybe, but we can't let fear stop us. We owe it to them and to ourselves to try. Besides, if we fail, at least we'll know we did everything we could," I said, a sense of purpose bubbling inside me.

As we exchanged ideas, planning our next steps with excitement and trepidation, a newfound energy filled the space around us. It was as if the fire had reignited, urging us forward, lighting the path ahead with possibilities. With each shared thought, our resolve strengthened, weaving our stories together into a singular narrative that defied the odds.

We made plans to dive into the mansion's vast library, where ancient tomes awaited our curious minds, and cryptic notes from long-gone ancestors whispered secrets of the past. There, we would hunt for clues that might lead us to a way to lift the curse, feeling our bond deepen with every shared moment of discovery.

As the fire dwindled to embers, casting a soft glow around the room, I felt a sense of belonging wash over me. I realized that this—Ethan by my side, fighting for something greater than ourselves—was where I was meant to be. With our hearts entwined, we were ready to face whatever storms the world threw our way, determined to forge a path through the shadows and into the light, together.

Chapter 17: Embracing the Journey

The city, with its cacophony of sounds and vibrant colors, welcomed me back like a long-lost friend. As I stepped onto the sun-drenched streets of Portland, the air was alive with the scent of roasted coffee beans wafting from corner cafes and the faint hint of rain that lingered just beyond the horizon. I could almost taste the electric energy buzzing in the atmosphere, a gentle reminder that every moment here was ripe with possibilities. My camera hung from my neck like an extension of myself, a silent partner ready to capture the world around me.

I had always viewed the lens as a window into others' lives, but now, it became a mirror reflecting my own emotions. My first few days back were spent wandering through the Pearl District, where the old brick warehouses had transformed into art galleries and hip boutiques, each corner offering a new story waiting to be told. I sought out the quieter moments amidst the bustle, those fleeting connections that often went unnoticed. The elderly couple sharing a bench, their fingers intertwined as they watched the world go by; the laughter of children echoing through the air as they chased each other in a park; or the whispered secrets shared between friends leaning against a graffiti-adorned wall. Each click of the shutter resonated deeply within me, grounding me in the present while allowing me to express my tangled emotions.

With every photograph, I felt a sense of catharsis. I immersed myself in the essence of connection—between people, between moments. I soon realized that capturing these bonds wasn't just an artistic endeavor; it was a lifeline, pulling me away from the shadows of self-doubt that threatened to creep in. My heart raced as I processed the images, pouring over them late into the night, the glow of my computer screen illuminating my determined expression. The images were more than just pictures; they were stories of resilience, of hope, of love flourishing against the odds.

But with each burst of inspiration came the familiar weight of anxiety. What if I couldn't sustain this happiness? What if the wellspring of creativity dried up, leaving me stranded in a desert of unfulfilled dreams? I shook my head, brushing aside the intrusive thoughts. Instead, I focused on what I could control, channeling my energy into organizing a community photography exhibit, a vibrant tapestry of connection that would not only showcase my work but also invite other local artists to share their visions.

I envisioned the gallery filled with photographs that spoke to the heart of Portland, each frame capturing an unguarded moment of affection or camaraderie. I wanted to create a space that radiated warmth, where strangers could become friends over shared experiences and where the laughter of children echoed alongside the soft strumming of a local musician's guitar. Ethan, with his unwavering support and infectious enthusiasm, became my rock throughout the planning process. Together, we navigated the logistics, hunting down the perfect venue that would not only accommodate the displays but also embody the spirit of community I hoped to foster.

The gallery we settled on was tucked away in a charming old building on Alberta Street, its exposed beams and rustic charm a fitting backdrop for our project. As we painted the walls a warm cream, the sound of laughter and the scent of fresh paint filled the air. Ethan had a knack for making even the most mundane tasks feel like an adventure. "You know," he said, leaning against the wall with a playful grin, "if this whole photography thing doesn't work out, we could always start a paint business. Clearly, we have the skills." I laughed, but my heart swelled at the thought of building something beautiful together.

As the exhibit day approached, the excitement in the air was palpable. Flyers fluttered around the city, showcasing our theme of connection. I felt a nervous flutter in my stomach each time I thought about the community coming together to celebrate art and love. The night before the opening, I lay in bed, Ethan beside me, his presence a soothing balm against my racing thoughts. "What if no one shows up?" I whispered, a tinge of vulnerability slipping through my bravado. Ethan turned to me, his gaze steady. "You're sharing something beautiful. People will want to be part of it. Just remember, it's about the journey, not just the end result." His words hung in the air like a promise, wrapping around me like a comforting embrace.

When the day finally arrived, the gallery buzzed with anticipation. Friends, families, and fellow artists filled the room, laughter and chatter blending into a symphony of connection. I stood in front of my photographs, heart racing as I watched people interact with the pieces. I felt like a proud parent watching their child take their first steps—each interaction, each moment of awe, a testament to the beauty I had aimed to capture.

The warmth in the room enveloped me, feeding my soul. I moved through the crowd, engaging with guests, their eyes lighting up as they shared their interpretations of my work. I reveled in the stories they told, each one adding another layer to the tapestry we were weaving together. The night was a kaleidoscope of laughter, conversations, and connections, a vivid reminder of the community spirit that thrived in this city I loved.

As the evening wound down and the last guests departed, I felt a profound sense of fulfillment wash over me. Ethan and I stood together amidst the remnants of the night, the glow of the lights reflecting in his eyes. In that moment, surrounded by our shared success, I felt an unshakeable bond solidify between us, rooted in trust, support, and a shared passion for embracing life's fleeting moments. I had learned not only to capture connection through my lens but also to appreciate it in every facet of my life.

As the weeks rolled on, the gallery buzz faded but left behind a warmth that cocooned me like the gentle embrace of a sunbeam on a chilly morning. The exhibit had been a resounding success, but I found myself wrestling with the echoes of uncertainty that crept back in, whispering doubts that tangled with the confidence I had begun to cultivate. Each day, I made my way through the vibrant city streets, my camera slung over my shoulder, eager to capture life as it unfolded before me. But beneath the surface, a persistent worry churned: Could I maintain this momentum? Could I continuously conjure the magic of connection through my lens?

Despite the occasional surge of self-doubt, I immersed myself in my work, venturing beyond familiar haunts to discover new neighborhoods brimming with stories. I wandered into North Portland, where the eclectic mix of cultures transformed each street into a canvas painted with the vivid strokes of humanity. The aroma of street tacos wafted through the air, mingling with the sound of a saxophonist playing a soulful tune on the corner. I paused, captivated by the musician's passion, the way he poured his soul into each note, weaving a melody that resonated deep within the hearts of passersby. I snapped a shot, freezing that moment in time, the saxophonist's eyes closed, lost in a world of his creation.

But it wasn't just the strangers I encountered that inspired me; it was also the connections forming around me. I spent countless afternoons with Ethan, exploring art shows and local coffee shops. Our discussions morphed into explorations of creativity and dreams, each conversation a brushstroke on the canvas of our relationship. Over steaming mugs of chai and frothy lattes, we dissected the nuances of our work, our laughter punctuating the air like the soft ping of a wind chime. There was an unspoken understanding between us, a shared passion that ignited my spirit and fueled my determination.

As I delved deeper into the world of photography, I found a sense of purpose blossoming within me. I began to collaborate with local organizations, documenting their community outreach efforts. I captured the faces of volunteers, their hands stained with paint as they transformed dilapidated spaces into vibrant community gardens. I followed the tireless workers at shelters, their eyes filled with compassion as they served meals to those in need. Each photograph told a story, a testament to the unwavering spirit of those who sought to uplift their community. The more I engaged with these narratives, the more I felt like a vessel through which their stories could flow, connecting me to a larger tapestry of humanity.

Yet, as the days passed, I couldn't shake the feeling of unease that lingered in the background. Every time I picked up my camera, a nagging thought whispered that I was an impostor in this world, that my art was merely a series of fortunate accidents. What if, one day, the inspiration vanished? What if I stood before my lens, unable to capture the beauty that had become my lifeblood? The fear crept in like shadows at dusk, settling in the corners of my mind.

Ethan sensed my struggle, and one evening, as we strolled along the waterfront, he turned to me, his expression earnest. "You know, it's okay to feel this way," he said, the moonlight casting a gentle glow on his features. "Every artist doubts themselves. It's part of the journey." I looked up at him, the honesty in his voice striking a chord deep within me. "But how do I keep going when the doubt feels so overwhelming?"

He paused, thoughtful, before responding, "Maybe it's not about silencing the doubt, but learning to work alongside it. Embrace it, let it guide you rather than paralyze you." His words hung in the air, a soothing balm for my restless soul. It was a reminder that even the most vibrant colors often emerge from the depths of uncertainty.

I began to shift my perspective, welcoming the doubts as part of my artistic journey rather than a hindrance. I understood that vulnerability could serve as fuel for creativity, a powerful force that could elevate my work to new heights.

Inspired by our conversation, I turned my lens inward. I began documenting my own experiences, capturing moments of vulnerability that had once felt too raw to share. I photographed myself in quiet moments—curling up with a book on my favorite armchair, the sunlight filtering through the window, or standing on my balcony, the city sprawling beneath me, alive with possibility. I found beauty in the mundane, the tender threads of life weaving together to create a tapestry of authenticity. Each photograph was a piece of me, a reflection of my journey through uncertainty and self-discovery.

This new direction in my work reinvigorated my passion. The stories I had previously captured in others began to resonate within me, revealing layers of my own narrative I hadn't fully acknowledged. I was learning to embrace my flaws, to celebrate the moments that made me human. The fear that had threatened to suffocate my creativity now transformed into a source of strength.

In the midst of this newfound clarity, I decided to host another event, this time focused on the theme of vulnerability. I reached out to fellow artists, inviting them to showcase their interpretations of authenticity and rawness. I wanted to create a space where we could share our truths, where the art could foster connection through the very act of revealing our imperfections.

Ethan was my steadfast partner in this venture, his unwavering support a constant reminder that I was not alone on this journey. We spent countless evenings poring over submissions, curating a collection that promised to inspire and resonate with the community. There was something magical about working alongside him, each decision forged in collaboration deepening our bond. Our laughter mingled with our shared aspirations, each moment a reminder of the journey we were embarking upon together.

As the date of the event approached, I felt a renewed sense of purpose coursing through my veins. I had learned to navigate the delicate dance of vulnerability and strength, embracing the uncertainty while allowing it to propel me forward. My camera had become a conduit for my emotions, a means to connect not only with others but also with myself. And as I looked ahead, I felt a flicker of hope igniting within me, ready to illuminate the path that lay before us.

The day of the exhibit arrived, cloaked in the soft hues of a Portland morning, as if the universe itself conspired to bless us with perfect weather. The sunlight spilled through the clouds, casting a gentle glow over the streets, and the air felt electric with anticipation. As I stood before the gallery, a sense of pride swelled within me, mingling with the familiar threads of anxiety that had become my constant companions. The building, with its rustic charm and worn wooden floors, exuded an inviting warmth that seemed to welcome both artists and patrons alike.

With Ethan by my side, I prepared for the influx of guests. He moved with an effortless grace, adjusting the positioning of a few frames while stealing glances at me, his encouraging smile igniting a spark of courage within my chest. The walls adorned with our curated collection, each photograph telling its own story of vulnerability, connection, and the beauty of human emotion. The images breathed life into the space, inviting everyone to step inside and engage with the moments we had captured.

As the clock ticked closer to opening, I took a deep breath, inhaling the scent of fresh paint mixed with coffee from the small café set up in the corner. This event was not just about displaying our art; it was a celebration of shared experiences, a reminder that in our chaotic world, we were all seeking connection in one form or another. I glanced around, the hum of conversation rising as artists mingled, laughter punctuating the air, their enthusiasm palpable. I felt a flutter of nerves, but it quickly morphed into excitement; this was our community, a vibrant tapestry woven with diverse threads of creativity.

When the doors finally swung open, a steady stream of people flowed into the gallery, their faces lighting up as they took in the artwork. I reveled in their reactions, watching as strangers leaned in close to examine the details of each photograph. A couple lingered over an image of two children sharing an ice cream cone, their faces a perfect mixture of delight and mischief, and I caught snippets of their conversation—a reminiscence of their own childhood adventures, which sparked a gentle nostalgia in the air.

Ethan moved among the crowd, engaging with guests, and I could see the way his natural charisma drew people in, much like the photographs we had displayed. I felt a warmth in my heart as I watched him, proud of the way he effortlessly bridged gaps between strangers, weaving connections in real-time. His passion for art and community mirrored my own, creating a bond that deepened with every shared smile and exchanged story.

Throughout the evening, I found myself gravitating toward the quieter corners of the gallery. In one such nook, I spotted an older woman studying one of my photographs—a close-up of a weathered hand holding a delicate flower. The lines etched on her face seemed to tell stories of their own, and as our eyes met, she smiled softly, her gaze twinkling with understanding. "This one speaks to me," she said, her voice rich with emotion. "It reminds me of my late husband. He always had a way with flowers."

I felt a lump form in my throat as she spoke, the weight of her memories resonating within me. "Thank you for sharing that," I replied, my voice barely above a whisper. "I wanted to capture not just the beauty of the flower, but the tenderness of the moment." We shared a connection forged in the understanding of love, loss, and the beauty of remembrance.

As the evening unfolded, I realized that my photographs were serving as bridges between lives, creating connections in unexpected ways. Each conversation, each shared laugh, and even the quiet moments of contemplation wove a rich tapestry of human experience that enveloped the gallery like a warm embrace. I moved among the guests, sharing the stories behind my images, connecting with their emotions, their laughter intertwining with my own.

But amidst the joy and warmth, a subtle tension lurked at the edges of my consciousness. The fear of losing this connection, of returning to the isolation I had once known, haunted me like a distant thunderstorm. Yet, as I glanced at Ethan, engaged in animated conversation with a group of fellow artists, I felt a flicker of reassurance. The bond we shared was stronger than my doubts; we were in this together, navigating the unpredictable waters of creativity and vulnerability.

As the night wore on, we prepared to unveil a collaborative piece—a collection of photographs by various artists, each one representing different facets of connection. I felt a surge of pride as I stood beside Ethan, our hands brushing against one another as we revealed the framed photographs to a hushed crowd. The gasps of awe that followed were music to my ears, each exclamation a testament to the power of our collective artistry.

Later, as the crowd thinned and the sounds of laughter faded into the background, Ethan and I began to clean up, our spirits buoyed by the success of the night. "You did it," he said, his eyes sparkling with pride as he tossed a crumpled napkin into the bin. "You created something beautiful tonight, something that resonated with so many."

I smiled, a warmth blooming in my chest. "I couldn't have done it without you," I replied, my voice earnest. "Your support has meant everything to me."

He paused, his gaze softening, and I could see the unspoken words lingering between us, a profound understanding that had developed through our shared journey. "We make a good team," he said, stepping closer, his voice low and sincere.

In that moment, I felt an overwhelming sense of gratitude for the connection we had forged, for the way our lives had intertwined through art and vulnerability. I realized that this was the essence of what I had been capturing in my photography—the beauty of human connection in its many forms. It was a reminder that even amidst uncertainty and fear, there was light to be found in our shared experiences.

As we locked up the gallery and stepped out into the cool night air, the city hummed with life around us. The streetlights flickered overhead, casting a warm glow on the pavement, and the sound of laughter drifted from nearby cafes. I took a deep breath, filling my lungs with the vibrant energy of the city. I had embraced my journey, and though the road ahead remained uncertain, I felt ready to navigate its twists and turns.

With Ethan beside me, I knew that whatever lay ahead, I could face it with open arms and an open heart, capturing each moment of connection along the way. Together, we would continue to explore the world, intertwining our paths and weaving our stories into the rich tapestry of life. The future held promise, and with my camera in hand and love in my heart, I was eager to embrace every fleeting moment.

Chapter 18: The Unexpected Visitor

The night of the exhibit unfurled like a rich tapestry of color and sound, the air thick with anticipation as the gallery buzzed with art enthusiasts and eager newcomers alike. It was one of those iconic New York nights, where the city's skyline glimmered like a diamond-studded crown against the dark velvet sky. Streetlights flickered like tiny stars, illuminating the bustling streets below as if to beckon inspiration into the hearts of those walking through the city. I stood on the cusp of this vibrant world, my heart racing in rhythm with the electric pulse of the city, a bundle of nerves hidden beneath a carefully crafted façade.

Ethan was my anchor in this sea of creativity and anxiety. His presence beside me, tall and reassuring, exuded warmth and confidence. I couldn't help but admire how the soft glow from the pendant lights reflected in his deep brown eyes, a comfort that settled my spiraling thoughts. We stood in front of my latest piece, a striking canvas splashed with hues of midnight blue and fiery orange, an abstract representation of the chaos and beauty intertwined in life. I had poured my heart and soul into this work, and for a brief moment, as I watched the admiring glances from the crowd, I allowed myself to bask in the glory of my artistic achievement.

As I reveled in the thrill of the evening, the door swung open, and Claire strolled in, her entrance heralded by a subtle hush that fell over the crowd. She was an embodiment of confidence, a dazzling figure adorned in a fitted red dress that clung to her every curve, a stark contrast against the soft pastels of the gallery's decor. The way she moved through the space was almost regal, her head held high, eyes glinting with a mixture of determination and playfulness. Instinctively, I tensed, the energy around me shifting as if the universe had conspired to send a storm my way.

Ethan noticed her almost immediately, his expression morphing into one of mild surprise that quickly masked itself with neutrality. The air thickened with tension, wrapping around me like an unwelcome embrace as I felt the weight of insecurity settle into my bones. Claire sauntered toward us, her gaze laser-focused on Ethan, and I could feel my heart plummeting, a heavy stone sinking in a vast ocean of doubt.

"Ethan!" she greeted, her voice smooth and melodic, a stark contrast to the jagged edge of my thoughts. I watched as her confident smile unfurled, directed solely at him. My stomach twisted uncomfortably, and I felt like a spectator in my own life, watching a play unfold that I never signed up for.

"Claire," he replied, his tone cordial yet laced with an undertone of caution. He turned slightly toward me, perhaps sensing the anxiety radiating from my being. "This is my girlfriend, Ava. Ava, this is Claire."

The introduction hung in the air, heavy with unspoken words. I extended my hand, forcing a smile to grace my lips, though it felt more like a mask than a genuine expression. "Nice to meet you," I managed, the words tasting bitter on my tongue. Claire's grip was firm, her gaze unwavering, and I couldn't shake the feeling that she was sizing me up, as if to determine whether I was a worthy adversary.

"Likewise," she replied, her smile widening, but there was something predatory in the way she looked at me. A flicker of amusement danced in her eyes, and I wondered what twisted delight she took in this encounter. The room around us buzzed with conversations and laughter, yet I felt entirely isolated, like a lone island amidst a bustling ocean.

As the conversation shifted between Ethan and Claire, my mind raced with insecurities that clawed at my confidence. I tried to focus on the sounds of the gallery—the gentle clinking of glasses, the soft murmur of admiration for the art—but my thoughts betrayed me. Memories flooded my mind, reminding me of Claire's history with Ethan, the way she had effortlessly charmed her way into his life. The whispers of their shared laughter, the glances that lingered just a moment too long, echoed in my thoughts, and I could feel the cracks in my self-assuredness deepen.

Suddenly, Claire turned her attention to me, her smile unwavering but her eyes sparkling with something that felt akin to challenge. "So, Ava, how did you get started in art?" Her question was innocent enough, but the way she asked it felt like a trap. I took a deep breath, gathering the scattered pieces of my resolve. I reminded myself of the trust that had been built between Ethan and me, the late-night talks, the laughter shared over spilled paint and wild ideas.

"I've always found solace in creating," I began, forcing the words out, my voice steady despite the turmoil within. "It's my way of processing the world around me. This piece," I gestured toward my painting, "is about finding beauty in chaos, how sometimes the messiest moments can lead to the most profound insights."

Claire's expression shifted, a flicker of genuine curiosity piercing through her confident façade. "That's beautiful," she said, the compliment almost unexpected. It disarmed me momentarily, and I couldn't help but soften. Perhaps there was more to her than the sharp edges I had imagined.

But just as I began to relax, I sensed a flicker of annoyance from Ethan, his brow slightly furrowed. "Ava's work deserves recognition, Claire. She's incredibly talented," he interjected, the protectiveness in his tone a balm to my fraying nerves.

Claire merely shrugged, her playful demeanor returning like a veil. "I've always believed that talent isn't enough in this world, darling. You need connections, too." She turned to me, her eyes glinting with mischief. "But you seem to have him wrapped around your little finger, so maybe you'll do just fine."

The words struck me like a bolt of lightning, illuminating the insecurities I had fought so hard to keep at bay. I watched as Ethan's jaw tightened, a flicker of frustration sparking in his gaze. The playful banter had turned sour, and I could feel the heaviness settling in the air again.

In that moment, I resolved not to let her words seep into my bones. I straightened my shoulders, reminding myself that I had earned my place in this world, that I was more than just a shadow in someone else's story. I wouldn't allow Claire to define my worth or my relationship with Ethan.

I took a step forward, my heart pounding in my chest. "You're right, Claire. Connections matter," I said, my voice steady as I glanced at Ethan, who was watching me with a mixture of admiration and concern. "But so does authenticity. I may not have the same history as you two, but I have something real with Ethan. That's what counts."

A moment of silence enveloped us, and I could feel the collective breath of the gallery holding onto my words. The atmosphere shifted slightly, the crowd's attention subtly redirecting toward our little standoff. I sensed Ethan's relief, and for the first time, I allowed myself to hope that perhaps, just perhaps, I could stand my ground against the specter of doubt that had haunted me for far too long.

The silence that enveloped us felt electric, humming with the unsaid and the uncertain, a tangible presence that made the hairs on my arms stand on end. Claire's smile faltered for a moment, the veneer of playfulness slipping as if she sensed the shift in the atmosphere. I stood my ground, heart thrumming like a drumbeat of defiance, every fiber of my being urging me to maintain this fragile confidence. I could almost hear the collective breath of the room—art lovers, critics, and fellow artists alike—waiting to see how this little tête-à-tête would unfold.

Ethan remained by my side, his presence a steadfast reminder that I was not alone in this. His hand brushed against my back, a subtle reassurance that sent warmth spreading through me. I could feel the tension coiling in the air, thickening like the paint on my canvas, each brushstroke adding layers to this moment of confrontation. Claire, unyielding and poised, wasn't backing down.

"Well, Ava, it's refreshing to see you so... assertive," she said, her tone laced with a mixture of sarcasm and intrigue.

"Confidence has a way of surprising people," I replied, a flicker of my own defiance glimmering in my voice. The corner of Ethan's mouth twitched upward, and I could sense his pride simmering just beneath the surface. I fought against the impulse to glance at him, fearing it would reveal the cracks I was desperately trying to hide.

"Isn't it funny how life brings us unexpected challenges?" Claire continued, her gaze flicking back to Ethan, who stood tall and firm, the very picture of loyalty. "You seem to be handling yours quite well, Ava. Or at least pretending to." Her words dripped with an underlying venom, and I could feel the knot in my stomach tighten.

"Pretending is part of the process," I shot back, feeling emboldened by the warmth of Ethan beside me. "Art isn't just about the final piece; it's about the journey and the messy emotions that come with it." I was surprised at the conviction in my voice, an echo of the artist I had fought hard to become. I refused to let Claire diminish that truth with her cutting remarks.

The corners of Claire's mouth lifted slightly, as if she appreciated the challenge. "Oh, darling, I don't doubt your journey. It's just that some people find it easier to hide behind a paintbrush than face the reality of who they are." The barb stung, and I felt the urge to recoil, but I steadied myself, drawing on the strength I had found through Ethan and my friends.

Suddenly, a bright voice broke through the charged atmosphere, slicing through our tension like a bolt of lightning. "Ava! Ethan! You both look stunning!" Jess, my best friend, bounded over, her energy a refreshing breeze against the brewing storm. Her bright floral dress fluttered as she approached, a whirlwind of positivity that had always been my safe haven.

"Hey, Jess!" I exclaimed, relief flooding my voice as she joined our little standoff. Claire's smile faltered again, her confidence slightly shaken by the unexpected interruption. "What do you think of the exhibit?" I directed the conversation toward Jess, grateful for her presence, which felt like a lifeline thrown into turbulent waters.

"It's amazing! I just love how you've captured the chaos in your piece," she gushed, her enthusiasm lighting up the room. "And don't get me started on the ambiance! The lighting here makes everything look like it's dipped in gold!" Her words flowed like the laughter we often shared, soothing the frayed edges of my nerves.

I could see Claire watching Jess with a mix of irritation and intrigue. "Isn't it fascinating how art can evoke such strong feelings?" Claire replied, her voice smooth yet edged with something sharp, like the glitter of broken glass. "It's like a window into the artist's soul."

Ethan's gaze flickered between us, a protective air enveloping him as he spoke up. "Ava's soul is filled with honesty and depth, something that shouldn't be undermined by mere opinion." He paused, letting the weight of his words settle. "Art is subjective, but what matters is the passion behind it."

The intensity of his support washed over me like a wave, momentarily drowning out the doubt that Claire had instilled. I felt the blush rise in my cheeks as I met his gaze, and for a fleeting moment, the world around us faded away, leaving just the two of us suspended in time, two souls entwined in the fabric of this chaotic night.

"Let's grab some wine," Jess suggested, her cheerful voice a beacon amidst the tension. "I need to celebrate your success! You're the star of the show tonight, Ava!"

I smiled, grateful for the distraction, and nodded. "Absolutely. I could use a glass to calm these nerves." The three of us moved toward the refreshment table, where crystal glasses glimmered like stars against the soft glow of the gallery lights. I poured a glass of Merlot, savoring the rich aroma before taking a long sip, letting the velvety liquid settle my frayed nerves.

"Did you see the other artists?" Jess continued, her excitement bubbling over as she chattered about their pieces. "Some of them are absolutely incredible! I met this one guy who paints landscapes that look so real, I swear I could step into them. And then there's that one installation with the flickering lights—it felt like being inside a dream."

Her words drew me in, allowing the earlier tension with Claire to slip into the background, relegated to the periphery of my thoughts. I began to relax, sinking into the comfort of Jess's presence, her infectious enthusiasm grounding me like an anchor against the relentless tide of uncertainty.

As we walked through the gallery, admiring the diverse range of artworks on display, I could feel the energy shifting once more. Claire had moved on, mingling with others, her earlier bravado now a distant memory. For the first time that night, I could breathe, absorbing the lively conversations and the vibrant colors that surrounded me.

Just then, Ethan sidled closer, his voice low, "You handled that beautifully. I'm proud of you." The sincerity in his words ignited a warmth within me, a gentle reminder that I was not alone in this world. The intensity of the night began to recede, replaced by a shared moment of quiet celebration, a reflection of the bond we had built through trust and vulnerability.

"Thank you," I replied, the sincerity evident in my tone. "It feels good to stand my ground. I just didn't expect her to be so..." I hesitated, searching for the right words.

"Challenging?" Ethan offered, a knowing smile on his lips.

"Exactly," I replied, rolling my eyes playfully. "But I guess every artist has to face their critics eventually."

"Especially the ones with a flair for the dramatic," he quipped, his voice teasing yet affectionate. We both laughed, the sound mingling with the lively ambiance of the exhibit, and for a moment, the weight of the evening lifted, leaving only the sweetness of the shared moment.

We meandered through the gallery, surrounded by friends and fellow artists, the warmth of camaraderie wrapping around us like a cherished blanket. I allowed myself to forget the earlier turmoil and simply enjoy the evening—the laughter, the art, and the deepening connection between Ethan and me. The world felt expansive, brimming with possibilities, and in that moment, I believed that perhaps I was enough just as I was.

As the evening unfurled around me, the gallery transformed into a vibrant tapestry of color and sound, each corner filled with stories waiting to be told. Conversations fluttered like butterflies, dancing from group to group, and laughter mingled with the soft strains of a live jazz band tucked away in a corner, the notes weaving a rich, melodic background that lulled my frayed nerves. With Jess by my side, her infectious energy pulling me into the rhythm of the night, I found solace in the camaraderie of fellow artists, their passion illuminating the room like the vibrant artwork displayed on the walls.

Ethan and I floated through the exhibit, the thrumming pulse of life around us beginning to feel like a warm embrace rather than an overwhelming tide. I pointed out different pieces that caught my eye, immersing myself in the stories behind each brushstroke, each carefully placed sculpture. It felt good to step away from the tension with Claire, if only for a moment, and dive into conversations that flowed easily, unencumbered by the weight of rivalry.

But the thrill of the night was short-lived, the shadow of Claire looming larger than before. I felt her presence even when I couldn't see her, an invisible thread tying her to my insecurities. I glanced toward the entrance where she had entered, half-expecting her to come striding back in my direction, ready to challenge me again. When I caught sight of her mingling with a group of well-dressed patrons, my heart sank slightly. Claire had a way of commanding attention, her laughter ringing out like a clarion call, drawing people to her as if she were a magnet.

As if sensing my gaze, Ethan turned to me, his brow furrowed with concern. "Hey," he said, his voice low and soothing, "don't let her get under your skin. You're incredible, and you've worked hard for this." His earnestness wrapped around me like a soft blanket, and I felt the tension in my shoulders ease, the weight of doubt lifting just a little.

"Thanks," I replied, the warmth of his words sinking in. "It's just hard not to compare myself, especially with someone like her around."

"Comparison is a thief," he mused, a teasing smile playing on his lips. "And you're no thief."

"Maybe not a thief, but definitely an amateur at best," I quipped back, a playful banter easing the gravity of the moment. The exchange was light and familiar, a reminder of the connection we had forged, built on laughter and mutual respect.

Just then, a flurry of energy erupted near the refreshments table, where Claire had now gathered a small entourage. I felt a wave of unease wash over me, and it was as if I could feel the ripple of her influence extend into my little oasis. I glanced over, only to see her regaling the crowd with a story, her hands animatedly painting a picture that captivated the listeners.

"It's not a competition," I whispered to Ethan, trying to push the knot in my stomach down further. "But she seems to thrive on it."

"Maybe she does," he replied thoughtfully, "but what matters is that you're here, sharing your art. That's what really counts." His gaze was steady, and for a moment, I allowed myself to believe him.

As the night wore on, the crowd continued to swell, the gallery buzzing with admiration for the works on display. I lost myself in the thrill of discussing my piece with curious onlookers, their questions a balm to my frazzled nerves. Each compliment felt like a brushstroke of confidence added to my canvas, painting over the insecurities that Claire's presence had tried to mar.

Jess, ever the cheerleader, had taken it upon herself to introduce me to anyone who wandered close, her enthusiasm infectious. "You have to see Ava's work," she would say, pulling strangers into the orbit of my latest piece. "It's breathtaking—truly a representation of the chaos we all feel." I couldn't help but blush at her exuberance, gratitude swelling in my chest.

Yet, no matter how I immersed myself in the evening, Claire's influence lingered like an ominous shadow. She floated through the crowd with an effortless grace, her laughter ringing out like a siren call. I could see her stealing glances at Ethan, a flicker of possessiveness dancing in her eyes, and I felt the heat of jealousy rise in my cheeks.

Just when I thought I could forget her, Claire approached again, her expression a carefully crafted mask of sweetness. "Ava," she said, her voice dripping with feigned warmth, "it's truly impressive how you've pulled this all together. The exhibit, the atmosphere—you've done a remarkable job."

"Thanks," I replied, forcing a polite smile even as my heart raced. The words felt like a double-edged sword, slicing through my defenses. "It's been a team effort, really."

She tilted her head, eyes glinting with a mixture of curiosity and challenge. "You know, it's easy to get lost in the excitement, isn't it? To forget the real reason we create?" Her words hung in the air, heavy with implications, and I felt the weight of them pressing down on my chest.

"Creating is about sharing, about expressing what's inside," I countered, holding my ground. "I think it's important to let others see that."

Claire's smile faltered for a moment before she regained her composure. "Of course, darling. But just remember, sometimes art can also be a battleground. A way to show who truly deserves the spotlight."

Before I could respond, Ethan stepped forward, his protective nature evident. "Art isn't a battle, Claire. It's a community. We lift each other up, not tear each other down." His words cut through the tension like a knife, his conviction unwavering.

Claire's expression hardened, a fleeting flicker of surprise crossing her features before she masked it with a practiced smile. "Of course, Ethan. I wouldn't dream of trying to create discord. Just a friendly reminder to keep one's eyes on the prize."

With that, she sauntered away, leaving an uneasy silence in her wake. I took a deep breath, trying to steady my racing heart. Ethan turned to me, concern etched on his face. "Are you okay?"

"I am now," I replied, grateful for his unwavering support. "But I can't help but feel that she's trying to play mind games."

"Let her try," he said, brushing his fingers against mine, the warmth a calming presence. "You have something she doesn't: authenticity. You create from the heart, and that's what will resonate."

His words lingered in the air, a gentle affirmation that pushed the shadows of doubt aside. I took a moment to breathe, grounding myself in the reality that I was surrounded by friends who believed in me. The hum of the crowd began to feel like a chorus, reminding me that I wasn't alone in this endeavor.

With renewed determination, I turned to the gallery, the vibrant paintings around me pulsating with energy. As the night unfolded, I found myself enveloped in conversations that sparked joy and curiosity. People were eager to learn about my creative process, to delve into the inspiration behind my work. Each inquiry ignited a fire within me, allowing the flickering flame of self-doubt to dissipate.

I moved through the space, engaging with attendees, my passion infectious. I spoke about the colors I had chosen, the emotions I had sought to capture, and the journey that had led me to this moment. It felt liberating, like shedding a second skin, and I relished the warmth of validation as others connected with my art.

Just when I thought the evening couldn't get any better, Ethan pulled me aside. "I have something for you," he said, his expression a mix of excitement and nervousness.

"Really? What is it?" I asked, my curiosity piqued.

He reached into his pocket and produced a small, intricately carved wooden box. "Open it."

I carefully lifted the lid, revealing a delicate silver necklace with a pendant shaped like a painter's palette, complete with tiny gemstones mimicking splashes of color. My breath caught in my throat, tears pricking at the corners of my eyes.

"It's beautiful," I whispered, overwhelmed.

"It's a reminder," Ethan said softly, "that your art is a reflection of you, and you deserve to shine."

In that moment, with the chaos of the night swirling around us, I felt a sense of clarity wash over me. I was not defined by Claire's perception or anyone else's expectations. I was an artist, a creator, and this was my time to shine.

As I fastened the necklace around my neck, I glanced around the gallery, the crowd bustling with energy and creativity. In the heart of the vibrant night, surrounded by friends and the warmth of Ethan's unwavering support, I finally felt at home. I was ready to embrace whatever came next, knowing that my journey was just beginning.

Chapter 19: Shattered Illusions

The gallery lights dimmed softly as the last visitors filtered out, their laughter echoing in the cavernous space before fading into the warm embrace of a summer night. My art, bathed in the golden glow of strategically placed spotlights, seemed to pulse with life—each piece a testament to countless hours spent wrestling with color and form, with love and despair woven into every stroke. But despite the triumphant success of the exhibit, an unsettling weight anchored itself deep in my chest, a feeling so alien amidst the jubilant chaos of the night.

    I stood alone in my studio, the remnants of my creativity scattered around me like fallen leaves in autumn. A tangle of paintbrushes lay abandoned in a jar, their bristles hardened and gnarled, as if echoing the frayed edges of my own emotions. Canvases leaned against the walls, some still bearing the promise of untapped potential, while others told stories I could no longer bear to look at. Each vibrant color, once bursting with hope, now felt like a cruel reminder of the fragile illusions I had spun around Ethan and me.

    The encounter with Claire lingered like a bitter aftertaste, her words cutting deeper than I cared to admit. She had appeared out of nowhere, a specter of my insecurities, her presence at the gallery a stark reminder that Ethan's past loomed over us like a thundercloud. In her confident demeanor, I saw the shadows of my own doubts, questions swirling like autumn leaves caught in a whirlwind. Did I truly understand Ethan? Had I merely crafted a narrative in my mind, one that glorified what I wished to see rather than the reality before me?

    As I wrapped my arms around my knees, I stared out the window, the dusky skyline of New York City sprawling before me, its glittering lights twinkling like stars scattered across a dark canvas. The city had always been a constant in my life—a chaotic symphony of sounds and sights, bustling with energy that seemed to invigorate my spirit. But tonight, it felt more like a distant planet, one I had become detached from as the echoes of Claire's laughter danced in my mind, mocking my vulnerability.

My phone buzzed on the cluttered table, a lifeline I hesitated to grasp. Ethan's name flickered on the screen, each syllable of his name resonating like a siren's call. In that moment, I felt the pull of familiarity, a magnetic draw that left me breathless. Yet, beneath that yearning lay a tangle of anxiety. What would we discuss? Would it be a confrontation? A reckoning of emotions? Or a desperate attempt to salvage what remained of our fragile connection?

Taking a deep breath, I forced myself to remember why I had fallen for him in the first place—the way his laughter seemed to brighten the most mundane moments, the warmth of his hand as it slipped into mine, and the depth of his gaze that always felt like home. But home was built on trust, and doubt crept in like an unwelcome guest, threatening to dismantle everything I held dear.

Deciding to face the music, I pushed away from the table, the chair scraping against the floor with a discordant shriek, breaking the quiet solitude that had enveloped me. My heart raced as I pulled on a light sweater, the fabric soft against my skin, and glanced at my reflection in the small mirror hanging beside my easel. My eyes, still reflecting the remnants of the evening's excitement, shimmered with uncertainty. I couldn't keep pretending everything was perfect; I needed to confront my fears, however daunting that might be.

The streets of Manhattan thrummed with life as I stepped outside, the heady mix of street food vendors, honking taxis, and distant music infusing the air with an intoxicating blend of chaos and exhilaration. Each footstep echoed my resolve, carrying me toward the café where Ethan had asked to meet. The familiarity of the neighborhood wrapped around me like a warm blanket, yet the butterflies in my stomach churned violently, each beat of my heart reminding me of what was at stake.

The café was a quaint little spot nestled between two towering buildings, its outdoor seating dotted with twinkling fairy lights that hung like tiny stars. I pushed through the glass door, the bell above tinkling softly as I entered. The aroma of freshly brewed coffee mingled with the sweetness of pastries, beckoning me to seek comfort in the bustling ambiance. Yet, I felt like an intruder, the warmth of the café contrasting sharply with the chill of uncertainty that gripped me.

Ethan sat at our usual corner table, his posture relaxed yet distant. The sunlight streamed through the window, casting a golden glow on his tousled hair, and for a fleeting moment, I was reminded of the boy who had captivated me with his artistic passion and charming wit. But the smile that usually danced on his lips was replaced by a thoughtful frown, his fingers absentmindedly tracing the rim of his coffee cup, as if seeking answers in the depths of the porcelain.

As I approached, my heart raced, the dialogue in my mind swirling chaotically. Should I dive right in, voicing my fears and uncertainties? Or would it be better to keep it light, pretending that the shadows looming over us didn't exist? I decided on honesty, fueled by the unrelenting urge to shatter the illusions I had been clinging to for too long.

"Hey," I greeted softly, taking a seat across from him. The moment felt electric, the air thick with unspoken words. He looked up, his eyes meeting mine, and in that instant, the world around us faded into a blur.

"Hey," he replied, a small smile tugging at the corners of his mouth, though it didn't quite reach his eyes. It was enough to ignite a flicker of hope within me, yet the weight of what lay ahead hung heavily in the air. As the café bustled around us, I realized that the real conversation was about to unfold, and with it, the potential for both healing and heartbreak.

The chatter of the café faded into a muted background hum, a gentle ocean of voices swirling around us as I grappled with the enormity of the moment. I fixed my gaze on Ethan, whose fingers now rested motionless against the cool ceramic of his mug. The familiar warmth of his presence was both a comfort and a reminder of the distance that had grown between us, threatening to swallow the affection we once shared.

"What's on your mind?" he asked, his voice a mixture of concern and curiosity, piercing the tension that had settled over the table like a dense fog. I could see the weight of my silence bearing down on him, and I had to remind myself that vulnerability, while frightening, was also liberating. This was my chance to untangle the knot of doubt that had taken root in my heart.

I took a deep breath, the scent of coffee and pastries wrapping around me like a shield. "I've been thinking a lot about… us," I began, my voice barely above a whisper, yet firm enough to carry the weight of my intentions. "About what happened at the gallery. About Claire."

Ethan's brow furrowed slightly, and I could sense the shift in his demeanor. The mention of her name sent a tremor through our conversation, like a pebble dropped in a serene pond. I had to tread carefully. "I didn't expect to see her there, and it caught me off guard. But what she said—"

"Are you really worried about what Claire thinks?" he interrupted, his tone sharp, cutting through the delicate web I was attempting to weave. "You know she's just trying to get under your skin, right? She always has."

His defensiveness was both comforting and disconcerting, but I pressed on, feeling the urge to bare my soul. "It's not just her. It's everything. I've been questioning if I misread you, if I've been too caught up in my own feelings to see the truth."

Ethan leaned back, a pained expression washing over his face. "You didn't misread me, Anna. Not at all." The sincerity in his voice broke through my uncertainty, and I felt my resolve waver. Yet, beneath his reassurance lay an undercurrent of tension, an unspoken acknowledgment of the complications that tangled our relationship.

As the minutes ticked by, I could almost hear the clock on the wall counting down to a confrontation I dreaded. "I care about you, Ethan. But every time I think we're moving forward, I see shadows creeping back in. Shadows of your past, and they terrify me." My confession hung in the air, heavy and palpable.

He sighed, the sound escaping his lips like a deflated balloon, leaving behind a lingering silence that filled the space between us. "Anna, my past is just that—my past. I'm trying to be present with you. I don't want you to doubt how I feel. You mean so much to me."

I studied his face, the furrow of his brow deepening, the way his lips pressed together in a tight line. It was then that I noticed the subtle shift in his demeanor. There was a vulnerability lurking beneath the surface, one that mirrored my own. "What if you don't know how to be present? What if your past still influences your future?" I ventured cautiously, probing into the depths of our uncertainty.

He met my gaze, a storm of emotions brewing in his dark eyes. "What if I'm terrified of losing you?" The raw honesty in his voice sent a shiver down my spine, igniting a flicker of hope in the depths of my uncertainty. "I've spent so much time guarding my heart, keeping people at bay. But with you, everything feels different. It scares me. You scare me."

The revelation hung there, electrifying the air around us. My heart raced as I processed his words, realizing that we were both teetering on the precipice of something profound, yet precarious.

"Then let's stop being scared together," I said, my voice steadying as I took a leap of faith. "Let's figure this out. I want to know the real you, Ethan, the one beyond the shadows."

A flicker of relief danced across his features, and for a moment, the world outside the café faded into insignificance. The clattering of cups, the laughter of patrons, all became background noise as our eyes locked in a shared understanding. "Okay," he said softly, his voice almost a whisper. "I want that too. I just don't want to hurt you."

The sincerity of his words wrapped around my heart, anchoring me to this moment. The doubt that had been gnawing at me began to unravel, replaced by a fragile sense of hope. We both carried scars, remnants of our pasts that had shaped us into who we were today. "We're both flawed, Ethan. But maybe that's what makes this real. Maybe we can learn from each other."

As I spoke, I felt the heaviness of my previous doubts begin to lift. The shadows that had loomed over us felt less daunting, less insurmountable. I wanted to believe that our shared vulnerabilities could bind us together rather than tear us apart.

Ethan reached across the table, his fingers brushing against mine, sending a warm jolt of electricity coursing through me. "I want to share my past with you, to let you in," he confessed, his thumb gently stroking the back of my hand. "But I need you to promise me that you won't run when things get tough."

"I promise," I replied, my heart pounding in my chest, the sincerity of my words ringing true. "I'm not going anywhere."

In that moment, I realized we were standing at a crossroads, poised to carve a new path together. The air was thick with unspoken possibilities, an intoxicating blend of fear and excitement that danced between us. For the first time in what felt like ages, I felt grounded in my truth, and the illusions I had built around our relationship began to dissolve like mist under the rising sun.

As the café bustled around us, I allowed myself to imagine a future where we could navigate the shadows together, a future filled with shared laughter, whispered secrets, and a love that could withstand the storms of our pasts. The connection we forged in that moment was fragile yet unwavering, a tentative truce against the chaos of our lives.

With the world continuing to whirl around us, I felt a newfound clarity settle over me like a comforting blanket. It wouldn't be easy, but we were willing to fight for this. And as we sat together, hands intertwined, I could almost hear the echoes of a love story beginning to unfold, the chapters unwritten but ripe with possibility.

The sunlight filtered through the café window, casting a warm glow on the chipped wooden table between us, illuminating the quiet intimacy of our moment. The soft clinking of spoons against porcelain seemed to underscore the weight of our conversation, each sound echoing like a heartbeat in the shared space. I glanced at Ethan, whose gaze was fixed on our intertwined hands, the warmth radiating from our fingers creating a fragile connection that felt both invigorating and terrifying.

"I want to tell you everything," he finally said, his voice steady yet laced with an undercurrent of vulnerability. "About my past, about the things I've done, and how I got here." He hesitated, as if the words were heavy stones lodged in his throat, waiting to be dislodged. I nodded, urging him to continue, feeling the knot of apprehension in my stomach twist tighter as I braced for what was to come.

Ethan leaned back, pulling his hand away just enough to create distance, but I sensed the invisible tether still binding us together. "It's not pretty. I've made choices I'm not proud of, things that still haunt me." His dark eyes bore into mine, searching for understanding, for forgiveness. "There was a time when I thought I could outrun my mistakes, but it only led to more regret."

I held my breath, captivated by his honesty, feeling the flicker of hope ignite within me once more. This was the raw truth I had longed to hear—the unvarnished story behind the guarded man who had captured my heart. "You're not alone in this," I whispered, my voice soft yet resolute. "We all have our ghosts, Ethan. The important thing is what we do with them."

He took a deep breath, the air seeming to swell with tension as he began to recount his story. "When I was younger, I got involved in a group that had a reputation for trouble. It was easy to get caught up in the excitement, the sense of belonging. But eventually, it spiraled out of control. I was so blinded by the thrill that I didn't see how it affected those around me." His voice trembled slightly, and I felt my heart clench at the pain etched across his features.

"I hurt people," he continued, his gaze dropping to the table. "Friends, family—people who cared about me. I thought I could escape, but the more I tried to leave it behind, the more it pulled me back in. I'm still dealing with the consequences of my actions, and I don't want you to be another casualty of my past."

Each word felt like a revelation, a glimpse into the soul of a man who had fought against the demons of his choices. My heart ached for him, for the weight he carried alone for so long. "You've changed, Ethan. You're not that person anymore," I said, my voice firm, desperate to reinforce the transformation I saw before me. "We all stumble, but it's how we rise that defines us."

His gaze lifted to meet mine, and for a brief moment, the walls that surrounded him crumbled, revealing the raw vulnerability underneath. "I want to believe that," he admitted, the flicker of hope evident in his tone. "But I'm terrified of hurting you, of dragging you into my mess."

"Then let me in," I urged, the words flowing from my heart. "Let's face it together. We can't change the past, but we can shape our future. We can decide what we want it to be." I reached out again, allowing our fingers to intertwine once more, feeling the warmth of his skin against mine, grounding me in the reality of this moment.

A small smile tugged at the corners of his lips, a hint of relief washing over his features. "You make it sound so easy," he said, though I could hear the gratitude in his voice. "But it feels like a mountain I have to climb. I just hope I don't lose you along the way."

"You won't lose me," I reassured him, the certainty of my words wrapping around us like a protective shield. "We'll find our way, one step at a time."

As we spoke, the café around us began to fade into a blur. The warmth of our connection eclipsed the bustling world outside, and I realized we were no longer just two individuals dancing around our fears—we were allies, facing our demons together.

The days that followed felt like an awakening. We began to share more than just our fears; we explored the depths of our dreams and aspirations. We filled the spaces between us with laughter and light, painting over the dark spots of doubt that had once clouded our hearts. Each conversation, each moment spent together, became a brushstroke on the canvas of our relationship, transforming it into a vibrant masterpiece filled with color and texture.

Ethan introduced me to his world—the art that inspired him, the music that ignited his spirit. We wandered through the streets of New York, hand in hand, discovering hidden gems that thrived beyond the tourist trails. An underground gallery tucked away in a forgotten corner of the city unveiled a collection of stunning murals, each piece alive with raw emotion. We laughed, marveled, and discussed our interpretations, losing ourselves in the colors and textures that echoed our evolving relationship.

One crisp afternoon, we ventured into Central Park, the leaves ablaze in shades of gold and crimson. We settled on a bench overlooking the shimmering lake, watching the sunlight dance on the surface like stars teasing their reflection. The world around us seemed to pause, a moment suspended in time as we shared stories of our childhoods, our hopes for the future, and the dreams we had once abandoned.

"What do you want, Anna?" Ethan asked suddenly, breaking the silence that had settled comfortably between us. His voice was earnest, laced with an intensity that made my heart race. "What do you really want?"

I took a moment to reflect, the weight of his question wrapping around me like a soft embrace. "I want to create art that resonates with people, that evokes emotion and sparks a connection," I replied, my voice steady. "But more than that, I want to build a life filled with love and laughter, surrounded by those who matter."

He nodded, a thoughtful expression crossing his face. "You have a gift, you know. Your art has the power to inspire. You're already doing it."

The warmth of his words wrapped around me like a cozy blanket, igniting a spark of confidence I had been missing. "I just hope I can keep it up," I confessed, the vulnerability creeping back in. "I don't want to falter again. I want to push through the shadows."

"You will," he said, his gaze steady and reassuring. "We'll push through together. I won't let you falter."

As the sun began to dip below the horizon, painting the sky in hues of pink and orange, I felt a surge of gratitude wash over me. We were creating something beautiful together, a narrative built on trust and understanding, and it was a story I wanted to explore to its fullest.

In that moment, I knew our journey was far from over. The past had shaped us, but it wouldn't define our future. Together, we would paint a canvas that would reflect our true selves—an intricate blend of colors, imperfections, and a shared commitment to embrace the complexities of love. The shadows may linger, but we were ready to face them hand in hand, determined to emerge into the light.

Chapter 20: Beneath the Surface

The air around us is thick with the scent of damp earth and decaying leaves, the signature aroma of autumn settling into the landscape. Lake Michigan stretches out before us, a shimmering expanse reflecting the fiery hues of the setting sun. The sky transforms into a canvas of oranges and purples, and as the warm colors bleed into one another, I can't help but feel a twinge of hope intermingled with my anxiety. Ethan sits beside me, his silhouette framed against the vibrant backdrop, but the tension in his posture reminds me that this moment is precarious.

I steal a glance at him, trying to decipher the emotions that swirl behind his hazel eyes. There's a familiarity between us, but the shadows of our recent past loom large, casting doubt over the tender connection we've forged. The last time we were together, words had escaped us, leaving behind a fragile silence that felt heavier than the world around us. My heart races at the thought of opening that door again, of revisiting the raw edges of our unspoken feelings. The bench creaks beneath us, as if echoing my unease.

"Ethan," I begin, my voice barely above a whisper. It catches in my throat, a tangible reminder of my insecurities. "I know things have been... complicated. I think about Claire a lot, and sometimes I wonder if I can really compete with memories." I hate how the admission feels like a confession of weakness. I glance at him, the sunset illuminating his features, making him look almost ethereal. Yet, the intensity of his gaze makes me feel exposed, vulnerable.

He leans forward, resting his elbows on his knees, the golden light casting long shadows on the ground. "Claire was a part of my life, yes, but she's not the one sitting next to me right now," he replies, his voice steady but warm, enveloping me like a soft blanket. "You're the one I want to be here with. I don't want to dwell in the past when I have something so real right in front of me."

My heart flutters at his words, a delicate dance of hope and uncertainty. There's a part of me that wants to believe him entirely, to let go of the fear that grips my chest like a vice. But another part, the more cautious side that has learned to tread lightly through emotional waters, hesitates. "But what if you wake up one day and realize you miss her?" I challenge, my voice trembling slightly as I pick at the frayed edges of my jacket. "What if I'm not enough?"

He runs a hand through his tousled hair, the gesture both familiar and frustratingly endearing. "You don't get it, do you?" Ethan looks at me, his expression softening, his voice low and earnest. "You're not meant to fill any space Claire left behind. You're creating a new one, with your own unique shape and light."

A breath hitches in my throat, and I feel the warmth spread through me like a gentle tide, washing away some of my doubts. But then the weight of reality crashes back. "It's just... hard. I've spent so long feeling like I'm always on the outside looking in. With you, everything feels different, but part of me is terrified of how much I care." The honesty spills from my lips before I can rein it in, a confession that lays my insecurities bare.

Ethan takes a moment to absorb my words, and as he does, the sun dips further into the horizon, leaving traces of dusk in its wake. He reaches for my hand, his fingers brushing against mine, igniting a spark that travels straight to my heart. "You care because it matters to you. And that's beautiful. I'm not asking you to be perfect. I'm asking you to be real with me."

The sincerity in his voice tugs at my heart, and for the first time, I feel a flicker of trust begin to emerge from the depths of my fears. "I don't want to ruin what we have," I murmur, squeezing his hand as if to ground myself in this moment. "But sometimes it feels so fragile, like it could shatter if we breathe too hard."

Ethan's thumb glides over my knuckles, and he leans closer, his voice barely a whisper against the backdrop of rustling leaves. "Then let's take a deep breath together. We can build something strong enough to weather any storm. I promise I won't let you go."

The warmth of his promise settles over me like the last rays of sun kissing the horizon. I nod, feeling the weight of my fears begin to lift, replaced by a sense of possibility that feels both exhilarating and terrifying. "I want that too," I admit, a smile breaking free as I allow myself to believe in the potential of what lies ahead. "I want to take this leap with you."

Ethan grins, the tension in his shoulders dissipating like mist in the morning sun. "Then let's do it together. No more holding back." The confidence in his voice intertwines with my hope, creating a thread that binds us in this moment, a promise of something deeper.

As twilight descends around us, the first stars begin to twinkle overhead, mirrored by the glimmering surface of the lake. I feel alive, like a canvas splashed with vibrant colors, ready to embrace whatever the universe has in store. The world around us fades, leaving only the soft sound of water lapping against the shore and the rhythmic thumping of my heart. This is where I want to be—here, with him, on this weathered bench, under a sky bursting with possibilities.

The sun continues its slow descent, painting the sky with deepening shades of indigo and violet, a breathtaking transition that feels almost intimate. The air carries a gentle chill, a harbinger of the evening, and I shiver slightly, not entirely from the cold. The warmth of Ethan's hand intertwined with mine offers a small comfort against the encroaching darkness. I can feel the heartbeat of the lake resonating in my chest, its waves lapping rhythmically against the shore, mirroring the rising tide of emotions swirling within me.

As we sit in companionable silence, a flock of geese honks overhead, their silhouettes carving a path through the twilight. I find myself drawn into Ethan's gaze, a mosaic of emotions shifting like the colors in the sky. His eyes, rich and expressive, seem to reflect the depth of the lake—a world of secrets and stories yet to unfold.

The tension that once felt so insurmountable begins to melt away, replaced by the undeniable chemistry that crackles between us. I can feel a warmth growing in my chest, an urge to lean in closer and let the world fade away.

"Do you ever think about how strange life is?" I ask, breaking the spell of silence that had enveloped us. The question surprises even me, but it feels appropriate, considering how surreal everything seems at this moment. "Like how we can be in one place and then, without warning, find ourselves somewhere entirely different?"

Ethan tilts his head, a playful grin spreading across his face as he considers my words. "Are you talking about physically or emotionally? Because both sound like a rollercoaster I'm not sure I'm ready for." He chuckles, the sound rich and melodic, sending a ripple of warmth through me.

"Both, I suppose," I reply, my heart racing as I meet his gaze. "I mean, here we are, just two people on a bench in a park, and yet it feels like we're at the center of something much bigger." I gesture toward the lake, its vastness representing all the unknowns ahead of us. "It's a little daunting, isn't it?"

"It is," he admits, his expression turning serious for a moment. "But sometimes those unknowns can lead to the best things in life." He pauses, the air thick with unspoken thoughts. "What if the chaos is what makes it all worth it?"

I ponder his words, feeling their weight settle within me. "You make it sound so easy," I say, a teasing note in my voice. "Like we should just embrace the uncertainty with open arms and a smile."

"Maybe we should," he counters, his gaze unwavering. "What's the worst that could happen? We fall? We get hurt? But isn't that part of living?"

There's a boldness in his voice, a fearless charm that captivates me. I can't help but admire the way he confronts the uncertainty, like a warrior charging into battle. His conviction ignites a fire within me, a desire to explore the unknown alongside him, to confront my fears rather than shy away. "You're right. It's about the journey, isn't it?"

"Exactly," Ethan replies, a spark of excitement lighting up his eyes. "And every journey has its bumps along the way."

Just then, a dog bounds toward us, tail wagging furiously, its owner trailing behind with a grin that seems to stretch from ear to ear. The dog stops right in front of us, looking expectantly at Ethan, as if he's waiting for a pat. Ethan chuckles, bending down to scratch the dog's ears. "See? Life brings unexpected joy even when we're not looking for it."

I watch the interaction, feeling my heart swell at the simple happiness emanating from this moment. The dog barks excitedly, nudging Ethan's hand, and in that instant, I realize how easily joy can seep into our lives if we let it. I think about Claire again, the specter of her memory looming over us, but I push it aside, focusing instead on the present, on the warmth blooming between Ethan and me.

"Maybe we should get a dog," I say playfully, the thought surprising me. "Something cute and fluffy to brighten our lives."

Ethan laughs, his eyes sparkling with mischief. "Only if you're prepared for the chaos. Dogs come with their own brand of craziness."

"Chaos is kind of what I signed up for," I respond, nudging him gently. "I'm already knee-deep in emotional whirlwind."

The playful banter unfolds like a comforting blanket, wrapping us in warmth against the chill of the evening air. The conversation drifts from dogs to dreams, and we share snippets of our lives—my aspirations to travel, his ambition to create art that resonates. With every word, every laugh, the distance between us shrinks, the past fading into the background as we carve out our own space in the present.

As the stars begin to pepper the night sky, I feel the shift in our connection, a palpable energy coursing between us. It's as if the universe has conspired to bring us together, to guide us through this tumultuous journey. The lake, calm yet teeming with life beneath its surface, mirrors the depths of my own feelings—hidden complexities waiting to be explored.

"Can I ask you something?" I say suddenly, my voice steady despite the flutter in my stomach. "What if things don't go the way we hope?"

Ethan meets my gaze, his expression earnest. "Then we adapt. We adjust our sails and find a new course. But I'll tell you this—whatever happens, I want you to be a part of it."

His words settle in my heart like a promise, a commitment that feels both exhilarating and terrifying. I nod slowly, absorbing the gravity of his declaration. It's a risk, but in this moment, I feel ready to embrace it, to dive into the depths of our connection, knowing that it's worth exploring—worth every chaotic twist and turn.

With the last slivers of sunlight giving way to night, I lean back, allowing myself to be swept away by the enchantment of the moment. The world fades to a soft murmur, the laughter of distant children mingling with the sound of the wind rustling through the trees. I glance at Ethan, the contours of his face illuminated by the glow of the streetlights, and for the first time, I feel a sense of belonging. We may be navigating uncharted waters, but I'm no longer afraid of the unknown. With Ethan beside me, I am ready to uncover the treasures hidden beneath the surface.

A soft hush falls over the park as the last of the daylight fades, leaving us cloaked in the gentle embrace of twilight. The distant sounds of laughter and splashing from a nearby playground seem to echo the joy sparking between us, a reminder that life continues its playful dance even as we grapple with our own emotions. I can feel the tension in my chest easing, replaced by a sense of belonging that I didn't realize I craved until this moment.

Ethan shifts slightly, leaning in closer as if to draw me into his world. "You know, I used to come here a lot as a kid," he says, breaking the spell of silence that had enveloped us. "There's something magical about watching the sun sink into the lake. It's like a promise that every day ends, but every new one is a chance for something better." His words hang in the air, a gentle reminder that endings can be beautiful in their own right.

I can't help but smile, warmed by the thought of young Ethan running through this park, carefree and full of dreams. "I wish I had known you then," I reply, imagining him racing down the path, hair tousled by the wind, laughter trailing behind him like a kite string. "I bet you were a little troublemaker."

"Maybe a little," he admits, a mischievous glint in his eyes. "But trouble usually leads to some of the best stories." He looks at me, and the weight of his gaze feels like an anchor grounding me in this moment. "What about you? What did you do for fun growing up?"

"Not much," I confess, shrugging lightly as if to dismiss the thought. "I was always the quiet one, the observer. I read a lot, lost myself in stories. It was safer that way." The admission leaves a slight taste of regret on my tongue, but Ethan's expression remains open and inviting, urging me to share more. "I never really ventured out of my comfort zone."

"Then consider this a leap," he suggests, gesturing to the vibrant landscape surrounding us. "You're not just observing anymore. You're living it." His words resonate, a subtle push towards embracing the present. The park feels alive, filled with whispers of potential, and as the first stars twinkle above, I realize that maybe, just maybe, I can allow myself to be part of this beautiful chaos.

The wind picks up, rustling the leaves overhead, and I shiver slightly as the chill seeps into my bones. Ethan notices and instinctively wraps his arm around my shoulders, pulling me closer.

The warmth of his body against mine sends a ripple of comfort through me. "Better?" he asks, a teasing lilt in his voice.

"Much," I reply, a flutter of something warm blooming within me. "You're like my personal space heater."

"Just doing my part to keep you comfortable." His voice is light, but there's an undercurrent of sincerity that makes my heart race. In this small park, with the world slipping into night, the barriers between us crumble, revealing a connection that feels both exhilarating and terrifying.

As the stars multiply overhead, I notice the first hint of moonlight spilling onto the lake, illuminating the water with a silver sheen. The scene before us transforms into something surreal, almost dreamlike, and I can't help but be captivated. "It's beautiful," I whisper, lost in the magic of the moment.

"It is," Ethan agrees, his gaze fixed on the horizon. "But not as beautiful as what's happening right here." He gestures between us, and the intensity of his words sends a shiver of anticipation coursing through me. "I want you to know, I'm all in. Whatever this is, I want to explore it with you."

My breath catches, and for a moment, I'm speechless, grappling with the enormity of his declaration. The warmth radiating from his body is nothing compared to the heat blooming in my chest. I lean in closer, tempted to close the distance that feels charged with unspoken words.

"What does 'all in' mean for you?" I ask, my voice barely a murmur, the question hanging delicately in the air.

He takes a deep breath, his eyes searching mine as if trying to decipher the depths of my soul. "It means I want to be here, in every moment, not just the easy ones. I want to be with you when the sun is shining and when it's storming outside." His honesty is both refreshing and intimidating, but beneath my apprehension lies a flicker of hope.

"What if I'm not ready for the storm?" I challenge lightly, a playful smile dancing on my lips despite the seriousness of the topic.

"Then we'll figure it out together. I won't let you drown." His sincerity sends a jolt of warmth through me, wrapping around my heart like a promise.

The world around us begins to fade as the weight of our conversation envelops us, creating a bubble of intimacy. "I've never really let anyone in like this before," I admit, the vulnerability spilling forth. "It's terrifying and exhilarating all at once."

"Trust me, I get it," he replies, his voice low and earnest. "But I think it's time we both take a risk. You don't have to face everything alone."

His words resonate with a truth I've been denying, and the realization washes over me, cleansing the doubts that have held me captive for so long. It's a gamble, but the thrill of the unknown stirs something deep within me, urging me to let go of my fears and embrace what lies ahead.

As we sit there, our breaths mingling in the crisp air, the stars seem to align above us, crafting a constellation of promises and dreams waiting to be realized. The park around us becomes a sanctuary, a place where we can be ourselves, unburdened by the weight of past mistakes or the fear of the future. Here, under the vast expanse of the night sky, I finally feel the freedom to explore the depths of my emotions.

With a newfound determination, I turn to Ethan, my heart racing with anticipation. "Okay, let's take this leap. Together."

His smile lights up his face, and I can see the joy dancing in his eyes. "Together."

In that moment, as the moon casts a silvery glow over the lake, I know we are standing on the precipice of something extraordinary. It won't be easy—life never is—but with Ethan by my side, I feel ready to face whatever storms come our way. Together, we will navigate the uncharted waters, crafting our own story amidst the chaos and beauty of the world around us. As the first stars twinkle above, I embrace the promise of new beginnings, knowing that this journey, fraught with uncertainty, is exactly where I am meant to be.

Chapter 21: The Turning Point

I stood at the edge of the farmers' market, the sun casting golden rays that danced across the bustling scene. Laughter bubbled up around me like the gentle flow of a nearby stream, and the air was thick with the sweet, earthy aroma of fresh produce mingling with the mouthwatering scent of baked goods. It was a sensory explosion, and I was there to capture it, my camera poised to immortalize fleeting moments of joy and connection.

The market stretched before me, a vibrant tapestry woven with colorful stalls that offered everything from heirloom tomatoes to handcrafted jewelry. Each vendor wore a smile, their faces glowing as brightly as the fruits and vegetables that surrounded them. I could hear the chatter of families, the playful banter of friends, and the occasional outburst of joy from children chasing after one another, their laughter mingling with the calls of vendors advertising their wares. It was a place where life unfolded in all its messy, beautiful glory, and I couldn't wait to document it.

As I moved through the crowd, I found myself drawn to the small interactions that often went unnoticed. A couple, hands intertwined, shared a moment of quiet affection as they browsed through a stand of sunflowers, their vibrant yellow petals standing in stark contrast to the soft blush of their cheeks. I raised my camera and snapped a quick shot, capturing the way they leaned into each other, as if the world around them had faded away.

With each click of the shutter, I felt the weight of my own heartache lift, replaced by a flicker of hope. Photography had always been my refuge, a means of expressing the emotions I sometimes struggled to voice. But today felt different; today, I was weaving a narrative of love and connection, and it filled me with a sense of purpose I hadn't felt in a long time.

In the midst of this kaleidoscope of life, my gaze wandered to a familiar figure standing just a few yards away. Ethan leaned against a wooden post, arms crossed, his smile genuine as he watched me work. There was something captivating about the way he observed the world, as if he were both a part of it and somehow apart from it. I couldn't help but feel a rush of warmth flood through me. His presence was comforting, a balm for the soul.

"Need a hand?" he called, stepping forward with a casual confidence that made my heart flutter.

I hesitated for a brief moment, caught off guard by his offer. Ethan had always been supportive, but the idea of working together on something so personal felt both thrilling and terrifying. Still, there was a spark in his eyes, an unspoken promise that this could be something beautiful. "Actually, I would love that," I replied, my voice betraying the excitement I felt.

Together, we began to navigate the market, weaving between stalls and capturing moments that felt both intimate and profound. I marveled at how naturally we fell into a rhythm, our laughter punctuating the air like music. Each click of the shutter felt like a step closer to bridging the gap that had formed between us in recent weeks. We explored the angles of love—from the tender glances shared between an elderly couple reliving their youth to the way a young mother cradled her child, both of them enveloped in a bubble of warmth.

As we continued to work, I found myself stealing glances at Ethan, admiring the way he approached each scene with a quiet intensity. He was not merely capturing images; he was preserving emotions, encapsulating the essence of love in a way that felt incredibly profound. His insights, the way he framed a shot, made me realize that we were two artists drawn together, our passions intertwining to create something meaningful.

"What do you think?" he asked as we reviewed a series of portraits on my camera. The sunlight danced across his features, illuminating the warmth in his gaze. "I think we're onto something here."

I nodded, exhilaration bubbling up inside me. "It's more than just photographs. We're telling a story."

His smile widened, and I felt a rush of exhilaration at the thought of us working together, side by side, building something beautiful from the fragments of our individual experiences. This collaboration was more than just a project; it felt like a turning point—a moment where our lives could intertwine in ways that went beyond friendship.

We paused by a small stand offering freshly made pastries, the rich scent of cinnamon and sugar wrapping around us like a warm hug. I couldn't resist grabbing a few, and Ethan's laughter filled the air as I took a bite of a flaky apple turnover. "You're going to have to work off those calories," he teased, winking.

"I'll take my chances," I replied, feeling bold as I brushed crumbs from my lips, the sweetness of the pastry lingering on my tongue. "I'd rather indulge than worry about every little bite."

Ethan's laughter faded into a softer smile, one that felt charged with unspoken words. For a brief moment, the world around us blurred, and it was just the two of us standing there, enveloped in the shared warmth of our burgeoning connection.

As the sun began to dip lower in the sky, casting a golden glow over the market, I took a step back and looked at the images we had captured. Each frame told a story—moments of connection, laughter, and love that resonated with the essence of what it meant to be human. I felt a swell of pride and hope, knowing that this experience had not only strengthened my bond with Ethan but had rekindled my passion for photography in a way I hadn't anticipated.

With every snap, every shared laugh, I was reminded of the power of connection, of the magic that comes when two souls come together to create something beautiful.

The vibrant symphony of the farmers' market pulsated around us as Ethan and I continued our creative exploration. Laughter erupted like fireworks, mingling with the crisp autumn air, a backdrop to our artistic endeavor. My camera became an extension of my soul, capturing not only the colors and textures of the market but also the very essence of human connection. Each click felt like a heartbeat, resonating with the stories unfolding in every corner.

We found ourselves gravitating toward a booth where a local artist displayed hand-painted mugs, their surfaces adorned with whimsical designs that danced under the sunlight. An elderly couple hovered nearby, their fingers brushing against the ceramic, as if searching for a memory hidden within the glazes. Ethan nudged me gently, nodding toward them, and I raised my camera instinctively. The way the man leaned in, whispering something that made the woman's eyes sparkle, was a moment that begged to be captured.

As the shutter clicked, I caught Ethan's gaze over the viewfinder, and in that instant, something shifted between us. It was a silent acknowledgment that our bond was not just about the project; it was about understanding and appreciating the layers of each other. There was a depth to our collaboration that ran deeper than the photos we took, a shared vision of what love looked like in its many forms.

We wandered further, the energy of the market sweeping us along like a river. The sounds of a nearby musician strumming a guitar lured us closer. A young woman danced playfully in the grass, her movements fluid and carefree, and her laughter echoed like a bell. It was an intoxicating scene, the kind that drew people in, and as I framed the shot, I felt Ethan's presence beside me, a steady warmth that radiated trust and encouragement.

"Get closer," he whispered, nudging my elbow. "Capture the joy, not just the moment."

I hesitated, feeling the rush of vulnerability that came with getting intimate with my subjects. But Ethan's enthusiasm was infectious, and with a deep breath, I stepped forward. The young woman spun around, her skirt flaring out like a blooming flower, and I could feel the magic in the air. As I pressed the shutter, the world around us blurred into a cascade of color, the joy of that fleeting moment preserved forever in time.

We continued our journey, the market's vibrant pulse guiding us through a tapestry of life. I watched as families huddled together, sharing treats and laughter, their love visible in the small gestures—an arm draped over a shoulder, a playful shove, the way a father would tousle his son's hair. Each scene was a testament to the connections we often took for granted, and with every photo, I felt myself becoming more attuned to the beauty around me.

At one stall, a young couple debated over which type of honey to buy, their playful bickering punctuated by laughter. I snapped a few shots, each frame encapsulating their easy chemistry. Ethan leaned against the stall, a look of admiration on his face as he watched me work. "You have a knack for this," he said, a hint of awe in his voice.

"Thanks," I replied, feeling a flush of pride wash over me. "But it's not just me. It's all about the moments we're capturing together."

He grinned, his enthusiasm infectious. "You know, I've always thought photography is about more than just a click. It's about telling a story—our story."

His words hung in the air between us, heavy with unspoken meanings. I felt a flicker of something deeper, something that crackled like static electricity. There was a palpable tension, an unarticulated desire for more than just friendship, but I pushed it aside, choosing instead to focus on the joy surrounding us.

As the day wore on, the golden hour approached, casting a warm, ethereal light over the market. I suggested we find a quieter spot, a hidden nook where we could capture the soft glow of the sunset mixed with the lingering warmth of the day. Ethan agreed, and we ventured to a small garden tucked away behind the stalls, filled with wildflowers that danced in the gentle breeze.

The serenity of the garden enveloped us, and as I set up my camera to capture the flowers illuminated by the fading sun, I felt Ethan's presence beside me. He leaned against a tree, his gaze focused on me, not the camera. "You're truly gifted, you know?" he said softly, breaking the comfortable silence.

"Just doing what I love," I replied, trying to sound nonchalant. But inside, my heart raced at his praise.

Ethan stepped closer, his hands sliding into his pockets, a hint of vulnerability in his demeanor. "What if we created something more? A project that not only captures love but explores what it means to us? Something we can share with the world."

I looked up, meeting his eyes, and in that moment, it was as if a veil had lifted. There was a sincerity in his expression, a desire to dig deeper than surface-level interactions. "You mean like a series?" I asked, my curiosity piqued.

"Exactly," he replied, a spark igniting between us. "We could explore different forms of love—friendship, family, the messy, complicated stuff. Not just the beautiful moments but the ones that challenge us too."

The idea sent a thrill through me, igniting my imagination. I could already envision a collection of photographs that chronicled the journey of love in its rawest form, capturing both its light and shadows. It was a profound undertaking, one that required vulnerability and trust—a leap into the unknown that both thrilled and terrified me.

"Are you in?" he asked, his voice steady but his eyes glimmering with hope.

"Absolutely," I said, my heart soaring at the prospect of creating something meaningful alongside him. This was more than just photography; it was a partnership that transcended our individual passions.

As the sun dipped lower, casting a warm glow that painted the garden in shades of amber, I felt a sense of belonging bloom within me. This project was not just about the art we would create; it was about the connection we were forging, a bond that felt undeniably special. In that tranquil moment, surrounded by the beauty of the world we were capturing, I realized that this was only the beginning of something extraordinary—a journey that promised to unravel the layers of love and life, one snapshot at a time.

As the afternoon sun continued its descent, the garden seemed to exhale, the warm air wrapping around us like a comforting embrace. The ambiance transformed, each moment becoming a brushstroke on the canvas of our collaboration. I felt invigorated, as if the world had opened up, revealing the intricate dance of love and vulnerability that lay just beneath the surface.

Ethan knelt beside a cluster of wildflowers, his fingers gently tracing the petals of a delicate violet. "You know, these flowers remind me of how unpredictable love can be," he mused, glancing up at me with an expression that blended mischief with sincerity. "One moment they're vibrant and full of life, and the next, they're wilting under the weight of a harsh reality."

I chuckled softly, finding truth in his words. "And yet, they always find a way to bloom again," I replied, a spark of inspiration igniting within me. "Perhaps we can incorporate that theme into our project—the idea of resilience in love. Moments of growth, decay, and rebirth."

Ethan's eyes sparkled, and he nodded eagerly. "Exactly! We can showcase couples who have weathered storms together, how they've evolved through challenges."

With renewed energy, we dove into the details of our project, brainstorming ideas that bubbled over like a pot on the stove. As we spoke, the world around us faded into a soothing blur of colors and sounds, creating a sanctuary where only our creativity thrived. It felt as if we were constructing something not only artistic but deeply meaningful—a mirror reflecting the complexities of love itself.

As dusk painted the sky in strokes of lavender and gold, we meandered back into the heart of the market, the vibrant atmosphere transformed into a cozy haven under the twinkling fairy lights that adorned the stalls. The energy pulsed around us, laughter mingling with the soft sounds of acoustic music drifting through the air, wrapping us in a tapestry of connection.

We paused by a cozy little café nestled between two stalls, the enticing scent of freshly brewed coffee wafting through the open windows. The café was an inviting nook, with its rustic wooden tables and mismatched chairs, a haven where conversations flowed freely. "Let's celebrate our new venture," Ethan suggested, his enthusiasm contagious.

We settled into a corner table, the hum of chatter surrounding us like a warm blanket. As we sipped our drinks, I couldn't help but steal glances at him. The way the dim light played on his features, accentuating the softness in his gaze, made my heart flutter with an excitement I hadn't anticipated.

"I was thinking," I began, a slight hesitation creeping into my voice. "Maybe we could interview the couples we photograph. Get their stories, the raw truths behind their connections."

Ethan leaned in, intrigued. "I love that idea! We could add their words to the images, intertwining their narratives with the visuals. It would create a deeper connection for those who view it."

The prospect thrilled me. It wasn't just about taking photos; it was about weaving together the rich tapestry of human experience, showcasing love in all its forms. With every conversation we shared, I felt our connection grow stronger, an invisible thread weaving our lives together in unexpected ways.

As the night unfolded, we discussed the logistics of our project, jotting down notes and ideas on a napkin that quickly became a chaotic canvas of our shared vision. I felt a spark of excitement dance within me, a flicker of hope that maybe, just maybe, this collaboration could lead us somewhere beautiful.

With our drinks finished and the market winding down, we stepped outside, the cool night air refreshing against my skin. The stars began to pepper the sky, twinkling like distant promises, each one a reminder of the vast possibilities that lay ahead.

"Let's start tomorrow," Ethan suggested, his voice low and filled with determination. "We'll head to the park first thing and see who we can find. There's bound to be couples enjoying the weekend, and we can ask if they're willing to share their stories."

I nodded, my heart racing with anticipation. "I can't wait," I replied, feeling a mix of excitement and nervousness swirl within me. The prospect of approaching strangers, inviting them to share their stories, felt daunting yet invigorating.

As we parted ways at the corner of the street, a sense of contentment washed over me. I could feel the energy of our project coursing through my veins, a blend of passion and purpose that ignited my spirit. I walked home, replaying our conversations in my mind, each detail a brushstroke adding to the masterpiece we were about to create together.

The next morning arrived with the promise of new beginnings. The sunlight streamed through my window, casting a golden glow across my room, and I could hardly contain my excitement. I dressed quickly, throwing on a comfortable sundress that swayed with each step. My heart raced as I grabbed my camera, a familiar weight in my hands that felt like a key to unlocking untold stories.

Ethan met me at the park, his smile bright and infectious. "Ready to change lives?" he quipped, his eyes glimmering with mischief.

I laughed, feeling the energy between us crackle like electricity. "Let's capture some love stories," I replied, determination swelling within me.

As we wandered through the park, we approached couples basking in the warm sun, sharing laughter and whispered secrets. Each interaction felt like peeling back layers of a beautifully wrapped gift, revealing the heart of each relationship. We heard stories of how they met, the obstacles they had overcome, and the little things that made their love special. Each story was a thread in the tapestry we were weaving, a testament to resilience, vulnerability, and the magic of connection.

With every photograph I snapped, I felt the weight of my past begin to lift. I was no longer just an observer; I was a participant in the intricate dance of love. My heart swelled with each story shared, a reminder of the beauty that could emerge from even the most chaotic of lives.

As the day unfolded, we found ourselves laughing and exploring the depths of human connection in a way I had never imagined. With each story and snapshot, I felt a bond growing between Ethan and me, a shared understanding that transcended words.

Our project blossomed into something profound, and with every frame captured, I realized that I was not only rediscovering my passion for photography but also forging a connection with someone who saw the world as I did. The journey we embarked upon together became a reflection of our lives, interwoven in a way that felt exhilarating and uncharted.

As dusk began to settle over the park, painting the sky in hues of orange and pink, I turned to Ethan, the realization dawning on me. This was more than just a project; it was a partnership that was redefining love and trust, shaping the narrative of our own lives. And as I stood there, camera in hand and heart wide open, I felt ready to embrace whatever came next, confident that together, we could capture the beauty of love in all its forms.

Chapter 22: A Storm Brewing

The wind swirled through the bustling streets of Chicago, weaving its way around the towering skyscrapers that stood like giants against the bruised sky. The scent of impending rain mingled with the fragrant air of roasted coffee and fresh pastries from the nearby café. I leaned against the cool glass of the gallery window, staring out at the people hurrying along the sidewalk, their umbrellas at the ready, as dark clouds gathered overhead, creating a foreboding backdrop for the evening ahead. My heart thudded in my chest, a drumbeat of anxiety that synced with the distant rumble of thunder. This was it—my art would finally be unveiled, a culmination of countless sleepless nights and fervent brushstrokes.

My mind was a tempest of thoughts, each wave crashing against the other, churning up insecurities and doubts. What if no one liked my work? What if I stood there, exposed and vulnerable, while the crowd whispered about how it failed to capture the essence of what I intended? The very idea made my stomach twist into knots. The gallery, typically a sanctuary of creativity, felt more like a stage where I would be put on display, my heart and soul painted onto canvas for strangers to scrutinize.

Yet, in the midst of my brewing storm, Ethan stood beside me, an unwavering anchor in the chaos of my mind. His calm demeanor was a balm for my anxiety, his presence reassuring as he adjusted the delicate collar of his shirt, preparing for the event with an air of nonchalance that I envied. He had been my steadfast supporter, a constant source of encouragement throughout this journey, reminding me that art was about expression, not perfection. "Just be yourself," he would say, his voice steady and warm. But "being myself" felt like an uphill battle when all I could think about was the impending storm—both in the skies and within me.

As the guests began to filter into the gallery, the atmosphere shifted. Laughter echoed off the polished concrete floors, mingling with the soft strains of jazz wafting from the corner where a small band had set up. I took a deep breath, trying to calm the raging tempest within. My heart fluttered as I caught glimpses of familiar faces—friends, mentors, and fellow artists—each one a beacon of support. Yet, as I scanned the room, my gaze landed on a figure that sent a chill through my veins. Claire.

She entered with the kind of confidence that seemed to part the crowd like a ship cutting through water. Her laughter rang out, bright and sharp, piercing through the fog of my insecurities. She was stunning, dressed in a crimson dress that hugged her curves and accentuated her fiery hair. My heart sank at the sight of her, a dark cloud looming over the evening. Claire was everything I felt I wasn't—glamorous, bold, effortlessly charming. She had a magnetic pull that drew people in, and I could feel their attention shifting as she engaged in conversation with Ethan.

My pulse quickened, and I fought against the urge to flee. My thoughts spiraled, images of her laughing with him while I stood in the shadows, a mere observer to the connection they shared. The knot in my stomach tightened, and the storm within me threatened to burst forth. What if Ethan preferred her? What if he saw me as nothing more than a passing fancy, a fleeting distraction? I tried to shake the thoughts away, to ground myself in the moment, but they clung to me like rain-soaked fabric.

With each passing moment, I felt more like an outsider in my own event. I watched as Claire and Ethan conversed animatedly, their chemistry palpable, and my heart sank further. The vibrant colors of my artwork, carefully selected to express my innermost thoughts and feelings, faded into the background. I could almost hear them—my canvases, pleading for recognition while I remained paralyzed by self-doubt.

"Are you okay?" Ethan's voice broke through my reverie, warm and concerned. I turned to him, forcing a smile that felt more like a grimace. The storm inside me raged on, but I didn't want him to see how vulnerable I felt. I shook my head slightly, hoping to banish the darkness that threatened to engulf me.

"I'm fine," I lied, my voice barely above a whisper. "Just a little nervous." I could hear the quiver in my words, betraying my façade of composure. Ethan studied my face, his brows knitting together in concern.

"Hey, you've worked hard for this," he reminded me gently, his gaze unwavering. "You deserve to shine tonight. Just look at how many people came out to support you." He gestured towards the room, and I noticed the crowd again, a sea of smiling faces and eager eyes. The momentary distraction helped to dull the edges of my anxiety.

"Yeah, I guess," I replied, forcing my focus onto the vibrant canvases lining the walls, each one a reflection of my journey, my struggles, and my victories. They were all I had poured my heart into, and yet, the weight of Claire's presence made me question their value.

As the minutes ticked away, my resolve wavered. Claire approached, her eyes sparkling with mischief, and I felt as if I were standing at the eye of a hurricane. "Ethan!" she called, her voice smooth and inviting. "I was just telling everyone how talented you are. Your support must mean the world to our dear artist." She gestured toward me, her words dripping with honeyed sweetness, but I could sense the undertone of competition—a challenge issued without a single word spoken.

I swallowed hard, the storm raging inside me amplifying her words. Ethan smiled, his expression softening as he turned to me, as if to shield me from the tempest she brought. "She's amazing, Claire. Her art speaks volumes," he said, his sincerity shining through.

But as I stood there, feeling like a small boat caught in a raging sea, I couldn't shake the feeling that the storm was just beginning.

The atmosphere in the gallery hummed with excitement, yet my heart felt like a stone, heavy and unyielding against the tide of anticipation washing over me. Each conversation flowed around me like a current, vibrant and alive, but I was adrift, isolated in my own whirlwind of emotions. I plastered on a smile, hoping to appear composed as guests admired my artwork, vibrant splashes of color mingling with whispers of admiration. But as I glanced toward Ethan and Claire, that cheerful façade crumbled.

Claire leaned in closer to Ethan, her laughter ringing like a bell, light and carefree. I could see the way he looked at her, a sparkle in his eyes that ignited the embers of jealousy flickering in my chest. They shared a moment that felt intimate, the kind of closeness that sent my heart spiraling. The warmth of the gallery seemed to dissipate, replaced by a chill that gnawed at my insides. I fought against the tide of insecurities threatening to pull me under, reminding myself of the journey I had undertaken to get to this moment. Each brushstroke on the canvas had been infused with my hopes and fears, a reflection of my spirit laid bare.

Taking a deep breath, I stepped away from the crowd, seeking refuge in a quieter corner of the gallery where the paintings hung like whispers in the air. I gazed at my work—a riot of colors that danced together in chaotic harmony. Each piece told a story, revealing fragments of my soul in shades of blue and gold, the textures evoking emotions I often struggled to articulate. Yet even amidst the pride swelling in my chest, Claire's presence loomed large, threatening to overshadow the very essence of my creations.

As I contemplated the colors swirling on the canvas before me, a soft voice broke through my reverie. "You have an incredible talent." I turned to find a woman standing beside me, her eyes alight with genuine admiration. She wore a tailored blazer and a soft smile that put me at ease.

"Thank you," I replied, a warmth spreading through me at her compliment. "It's just—" I hesitated, glancing over my shoulder at Ethan, who was now animatedly discussing my work with Claire, their shared laughter echoing like a taunt. "It's just a reflection of what I feel."

"I can see that. Art has a way of capturing emotions we often can't express," she said, her gaze lingering on my pieces. "I'm a curator for a few galleries in the area, and I believe you have a unique voice. Your work deserves to be seen."

Her words wrapped around me like a soothing balm, easing the tumult within. "Really? You think so?" I asked, my heart quickening at the thought of opportunities beyond this night.

"Absolutely. Don't let anyone dim your light. Keep creating," she encouraged, her sincerity cutting through the fog of doubt clouding my mind.

Just then, the ambient chatter faded as the gallery lights dimmed slightly, drawing everyone's attention to a makeshift stage where a local artist was about to give a speech. The curator smiled warmly before drifting away to mingle with other guests, leaving me alone with my thoughts.

I turned my gaze back to Ethan and Claire. The sound of her laughter mixed with the low hum of the crowd, and I felt a mix of envy and longing. I wanted that easy connection, that effortless camaraderie. But what I craved even more was for Ethan to look at me like that, to see the depth behind my colors and not just the surface. The flutter in my stomach morphed into a tempest, tossing me between despair and hope.

As the speech commenced, I took a step back, retreating into the shadows to gather my thoughts. The room buzzed with energy, but my heart felt like a muted drum, drowning beneath the noise. I wished for the storm to pass, for the sun to break through the clouds and illuminate my moment instead of shrouding it in doubt.

Suddenly, a presence pulled me back to reality. "Hey," Ethan said softly, stepping away from Claire and slipping beside me. The warmth radiating from him felt like a beacon amidst the storm. "You okay? You've been quiet."

"Just taking it all in," I replied, forcing a smile that didn't quite reach my eyes. "It's a bit overwhelming, isn't it?"

He studied me for a moment, his brow furrowing in concern. "You've put so much into this. Don't let anyone, including Claire, take away your joy. You should be proud."

His words sparked a flicker of resolve within me. "You're right. I just wish—" I hesitated, my voice trailing off as I glanced at Claire, who seemed to have her claws sunk into him with the ease of someone who had always been there. "I wish I could feel more confident."

Ethan's expression softened, and he stepped closer, leaning in so only I could hear. "You are incredible. The way you see the world, it's unlike anything I've ever known. Your art, it's not just good; it's powerful. Trust in that."

His encouragement enveloped me like a warm embrace, pushing back against the chill Claire had cast over my heart. For a moment, I allowed myself to bask in his unwavering belief in me, a comfort I desperately needed.

As the speech came to an end, applause erupted, a wave of sound washing over us. I turned back to my paintings, taking a deep breath, letting the vibrant colors fill my senses. My heart quickened with renewed determination, a resolve blossoming within me.

Ethan's gaze lingered on me, and I could feel his energy, a tether anchoring me to the moment. "Shall we?" he asked, gesturing toward the center of the gallery where people began to gather.

I nodded, taking his hand, feeling a jolt of electricity at the contact. Together, we stepped into the sea of people, ready to face whatever storm lay ahead. The clouds outside threatened to burst, but in that moment, with Ethan beside me, I felt ready to dance in the rain.

The gallery pulsated with life, a canvas of conversations and laughter that filled the air like a sweet perfume. I stood there, surrounded by the vibrant colors of my art, but my focus remained tethered to Ethan, who appeared to be entirely captivated by Claire. Their animated dialogue painted a picture I didn't want to see—a perfect snapshot of a connection I feared I could never replicate. Yet, amidst the swirling thoughts of envy and inadequacy, the chatter of the crowd began to blend into a soothing hum, grounding me in the moment.

As I caught glimpses of the artworks hanging around the room, I realized that each piece held a fragment of my journey. My fingers had danced over the canvas with joy and despair, the brushstrokes representing a tapestry of emotions that I had poured into my work. I recalled the quiet nights spent in solitude, lost in a world of color and creativity, the soothing sound of my paintbrush gliding across the fabric as I sought to make sense of my own chaotic feelings. The beauty of the gallery, with its high ceilings and soft lighting, felt like a cocoon—each artwork a testament to my growth, my trials, and my triumphs.

But as the evening wore on, I could feel the air shift, the storm outside becoming a metaphor for the turmoil inside me. My heart raced when I noticed Ethan and Claire moving closer together, their proximity tightening the knot of anxiety in my chest. Claire leaned in, her laughter pealing like a bell, and I felt a pang of longing—longing not just for Ethan's affection, but for the kind of confidence that radiated from her, like sunlight piercing through heavy clouds.

With a resolute breath, I decided I couldn't stand idle any longer. I had come too far to let self-doubt ruin this night. I slipped away from my corner, where shadows clung like old memories, and made my way toward my paintings. The rhythmic thrum of the crowd surrounded me, but I focused on my pieces, recalling the stories behind each one. One canvas depicted a stormy ocean, the waves crashing violently against the rocks—an embodiment of my fears and frustrations. Another showcased a serene landscape bathed in sunset hues, a reminder of the hope and calm that followed every tempest.

As I stood before my work, an unexpected presence interrupted my thoughts. "Your pieces are stunning." A tall man with tousled hair and an easy smile approached, a glass of wine cradled in his hand. "I've been drawn to them since I walked in. They speak with such authenticity."

"Thank you," I said, my voice steadying as I turned to meet his gaze. "It means a lot to hear that. Art is...well, it's my way of processing everything."

"I can see that," he replied, gesturing toward the painting of the ocean. "This one in particular resonates. The chaos, yet the beauty in it."

I smiled, feeling a flicker of pride igniting within me. "It reflects a part of me," I confessed, the words spilling out before I could stop them. "Sometimes, life feels overwhelming, like it's pulling me under, but there's beauty to be found even in the storm."

He nodded, his expression thoughtful. "That's the magic of art. It connects us through our shared experiences. I'm Michael, by the way."

"Nice to meet you," I said, extending my hand.

As we spoke, I found my confidence gradually returning, the knot in my stomach loosening with each exchange. Michael was easy to talk to, his passion for art evident in the way he discussed various techniques and styles. He asked questions about my creative process, and with each response, I felt myself stepping further into the light, leaving the shadows of self-doubt behind.

Meanwhile, I caught sight of Ethan again, standing at the center of the gallery with Claire, their chemistry as undeniable as the electricity in the air. But instead of crumbling under the weight of jealousy, I turned my attention back to Michael, who was now animatedly explaining his own artistic endeavors. I found solace in the way he spoke about his experiences, weaving tales of inspiration that resonated deeply within me.

"Art isn't just about what you see; it's about what you feel," he said, a fervor igniting his words. "It's about translating those emotions onto the canvas, letting the viewer feel something profound."

The more we talked, the more I began to realize that this night was not just about my art, but about connecting with others who understood its power. I stole another glance at Ethan, who was now engrossed in conversation with Claire, but instead of the familiar pang of jealousy, I felt a spark of hope. This was my moment to shine, to embrace the recognition I deserved.

Before long, the evening began to take on a different shape. Laughter rang out, conversations flourished, and I felt the gallery transforming into a vibrant community of art lovers. People drifted from painting to painting, their whispers of admiration filling the room, and I found myself swept up in the excitement. Each compliment and shared story brought me closer to the realization that I was not alone; my journey resonated with others.

And then, as if scripted by the universe, the lights dimmed once more, signaling the official opening of my exhibition. Ethan stepped forward, his gaze sweeping over the crowd, a beacon of confidence that I hoped to emulate. "Thank you all for being here tonight," he began, his voice strong and steady. "This exhibition showcases not just the art itself, but the heart behind it—an artist's journey of self-discovery."

I stood there, a whirlpool of emotions surging within me. As Ethan spoke, I felt the weight of Claire's presence diminish, replaced by a growing sense of belonging. I realized that this was my moment to embrace—not only my art but my own self-worth. With each word he spoke, I felt the storm outside echo the one within, building toward a powerful crescendo.

"Art is a reflection of our experiences, our dreams, and our struggles," Ethan continued, his eyes locking onto mine for a brief moment, igniting a warmth that spread through me. "Tonight, we celebrate not just the colors on these canvases but the journey of the artist who created them."

Applause erupted, ringing through the gallery like music, and I couldn't help but feel a swell of pride rising within me. This was what I had fought for—the opportunity to share my voice, my art, and my truth with the world. As the crowd cheered, I took a step forward, no longer just an observer but a participant in my own story.

With every heartbeat, I felt the storm begin to settle, the clouds parting to reveal a sky painted in hues of possibility. I had emerged from the shadows, no longer weighed down by insecurity but buoyed by the love of art, the support of friends, and the unexpected connections formed on this electrifying evening.

In that moment, I knew that even amidst the storms that life would inevitably bring, I had the strength to weather them. I had my art, my voice, and, perhaps most importantly, I had found my place in the world. And as I stood there, bathed in the warm glow of acceptance and possibility, I felt ready to embrace whatever came next.

Chapter 23: Through the Rain

The gallery buzzes with excitement, a whirlpool of voices, laughter, and clinking glasses that blend into a symphony of art appreciation. Vibrant canvases drape the walls, each piece a window into someone else's soul, but in this moment, I can hardly focus on them. My own heart thuds insistently against my ribcage, a frantic drummer in a parade that refuses to end. I weave through the crowd, my fingers grazing the cool, smooth surface of the artwork, seeking solace in the textures and colors. Every step feels heavier, and I can almost hear my self-doubt whispering in the background, a nagging presence I can't quite shake off.

Suddenly, the atmosphere shifts. A cacophony of thunder rumbles in the distance, and the rain begins to fall—a torrential downpour that sends the gallery's patrons glancing uneasily toward the large glass windows. The storm becomes a backdrop to my internal turmoil, mirroring the chaotic swirl of emotions within me. Each raindrop pounds against the glass like a tiny drumbeat, a steady reminder of the fears I've kept at bay. Just when I think I might lose myself entirely in this tempest, I feel a presence beside me.

Ethan emerges from the throng, his expression a mix of concern and admiration that sends a surge of warmth through my veins. He's like a lighthouse in the storm, guiding me back to safety. "Hey," he says softly, his voice cutting through the clamor. "You look like you could use a break." With a gentle tug, he leads me away from the chaos, his hand warm and reassuring around my wrist. I follow him into a quieter corner of the gallery, where the noise dims to a distant hum, and the shadows embrace us like a comforting blanket.

The air here is thick with the scent of paint and varnish, a fragrance I've grown to love, and I take a deep breath, trying to center myself. Ethan turns to face me, his blue eyes brimming with sincerity, and I can feel the weight of my worries begin to lift, even if just a little. "I just wanted to say," he begins, a small smile playing on his lips, "I'm so proud of you. Your work is absolutely stunning. You've captured the essence of love in a way I've never seen before."

His words envelop me like a warm embrace, washing over my insecurities like the rain outside. I've poured my heart into this collection, each brushstroke a piece of my soul, but hearing him say it out loud somehow makes it all feel real. My cheeks flush with warmth, and I can't help but smile back at him, feeling a spark of hope. "Thank you," I reply, my voice steadier than I expected. "It means a lot coming from you."

He steps a little closer, the distance between us narrowing, and I can feel the air crackle with unspoken words. The chaos of the gallery fades into the background as we stand there, two souls adrift in a storm. "I mean it," he insists, his gaze steady and unwavering. "You've taken something as complicated as love and made it beautiful, tangible. It's more than art; it's a testament to what we all long for."

I can't help but glance down, a mixture of embarrassment and pride swelling within me. He sees me, truly sees me, and that realization sends my heart racing. The doubts that had clawed at the edges of my mind retreat momentarily, unable to withstand the warmth of his belief in me. "I just… I wanted to express something real," I confess, my voice softening. "It's hard to put into words sometimes."

Ethan steps back slightly, leaning against the cool wall as the rain beats down like a heartbeat in the background. "You've done it, though," he replies, his smile brightening the dim light of our corner. "Every piece tells a story—stories that need to be heard." I can see the rain cascading outside, each droplet weaving a tapestry of chaos and beauty, much like my own emotions. It's as if the universe is conspiring to remind me that even storms can yield something remarkable.

The storm outside intensifies, rattling the glass and casting shadows that dance across the floor, but in this moment, with Ethan's unwavering gaze fixed on me, the storm within begins to quiet. "It's just hard not to feel overwhelmed sometimes," I admit, my voice barely a whisper as I brush a stray lock of hair behind my ear. "I worry that maybe I'm not good enough."

Ethan shakes his head, a look of fierce determination etching his features. "You are more than enough. You're a force, a storm of creativity and passion. Don't let the chaos drown you." His words ignite a fire within me, and for the first time, I begin to believe them. The storm outside feels like a distant echo as I stand here, tethered to him by something greater than just the moment.

As the rain continues to pour, each drop a reminder of the tempest outside, I feel a different kind of storm brewing—one of hope and possibility. I take a deep breath, and for the first time, I allow myself to imagine a future painted with the vibrant colors of my dreams. In this corner of the gallery, amidst the chaos of the world outside, I find clarity. With Ethan by my side, I realize that I can weather any storm and come out stronger on the other side, my heart full of love and creativity.

The air is thick with anticipation as we linger in the shadows of the gallery, the rhythmic patter of rain creating a soothing cadence that contrasts sharply with the earlier chaos. The storm outside blurs the world, transforming the vibrant cityscape into a watercolor painting, the colors bleeding into one another under the weight of the downpour. It's as if nature has conspired to provide a fitting backdrop for the emotions swirling within me. I steal a glance at Ethan, whose presence feels both calming and exhilarating, a paradox that sends a shiver of excitement down my spine.

"Let's step outside for a moment," he suggests, and I nod, intrigued by the idea of facing the elements together. We weave through the throng of art enthusiasts, their faces illuminated by the soft glow of the gallery lights, each absorbed in their own reverie. The moment we reach the door, a blast of cool air greets us, mingled with the earthy scent of wet pavement. The rain slants down in sheets, drenching the streets, but I feel an inexplicable urge to embrace it.

Once outside, we stand beneath the overhang, sheltered from the worst of the storm while still able to feel its power. The world beyond is alive, a vibrant spectacle of swirling raindrops and shimmering reflections. The glow from the streetlights transforms the streets into a dance floor of light and shadow, where every puddle becomes a portal to another world. I can't help but laugh, the sound bright and unrestrained, echoing in the midst of the rain's symphony.

Ethan grins at me, his expression a mixture of admiration and mischief. "You look radiant out here," he says, his voice low and sincere, as if sharing a secret meant only for me. I feel warmth creep up my cheeks, a blush that seems absurd in the face of the torrential rain. "It's just the rain," I respond, though the spark in his gaze makes me reconsider.

"Maybe it's a little of both," he replies, stepping closer until the distance between us feels charged with unspoken possibilities. "You should let yourself feel that way more often. You have this way of lighting up even the darkest corners." I glance down, contemplating the compliment, trying to weave its meaning into the tapestry of my self-image. Am I really capable of bringing light to darkness?

The rain intensifies, and without thinking, I take a small step into the storm, letting the droplets drench my hair and clothes. "It feels alive," I exclaim, spinning in a small circle, my laughter ringing out like a bell. Ethan watches me, a bemused smile playing on his lips, and I can see the admiration in his eyes evolve into something deeper, something that sends a thrill through my entire being.

"Maybe it is alive," he muses, stepping into the rain beside me, his laughter harmonizing with mine as we both surrender to the storm. It's liberating to let go of the weight of expectation, to become part of something larger than ourselves. The world shrinks to just the two of us, lost in a tempest of joy and connection. I feel like a child again, unburdened by worries, if only for a moment.

As the rain pours, the space between us collapses further, and I can feel the heat radiating from him, mingling with the coolness of the rain-soaked air. The chemistry between us is palpable, an electric current that pulses with every shared glance, every laugh. I find myself wanting to bridge that distance entirely, to feel his warmth envelop me in this chilly downpour. But a flutter of uncertainty rises within me, a whisper that questions whether this moment is merely an illusion, a fleeting escape from the reality that awaits us inside.

"Do you ever think about how life is like this storm?" I ask, surprising myself with the profundity of the question. "How it can be so chaotic yet strangely beautiful?" Ethan cocks his head, his expression thoughtful. "I do now. I guess we just have to dance in the rain and embrace it." He reaches for my hand, and I feel a rush of exhilaration as our fingers intertwine, the warmth of his skin grounding me amidst the tempest.

Our laughter mingles with the sounds of the rain, and as we begin to sway, I realize we're not just dancing in the storm; we're creating our own rhythm, a melody that speaks to the connection we've forged. With each movement, the boundaries between us dissolve further, and I can almost forget the uncertainties lurking just beyond our bubble of laughter. The world feels far away, a distant memory blurred by the rain and the electricity that crackles in the air around us.

Just then, a flash of lightning illuminates the sky, followed by a thunderous boom that reverberates in my chest. I gasp, half in surprise and half in delight, and Ethan pulls me closer, his breath warm against my ear as he whispers, "I think we should head back inside before we're completely soaked." But I don't want to go back just yet; I want to savor this moment, this whirlwind of emotion and connection.

"Just a little longer," I plead, my voice soft and earnest. "Let's stay out here a bit more." He studies me for a heartbeat, as if weighing my request, before nodding slowly, a smile spreading across his face. "Okay, but only if you promise to keep dancing."

We spin and twirl, lost in our own world, the rain washing away the remnants of doubt and fear. I can feel the vibrant energy between us crackling like the storm itself, and I find solace in the rhythm of our laughter. In that moment, I realize that sometimes, amidst the chaos of life, you just need to embrace the storm and dance. The outside world fades, and the only truth is the unbreakable bond we're forming—a testament to love, vulnerability, and the beauty of simply being alive.

As the rain continues to cascade around us, I lose myself in the moment, letting the rhythm of our laughter and the downpour blend into a melody that feels almost sacred. Ethan's presence beside me feels electric, like the very storm that surrounds us, each drop of rain dancing in the glow of the streetlights. We create our own bubble, a vibrant world suspended between the chaos of the gallery and the intensity of the storm. I find myself wanting to remember every detail—the way his hair clings to his forehead, the laughter lines that crinkle at the corners of his eyes, the warmth radiating from him that feels like a lifeline.

We take a step back from the edge of the overhang, letting the rain envelop us. I close my eyes, tilting my face toward the sky, letting the droplets pelt my skin like tiny kisses from the universe. "You know," I say, my voice rising above the sound of the storm, "there's something exhilarating about just letting go."

Ethan nods, his gaze thoughtful. "It's like shedding the weight of expectations. In moments like this, you realize the world can be messy and beautiful at the same time." His words resonate deeply within me, as if he's plucking the strings of a hidden chord in my heart. It's a revelation I've been seeking, and his insight somehow makes it all feel more attainable.

We retreat beneath the awning, panting slightly from laughter and exertion, our shoulders brushing against each other. The wind shifts, and I can feel the chill creeping back in, contrasting with the warmth that has enveloped us. I shiver, more from the abruptness of reality than from the temperature, and Ethan glances at me, his expression shifting to one of concern. "Let's get you back inside before you catch a cold," he suggests, reaching for my hand again.

Reluctantly, I allow him to guide me back into the gallery, but as we step through the doorway, the ambiance shifts. The gallery feels transformed, a warm sanctuary bursting with vibrant art and animated chatter. The storm outside might rage on, but inside, the atmosphere is thick with camaraderie and creativity. I catch glimpses of my pieces, each canvas alive with color and emotion, glowing under the soft, flattering lights. I wonder if I truly belong here, surrounded by such talent and vision.

Ethan leans closer, his voice low, almost conspiratorial. "You know, I think your work is already making waves. I overheard someone mention wanting to buy one of your pieces." My heart skips a beat. The thought of someone wanting to own a piece of my soul is both thrilling and terrifying. "Really?" I stammer, my mind racing. "Which one?"

"The one with the couple in the rain," he replies, a soft smile gracing his lips. "It's stunning. You've captured a fleeting moment in time, and it feels so raw and real." I glance over at the painting, a swirl of blues and grays intermingled with vibrant strokes of crimson and gold. I remember the inspiration behind it, a memory of laughter shared under an umbrella, the weight of worries lifted by simple joy.

"I can't believe someone would want to buy that," I murmur, my voice tinged with disbelief. "It feels so personal."

"That's the beauty of art," Ethan replies, his gaze unwavering. "It resonates with others because it reflects the truths we sometimes struggle to articulate. You've poured your heart into this, and that authenticity shines through."

His words wrap around me like a warm embrace, pulling me back from the edge of doubt. I realize then that I'm not just an artist—I'm a storyteller, weaving narratives through color and form. In that moment of clarity, I understand that the storm outside and the storm within are part of the same journey, a journey toward authenticity and connection.

With newfound confidence, I decide to mingle with the guests, to engage in conversations about my work. Ethan stays close by, an unwavering support, and as we navigate the crowd together, I can feel the energy shifting. People approach me, curious and excited, asking questions and sharing their thoughts about my pieces. I share stories about my inspiration, the struggles behind each stroke, and as I talk, I see their eyes light up, reflecting the emotions I've poured into my work.

The storm outside begins to subside, the rain reducing to a gentle patter against the windows. I find a moment to step back and take it all in, the gallery alive with chatter and laughter, each person a thread in the tapestry of the evening. I glance at Ethan, who is engaged in conversation with a group of patrons, his smile warm and inviting. My heart swells with gratitude—this moment, this night, feels monumental.

Just as I'm about to rejoin him, the gallery doors swing open, and a rush of wind sweeps through the entrance, bringing with it the scent of rain-soaked earth. A figure appears, silhouetted against the darkened sky, their expression unreadable. The atmosphere shifts, a collective intake of breath rippling through the crowd as the figure steps inside. My heart races; the room buzzes with uncertainty.

Ethan catches my eye, a flicker of concern crossing his features as the figure draws closer. The tension is palpable, and I can feel a knot forming in my stomach. I recognize the newcomer—an art critic known for their sharp tongue and discerning eye. My pulse quickens as they survey the room, their gaze finally landing on me.

"Ah, the artist of the evening," they say, their voice smooth yet commanding. The crowd parts slightly, as if they sense the gravity of the moment. "I've heard much about your work. The piece with the couple in the rain—an intriguing choice."

I swallow hard, unsure whether to feel flattered or intimidated. "Thank you," I reply, my voice steadier than I feel. "I wanted to capture a moment of connection amid chaos."

Their expression shifts, and for a brief second, I catch a glimpse of something softening in their eyes. "Art should provoke thought and stir emotion. It seems you've accomplished that," they concede, before turning their attention back to the crowd.

As the critic moves on, I feel a wave of relief wash over me. I've faced the storm, both inside and out, and emerged with my head held high. Ethan steps up beside me, his eyes sparkling with pride. "You handled that beautifully," he says, his voice warm with admiration.

"I couldn't have done it without you," I admit, feeling the weight of his support as if it's a tangible force anchoring me. The night stretches on, filled with laughter, conversations, and art. I realize that this journey is just beginning, and while storms may come and go, I'm learning to embrace each moment, to find beauty in the chaos, and to dance through the rain.

Chapter 24: When the Floodgates Open

The sun dipped low over the sprawling landscape of Silverbrook, casting a warm golden hue across the neatly manicured lawns and brightly colored flower beds that bordered the grand estate. The air hummed with laughter and chatter, a symphony of joy that danced alongside the intoxicating aroma of fresh hors d'oeuvres being served on delicate china. I stood at the edge of the lively crowd, a glass of sparkling cider in hand, savoring the effervescence as it tickled my nose. My heart swelled with pride; this night was a celebration of my hard work, and I couldn't let a whisper of doubt dampen my spirit.

Ethan was nearby, a constant presence that grounded me amidst the excitement. He moved through the gathering with effortless charm, his laughter ringing out like music, pulling in guests as if he were the sun around which they revolved. It was in these moments that I felt invincible, buoyed by his unwavering support. His eyes, a deep shade of amber that reminded me of the autumn leaves, glinted with pride as he caught my gaze, offering a warm smile that made my heart flutter. The world around us melted away, and for a brief instant, it felt like we were the only two people in existence.

I laughed, tossing my hair back, trying to blend into the lightheartedness of the evening. Friends and colleagues approached, their eyes sparkling with admiration for the work I had poured my heart into. The project—a collaborative effort that had consumed months of our lives—had finally come to fruition. The overwhelming sense of accomplishment coursed through me like a heady rush, filling the cracks of self-doubt that I often found creeping in.

However, the illusion of tranquility shattered when I overheard Claire's voice, melodic yet laced with an edge, discussing our project with a group of guests. "It's stunning, truly. The way she captured the essence of the theme…" My stomach churned. Claire's lingering presence in Ethan's life felt like a storm cloud on an otherwise clear day. The very name that had once echoed with camaraderie now sliced through the air, sharp and unwelcome.

In a moment fueled by an unsettling blend of insecurity and determination, I found myself striding toward her, my heart racing. Each step felt heavy with the weight of unspoken words, emotions teetering on the edge of eruption. "Can we talk?" I blurted out, my voice sharper than I intended. A hush fell over the group, eyes darting between us, the air thick with tension.

Claire turned, surprise flickering across her features before it settled into a calculating look. "Sure," she replied, her tone smooth, though the underlying edge hinted at her awareness of the discomfort I felt. We stepped aside, and the noise of the party faded into a distant hum.

"What's going on with you?" I started, the question tumbling out more forcefully than I had anticipated. "You keep hovering around Ethan, and I can't shake the feeling that you're... I don't know, trying to make something happen."

Claire crossed her arms, her expression shifting from confusion to defensiveness. "You think I'm after him?" The challenge in her voice made me hesitate, but the honesty bubbling up inside propelled me forward.

"I just—" I paused, searching for the right words. "It feels like you're... still a part of his life, and I don't know how to fit into that. It's like I'm competing with a ghost."

Her eyes narrowed, and for a fleeting moment, I feared I had miscalculated. But then, to my astonishment, she sighed, the tension in her shoulders relaxing slightly. "You're not the only one with insecurities, you know." Her voice softened, a hint of vulnerability breaking through the facade. "I've been trying to figure out my place since things ended with Ethan. It's hard seeing someone move on."

I blinked, momentarily taken aback. "You're still affected by that?"

"Of course." Claire looked away, her gaze falling to the ground as if the weight of her words pressed her down. "Ethan was my best friend before we dated. Losing that connection... it's been tough."

A flicker of empathy ignited within me, igniting a bond I hadn't anticipated. "I didn't know. I thought you were... I don't know, completely over it."

Claire's laughter was a dry chuckle, devoid of humor. "I wish it were that simple. Watching him with you is like watching a part of my past I can't quite let go of."

The unexpected clarity in her confession soothed the tempest brewing in my heart. This wasn't just about competition; it was about two women caught in the wake of a shared history. I felt a strange kinship with her, understanding the delicate balance of friendships and romantic entanglements.

"I didn't mean to intrude on something that mattered to you," I admitted, my voice softer now, tinged with sincerity. "I care about him, but I also don't want to step on anyone's toes. I just want us all to be happy."

Claire nodded slowly, her posture shifting from defensive to contemplative. "Maybe we can figure this out together? I don't want to be at odds with you. You seem great, and if he's happy with you, then..." She trailed off, the words hanging in the air.

I felt a warmth blooming in my chest, a sense of relief washing over me like the gentle tide. "I'd like that. Let's try to be allies instead of enemies."

In that moment, the floodgates of understanding opened wide, washing away the tension that had lingered like a shadow between us. We talked, and the conversations flowed with unexpected ease, as if the barriers that had kept us apart crumbled, revealing a shared desire for happiness and acceptance.

PICTURE PERFECT   249

    As I stepped back into the celebration, the laughter of friends enveloped me once more, but this time, it felt different. Lighter. I had faced my insecurities and found common ground with Claire, a step toward healing not just for her, but for me as well. Ethan caught my eye from across the room, and the warmth of his smile reassured me that I was where I belonged, not just with him, but within myself.

    The night shimmered with the kind of magic that can only be conjured by laughter and soft music, each note curling into the air like wisps of smoke, lingering just long enough to tease the senses. As I moved through the throng of guests, the atmosphere enveloped me like a warm embrace. Each conversation bubbled with excitement, a mixture of praise and hopeful anticipation for the future. My heart, still buoyant from my earlier exchange with Claire, beat in sync with the rhythm of the evening, and for the first time in what felt like an eternity, I allowed myself to bask in the warmth of accomplishment.

    Ethan was a stone's throw away, mingling effortlessly as he engaged in conversation with a group of friends. His charisma radiated like the soft glow of the chandeliers that adorned the ceiling, illuminating his every gesture. I felt a surge of pride as I observed him, marveling at the way he drew people in with his laughter, his easy charm making the world around us seem just a little brighter. It was as if, in this enchanted moment, all my insecurities had taken a back seat, allowing me to revel in the genuine connections that filled the room.

    Suddenly, the laughter crescendoed, drawing my attention to a nearby group where Claire stood, her laughter ringing out like a silver bell. I couldn't help but notice the way her smile lit up her entire face, her animated gestures painting vivid images in the air. The unease that had briefly subsided within me resurfaced like a phantom, gnawing at the edges of my newfound joy. It was in that moment, surrounded by admiration and compliments, that I felt the sharp sting of jealousy creeping in, a dark shadow that threatened to obscure my happiness.

Yet, instead of retreating into my insecurities, I inhaled deeply, savoring the fresh scent of jasmine that wafted through the evening air. With each step, I reminded myself that I was not competing for Ethan's affection; I was simply trying to navigate a world filled with complicated emotions. I leaned against the railing of the balcony, the cool metal grounding me, the city's lights twinkling like stars scattered across a vast ocean.

"Enjoying the view?" Ethan's voice broke through my reverie, and I turned to find him standing beside me, his presence a soothing balm against the turmoil inside.

"Always," I replied, unable to hide my smile. "It's beautiful up here."

His gaze shifted to the horizon, where the last traces of sunlight surrendered to the encroaching night. "Just like you," he mused, and my heart fluttered, feeling both exhilarated and vulnerable under his gaze.

As we shared a comfortable silence, I allowed myself to soak in the warmth of the moment, feeling the soft breeze caress my skin. Just then, Claire emerged from the crowd, her expression a mix of determination and unease as she approached us. The atmosphere shifted, a palpable tension hanging in the air, but instead of feeling threatened, I resolved to stand my ground.

"Can we have a moment?" Claire asked, her tone polite but direct, catching Ethan slightly off-guard.

"Sure," he replied, sensing the gravity in her voice, and took a step back, giving us space. I could see his concern mirrored in his eyes, but I needed this moment with her, if only to clarify the air between us.

"What's on your mind?" I inquired, keeping my tone even, despite the slight quiver of anxiety within me.

"I wanted to apologize," Claire began, her gaze earnest. "For the way I've acted. I didn't mean to make you feel uncomfortable or threatened."

Her sincerity cut through the last of my defenses, and I felt the walls I had built around my heart start to crumble. "Thank you for saying that. I didn't mean to confront you out of nowhere, but I was feeling overwhelmed. I guess it's easy to misinterpret things when insecurities creep in."

Claire nodded, a soft smile breaking through the seriousness. "I know what you mean. I've been in a similar position, watching someone I care about move on. It's... complicated."

A shared understanding blossomed between us, blooming like wildflowers breaking through concrete. "I didn't realize how much we had in common," I admitted, feeling a flicker of hope igniting within me.

"Believe it or not, we're not so different," she said, her tone lightening. "I've spent too long trying to hold onto something that was slipping away. It's exhausting."

"Right? It's like carrying around a weight that you don't even notice until someone helps you set it down," I mused, and she laughed softly, the sound lifting the heaviness of our earlier conversation.

"Exactly. And I think we both need to let go of that weight. It's exhausting being in competition when we could actually be friends."

The prospect of friendship felt surreal, yet liberating. I nodded, my heart racing at the idea of finding common ground rather than remaining adversaries. "I'd like that. It would be nice to support each other instead of feeling like we're in each other's way."

As we talked, the walls that had once divided us dissolved into nothingness, replaced by a genuine connection that blossomed in the open air. In the distance, fireworks erupted, illuminating the night sky in bursts of color, each explosion a reminder that beauty often lies just beyond the horizon of our fears.

"See?" Claire gestured toward the sky, her eyes bright with wonder. "That's exactly what I mean. We don't have to be enemies. We can share the spotlight instead of competing for it."

"Agreed. Here's to sharing the spotlight," I declared, raising my glass in a toast. She laughed again, the sound ringing out in harmony with the fireworks above.

With each passing moment, I felt lighter, unburdened by the weight of jealousy and competition. It was liberating to realize that I didn't have to navigate this world alone. I could find camaraderie even with those I had once viewed as rivals.

The evening unfolded like the petals of a flower, revealing layers of complexity and beauty. I glanced over at Ethan, who had returned to the group of friends, his laughter carrying across the distance, each sound threading itself into the fabric of the night. The flicker of fireworks mirrored the excitement in my heart, the possibilities of what lay ahead stretching infinitely before me.

As the celebration continued, I felt a sense of clarity wash over me, one that resonated with the rhythm of the evening. My life was no longer just a series of competitions and insecurities; it was a tapestry woven with friendship, understanding, and the promise of brighter days. I was ready to embrace it all, confident that together, Claire and I could navigate this complex web of emotions and experiences.

The stars above twinkled like a million tiny promises, each one beckoning me to step forward, to embrace the unexpected. In that moment, I realized that even amid uncertainty, there was beauty to be found.

With the celebration in full swing, I turned my attention back to the vibrant gathering, where the laughter of friends and acquaintances melded into a rich tapestry of sound, punctuated by the occasional clink of glasses and the soft strains of music wafting from the grand piano in the corner. Each note floated through the air like a gentle caress, inviting everyone to let their guard down and simply enjoy the moment. I could feel the adrenaline from my earlier confrontation with Claire fading, replaced by a newfound sense of camaraderie and purpose.

As I weaved through the crowd, I took in the faces illuminated by the soft, golden glow of string lights that adorned the patio. Familiar and unfamiliar faces smiled at me, their admiration genuine and warm. Each compliment felt like a gentle nudge, encouraging me to embrace the confidence that had been bubbling beneath the surface for far too long. I caught sight of Ethan again, effortlessly commanding the room with his infectious enthusiasm, his laughter rising above the chatter like a beacon.

Just then, a gentle tap on my shoulder pulled me from my reverie. I turned to find Julia, one of my closest friends, her eyes sparkling with excitement. "You did it! The project looks amazing, and everyone is raving about it!" she exclaimed, her enthusiasm infectious.

"Thanks, Julia! I couldn't have done it without the team. We really pulled together," I replied, my heart swelling at her words. It was a testament not only to our hard work but to the friendships that had blossomed along the way.

She beamed at me, her dark curls bouncing as she swayed to the rhythm of the music. "We should celebrate properly! How about we head to the dance floor? You need to show off those moves I know you've been hiding!"

I laughed, the sound spilling out like bubbles from a shaken soda. "Dance floor? You might regret that, but let's do it!"

We made our way to the center of the patio, where a makeshift dance floor had formed. Couples swayed in time with the music, their movements a blend of grace and uninhibited joy. As I joined them, I felt the rhythm seep into my bones, igniting a spark that coaxed my feet to move. The world around us blurred into a whirl of color and sound, the laughter and music wrapping around me like a warm embrace.

With every step, I let go of the tension that had clung to me throughout the evening. The freedom of the moment washed over me like a cool breeze, refreshing and exhilarating. Julia twirled, pulling me into a spin, and for those blissful minutes, all my worries faded into the background. I felt liberated, unencumbered by self-doubt, and the thrill of the moment carried me higher.

Just as I was lost in the joy of movement, I noticed Ethan watching me from the sidelines, a smile playing on his lips. He looked like he belonged there, his presence grounding yet uplifting all at once. As if sensing my gaze, he stepped onto the dance floor, his confidence electrifying the air around us. He reached out, his hand extended toward me, inviting me to join him in this dance of unrestrained celebration.

I took his hand, feeling the warmth radiating from him as he pulled me close. The world around us faded further, and it felt like we were suspended in time. We danced as if no one else existed, the soft music wrapping around us like a cocoon, shielding us from the outside world. In that moment, it was just the two of us—two souls finding rhythm in each other's presence.

"You're a natural!" he complimented, his voice low and smooth against the backdrop of the lively crowd. "I love watching you let loose like this."

A blush crept up my cheeks, warmth spreading through me at his praise. "Thanks! It's easier when I'm with you. You make it feel... effortless."

Ethan grinned, his eyes sparkling with a mischief that sent butterflies fluttering in my stomach. "Well, I'll take that as a compliment. You inspire me to dance, and believe me, that's saying something."

Just then, a chorus of cheers erupted from the guests, drawing my attention to Claire, who had joined us on the dance floor. She was moving with grace, her laughter infectious as she twirled away from her group, inviting others to join in. For a moment, I felt a pang of hesitation, but I reminded myself of our earlier conversation. Instead of viewing her as a rival, I could see her as an ally—a reminder that connections could evolve in unexpected ways.

As the night wore on, I found myself alternating between dancing with Ethan and Julia, my laughter mingling with theirs like a melody woven through the night. Each spin and sway felt like a celebration of not only my achievements but the relationships I was nurturing, relationships that transcended jealousy and competition.

The celebration seemed endless, a joyful blur of colors and laughter, but as the clock ticked toward midnight, I sensed a change in the atmosphere. The music slowed, transitioning to softer tunes that wrapped around us like a comforting blanket. Couples gravitated toward one another, lost in the magic of the moment, while I found myself standing close to Ethan, the space between us charged with an unspoken connection.

"Can we take a breather?" he suggested, his voice barely above the gentle strains of the music. "I need a moment to catch my breath."

"Absolutely," I agreed, grateful for the chance to step away from the whirlwind of the dance floor. We wandered to the edge of the patio, where soft lanterns hung like stars, casting a warm glow over the seating area.

As we settled onto a bench, the night air wrapped around us, fragrant with hints of jasmine and the lingering aroma of summer. "What a night," I said, leaning back against the wooden slats, letting out a contented sigh. "I feel like I've been swept away by a wave of joy."

Ethan chuckled softly, his gaze fixed on the horizon. "You deserve every bit of it. You worked incredibly hard for this, and it shows. Watching you shine tonight has been one of the highlights of my year."

I glanced over, surprised by his sincerity. "Thank you, Ethan. That means so much, especially coming from you."

He turned to me, his expression shifting as if contemplating something deeper. "You know, there's a kind of beauty in vulnerability. The way you confronted Claire, the way you've embraced this moment—it's all part of what makes you special."

His words resonated with me, and I felt a swell of gratitude. "I've always been afraid to be vulnerable. I think it's something I'm learning to embrace. It's easier when I have people like you around, cheering me on."

Ethan's gaze held mine, his expression steady and sincere. "I'll always be in your corner. You've got this incredible light in you, and I can't wait to see where it takes you."

As his words sank in, a warmth unfurled within me, mingling with a sense of possibility that stretched far beyond the confines of the night. The doubts that had once plagued me seemed to dissipate in the soft glow of his encouragement, revealing a landscape rich with opportunities and dreams waiting to be realized.

In that moment, beneath the starlit sky, I felt as though the universe had opened its arms to welcome me into its embrace. It was a new beginning, a reminder that even amid uncertainty, there existed a world filled with promise and connection. And as I sat beside Ethan, the possibilities unfurling like the petals of a blooming flower, I realized that the journey ahead would be an adventure worth embracing, one where I could learn to navigate the intricate dance of life with grace and courage.

Chapter 25: Finding Common Ground

The soft hum of jazz floated through the air as I stepped into the small restaurant, the scent of garlic and fresh herbs wrapping around me like a warm embrace. Nestled in a vibrant corner of the city, this hidden gem, with its rustic wooden beams and exposed brick walls, felt like a sanctuary away from the hustle and bustle outside. The intimate lighting flickered like a constellation of stars, casting a golden glow that danced across the faces of patrons lost in their own worlds of conversation.

I spotted Ethan sitting at a table tucked in the back, his dark hair slightly tousled, the corners of his mouth curling into a shy smile when he caught my eye. I couldn't help but feel a flutter of excitement in my chest—a familiar warmth that had become my solace over the past few weeks. He stood to greet me, and in that moment, the world outside faded away.

As I settled into my seat, I noticed the way the candlelight flickered against his skin, illuminating the strong line of his jaw and the warmth in his hazel eyes. It was a look I had grown to cherish, the kind that made me feel as if I were the only person in the room, even in the midst of the restaurant's gentle chatter. I ordered a plate of spaghetti, the waiter's crisp manners adding to the ambiance, while Ethan opted for a seafood risotto that smelled heavenly.

"So," I began, stirring the strands of pasta on my plate, "how are you feeling after the exhibit? I know it was a big night for both of us."

His brow furrowed slightly as he pondered my question, the flicker of candlelight reflecting uncertainty in his gaze. "Honestly? It was incredible, but a little overwhelming too," he admitted. "Seeing all those people admiring your work... it made me realize how much pressure I put on myself. I sometimes feel like I'm just in the background, you know?"

His confession surprised me. I had always seen Ethan as someone who exuded confidence, but now I was confronted with the vulnerability he rarely revealed. My heart ached at the thought that he could feel overshadowed by my success.

"I never wanted you to feel that way," I said softly, leaning forward to bridge the distance between us. "You've been such a crucial part of this journey for me. Your support has been everything."

He smiled, a hint of relief washing over his features. "I appreciate that. It's just hard to shake the feeling sometimes. I guess we both have our insecurities."

We shared a laugh that mingled with the sound of clinking glasses and soft laughter from nearby tables. The sound was soothing, a backdrop to the rhythm of our conversation, as if the universe conspired to create this perfect moment just for us.

"I've always admired your dedication," I said, hoping to uplift him. "Your art has this raw, genuine quality that resonates with people. It's beautiful."

His cheeks flushed slightly, and I could see the vulnerability transforming into something stronger—a sense of pride in his craft. "Thanks. I've always wanted to create something that makes people feel, you know? But sometimes I wonder if I'm good enough. With everything you've accomplished, it's hard not to compare."

The realization struck me then—how both of us, despite our different paths, were trapped in our own minds, constantly measuring our worth against one another's achievements. It was a race we hadn't signed up for, yet here we were, caught in a loop of self-doubt.

"I think we need to redefine what 'enough' means for us," I suggested, swirling my fork in the spaghetti, watching the noodles twirl around with a certain elegance. "We should be each other's cheerleaders, not competitors. Your art deserves to shine just as much as mine does."

He nodded thoughtfully, a spark igniting in his eyes. "I like that. We could really use each other's strengths to build something amazing."

Our conversation flowed easily, like the gentle current of a river, as we shared our dreams and fears. With each passing moment, the barriers we had built around ourselves began to crumble, replaced by an unspoken promise to support one another. I could see a renewed determination reflecting in Ethan's eyes, and it filled me with an overwhelming sense of hope.

The waiter arrived with our meals, and the aroma filled the air, momentarily drawing us back to reality. We took a moment to appreciate the dishes in front of us, allowing ourselves to indulge in the sensory delight of flavors and textures. As I twirled the spaghetti onto my fork, I felt the warmth of Ethan's gaze on me, a reminder of the bond we were forging.

Between bites, we exchanged stories of our artistic journeys—Ethan recounting the countless hours spent perfecting his latest pieces, the struggles he faced to find his unique voice. I shared my experiences in the gallery, the nerves that had nearly consumed me before stepping into the spotlight, and how much I had learned about my own resilience.

Each story revealed layers of ourselves, peeling back the insecurities that had kept us at arm's length. As the evening wore on, laughter became our constant companion, each chuckle weaving a tapestry of connection that felt unbreakable. I realized then that this was more than just a meal; it was a moment of clarity, a turning point in our relationship.

In that cozy restaurant, under the warm glow of flickering candlelight, we found common ground—our dreams intertwined, each ambition a thread in the fabric of our shared journey. We vowed to lift each other, to celebrate our successes without letting the shadow of comparison creep in. The warmth of our conversation enveloped us, a shield against the world outside, and I couldn't help but feel that perhaps we were meant to navigate this path together, hand in hand.

The restaurant buzzed with soft conversations and the clinking of cutlery against plates, a cozy sanctuary that felt like it was carved out of the very heart of the city. As we savored our meals, the atmosphere shifted from casual pleasantries to something deeper, a shared acknowledgment of our unguarded selves. Each bite of food became a deliberate act of celebration, marking not just the successes we had recently achieved, but the courage it took to admit our vulnerabilities.

Ethan leaned back in his chair, his fingers interlaced behind his head, a posture that spoke of relaxation yet hinted at the myriad thoughts swirling in his mind. "You know, I've always admired how you seem to glide through life," he mused, a playful glint in his eyes. "Like you're always one step ahead, even when you don't realize it."

I couldn't help but chuckle, shaking my head at his words. "If only you knew how many times I've stumbled over my own feet. It's like a dance where I keep stepping on my partner's toes." I took a sip of my sparkling water, feeling the bubbles tickle my nose, an unexpected delight that added levity to our conversation.

He raised an eyebrow, intrigued. "Really? I always thought you had everything figured out."

"Trust me, I'm just a mess with a decent artist's resume," I replied, leaning closer, my voice dropping to a conspiratorial whisper. "Behind the scenes, it's a little chaotic. My sketchbooks are filled with half-finished ideas and doodles that never made it past my desk."

He nodded, a knowing smile creeping across his face, and I felt a warm sense of camaraderie envelop us. In this intimate bubble, it felt safe to share our insecurities, to peel back the layers we had built around our hearts.

"I guess that's the funny thing about art," he said, his tone growing more contemplative. "We put ourselves out there, raw and exposed, but nobody sees the countless hours of self-doubt that go into each piece."

The truth of his words resonated deeply within me. I had spent countless nights staring at blank canvases, paralyzed by the fear of failure. "Exactly. It's like standing in front of a crowd, waiting for someone to throw tomatoes at you for not being good enough."

"Or worse," he added, his eyes sparkling with mischief, "getting hit by a rogue tomato when you're trying to impress someone special."

Laughter bubbled between us, filling the space with a warmth that drove away the lingering chill of insecurity. We found ourselves lost in a dance of banter, the intimacy of our shared laughter transforming the restaurant into our own private universe. Each witty remark was a stepping stone, bridging the gap between us, making the world outside feel distant and irrelevant.

As our plates emptied, I noticed the way Ethan's fingers fidgeted with the edge of his napkin. It was a telltale sign that he was about to dive into something serious. I leaned forward, ready to listen.

"Can I be honest with you?" he asked, his voice lower, a hint of hesitation threading through his words. "It's hard sometimes, you know? To feel like I'm standing in the shadows of your success."

His admission hung in the air, heavy yet liberating. I reached across the table, my hand brushing against his. "You don't have to feel that way. I want you to shine as brightly as you can. I never want to overshadow you."

Ethan's eyes met mine, a flicker of gratitude igniting within them. "It's just... I've spent so much time trying to carve out my own space in this world, but I can't shake the feeling that I'm still just a sidekick in your story."

"Ethan," I said softly, squeezing his hand, "you're not a sidekick. You're the hero of your own journey. We're just on parallel paths right now."

His smile returned, a little brighter this time, and I felt a swell of pride that we could have this conversation—one that felt less like a confrontation and more like a collaborative effort to understand one another.

"I want us to be a team," he said, his resolve solidifying with each word. "Let's inspire each other instead of comparing ourselves."

"Deal," I replied, my heart fluttering with excitement at the thought of our newfound alliance. "Let's build something beautiful together."

As the waiter approached to clear our plates, I noticed the glow of candlelight illuminating Ethan's features, making him look almost ethereal. It was in this moment that I understood how crucial it was for us to embrace each other's strengths, to let our individual lights shine without fear of dimming one another.

Over dessert—a decadent chocolate torte that melted in our mouths—we exchanged dreams and aspirations like secret wishes tossed into a wishing well. I spoke of my desire to showcase a collection inspired by the city's vibrant pulse, each piece a reflection of its art, its culture, its people.

"I want to capture the essence of what it means to be alive in this moment," I explained, my voice laced with passion. "There's so much beauty in our everyday lives that goes unnoticed."

Ethan nodded, his expression thoughtful. "That sounds incredible. I've been toying with the idea of a series that explores the concept of identity—how we see ourselves versus how others perceive us. It's messy and complicated, just like real life."

His words hung in the air, heavy with promise and potential. "I'd love to help," I offered, feeling an undeniable excitement at the prospect of collaborating. "Let's brainstorm together."

The thought of us creating something that reflected both our journeys sent a thrill racing through me. Here we were, two artists navigating the complexities of our dreams, determined to rise together instead of apart.

As the evening wore on, we lingered over our drinks, the intimate setting allowing for quiet moments where words weren't necessary. Just being together felt like a silent vow, a promise to support one another unconditionally. With the glow of the candle flickering softly between us, I realized that our connection had evolved into something truly special—a bond fortified by honesty and a shared commitment to uplift each other.

When we finally left the restaurant, the cool night air enveloped us, contrasting sharply with the warmth we had cultivated inside. The city sparkled with life around us, each streetlight a star in our own galaxy, illuminating the path ahead. As we walked side by side, I felt the weight of uncertainty begin to lift, replaced by a sense of possibility. Together, we would carve out our own narrative, one where our dreams intertwined and our voices harmonized in a beautiful crescendo.

The brisk night air felt invigorating as we stepped outside the restaurant, the city stretching before us like a living tapestry, each street a vibrant thread woven into the fabric of our shared existence. The distant sound of laughter and music spilled from nearby bars, a siren call of life that beckoned us to join in. I caught the hint of a smile on Ethan's face as we navigated the bustling sidewalks, our footsteps harmonizing in a dance that felt both familiar and new.

"Where to now?" he asked, a playful gleam lighting up his eyes.

"Let's wander," I suggested, an impulse igniting within me. The city was a canvas, and tonight, it was begging for exploration. "I've always wanted to discover hidden gems—the kind of places that feel like they hold secrets."

"Secret places, huh?" he mused, feigning deep contemplation. "What are we, explorers of the urban jungle?"

"Absolutely," I replied, grinning as I linked my arm through his. "Let's find the most picturesque corner of this concrete paradise."

As we strolled, the city revealed itself in fragments—neon lights flickering above, casting colorful shadows that danced across the pavement. I pointed out a mural, its vibrant colors splashed against an aged brick wall, a chaotic explosion of artistry that seemed to echo our own journeys. "Look at that! It's breathtaking," I exclaimed, taking a moment to appreciate the skill and emotion woven into the design.

Ethan leaned in closer, studying the mural's intricate details. "It's a perfect reflection of how messy life can be," he observed, his voice thoughtful. "Beautiful, yet chaotic."

His words resonated within me, mirroring the complex tapestry of our lives. I felt a wave of appreciation wash over me, recognizing that we were forging a shared understanding, one where each color and line represented our individual struggles and triumphs. "Exactly! Just like us, right?" I replied, nudging him playfully.

"Right," he chuckled, his laughter mingling with the city sounds.

We continued our journey, wandering through a narrow alleyway adorned with twinkling fairy lights that hung like stars against the night sky. The air was tinged with the rich scent of roasted coffee, wafting from a quaint café tucked away in the corner. I paused, captivated by the warmth emanating from within. "Can we stop there?" I asked, pointing toward the inviting glow.

"Of course," he replied, his eyes lighting up at the prospect of another shared moment.

The café was a charming hideaway, its wooden interior alive with chatter and the clinking of mugs. We settled into a cozy booth by the window, the dim light creating an intimate cocoon around us. As I sipped my mocha, the rich chocolate notes melting on my tongue, I glanced at Ethan, who was gazing out at the world beyond the glass.

"What are you thinking?" I asked, intrigued by the contemplative look on his face.

He turned to me, a hint of a smile playing at the corners of his lips. "Just how surreal this all feels. Here we are, two artists finding our way in a city that never sleeps."

"It's magical, isn't it?" I replied, savoring the moment. "Every corner has a story, and we're part of it now."

We spent the next hour lost in conversation, our words flowing like the steam rising from our mugs. We spoke of our dreams, our fears, and the inevitable uncertainties that accompanied the life of an artist. I shared my hope to showcase a new collection that reflected our vibrant city, infusing each piece with the energy I felt around us. Ethan, in turn, expressed his desire to delve into the complexities of identity through his work, revealing the intricate layers that formed our sense of self.

As the night wore on, the café began to empty, leaving just a few dedicated patrons still engrossed in their conversations. The hushed atmosphere allowed us to share our ambitions without distraction, each word grounding us further into our newfound alliance.

"Do you think we'll ever make it?" he asked, his voice soft but laced with sincerity. "Like, truly make a mark in this world?"

"Absolutely," I said, my conviction unwavering. "If we support each other and stay true to our visions, there's no limit to what we can achieve."

He leaned back, a look of admiration crossing his face. "I love that. I can already see us at our own gallery opening, showcasing a collection that tells our story."

The thought ignited a fire within me, and I couldn't help but envision the vibrancy of such an event—the walls adorned with our combined artistry, our friends and family celebrating alongside us. It felt not just like a dream, but a tangible possibility, one we could actively create together.

"Let's do it," I said, my voice filled with excitement. "Let's make that our goal. We'll start planning, brainstorming ideas, everything."

"Together," he echoed, a sense of determination settling over us like a warm blanket.

After finishing our drinks, we reluctantly stood to leave, but the city still beckoned, its magic irresistible. We wandered back outside, the air cooler now, the night alive with the distant sounds of laughter and music. I felt a rush of exhilaration, a surge of possibilities unfurling like a tapestry before us.

As we strolled through the streets, hand in hand, the world felt more vibrant, the lights more dazzling. I could sense a shift in our dynamic, an unspoken promise to be each other's biggest supporters, to nurture our dreams without letting competition tarnish the bond we had forged.

In that moment, I knew that our connection was rooted in more than just love; it was a partnership grounded in shared experiences and aspirations. As we approached a park bathed in moonlight, I paused, my heart swelling with the realization of how far we had come.

"Look at the stars," I breathed, tilting my head back to gaze at the night sky. "They seem to be shining just for us."

Ethan laughed softly, his fingers tightening around mine. "They always do when you're around."

With that, we ventured deeper into the park, our laughter echoing against the trees, the weight of the world lifting from our shoulders. This was the beginning of something extraordinary, a journey defined not just by our individual paths but by the love and support we vowed to give one another.

Together, we would navigate the complexities of our dreams, transforming the chaos into beauty, and every moment shared would be another brushstroke on the canvas of our lives.

Chapter 26: The Calm Before the Storm

Ethan and I leaned over a large canvas stretched across the living room floor of my apartment, sunlight filtering through the sheer curtains, casting playful shadows that danced alongside our ideas. The aroma of fresh coffee mingled with the faint scent of paint, creating an intoxicating atmosphere that made my heart race with anticipation. He had a way of igniting my creativity, his enthusiasm infectious as we shared our thoughts and dreams. Today's project wasn't just another art installation; it felt like a love letter to everything we'd been through together—a celebration of our journey, our connection, and the vibrant world we lived in.

"I was thinking we could incorporate a series of small sculptures scattered throughout the city," I suggested, my fingers brushing against a brushstroke of deep crimson on the canvas. "Each one could represent a different aspect of love—familial, romantic, platonic. We could place them in unexpected locations, inviting people to discover them."

Ethan's eyes sparkled with inspiration, and for a fleeting moment, the worry I had sensed in him melted away. "What about using mirrors?" he proposed, his voice animated. "Mirrors can symbolize self-love, reflection, and how love is often a two-way street. We could create installations that encourage people to interact with them."

I could see the ideas swirling in his mind, and it felt as if we were weaving a tapestry of creativity together, thread by thread. The city was our playground—its cobblestone streets and bustling parks were canvases waiting to be splashed with colors of emotion. I envisioned us, hand in hand, leaving a trail of beauty that would not only captivate passersby but also prompt them to reflect on their own relationships. The thought made me giddy, as if we were planning an adventure in a world filled with possibilities.

Yet, despite the excitement that crackled in the air, I couldn't shake the feeling that something was amiss. Ethan's smile was genuine, but there was a shadow lurking behind his eyes, a flicker of something I couldn't quite put my finger on. I decided to let it go for now, not wanting to mar the vibrant moment we had created, but the sensation nagged at me, like a soft whisper in the back of my mind.

As the afternoon melted into evening, we ventured outside, determined to explore the city and find inspiration in its corners. The sun dipped low in the sky, painting everything in hues of amber and gold. I took a deep breath, savoring the crisp autumn air that wrapped around us like a warm embrace. The streets were alive, filled with the laughter of children and the rhythmic clattering of heels on pavement. Each sound blended into a symphony of life, fueling our creative spirits.

Ethan pointed out a quaint alleyway adorned with murals, the vibrancy of the artwork calling to us. "What if we placed a sculpture here, something that resonates with the idea of community love?" he mused, his eyes glimmering with excitement. I nodded in agreement, feeling a sense of purpose blooming within me.

As we wandered deeper into the heart of the city, I couldn't help but marvel at how it thrived with stories. The old brick buildings bore witness to decades of love, loss, and everything in between. Couples strolled hand in hand, sharing secrets beneath the glow of streetlights. Friends gathered at cafes, laughter spilling out onto the streets like confetti. It was a living tapestry, rich with emotion and experience, and I felt honored to be part of it, creating something that could contribute to this narrative.

Our steps led us to a small park, where the leaves crunched beneath our feet, the golden foliage creating a carpet of warmth. I paused, taking in the scene before me. Children played, their laughter ringing through the air, while couples sat on benches, lost in each other's gaze. It was the epitome of love in its many forms, a snapshot of life unfolding before us.

"This place feels perfect for an installation," I said, my voice barely above a whisper, as if I were afraid to break the spell. "We could create a garden of love, a space where people can come together, reflect, and share their stories."

Ethan smiled, his expression softening as he glanced around. "I love that idea," he replied, his voice warm and inviting. "It could become a sanctuary for people, a reminder that love is everywhere if you just look for it."

Just then, as we began sketching ideas in the margins of our minds, I caught a glimpse of something flicker across Ethan's face—a shadow, a momentary slip that reminded me of the tension I had noticed earlier. I wanted to reach out, to pull him back into the light with me, but something held me back. I feared that pressing him too hard would only push him away. Instead, I let the moment linger, filled with the hopes of our creative endeavor, and allowed myself to bask in the comfort of his presence.

As night began to drape its velvet cloak over the city, Ethan and I settled onto a bench, our shoulders brushing together. The moonlight cast a soft glow around us, illuminating the contours of his face, making him look almost ethereal. I could feel the warmth radiating from him, a solid presence that anchored me in a world that sometimes felt overwhelming.

"I know you're feeling something," I said gently, my voice laced with concern. "You can talk to me, you know. Whatever it is, I'm here."

He took a deep breath, the tension in his shoulders easing slightly. "It's just... sometimes I feel like I'm being pulled in two directions. This project is exciting, but there are other things—family stuff—that's weighing on me." His words hung in the air, heavy with unspoken fears.

"Ethan," I began, instinctively reaching for his hand, "you don't have to carry that alone. We're in this together."

He turned to me, a flicker of gratitude mingling with the unease in his gaze. I could see the gears turning in his mind, the struggle between vulnerability and the desire to protect those he cared for. In that moment, I wanted nothing more than to shield him from the storm brewing within. We sat together in silence, the world around us bustling with life, yet we were cocooned in our little bubble of unspoken understanding, the weight of our connection palpable in the cool night air.

The lingering moonlight enveloped us, casting a silvery sheen across the park as Ethan and I sat in contemplative silence. The hum of the city provided a comforting backdrop, the distant sounds of laughter and music wafting through the night air, intertwining with the rustle of leaves overhead. I could feel the warmth of his hand in mine, a simple connection that sparked warmth deep within my core. Yet, as the moments stretched, I sensed that the weight of unspoken words pressed heavily between us, a palpable tension that seemed to tug at the edges of our shared happiness.

"I never really thought about how love could be expressed through art until we started planning this project," I said, hoping to lighten the mood, to redirect Ethan's swirling thoughts. "It's like we're on the cusp of something magical, something that could resonate with so many people. The idea of creating a space where others can reflect on their own experiences of love—it's beautiful."

Ethan smiled, but it didn't quite reach his eyes. "Yeah, it is. It feels like we're crafting something significant." He hesitated, his gaze drifting toward the shimmering cityscape before us, as if searching for clarity among the twinkling lights. "But sometimes I wonder if we can truly capture the essence of it all. Love is messy, complicated. What if we fail to represent that?"

His vulnerability tugged at my heartstrings, and I squeezed his hand, willing my warmth to seep into his doubts. "But isn't that the point? Love isn't always perfect. It can be chaotic, confusing, and even painful, but it's also beautiful in its own right. Every experience shapes our understanding of it. We can explore those complexities through our art."

Ethan turned to me, his expression softening. "You always know how to put things into perspective." His voice was thick with gratitude, and the corners of his mouth lifted just a little, chasing away some of the shadows that had lingered. "I guess I'm just worried that my experiences aren't enough to convey what I feel. Like I'm not worthy of creating something meaningful."

"Don't ever say that," I replied, my voice firm yet gentle. "Your feelings matter. Your perspective is uniquely yours, and that's what makes it valuable. Every brushstroke, every sculpture tells a story—your story. We all carry our burdens and joys, and that's what makes art resonate with others. Trust yourself."

Ethan's brow furrowed slightly, a flicker of doubt still hanging in the air, but there was a glimmer of hope dancing in his eyes as well. I wanted to pull him closer, wrap him in my warmth, and shield him from whatever storm was brewing inside him. Instead, we remained seated, allowing the quiet intimacy of the moment to envelop us, giving him space to unravel his tangled thoughts.

As the night deepened, we returned to our brainstorming session, scribbling down ideas on scraps of paper and the back of an old receipt I'd found crumpled in my pocket. Each suggestion ignited a new spark, a delightful exchange of thoughts that flowed freely between us like the river winding through the city.

"What if we created a series of interactive installations?" I proposed, excitement bubbling within me. "Something that encourages people to share their own stories. We could have a wall where visitors can write love letters, or a space where they can leave tokens representing their relationships—like a community shrine of sorts."

Ethan's face lit up at the idea. "I love that! It could be a living piece of art that evolves with each new story. We could even have a spot where people can record their experiences, capturing the voices of our community."

As the ideas flowed, the park around us transformed into a vivid tapestry of inspiration. I imagined vibrant colors splashed against the dull concrete, love notes fluttering in the breeze, and the gentle murmur of voices sharing their truths. It was exhilarating, breathing life into a concept that had begun as a mere spark in our minds. Yet, even amid the excitement, I couldn't shake the underlying current of unease that seemed to tether Ethan to a darker place.

We finally decided to take a walk, letting the cool breeze kiss our cheeks as we strolled through the park. The shadows of trees danced in the moonlight, their branches swaying like hands reaching for the sky. I admired the beauty of the moment, the way the stars flickered above, each one a tiny beacon of hope, illuminating the darkness surrounding us.

"Do you ever feel overwhelmed by everything?" I asked, seeking to understand the turmoil that had been hidden beneath Ethan's composed exterior. "Like, as if the weight of the world is pressing down on you?"

He paused, taking a moment to gather his thoughts, the rhythm of his breaths audible in the stillness. "Sometimes," he admitted, his voice barely above a whisper. "It's like the world expects so much from us—creatively, emotionally. And I find myself struggling to keep up. It feels like there's always something more I should be doing, someone else I should be for others."

I nodded, understanding the pressure that came with pursuing our passions and the expectations we placed upon ourselves. "It's okay to feel that way. We're all trying to navigate this chaos, and it's easy to lose ourselves in it. But you have to remember that you're enough, just as you are. You don't have to carry the weight of the world on your shoulders. We can share that burden."

Ethan stopped walking, turning to face me. There was a vulnerability in his eyes that cut through the night, a rawness that made my heart ache. "Thank you," he said softly, his voice trembling slightly. "I don't know what I would do without you."

We stood there for a moment, suspended in time, the air thick with unspoken emotions. I wanted to bridge the distance, to assure him that he wasn't alone, but something deep within me warned against pushing too hard. Instead, I took a step closer, allowing our hands to remain intertwined, a quiet promise that we would face whatever came our way together.

As we resumed our stroll, the weight of our conversation lingered, yet I could feel a shift in the air. The shadows seemed to recede just a little, replaced by the possibility of brighter days ahead. Each step we took felt lighter, a testament to the power of connection and the strength that blossomed from shared vulnerability. In that moment, amid the chaos of the city, I felt a glimmer of hope—a belief that we could navigate the storm brewing in Ethan's heart and emerge stronger on the other side. The city was alive with stories waiting to be told, and ours was only just beginning.

The moon hung high, a luminous sentinel watching over us as we wandered through the dimly lit streets, our conversation trailing like the shadows cast by the flickering streetlights. Ethan and I had crafted a makeshift world of our own amidst the chaos of the city, where ideas floated like confetti in the air, but the reality of our lives loomed ever closer, pressing against the fragile bubble of creativity we had forged.

As we meandered, the city transformed into a living entity, each corner steeped in stories waiting to unfold. The aroma of fresh-baked bread wafted from a nearby bakery, mingling with the sweet scent of blooming night jasmine that lined the sidewalks. I paused to inhale deeply, letting the mix of sensations wash over me, grounding me in the moment. This was the backdrop for our installation, a vibrant tapestry that pulsed with life, just as our project aimed to capture the essence of love in all its multifaceted glory.

"What if we made a section dedicated to unrequited love?" I suggested, excitement bubbling within me as I imagined the possibilities. "We could create a beautiful yet heart-wrenching installation—something that evokes the bittersweet nature of loving someone who doesn't love you back."

Ethan's brows furrowed slightly, a flicker of discomfort crossing his face. "That's a powerful idea," he said slowly, the weight of his words underscored by the hint of vulnerability I had come to recognize in him. "But do we really want to dive into the darker aspects of love? It's heavy, and I'm not sure I'm ready for that."

I sensed the storm within him rising, threatening to eclipse our creative flow. "It's important, though. Love isn't just sunshine and roses. It's the thorns that often leave the deepest scars. Maybe by acknowledging those feelings, we can create a deeper connection with people."

He nodded, though I could tell my words had not completely alleviated the worry etched on his features. "You're right. It just feels... personal, I guess." His voice trailed off, and I sensed that this topic hit closer to home than he was willing to admit.

As we walked, I tried to bring our focus back to the project, to channel the energy buzzing between us into something beautiful and inspiring. "What about a section that celebrates friendship?" I proposed, my enthusiasm reigniting. "We could create an interactive mural where people can write their favorite memories with friends, or even share what their friends mean to them. Imagine the colors and the joy of that!"

Ethan's eyes lit up at the idea, his features softening as he considered it. "That could really resonate with people. Everyone has friendships that shape their lives, and celebrating that could bring so much warmth to our installation."

The energy between us shifted, the heaviness lifting just a little as we continued to brainstorm, our laughter echoing through the empty streets. Each idea flowed seamlessly into the next, our imaginations intertwining like the ivy creeping up the brick walls of the buildings surrounding us. We painted vivid pictures of our installation, crafting a vision that felt grand and transformative, a gift to the city and its inhabitants.

In the midst of our excitement, I couldn't shake the sensation that Ethan was still holding something back. We were forging a path together, but I could sense a fork ahead where his thoughts diverged from mine, where the winds of his internal storm threatened to veer him off course. I wanted desperately to reach that part of him, to peel away the layers of hesitation that seemed to bind him, but I understood that it was a journey he had to undertake in his own time.

As the night wore on, we found ourselves at the edge of a small park, its lush greenery stark against the urban backdrop. The silence was punctuated only by the rustle of leaves and the distant hum of traffic. I leaned against the cool metal railing, gazing out at the cityscape, my heart full of hope and apprehension.

"Do you think we're ready for this?" Ethan asked, breaking the silence that had settled around us. "What if we pour our hearts into this and it falls flat? What if people don't connect with what we create?"

I turned to face him, the moonlight illuminating his features, revealing the turmoil beneath his bravado. "What matters is that we're honest. This installation is our story, a reflection of who we are and what we've experienced. Even if it doesn't resonate with everyone, it will still be a part of us—a piece of our journey that we can be proud of."

He considered my words, the tension in his shoulders gradually easing as he absorbed the truth in them. "You always seem to know exactly what to say," he remarked, a ghost of a smile playing on his lips. "It's like you have this magical ability to turn my fears into something tangible."

"Maybe it's just that I have a habit of living in my own head too much," I replied, returning his smile, the banter serving as a balm to the heavier conversation we had just navigated. "Or perhaps it's because I believe in us. Together, we can create something meaningful."

With renewed determination, we resumed our walk, brainstorming ideas that ranged from whimsical to profound. The park became our sanctuary, a place where our dreams unfurled like the petals of the flowers blooming around us. We sketched out plans for the interactive elements of our installation, crafting a narrative that was vibrant, multifaceted, and deeply human.

As we stepped away from the park and back into the thrumming heart of the city, the air shifted, crackling with energy and possibility. We passed by bustling cafes and street performers, the pulse of life invigorating our spirits. I could feel the excitement radiating between us, a tangible force that propelled us forward.

Just as we turned a corner, a sudden flash of movement caught my eye—a fleeting silhouette darting into an alleyway. My heart skipped a beat as unease settled back into my chest. "Did you see that?" I whispered, my voice barely above a breath.

Ethan paused, his expression shifting from excitement to concern. "What was it?" he asked, scanning the dimly lit alley.

"I'm not sure," I replied, instinctively taking a step closer to him. The thrill of creativity had ignited a fire within me, but now, an unfamiliar chill crept along my spine. "It felt... off. Like something wasn't right."

Ethan and I exchanged worried glances, the warmth of our earlier conversation cooling as we stood on the precipice of uncertainty. Whatever had flickered in the shadows was a reminder that life was not only composed of beautiful moments and shared dreams but also of the lurking mysteries that could reshape our reality in an instant.

Our world, once filled with vibrant ideas and dreams, now felt tinged with caution. The city, which had served as our canvas, was also a labyrinth filled with hidden corners and secrets that remained veiled, waiting for us to uncover them. With hearts pounding, we took a deep breath and stepped forward, ready to confront whatever lay ahead. We were embarking on a new journey, one that promised not only the beauty of creation but the potential chaos that life inevitably brought. And as long as we faced it together, I held onto the belief that we could weather any storm.

Chapter 27: The Breaking Point

The vibrant sun dipped low in the sky, casting a golden hue over the sprawling landscape of Charleston, South Carolina. I stood on the balcony of my apartment, the salty breeze tousling my hair, mingling with the sweet scent of blooming magnolias wafting from the garden below. The old city was a canvas of pastel-colored buildings, their weathered facades whispering tales of a bygone era. This was home—my sanctuary amid the chaos of the world and my blossoming photography career.

Each morning, I would rise with the sun, clutching my trusty camera, which had become an extension of myself. Its worn leather strap felt familiar against my palm, and I found solace in the way the shutter clicked, capturing fleeting moments that would otherwise vanish. Whether it was the laughter of children playing tag in the park, the sun-drenched cobblestone streets glistening after a summer rain, or the delicate lace of a Southern woman's dress swaying in the wind, I felt the pulse of life through my lens.

Yet, beneath the surface of my artistic triumphs lay a shadow that threatened to eclipse everything I cherished—Ethan. My partner in creativity, my muse, and the one person who understood the deepest corners of my heart. At first, our late-night brainstorming sessions brimmed with ideas and laughter, our minds dancing in unison like fireflies on a warm summer night. But recently, a quiet dissonance had crept into our conversations, a tension that gnawed at the edges of our connection.

The late nights had morphed into something akin to a silent standoff. I'd catch Ethan staring out the window, lost in thought as the world around him blurred into a background hum. His once-bright eyes, full of curiosity and mischief, had dulled, shadowed by an invisible weight. I tried to reach out, to break the invisible barrier he'd constructed, but every time I approached, he'd retreat further into himself, a walled fortress against my concerns.

"Do you ever think about just letting go?" I'd asked him one night, the flickering candlelight casting playful shadows on the walls of my tiny studio apartment. I was eager to dig into his thoughts, to pull him back from the edge of whatever chasm had opened between us. "You know, to let the art flow without judgment?"

His response was an absent shrug, a motion that felt more like a dismissal than an invitation to share. The warmth of his presence faded, leaving an aching chill where our laughter used to flourish. It was as if he was slipping through my fingers, sand on the shore, impossible to grasp as it tumbled into the vast ocean of our unspoken fears.

The day the local newspaper featured my photography was a moment I had longed for. I stood in front of the counter at the café, the scent of freshly brewed coffee mingling with the sweet aroma of pastries. My heart raced as I flipped through the glossy pages, a sense of pride swelling in my chest. There, among the articles and advertisements, my work shone like a beacon. Yet, in that same breath, I felt a pang of guilt when I realized Ethan's contributions had been cast aside, overlooked as if they were mere shadows to my spotlight.

As I cradled the newspaper, my fingers trembled, and the sense of elation I had anticipated turned sour. The café buzzed around me, but I felt isolated, the cheers and laughter fading into a dull roar. I knew how hard Ethan had worked, pouring his soul into our project. Each piece of his art was a reflection of himself, yet here I was, basking in the light while he stood in the shadows.

Later that evening, as we sat together on the floor of my studio, the walls adorned with our dreams and aspirations, the silence thickened like fog rolling over the marshes. I could no longer hold back the frustration that bubbled inside me. "Why aren't you more excited for me?" I blurted, the words spilling from my lips before I could contain them. "You should be celebrating too."

Ethan's eyes flashed, and for a brief moment, I thought I saw a flicker of the boy I had fallen for—the one with a smile that lit up the darkest corners of my heart. But it quickly faded, replaced by something more sorrowful. "You think it's easy for me?" he snapped, the intensity in his voice striking like lightning. "Do you have any idea what it's like to feel overshadowed by someone you care about?"

His words hung in the air, a weight that bore down on my chest. I felt my heart clench, the ache sharp and unexpected. "Ethan, I never meant to overshadow you," I whispered, my voice trembling as I tried to reach for his hand. "I just wanted to share this journey with you."

He pulled back, retreating into himself like a turtle withdrawing into its shell. The vulnerability in his eyes made my heart ache deeper. "You don't get it," he said, his voice barely above a whisper. "Every time I see your name in lights, it reminds me of how I'm just... not enough. I pour my heart into this, but it never feels like it's enough."

The realization struck me hard, an emotional slap that left me breathless. I had always believed we were partners in this creative endeavor, but in my quest for success, I had failed to see the toll it was taking on him. My achievements had become a mirror reflecting his insecurities, and suddenly I was struck with the terrible understanding that I had fed his doubt, not only mine. In my pursuit of recognition, I had inadvertently compounded his struggles, a painful twist of fate that left us both feeling lost.

As the shadows lengthened in my studio, I felt a deep yearning to bridge the growing chasm between us. My heart swelled with compassion for the boy I loved, the boy who had stood beside me through every moment of doubt and despair. I had to show him that his worth was not defined by my success, that together we could rise above the noise and find our voices anew.

The silence between us felt like a heavy curtain, drawn tight against the light, casting everything in shadows. I could see the tension curling in the corners of the room, wrapping around us like a dense fog. I held onto the remnants of our previous discussions, desperate to grasp the threads of our camaraderie, but every attempt to bridge the widening gap seemed to evaporate before my eyes.

One evening, after what felt like a thousand unspoken words hung between us, I decided to break the monotony that had taken root in our home. I slipped out of my apartment, the crisp evening air washing over me like a refreshing wave. The world outside was painted in shades of indigo and silver, the stars flickering like distant promises. I knew exactly where to go—King Street, with its eclectic mix of boutiques, cafés, and street performers, would be the perfect antidote to our stagnant atmosphere.

As I strolled down the cobblestone path, the sounds of laughter and music intertwined, creating a symphony that seemed to coax the very walls of Charleston into dancing. I paused to watch a musician strumming his guitar, the notes drifting through the air like warm whispers. A small crowd gathered, swaying to the rhythm, their worries momentarily forgotten. I felt a twinge of longing for that carefree spirit, the joy that came from losing oneself in the moment.

I made my way to a quaint little café, the scent of freshly baked pastries wafting from the open door. The dimly lit interior beckoned me with its cozy charm, a refuge from the evening chill. I settled into a corner booth, ordering a slice of decadent chocolate cake and a steaming cup of coffee. As I waited, I pulled out my camera, absentmindedly snapping shots of the barista's quick hands and the delicate latte art swirling atop foamy milk. Each click was a reminder of the life bustling around me, vibrant and unrestrained, a stark contrast to the quiet unease I had left behind.

When I returned home, the atmosphere felt different. The door creaked open, and the familiar scent of paint and linseed oil greeted me. Ethan was hunched over his easel, the soft glow of the lamp illuminating his furrowed brow. The tension still lingered, but there was a flicker of something else in his eyes—a spark of creativity that had been dulled but not extinguished.

"Hey," I ventured, the word slipping from my lips like a fragile promise. "I brought back something sweet." I held out the box, the tempting aroma of chocolate filling the air between us.

He turned, a slight smile breaking through the clouds that had settled over his features. "You know the way to my heart," he quipped, a playful glimmer in his eye that made my heart flutter. It was a small victory, but I clung to it, hoping it would usher in a new conversation.

As we shared the cake, I leaned against the wall, feeling the warmth of the room seep into my bones. "I was thinking... maybe we could go out tomorrow? Just us. Let's take our cameras and see what Charleston has to offer," I suggested, infusing my voice with enthusiasm. "We could capture the sunset at Waterfront Park, maybe grab dinner at that little seafood place by the pier."

Ethan paused, his fork hovering mid-air. "Sounds nice," he replied, though his tone was more reserved than I had hoped. I recognized the hesitation in his eyes, the way he seemed to be evaluating my proposal like a carefully crafted photograph.

After a moment of silence, he set down his fork and sighed. "I'm not sure I'm in the right headspace for that. I've got... things to figure out."

My heart sank at his words, the familiarity of rejection washing over me. "Ethan," I started, my voice softening, "you don't have to go through this alone. Whatever it is, we can face it together. I can help."

He leaned back, crossing his arms as if bracing himself against a sudden chill. "It's not that simple. You've got all this momentum, and I feel like I'm just... stuck. I can't keep riding your coattails. It's not fair to you."

"Stop it!" I exclaimed, the urgency in my voice startling us both. "This isn't about fairness; it's about us. I want to share this journey with you, and I want you to know that your art is just as valuable. You're not just a background character in my story. You're a co-creator."

Ethan's expression softened, the tension in his shoulders easing slightly. "You don't know what it feels like to have everyone look at you and only see the other half. When they see your photography, they don't think about me. They think about you."

"Then let them think whatever they want!" I shot back, my heart racing as I felt the heat of the moment swell around us. "What matters is what we know. We're in this together. You're my partner. Always."

There was a flicker of something in his gaze, a spark that ignited a small flame of hope within me. But it quickly flickered, and a shadow of doubt crept back in. "I want to believe that," he murmured, his voice barely above a whisper. "But it's hard when you're the one everyone admires, and I'm just... here."

My heart ached at the weight of his vulnerability. I reached across the table, my fingers brushing against his, feeling the warmth of his skin. "Ethan, look at me. You are not 'just here.' You're everything to me. I see you. I see your talent, your passion. And I promise, we'll figure this out together."

As the last rays of sunlight slipped beneath the horizon, casting a dusky glow around us, I hoped that my words had pierced the darkness that had enveloped him. I could feel the energy between us shifting, like a canvas catching the first strokes of paint, hinting at the beauty yet to unfold. Perhaps it wasn't too late to reclaim what we had lost, to reignite the creative spark that had drawn us together in the first place.

In that moment, amid the shadows and uncertainty, I vowed to fight for us—because sometimes, the most beautiful art comes from the rawest emotions, the deepest struggles, and the bonds that refuse to break. The evening air grew thick with possibilities, and I was determined to uncover them, one click at a time.

The atmosphere felt charged as I watched the shadows dance across the walls of my apartment, a mixture of uncertainty and determination swirling within me. I couldn't shake the image of Ethan's furrowed brow, the way his fingers brushed against the edges of his canvas, as if searching for something just beyond his reach. Each moment I spent with him was a delicate balance, a tightrope walk between the fear of losing him and the hope of rekindling the spark that had initially brought us together.

The next day dawned with a sense of renewed purpose. I had resolved to show Ethan just how much he meant to me—not only as my partner in art but as the beating heart of my world. Charleston was alive with possibilities, and I would not let the darkness encroach upon our creative sanctuary any longer.

I gathered my camera gear, ensuring every lens and filter was ready to capture the magic of the day. With a gentle nudge, I coaxed Ethan into stepping outside, promising him an adventure in our beloved city. As we wandered the cobblestone streets, I kept a close eye on him, hoping to catch glimpses of the light I knew still resided within him.

We strolled past historic mansions draped in Spanish moss, the sun filtering through the leaves, casting intricate patterns on the ground. The vibrant colors of the flowers bursting from window boxes added a whimsical touch to the old-world charm. As I snapped photos, I encouraged Ethan to join me in the creative process, coaxing him to capture his perspective. "Look for the stories hidden in the ordinary," I urged, hoping to spark the inspiration I felt was still smoldering beneath the surface.

He hesitated at first, his camera resting lightly in his hands, as if he were unsure of its weight. But slowly, the world began to unfold before him, and I watched as the tension in his shoulders eased with each click of the shutter. I pointed out the way the light caught a seagull perched on a lamppost, or how a child's laughter echoed in the distance, bringing forth the beauty of the mundane.

"See that?" I said, gesturing toward a couple dancing in a small square, lost in their own world. "Capture the joy they're sharing." Ethan raised his camera, and as he framed the moment, I caught a flicker of the passion I had feared was extinguished.

As we made our way to Waterfront Park, the rhythm of our footsteps fell into sync, the silence between us no longer heavy with unspoken words but alive with the possibility of new memories. We found a quiet spot on the grass, overlooking the water, the evening sky painted in hues of orange and pink. It was as if the world had paused to allow us this moment of tranquility, and I seized it.

"Ethan," I began, my voice steady but laced with vulnerability. "I know things have been hard lately, and I don't want to make them harder. But I need you to understand that I see you. I see the way your art breathes life into everything around us. You're not just my partner; you're my muse. I don't want to lose you to your doubts."

He turned to me, his gaze penetrating as if he were peeling back the layers of my heart, searching for truth among my words. "You make it sound so easy," he replied, his voice heavy with emotion. "But every time I try to create, it feels like I'm fighting against an invisible force. It's like I'm drowning in my own insecurities, and I don't know how to swim to the surface."

I felt the weight of his honesty, an echo of the fears that had haunted me since the beginning of our journey. "Then let's swim together," I urged, leaning closer, reaching for his hand. "We'll find our way out of this. I promise you're not alone. Not now, not ever."

As the sun sank lower on the horizon, casting a warm glow around us, Ethan's hand slipped into mine, and a surge of electricity coursed through me. In that moment, everything felt right. I could sense the barriers between us beginning to crumble, the walls that had kept our hearts distant slowly disintegrating like sandcastles at high tide.

We spent the golden hour capturing the beauty around us, each photograph a testament to our shared experience. The laughter of children, the gentle rustle of leaves, and the distant call of seagulls became our soundtrack, a reminder that life continued to unfold in all its messy glory. With each click of the shutter, I saw Ethan begin to relax, his creativity unfurling like the petals of a blooming flower.

As the sky darkened and the stars began to twinkle, we wandered back toward my apartment, our conversations flowing freely like the water of the nearby harbor. Ethan opened up about his childhood, the pressures he had faced, and how they had woven themselves into the fabric of his identity. I shared my own insecurities, the doubts that occasionally crept in and threatened to overshadow my achievements.

In that exchange of vulnerability, we forged an unspoken bond, an understanding that neither of us had to bear our burdens alone. It was liberating, and as we reached my apartment door, I felt lighter, as if a heavy cloak had been lifted from my shoulders.

The next morning, the sun spilled into the room, illuminating the remnants of last night's creative frenzy. My camera was propped against the wall, still buzzing with the energy of our shared moments. I turned to find Ethan already awake, his eyes scanning the photos we had captured together, a smile creeping across his face. "These are incredible," he said, his voice warm and inviting. "I think I've found a new way to see things."

The realization washed over me, filling my heart with warmth. It wasn't just the photographs; it was the understanding that we were both evolving, both growing into something greater than we had been alone. Together, we were an unstoppable force, our talents weaving together to create a tapestry of color and light.

I moved closer, slipping my arm around his shoulder as we reveled in the moment. "And we can keep creating, keep exploring," I whispered. "As long as we face it all together."

With that, I felt the weight of our previous struggles beginning to lift. The world outside was bursting with life, and I knew we were ready to embrace it, hand in hand. The journey ahead would undoubtedly be fraught with challenges, but for the first time in what felt like ages, I was filled with a sense of hope and excitement, a belief that together, we could weather any storm. The canvas of our lives awaited us, ready to be painted with the vibrant colors of our shared experiences and newfound dreams.

Chapter 28: The Eye of the Storm

The scent of damp earth fills the air as I step onto the winding path leading to the lakeshore. Each footfall is a reminder of how lost I've felt without Ethan by my side. The trees, with their vibrant green leaves glistening under the late afternoon sun, seem to whisper secrets I'm too distracted to comprehend. I take a deep breath, trying to steady the tumult within me, but my heart races with both excitement and apprehension. The world feels heavy, charged with electricity, as if nature itself is holding its breath, waiting for something—anything—to happen.

As I reach the familiar clearing, a sense of nostalgia washes over me. The lake stretches out like a shimmering blanket of glass, reflecting the vivid hues of the sky as it begins to shift from gold to a deep cerulean. Our spot, nestled between two gnarled oaks that seem to have witnessed the unfolding of every moment we've shared, is untouched by time, holding a sacred place in my heart. I can almost hear the echoes of our laughter, the warmth of our conversations lingering in the air like a forgotten melody.

I scan the horizon, searching for any sign of him. The wind picks up, swirling leaves around my feet and tousling my hair. A storm brews in the distance, dark clouds gathering like a curtain drawing closer, threatening to unleash its fury. My heart sinks at the thought that this might be our final meeting, the storm within me echoing the one outside. Just as doubt begins to creep in, I catch a glimpse of his silhouette against the backdrop of the water. He stands at the edge, hands shoved deep into the pockets of his jeans, a familiar pose that sends a rush of warmth through me.

The sight of him brings a mix of relief and longing, and I can't help but notice the way the fading sunlight dances across his features, casting shadows that enhance his strong jawline and soft, troubled eyes. In this moment, I realize how much I've missed him—his laughter, his kindness, and even the way he could challenge me without reservation. I take a tentative step forward, feeling like I'm walking on the edge of something monumental, my heart thundering in my chest as the distance between us shrinks.

"Lily," he calls softly, his voice breaking the fragile silence that envelops us. It's a sound that has always had the power to soothe me, yet now it feels weighted, as if it carries the weight of all our unspoken words. I draw closer, feeling the magnetic pull of our connection, and for a brief moment, it feels like the world falls away, leaving just the two of us suspended in time.

"I got your message," I reply, my voice barely above a whisper. The honesty of my admission hangs in the air, intertwining with the approaching storm that now rumbles ominously overhead. He shifts his weight, glancing at the lake before meeting my gaze again. The tension in the air is palpable, a silent acknowledgment of the unresolved issues that linger like an impending downpour.

"I know things have been… complicated," he starts, his brow furrowing slightly as he searches for the right words. I can see the turmoil brewing within him, mirroring the chaos in my own heart. "I just wanted to see you, to talk." His admission is both a balm and a burden, and it takes all my strength not to reach out and close the gap between us.

The wind picks up again, rustling the leaves and sending ripples across the lake's surface. I wrap my arms around myself, seeking comfort in the familiarity of my own embrace. "I've missed you," I admit, the vulnerability in my voice a reflection of the tempest within me. It feels good to say the words, to finally acknowledge the depth of my feelings.

"I've missed you too," he replies, the sincerity in his voice cutting through the tension. "More than I thought possible." The weight of his confession hangs in the air like a heavy fog, shrouding us in uncertainty yet offering a glimmer of hope. In that moment, it feels as if we're both standing at the precipice, teetering on the edge of what could be—a chance to bridge the chasm that has formed between us.

As the first drops of rain begin to fall, I glance up at the sky, my heart racing as I feel the electric charge of the storm surging around us. It feels fitting, somehow, that as we confront our feelings, nature mirrors our emotional upheaval. I take a step closer, drawn to him like a moth to a flame, the warmth of his presence igniting something deep within me that I thought had dimmed.

"Ethan, we need to talk about what happened. About us," I say, my voice steady despite the turmoil churning inside. He nods slowly, his expression shifting from uncertainty to determination.

"Let's get out of the rain first," he suggests, a hint of a smile breaking through the tension. With a shared understanding, we begin to walk along the shore, the sound of our footsteps mingling with the soft patter of rain as it begins to fall more steadily. The air is charged with anticipation, and I can feel the storm within me building, echoing the one raging above.

With each step, I feel the weight of our unspoken words lifting, replaced by the promise of revelation. The world around us fades into the background as we navigate the delicate terrain of our relationship, the storm and our emotions intertwining in an intricate dance that feels both terrifying and exhilarating.

The air thickens with tension as we find ourselves sheltered beneath the sprawling branches of a nearby oak, rainwater dripping from the leaves like a gentle symphony of nature's percussion. The world is a blur of gray and green, the lush foliage glistening with the fresh scent of rain. I can't help but marvel at how the storm transforms the landscape into something magical, every droplet a reminder that beauty can exist even amidst chaos. The cacophony of raindrops mingling with the soft lapping of the lake is a melody I never knew I needed until this moment.

Ethan's presence beside me is both a comfort and a challenge. His shoulder brushes against mine, igniting an electric spark that travels straight to my heart, each pulse echoing the unspoken words hanging between us. It's as if the universe has conspired to bring us to this exact moment, a perfect storm of emotions that threatens to engulf us, yet promises something beautiful at the same time.

"I'm glad you came," he says, his voice a low murmur, barely rising above the sound of the rain. I catch a glimpse of vulnerability in his eyes, a rare peek into the tumult within him. It's an opening, a gateway to the conversation we desperately need. My heart skips a beat, a tumultuous mix of hope and anxiety swirling inside me like the clouds overhead.

"I didn't want to miss this," I reply, my voice steady despite the nervous flutter in my stomach. I take a breath, the cool air invigorating, grounding me as I prepare to plunge into the depths of our shared uncertainty. "We've both been avoiding the truth, Ethan. We can't keep dancing around it."

He exhales slowly, and I can almost see the weight of our shared past, the misunderstandings and unspoken words hanging between us like storm clouds ready to burst. "You're right. I... I've been scared," he admits, his gaze dropping to the ground. "Scared of losing you. Scared of what this—what we—could mean."

The confession strikes me like lightning, illuminating the shadows in my mind. I want to reach out, to cup his face and reassure him that he's not alone, that I'm right here, but the storm inside me swells with conflicting emotions. I want to comfort him, but I also want to challenge him. "You're not going to lose me unless you push me away," I say, my tone firm but gentle. "I care about you, Ethan. You know that."

He looks up, his eyes searching mine as if trying to decode the very essence of what I'm saying. "But what if I'm not enough?" The question hangs in the air, heavy with the weight of uncertainty. My heart aches at his admission, for I can see the echoes of past disappointments etched in his features, the fear that perhaps he's unworthy of love or connection.

"Enough for what?" I ask, my brows furrowing as I step closer, the rain drenching us both, but I hardly notice. "Enough to be someone I want by my side? You already are." The clarity of my words ignites something within me, a fierce determination to pull him from the depths of his insecurities. "It's not about perfection; it's about understanding each other and being willing to navigate the storm together."

Ethan's lips curl into a hesitant smile, and I feel my heart leap in response. It's not the carefree joy I've seen from him before, but it's a start—a flicker of light in the darkness that envelops us. "You really mean that?" he asks, the vulnerability in his voice making me want to wrap him in my arms and shield him from every fear he holds.

"I do. I mean it more than anything," I reply, my voice steady, grounding us both in this moment of clarity. The rain begins to fall heavier now, each drop a reminder of the tears and struggles we've faced, but also a promise of renewal. The storm is cleansing us, washing away the remnants of doubt and confusion that have held us captive for far too long.

The air shifts around us as I step even closer, my heart racing as I bridge the gap between us. "Ethan, we're both scared, but we can't let that fear dictate our lives. I don't want to lose what we have because of what-ifs." My voice wavers slightly, the gravity of my words anchoring me in this moment. "I want to explore this… whatever this is. Together."

A flicker of hope ignites in his eyes, and the tension that has clung to us begins to dissolve, leaving only the essence of possibility. "You really think we can?" he asks, his voice a mixture of disbelief and yearning, the two emotions woven together like the branches of the oak above us.

"Absolutely," I respond, the conviction in my voice solidifying my resolve. "Life is full of storms, Ethan. But it's also filled with moments of beauty, connection, and growth. If we're willing to weather the storms together, we can create something beautiful."

The moment stretches, charged with unspoken promises as we stand beneath the oak, the rain pouring down around us, enveloping us in our own world. I take a step back, giving him space but not wanting to break the connection we've forged. "I want to understand you, to support you, but I need you to be open with me too," I add, my heart racing at the thought of what might come next.

He nods slowly, the tension in his shoulders easing just a fraction. "You're right. I haven't been completely honest, not just with you but with myself." His admission feels like a weight lifting, and I can see the gears turning in his mind. "I think I've been so focused on my fears that I forgot to embrace the possibilities."

"Then let's embrace them," I urge, my heart pounding as I step closer again, a newfound determination igniting my spirit. The rain continues to pour, washing away the remnants of our past confrontations and misunderstandings, leaving us standing at the precipice of something new and vibrant.

Ethan's gaze softens, and I can see the flicker of hope reflecting in his eyes. "Okay. Let's do this." The words slip from his lips like a promise, and with that, I can feel the storm within me begin to calm, replaced by a quiet sense of determination that anchors us both.

As the clouds gather overhead, we stand together, ready to face whatever comes next. The chaos surrounding us feels less daunting with him by my side, and for the first time in what feels like an eternity, I can see the path ahead illuminated by our shared resolve. In the midst of the storm, I feel the spark of something beautiful begin to grow.

The rain tapers off, leaving behind a world washed clean and glistening. Droplets cling to the leaves like diamonds, and the air is saturated with the scent of wet earth and pine—a balm for the soul. The rhythmic lapping of the lake against the shore provides a serene soundtrack, a comforting reminder that life continues despite the storms we endure. As I stand there, my heart still thrumming from our earlier conversation, I glance sideways at Ethan, his face still lit by the afterglow of our newfound understanding.

"I've been thinking about us," he says, breaking the silence that has become a fragile thread between us. I turn to him, encouraged by the sincerity in his tone. "I don't want to live in fear anymore. I've spent too long hiding parts of myself, afraid of what might happen if I let anyone in." His vulnerability shines through, and I can't help but admire the courage it takes to expose oneself to another, especially after the rift we've faced.

I take a step closer, wanting to assure him that I, too, have my fears but that they pale in comparison to the brightness of what we might share. "You don't have to hide from me, Ethan. I want to know you, the real you—the dreams, the quirks, the scars." I say this softly, as if my words could soothe the lingering worries within him.

He watches me for a moment, the weight of his thoughts heavy in the space between us. "There's a lot you don't know," he finally replies, his gaze drifting to the horizon, where dark clouds have begun to dissipate, leaving a hazy light in their wake. "I've been running from my past, from the parts of me that I thought would scare you away."

"What if those parts are what make you extraordinary?" I ask, emboldened by the glimmer of hope sparking between us. "What if they're what makes you, you?"

Ethan lets out a breath, the tension in his shoulders easing slightly. "I've always been the 'quiet guy' in the background. The one who observes rather than participates. I thought being that way would keep me safe." His voice wavers slightly, revealing the turmoil he's carried for far too long. "But maybe it's time for me to step into the light, even if it's scary."

"Maybe it's time for both of us," I counter gently, realizing the truth of my own words. I've spent so much time tiptoeing around my insecurities, afraid of stepping into the unknown. "We can do this together."

The lake glimmers, reflecting the fading sunlight like a million tiny stars, as if the universe is encouraging our leap of faith. "How do you want to start?" he asks, a flicker of excitement igniting in his eyes.

"Let's take a walk," I suggest, gesturing toward the winding path that hugs the shoreline. We set off side by side, the silence between us now comfortable, filled with the promise of shared discovery. As we stroll, I find myself noticing the little things—the way his hair curls slightly at the nape of his neck, the thoughtful crease between his brows, and how his fingers flex and relax at his sides as if they're eager to reach out but unsure of where to go.

"I used to come here to think," I share, my voice soft against the backdrop of nature. "Whenever life felt overwhelming, the lake was my escape. It felt like the water could wash away my worries."

"I get that," he replies, a smile tugging at the corners of his lips. "There's something about being near water that just calms the chaos."

"I think it's because it reminds us that life ebbs and flows," I say, a sudden clarity washing over me. "Like the tides, we experience highs and lows. Sometimes we're swept away; other times, we find our footing again."

His expression shifts, reflecting a deeper understanding of what I'm trying to convey. "Maybe we're both just learning to navigate our own tides," he muses, his voice thoughtful. "It's okay to ride the waves and to stumble along the way."

The path meanders ahead, flanked by wildflowers that sway gently in the breeze. Their colors pop against the backdrop of lush green foliage, a riot of purples, yellows, and pinks that seem to dance in celebration of our budding connection. I reach out to pluck a flower, twirling it between my fingers as I watch him.

"What about you? What do you want?" he suddenly asks, his eyes locking onto mine with an intensity that sends a shiver down my spine.

The question catches me off guard, and I pause to consider it, the flower still spinning between my fingers. "I want... to create," I say finally, my voice steady. "To capture the beauty in the chaos, to transform the ordinary into something extraordinary. I want to explore life and all its intricacies, but I also want someone to share that journey with."

The corners of his mouth lift, and I feel a warmth spreading through me as he steps closer, our shoulders brushing again. "I think you're already doing that," he replies, admiration etched into his features. "Your art—it captures moments that most people overlook. You see the world differently."

"Maybe that's why I'm drawn to you," I say with a teasing glint in my eye. "You're like a walking piece of art—full of depth, complexity, and mystery."

He laughs, a sound that resonates in the stillness around us. "Well, I guess it takes one artist to appreciate another."

As we walk further along the shore, I notice the way the sky shifts, the colors transforming from muted pastels to bold hues of orange and crimson as the sun dips lower. The golden light bathes us, wrapping us in warmth and illuminating the path ahead.

"Ethan," I begin, my heart racing with the weight of my next words, "what if we promised to always be honest with each other? To share our fears, our dreams, even the parts we hide?"

"I'd like that," he replies, his expression turning serious yet hopeful. "No more hiding. Let's lay everything out on the table."

The thought of shedding the layers that have kept us apart sends a thrill through me. "Together, we can weather any storm," I say, feeling emboldened by our shared resolve.

As twilight descends, we find ourselves at the edge of the lake, where the water glistens like a blanket of stars fallen from the heavens. I turn to Ethan, who stands beside me, his gaze fixed on the horizon. "Do you think we're ready for this?" I ask, my heart fluttering with anticipation.

"We'll never know until we try," he replies, his voice steady, confidence radiating from him. "And I'd rather face the unknown with you by my side than alone."

His words strike a chord deep within me, a truth I've longed to embrace. The storm may have raged around us, but standing here together, I realize we are not just weathering it; we are emerging stronger, ready to face whatever comes next, hand in hand.

Chapter 29: The Aftermath

The lake stretches before us, a vast expanse of shimmering silver, its surface occasionally breaking into ripples as the wind stirs. The storm clouds that loomed ominously above have finally begun to disperse, unveiling a canvas of vibrant blues and soft whites, reminiscent of the early morning sky. The air carries a cool freshness, scented with the earthy musk of wet soil and the delicate perfume of pine trees lining the shore. I can hear the distant call of a lone heron as it glides gracefully above the water, its silhouette cutting through the last remnants of the storm.

Ethan stands beside me, his figure outlined against the vivid backdrop of the newly revealed sun. His expression is a mixture of vulnerability and strength, a portrait of the boy who had once seemed so distant and unreachable. I can see the conflict swirling in his deep-set eyes, those pools of dark brown that often reflect a kaleidoscope of emotions. His brow furrows slightly, and for a moment, I'm reminded of the jagged peaks surrounding this lake, steadfast yet seemingly fragile beneath the weight of the storm.

"Sometimes, I feel like I'm standing in the shadows of everything you've accomplished," he confesses, his voice barely rising above the sound of the lapping waves. "It's like... I'm constantly measuring myself against your success, and I fear I'll never measure up."

The raw honesty of his words pierces through the thick air between us, pulling at my heartstrings. I step closer, feeling the warmth radiate from his body, contrasting the coolness of the post-storm air. My fingers curl around his, grounding us both in this moment. I search his eyes for a flicker of understanding, hoping he can see the sincerity in my gaze.

"Ethan," I say softly, my voice trembling slightly, "you are more than enough. Your strength, your kindness—those are things I admire about you. It's not a competition. We're on the same team, navigating this unpredictable sea together."

As I speak, I can see the tension in his shoulders begin to ease, his posture shifting from defensive to open. The weight of his fears hangs visibly between us, yet I feel an unspoken connection growing stronger, as if the very air around us is humming with the energy of our shared vulnerabilities. The clouds that had once threatened to engulf us are slowly giving way to rays of sunlight, painting the landscape in golden hues that dance on the surface of the water.

With a gentle squeeze, I pull him closer, our fingers intertwining, creating a bridge between our hearts. "We both have our storms," I continue, my voice steady. "I've faced my own doubts, my own fears. But together, we can weather anything. You uplift me in ways you can't even begin to understand, just by being you."

His eyes glisten with unshed tears, and for a moment, I feel as though we are the only two souls in this vast world, bound together by our shared struggles. I lift my other hand to brush a stray lock of hair from his forehead, and the simple touch sparks a warmth that radiates through my body. This small act of intimacy is powerful, reminding me that we are not defined by our pasts but by our choices in the present.

A gust of wind sweeps across the lake, sending a flurry of leaves dancing through the air. The storm is truly gone now, leaving behind the promise of something new—a fresh beginning that smells of rain and sun. The landscape has transformed, just as we have. The lake, once a churning tempest, now glimmers invitingly, as if beckoning us to dive into its depths, to embrace the uncharted waters of our futures.

"Let's not hide anymore," Ethan murmurs, his voice a tender whisper, echoing my own thoughts. "Let's be honest with ourselves and with each other."

With those words, a sense of clarity washes over me. The fear of vulnerability no longer feels insurmountable; instead, it transforms into a catalyst for growth. I nod, feeling a surge of determination. Together, we can face whatever lies ahead—together, we can redefine what love means, breaking free from the constraints of fear and insecurity.

The rain begins to fall softly, like a gentle blessing from the heavens. Each droplet dances upon the surface of the lake, creating ripples that mirror the shifting currents of our hearts. As the first few drops land on our skin, I laugh, the sound bright and pure, a melody carried away by the wind. Ethan joins me, his laughter mingling with mine, and in that moment, I feel the weight of our pasts slipping away, washed clean by the cleansing rain.

Leaning in closer, I can feel the heat radiating from him, our breaths mingling in the crisp air as the world around us fades into a blur of color and sound. Our lips meet in a gentle kiss, one that starts tentative but quickly ignites into something deeper, something profound. This is not just a promise sealed with a touch; it is an unspoken vow that we will face the storms of life hand in hand.

As we pull away, breathless, the sun breaks through the clouds, casting a warm glow over the lake, illuminating the world around us. In this vibrant landscape, we are not merely survivors of our storms; we are warriors, ready to embrace the challenges ahead. I can feel the weight of my fears dissipating, replaced by a sense of hope that flutters within my chest like a bird newly freed from its cage. This moment marks the dawn of a new chapter, not just for us, but for all that lies ahead.

The rain drizzles softly around us, each drop a tiny messenger, washing away remnants of the storm that had threatened to unravel everything. It's a peculiar feeling, standing there under the overcast sky, the cool water kissing our skin while warmth radiates from the connection between our hands. I take a moment to soak in the tranquility, the symphony of nature settling into a gentle rhythm. It's almost as if the universe, in all its chaotic beauty, is giving us a second chance.

As we pull apart from that first kiss, Ethan's gaze doesn't waver. There's a flicker of hope mingled with uncertainty, and I can feel the weight of our pasts lingering in the air, like the humidity that envelops us. "Can we really do this?" he asks, the question hanging between us like a fragile thread, ready to snap under the slightest tension. His vulnerability is palpable, a raw honesty that tugs at my heartstrings.

"Why not?" I reply, forcing a confidence I don't fully feel. "We've already weathered a storm, haven't we?" The words sound better in the air than they feel in my heart, but the truth is that every heartbeat in this moment feels like an adventure, teetering on the edge of possibility.

He nods slowly, contemplating my words as we begin to walk along the shoreline. The sand is damp beneath our feet, squelching slightly with each step, and the occasional splash of a wave sends a spray of cool droplets in our direction, making us laugh. It's a joyous sound that bounces off the trees lining the lake, echoing in the fresh air, a stark contrast to the heaviness we had just shared.

Our conversation flows easily, intertwining our fears and dreams like the roots of the ancient trees that surround us. I find myself sharing things I've never spoken of before, thoughts I've tucked away in the corners of my mind, where shadows linger. "I often feel like I'm in a constant battle with myself," I confess, my voice soft but resolute. "It's like I'm on this endless treadmill of expectations, and sometimes I can't tell if I'm running towards something or just trying to escape."

Ethan listens intently, his brow furrowing in empathy. "I get that," he responds, his voice low and steady. "It's as if we're all trying to outrun ghosts of who we think we should be, while missing out on just... being."

With every shared thought, a layer of tension begins to peel away. I realize that our fears are not so different after all. Beneath the surface of our experiences lies a shared desire to be seen, to be understood, and to find peace in our own skins. This realization brings a warmth to my heart, one that spreads like the sun finally breaking through the clouds, illuminating the hidden beauty of our connection.

As we stroll along the water's edge, I notice how the rain has brought a different kind of life to the landscape. The vibrant greens of the grass seem to dance in the breeze, and the wildflowers that dot the shoreline stretch toward the sky, drinking in the cool moisture. It's a reminder that beauty often follows adversity, and in this moment, I see the world anew, through the lens of possibility.

"Do you remember that summer we spent at the cabin?" I ask, my mind drifting back to lazy afternoons filled with laughter and campfire stories. Ethan's face lights up at the memory, and I can't help but smile at the way his eyes twinkle. "I thought we were going to have to deal with bugs and bad Wi-Fi, but it ended up being one of the best weeks of my life."

"Yeah," he chuckles, the sound rich and genuine. "And you still managed to burn the marshmallows every night. How is that even possible?"

I laugh, my heart swelling at the camaraderie we've built, layer upon layer, through shared experiences and the little idiosyncrasies that make us who we are. "In my defense, I was busy trying to roast the perfect hot dog!"

As we continue our playful banter, I can feel the darkness that once hovered around us slowly dissipating. It's as if the lake itself is a mirror reflecting our journey, a testament to the trials we've faced and the joy we've found in each other. The air becomes thick with the scent of earth and rain, an intoxicating perfume that grounds me, reminding me of the beauty of resilience.

Ethan glances at me, his expression shifting to something more serious. "You know, it's not just about what you accomplish. It's about how you choose to live in the moment." His words hang in the air, each syllable weighted with meaning. "I've seen how you light up a room, how you inspire people just by being you. Don't ever forget that."

The sincerity in his voice washes over me, soothing like a balm on a bruised heart. It's the kind of compliment that sinks deep, settling into the crevices of my insecurities and transforming them into something beautiful. "Thank you," I whisper, my voice catching in my throat. "That means more to me than you'll ever know."

Ethan smiles, and the warmth of his gaze envelops me like a cozy blanket. We pause at a rocky outcropping, the remnants of the storm evident in the scattered debris—a testament to nature's power. Yet, amidst the chaos, I spot a delicate wildflower, resiliently blooming among the stones, vibrant against the stark gray. It's a perfect metaphor for our lives, both fragile and strong, capable of growing even in the harshest of conditions.

"Look at that," I say, pointing toward the flower. "It's beautiful, isn't it? Just like us, in a way."

Ethan's eyes follow my gesture, and he nods. "It is. We might not have everything figured out, but we're still here, growing."

A comfortable silence envelops us, filled only with the gentle sound of water lapping against the shore and the occasional rustle of leaves in the breeze. In that quiet space, I feel a profound sense of gratitude swell within me. The storm may have come and gone, but what remains is the promise of new beginnings, wrapped in the warmth of connection and the power of love.

As the sun begins to dip below the horizon, painting the sky in strokes of orange and purple, I know that whatever challenges lie ahead, we'll face them together. This moment, this laughter, and the unbreakable bond we've formed—these are the things that will carry us forward. And in this vibrant world, I can't help but believe that love, like the wildflower, will flourish even in the most unexpected places.

The sun dips lower on the horizon, casting a golden hue across the lake, each ripple catching the light like a thousand tiny diamonds scattered on its surface. As we continue to walk, the air fills with a crisp freshness, mingling with the faint scent of pine and damp earth, grounding me in this moment of clarity. The rain has become a mere whisper in the background, and the world seems to exhale a sigh of relief, as if nature itself is celebrating our newfound resolve.

Ethan and I wander further down the shore, our feet sinking into the wet sand with each step. I can feel the pulse of the earth beneath me, a steady rhythm that echoes the unsteady beats of my heart. The intimacy of our shared space draws us closer, and I find myself marveling at the way he moves, effortlessly gliding through this landscape that is both familiar and foreign. There's a certain grace in the way he navigates the rocky shoreline, as if he were born to be here, in this wild, untamed beauty.

"Do you ever think about what's next for us?" I ask, my curiosity bubbling over as I scan the horizon, where the sun kisses the edge of the water, creating a fiery spectacle. "I mean, after everything we've been through, what does the future look like?"

Ethan pauses, his eyes narrowing slightly as he contemplates the question. The corners of his mouth turn up into a soft smile, one that holds promise and uncertainty in equal measure. "Honestly? I see us creating our own adventures, like exploring the world beyond this lake, discovering new places, and making memories that don't feel like a shadow of what came before."

His words resonate deeply within me, igniting a spark of wanderlust I hadn't fully acknowledged until now. The thought of venturing beyond the familiar confines of our lives, of stepping into the unknown hand in hand with him, sends a shiver of excitement down my spine. "That sounds amazing," I breathe, feeling the weight of past insecurities begin to lift, replaced by the exhilarating thrill of possibility.

Ethan takes a step closer, the warmth of his presence enveloping me like a cherished blanket. "But," he continues, his tone shifting to something more serious, "it's not just about the adventures. It's about how we choose to face the challenges that come our way. I want us to be partners, really partners. Not just in the fun stuff but in the hard stuff, too."

I nod, understanding the gravity of his words. Life isn't always a picturesque sunset over a tranquil lake. There will be storms, hidden currents, and obstacles we can't foresee. But there's a certain strength that comes from facing those challenges together. "I agree," I reply, my voice steady. "Whatever comes next, I want us to face it side by side."

With a shared resolve igniting our hearts, we venture deeper into our conversation, weaving our dreams and aspirations together like a tapestry rich with color and texture. I share my hopes of traveling to places I've only read about in books, where the air is thick with culture and history, and the food is a symphony of flavors. Ethan talks about his love for music and how he dreams of one day performing on a stage, not just for the applause but for the joy of sharing his passion with others.

"Imagine it," he says, his voice rising with excitement. "A small café in Paris, the smell of fresh pastries in the air, and me playing a tune that makes people feel alive."

I can see it, vivid and bright in my mind's eye. The soft glow of fairy lights strung across a rustic café, laughter mingling with the gentle strumming of his guitar. The thought sends warmth pooling in my chest, a surge of inspiration flooding my senses. "And I'll be right there, sipping a café au lait, cheering you on," I promise, feeling a sense of belonging blossom between us.

As we talk, time slips away, and the world around us fades, leaving just the two of us standing at the intersection of hope and dreams. The sun finally sets, painting the sky in hues of purple and indigo, as the stars begin to twinkle overhead, shyly peeking out from the fabric of night. It's a mesmerizing sight, a canvas so stunning it steals my breath.

"Look at the stars," Ethan says, pointing upward, his voice tinged with awe. "They're like a map of possibilities."

I follow his gaze, captivated by the constellations that blanket the sky, each star a reminder of the infinite potential that lies ahead. "Do you think they can guide us?" I ask playfully, leaning into him, reveling in the warmth radiating from his body.

"Only if we're brave enough to follow them," he replies, his voice low and thoughtful. The sincerity in his tone makes my heart flutter, igniting a flame of courage within me.

In that moment, the world feels impossibly vast yet intimately small, as if our dreams and the universe are aligned in a cosmic dance. I take a deep breath, inhaling the fresh scent of the earth mixed with the fading aroma of rain, and feel a surge of determination flood my veins. I want to explore every corner of this life we're beginning to carve out together, to dive into the unknown with the fierce love that binds us.

As we make our way back along the shoreline, I can't help but reflect on how far we've come. The storms that once threatened to drown us now feel like distant echoes, reminders of our strength and resilience. The laughter and lightness we share now serve as a testament to our journey—a vibrant celebration of love and partnership that has flourished amidst the chaos.

With each step, I feel more grounded, more alive, and more sure of the path that lies ahead. The darkness of the past no longer has a hold on me; instead, I'm enveloped in the warm glow of the future, bright and inviting. And as the stars shimmer above us, I know that whatever challenges we face, we will navigate them together, hand in hand, heart to heart.

Ethan stops suddenly, turning to me with a mischievous glint in his eyes. "Race you to the car?" he challenges, a playful grin breaking across his face.

"Last one there has to do the dishes!" I laugh, and with that, we take off, our footsteps echoing against the shoreline, hearts racing in sync with the thrill of the chase. In the cool night air, as we sprint across the sand, I can't help but feel that this is only the beginning of our greatest adventure yet, filled with love, laughter, and an endless horizon of possibilities.